M
Next Door

CW01597660

by

Rebecca Black

The Hearsay Series, Volume 2

To Dominique

Enjoy!

This is a work of fiction. Similarities to real people, places, or events are entirely coincidental.

MY GIRL NEXT DOOR

First edition. July 14, 2023.

Copyright © 2023 Rebecca Black.

Written by Rebecca Black.

Rough

*

Author's Note

This book is intended for an adult audience as there are scenes of a sexual nature.

Chapter 1
Lucy

He loves me?

I read the short text over and over. *Please pick up, Lucy. I love you x*

He loves me? But did he, though? Because that picture of him by the hospital bed showed a different story. And what is it they say? A picture is worth a thousand words. He might think he was in love with me, but his body language and facial expression said he was in love with Alysa.

I pressed dial and waited for Steph to pick up.

'Yeeee! Oh my God, I've literally been pacing up and down, waiting for you to call. I didn't want to call you because I didn't want to interrupt any hot sex you might be having now that you're publicly Will's girlfriend...'

She trailed off.

'I broke up with him,' I said flatly.

'What? Are you okay? What happened?'

'Are you around later? I need to decompress.'

I really didn't want to go over everything on the phone.

'Of course, I've already organised for us to have drinks with the girls, but I can relocate it to mine if you'd prefer?'

'Really?' I asked, a little perplexed.

'Well, I thought we'd be getting a full rundown of the G.A.M. awards, not a crisis meeting.'

'Oh, I see.'

'Or I can cancel? Just you and me?'

'No, it might be good getting their perspective. I'm so torn.'

'Okay, mine at seven and then if you feel up to it, we can pop out for a late one.'

She hung up, and I looked back at Will's message. Suddenly, my phone started ringing again. It was Will. I dropped it onto the bed like it was a hot potato and stared at it until it rang out. I wasn't ready to speak to him. I needed to speak to the girls and get their opinion. My brain was swimming with the comments Katia had made, the images ingrained in my mind, and the judgement from all the readers of that article.

It started ringing again.

For Christ's sake.

I closed my eyes until it stopped, and then I quickly picked up my phone and blocked him. I didn't know what else to do. I just needed some space. Some time to get my head straight.

Will

'Grrraaaggghhhh.'

I hurled my cell right across the room from the kitchen into the seating area, turned and thumped the wall with my fist in frustration.

We were back at my apartment in Brooklyn. I had been trying to get hold of Lucy since I got her text message. But after Terry had discovered that she'd left the hotel and Alysa had eventually been discharged, we'd run out of time and had to go straight to the airport.

I couldn't even look at Alysa on the way home. She spent most of the time asleep. She'd had her stomach pumped, so I'd imagined she was feeling pretty worse for wear. But boy, was I pissed with her. Alysa had inadvertently completely screwed everything up... again.

'Will, you're gonna break your goddamn hand,' Jake said calmly from the stool he'd stationed himself on at the island.

Rolling my eyes, I sighed with exasperation. His sangfroid demeanour amplified my anger.

'She's fucking blocked me,' I stated, turning back and leaning my elbows on the island, putting my head in my hands.

I knew Paul had sent Jake back there to keep an eye on me and make sure I didn't do anything stupid. He had good reason to because that was a high possibility if I didn't get a hold of myself. Paul would've normally come back with me, but after we'd dropped Alysa at her parents, he needed to get home to Hannah, who was already pissed that we'd extended the tour by a week for the G.A.M. Awards.

And Jake had seen me at my worst, but I knew damn well he'd far rather be balls deep in some chick than be there with me, so he was just pressing my buttons instead.

'Why are you getting so worked up about it?'

'Because I fucking love her!' I blurted out.

Jake's eyes locked with mine. He looked like he'd been sucker-punched. I knew he'd be shocked. That word was like the fuck of all evils to him.

'You *love* her?' he asked in disbelief.

'Yes!' I hissed. 'And I fucking text it to her,' I added, closing my eyes at my self-loathing, and there was a long pause.

'You dick.' He laughed patronisingly. 'So let me get this straight. You invited her to an awards night to announce to the world that she's your girlfriend. Whilst there, your ex-girlfriend ODs. Then Katia tells Lucy you fucked her one time, and you left Lucy there?'

I stared at him, fuming that he was actually spelling out my misdemeanours. He was goading me.

'And then.' He laughed again. 'You *text* her that you love her. I'm not surprised she's blocked you.'

I stood there staring at him, my breathing laboured. He was supposed to be helping me to calm down, not piss me off. I began to pace.

'Fuck!' I gritted out and put my hands on my hips. 'What the fuck am I gonna do?'

'Oh, Mr Charisma wants girl advice now.'

I shook my head and physically bit my tongue, but it was no use.

'Fuck you.'

'No, fuck you,' he said, pointing at me, and then grabbed his wallet and keys. 'You know, if I was in love with a girl, like, truly in love with her, I wouldn't be pacing around my apartment. I'd be hunting her down.'

I looked at the floor, not wanting to make eye contact with him because I knew he was right. I heard the elevator doors open, and I stole myself to look up.

'You shared her with the world and left her high and dry.'

He shook his head, and I closed my eyes as the doors rolled shut.

Why in the fuck had I gone back there to the apartment? I knew damn well why. We had a meeting with the record label and some futile event Alysa had accepted on our behalf. All my life, I had put the band first. I'd lost shit loads of girls over the years because of my ridiculous schedule. Girls that clearly didn't mean anything to me, otherwise, it would have bothered me before.

I thought I'd got it right with Alysa, but, looking back, it was just easy because we worked together. I'd never met someone I'd wanted to fight for until I met Lucy. I knew the second I laid eyes on her. The way she looked at me, taking every inch of me in but unable to look me in the eye. I was sure she'd recognise me, but she didn't. She was looking at *me*.

I bit my lip, thinking about it.

I had royally fucked up. This whole love thing was completely new to me. I'd only ever said it once before, and that was to Alysa, and only because I thought I should under the circumstances. I'd text the words to Lucy. Who the fuck does that? I should have said it at sunset, under a starlit night or with a fucking string quartet in accompaniment.

Jake was right.

I needed to find her, and if I played my cards right, I could be back in the UK within ten hours. I needed to schedule a flight. Retrieving my phone from under the coffee table, I called Terry in the hope he hadn't made it home.

Lucy

I arrived at Steph's just after seven. My thoughts had been swaying one way to the other all day. One minute I was on the brink of tears, angry with myself because the upset was self-inflicted, as I'd broken it off. The next I was positive I'd made the right decision because he was still in love with Alysa.

'Sorry, I'm late. Time just ran away with me.'

The girls were already sitting in the kitchen, and Steph was busy making drinks for everyone.

'You're here. That's the main thing,' Steph said, handing me a glass.

'What is it?' I asked.

'This one's called rum tropical,' she said in a silly accent as she wedged a slice of lime over the rim.

I frowned. Steph was clearly making cocktails on the fly as she had all the spirits out and several mixers. I sipped and was pleasantly surprised.

'So, what's this I hear about you breaking things off with Will?' Claire asked, getting straight to the point. 'Did we not just spend last weekend getting you two back together?'

I perched on one of the bar stools, knowing I was going to have to explain *everything* that had happened in fine detail to appease her curiosity. But then again, I did want their advice.

I couldn't help but laugh at the three of them as they sat there with their jaws slack. I finished by showing them the text Will had sent.

'And how do you feel now, knowing he loves you?' Zara asked.

'I don't think he does. He's still in love with Alysa. It's written all over his face in that photo.'

'That was just one report, Lu,' Zara said. 'Did you see any of the other pictures?' I looked at her and then down at my glass as I swirled the remainder of my rum tropical around the ice. 'That one of you two kissing by the bar... if you're looking for a picture of a man in love, that's it.'

'And that one of you on the red carpet where Will is whispering something in your ear,' Claire added, placing a hand over her heart.

I hadn't seen them. I really didn't need to torture myself. I wasn't one to trawl through the gossip sites, and I wasn't about to start now. Besides, they had been taken before Alysa had OD'd.

Steph handed me another drink. 'How do *you* feel about him?' she asked.

I sighed, not really wanting to admit my feelings because it didn't change anything, despite how I felt. My silence spoke volumes, and they all glanced at each other, conceding not to push me. I spent the next hour or so asking the girls about what they'd been up to, avoiding the subject completely.

'Come on. Drink up. We're going out,' Steph announced.

'What? I thought we were staying here?' I said, looking down at myself.

I was wearing a pair of floaty cotton trousers with a batik print on them, a clingy raspberry-coloured camisole, and some sandals. I was not dressed for going out-out. It was no use. Steph was already hollering up the stairs to tell her girls we were heading to the pub. Zara was gathering her belongings, and Claire was reapplying her lipstick.

We arrived at the pub ten minutes later. It was fairly busy, but Claire spotted a free booth, and we all slid in. Zara was next to me, Steph and Claire opposite. I was thankful for the semi-private area, as I was feeling self-conscious after the media exposure. Better still, we were able to order via an app from the table, so none of us had to go to the bar.

Zara swiped her mobile over the QR code. 'Shall we get a bottle of something?'

'The Viognier is nice in here,' Steph piped up, and Zara scrolled through until she found it, ordering two bottles.

As we sat waiting for our order, I glanced around the room. An uneasy feeling came over me as I realised several people were looking in our direction.

I leaned in.

'Do you think they recognise me?' I asked.

'Of course they do. There are pictures of you everywhere, Lu. The local press is having a field day.' Zara declared as she squeezed my thigh.

Oh God, now I had people staring at me even when I wasn't with Will.

As the evening went on, the pub became busier and louder, but the effects of the alcohol were helping to dampen my concern over the gawkers. Claire was just finishing up a hilarious story about one of her kids going on a blind date when Steph's phone started to ring.

'Hold that thought. It's the girls. Hiya, everything okay?'

She listened and then slowly raised her eyes to me.

I frowned.

'Right, and what did you say to him?'

There was a pause.

'Did you say which pub we were in?'

As she listened again, her eyes left mine, and so did Claire's, and lifted above my head, looking towards the main entrance.

My stomach dropped just as the general chit-chat of the pub did, and I knew, I could sense him.

Will was there.

I stood up as he came into view, but Zara stayed put, blocking my exit from the booth.

'Lucy,' he said in greeting, nodding his head warily, probably unsure of the response he was going to receive.

I just swallowed, the lump in my throat almost making it audible. I didn't know what to say. I glanced around the room nervously as all the patrons were over-enthusiastically pretending they were doing anything but listening in.

'Hi,' I murmured. 'You're... here.'

The slightest curl formed at the corner of his lip as he took me in, scanning my entire body.

'I just thought I'd... *pop* over.'

The curl turned into a small smile as he referred to a conversation we'd had a couple of weeks ago about being unable to just pop over when three thousand miles were between us.

He bit down on his lip to resume his placid expression. 'We need to talk.'

'You came all this way to talk?' I half-laughed, half choked back a sob in disbelief.

He glanced around and stepped in a little closer, placing a hand on top of the booth, caging Zara and me in.

'I didn't have much choice, Lucy. You weren't taking my calls or replying to my messages,' he said as tempered as possible, offsetting his jaw to hide his frustration.

'I, um...'

I shot a look at Steph, who could sense my agony. The awkward tension I felt mirrored in the girls.

'Why don't you two step outside,' Steph suggested.

Will's intense gaze didn't leave mine. I could tell by the look on his face that he couldn't care less where this conversation took place. He was far more accustomed to the high levels of attention.

Zara suddenly stood, ducking under Will's arm to make way for me. I quickly grabbed my bag as Will released his hand, standing tall to allow me out. He glared at all the on-lookers as I moved in front of him, and he followed me out of the door, Terry in close pursuit.

I quickly walked around to the side of the building. It was dark, and Terry hung back by the corner to give us some privacy. I stopped and turned as the passageway became too dark to see where I was going. Will's proximity was almost intimidating, but he didn't touch me. He didn't say anything. He was waiting for me to continue.

'I thought it was best I left so you could... be with Alysa.'

It was difficult for me to say her name without the picture popping into my head, and I looked past Will toward the street to evade his stare.

'*Be* with Alysa,' Will repeated questioningly, taking hold of my jaw and directing my gaze back to him. 'What do you mean by that?'

I stepped back out of his grasp, the sensation of his touch raw on my face, and folded my arms across my chest protectively.

'The picture.'

'What picture?'

'Of you by the hospital bed,' I said, and he frowned.

Maybe he hadn't seen it, or maybe he was just in denial over being in love with her.

'You looked heartbroken,' I stated, looking into his eyes briefly and then back to the street.

'Show me,' he said suddenly, and I looked back.

He wanted proof?

He pulled his phone out of his back pocket and typed something into the search engine before handing it to me.

'Show me the picture,' he demanded.

I went to say no and then thought better of it. He was here in Clevedon. He wasn't about to turn back without answers. I scrolled through, wincing at the number of pictures of him and Alysa together until I found it, and lifted it to show him.

Rather than taking the phone back, he pivoted around me to look at it over my shoulder.

I tensed.

I could feel the heat from his body and smell his aftershave and the leather of his jacket. His scent was intoxicating. I closed my eyes in an attempt to find the strength within me not to turn and kiss him. Despite the warm evening, my skin scattered with goosebumps.

'Yeah, heartbroken,' he confirmed.

His admission made me catch my breath. Was he mocking me? But then he moved in closer to access the screen and zoomed in on the picture. While one of his hands was holding Alysa's, the other was holding his phone.

'Heartbroken because I'd just received your text,' he added, and I could tell by his tone that he was trying to keep his voice level.

I exhaled, my mouth open. The earth seemed to shift under my feet, and I somehow lost my balance despite standing still.

Will was heartbroken because of me?

I had thought the look on his face was because of Alysa's predicament. Will automatically steadied me, and the moment his hand touched my forearm, I jumped with the sparking sensation that resonated through my body. I'd barely had time to process the information when Will suddenly used my arm to spin me around to face him. His other arm wrapped around my waist and yanked me flush to his body.

'Will?'

I'm not sure why I made his name a question. Maybe I was asking him what his intentions were, but I didn't need to, as his body was making it perfectly clear. My breathing was coming in quick breaths, and my face contorted with shock. His was serious, his eyes dark, demeanour challenging. Almost overbearing. He was a man on a mission, but I was fighting to stay focused. It wasn't just Alysa. It was all the other stuff.

'Lucy,' he said. 'Why do I get the feeling you're about to spill a whole bunch of reasons about why we shouldn't be together again?'

I shook my head slightly, annoyed that he read me so easily, but his countenance didn't change.

'I tried to fit in at the awards, but I'm not the person you need me to be.'

He shook his head in disagreement and was about to say something, but I needed to finish.

'Everyone just stared, Will, they stared because I'm... a pathetic mother of two who wears a jumpsuit. Shock, horror...' the words thick as I spoke them, as the shame and embarrassment bubbled up to the surface. '... from a high street store,' I choked out.

I could feel the tears burning, but I was determined to say what I needed to. 'I guess I felt protected when you were with me, but I felt vulnerable the moment I was on my own.'

'I should have stayed with you. I'm sorry,' he said, gliding his thumbs under my eyes to catch the tears before they fell.

'No, you did the right thing. Alysa needed you, and you've practically known her all your life.'

His head dipped, and he scrunched his eyes shut for a second, placing his hands on his hips.

'But I don't love her,' he gritted out, his gaze flicked from my eyes to my lips and back. 'I love you.'

My breath hitched.

'And I'm not expecting you to say it back, but this distance thing is fucked up, and I need to start being brutally honest with you... with myself. And you,' he said, pointing at me, 'You've gotta stop holding out on me. I just thought you were nervous. Not *vulnerable*.'

He pushed a hand through his hair in frustration.

'Fuck!' He spat out, looking up at the stars. 'Not harbouring feelings of unworthiness while you were sitting amongst a whole bunch of useless, plastic, talentless reality TV contestants.'

A small smile started to appear on my face as he took a huge breath in to compose himself.

'Lucy, you're perfect, and I'm sorry I text...'

'I love you too,' I said quickly.

Silence.

Will just stared at me, a mix of shock and wonder, and then, after a couple of moments, he choked out a short laugh.

'S-say that again,' he breathed.

I looked down, the enormity of the moment almost consuming, agitated that he was making me say it again. I took a staggered breath in and looked straight into his eyes.

'I love you.'

As the last word left my mouth, Will crushed his lips against mine, simultaneously pulling me into him with such force I dropped my bag. Pressing himself against me, making me step back, and pinning me against the wall of the pub.

His kissing was merciless. He lifted one of his hands, and out of the corner of my eye, I saw his outstretched palm flying through the air as if he was going to slap me, but he stopped less than a millimetre away from my skin on the side of my face. I flinched, but he gently pressed his palm against my cheek.

He was trembling.

He hooked his thumb under my chin, forcing my head back against the stone wall, but that wasn't where I felt the pain. I yelped as he bit into my neck, marking me. I gasped. His teeth scraped up my neck as I tried to calm my ragged breathing. Smoothing the hair away from my face as my head dropped forwards with exhaustion after his sweet assault. He gently held his forehead against mine, but his eyes were ablaze with a dark intensity.

'Next time there are three thousand miles between us, don't fucking block me,' he said in a measured but firm tone.

I swallowed. He was deadly serious, and a deep part of me wondered if his assault had been punishment.

'I won't,' I whispered.

He kissed me again, but this time it was delicate and loving. Oh, so gentle. His hand firmly smoothed its way up the back of my neck, his fingers pushing into my hair.

'Can I take you home?' he asked calmly.

I nodded. 'What time's your flight back?' I asked with mild trepidation.

He grinned. 'I didn't schedule a return.'

I looked at him, my eyes huge. 'But I thought...'

He placed a finger over my lips.

'Let's just see what happens,' he whispered, and I smiled against his finger.

Chapter 2

I'd sent a text to Steph to let her know I was on my way home. The boys had been expecting us when we snuck into the house through the back. Will had tried the house first, they had sent him around to Steph's, and her daughter had directed him to the pub. Within that time, the press had set up camp outside again.

Being that we'd only really been apart for twenty-four hours, we had so much to catch up on. He told me what had happened with Alysa, and how Jake had gone back with him to his apartment and made him realise that he needed to come and find me. Shortly after I'd blocked him, he'd flown back.

'It was lucky they had a flight at the time you wanted to return,' I thought out loud.

It was late. We were lying on the sofa, Will on his back, me on my side. The boys had gone to bed hours ago, and I was absentmindedly tracing the veins on Will's arm as he played with my hair at the nape of my neck.

'Hmm,' he said, frowning, a strange look in his eyes. 'You know, I knew deep down the second the plane took off that I shouldn't have left. I never really considered that I had a choice. I just automatically went back.'

'Didn't you say you had a meeting with the record label?'

'Yeah, but I don't have to be there in person. Lord knows I've attended enough meetings online when I'm in...' He stopped short and then bit his lip.

'What?' I asked.

'Nothing,' he said, looking up at the ceiling. I got the feeling he was hiding something from me, but it was so lovely to have him back. I didn't want to rock the boat by asking what it was.

We lay there for a while, both lost in thought, and my mind came back to a conversation I'd had with the girls a while ago.

'Can I ask you something?'

'Anything. Shoot.'

I stalled, trying to find the right words, and Will looked at me, drawing his eyebrows together. I just needed to come out with it.

'Where's Ben?'

He paused and then took a deep breath.

'He's gone back to the States, and he's currently staying at a rehab facility in East Hampton. I promise you're safe, and I'll let you know when he comes out, okay?'

'Did you organise that?' I asked, looking at him.

'Yes,' he replied simply.

He looked at me, searching my eyes.

'Anything else?' he asked, a faint smirk passing over his face.

I pursed my lips.

'Do you ever want kids?'

He laughed.

'Well, we haven't ever talked about it, and apparently, we should have had this conversation by now.'

'Really. Says who?'

'The girls,' I admitted.

'You are gonna have *thought too much* on your gravestone at this rate.' He took another deep, steadying breath. 'For a while, I thought I might want kids, but it was either the wrong time or I wasn't in a relationship, and then a couple of years ago, I just accepted that it wouldn't happen, and I'm cool with that.'

'When you split from Alysa?'

'Yes.'

'So, you wanted kids with Alysa?'

'For a time, but I'm really glad we didn't... and then I met you.'

'And you don't want to have kids with me?'

'Is that a trick question?'

'What?'

Why would I be tricking him at a time like this?

'To be honest, I assumed you didn't want any more kids, and I'm cool with that, but if you're asking whether I want to have kids with you because you're comparing yourself to Alysa, then yes, I'd have kids with you.'

Oh, he was good and sneaky because he hadn't actually confirmed yes or no.

'Why? Do you wanna have kids with me?'

There was a pause, and I looked down at his arm. He lifted my chin, and I batted him away. This was definitely a looking-down conversation, but I could feel his eyes boring into me.

'If I had my time again, then yes, but I feel like I've finished that chapter of my life. The boys are amazing, but it won't be long before they fly the nest, and I'm ready to get my life back.'

'So... I think we've agreed that we don't wanna have kids?'

I rolled my eyes and smiled.

'You see, that wasn't so bad,' he said, smiling too, knowing it had taken a lot for me to ask.

Suddenly, he propped himself up on his elbows, bringing his eyes in line with mine.

'As we're addressing a few... subjects this evening...'

I looked at him, wondering what he was going to say. I was sure the baby conversation was the most awkward issue to tackle, but Will looked hesitant.

'I wanna organise some security for you.'

'Errr, that won't be necessary. I don't need a Terry.'

He laughed, but I couldn't find humour in the conversation.

'I don't mean that. I'm talking about here, your home. I want you and the boys to feel safe. I'm thinking a secure fence, cameras, a decent alarm.'

I had barbed wire and 1980s security cameras passing through my mind.

'Your face is a picture,' he laughed. 'They're super discreet, and you'll be able to choose exactly what you want.'

'I... I really don't think that's necessary.'

'Lucy, I can guarantee you're gonna get pretty fed up with the camera crew outside. And they can be brutal sometimes. I just wanna protect you.'

I sighed, biting the side of my cheek.

'Fine, I'll speak to them.'

He clutched the side of my face with his hand, brushing my lip with his thumb.

'Good,' he said, biting his bottom lip and looking at me with a twinkle in his eye. 'Now, where am I putting my rucksack? Are we still going along with the façade that we're together, but not actually fucking? Because if that's the case, I might need to fuck you right here before we go to bed.'

He ran his fingers down my neck and pushed the strap of my camisole off my shoulder as his fingers continued their journey down my arm. He lifted his eyebrow, trying not to smirk because he knew he was testing my motherly morals.

I had actually been thinking about that as Terry drove us back. I didn't think the boys would mind. I mean, I let Emily stay over in Frankie's room, for goodness sake. And we had actually had sex in my bed the night he surprised me on his way to France. It just felt weird.

'What is it?' he asked, mischief dancing in his eyes.

'I'm good with us sleeping in the same room...' I began, but I didn't quite know how to explain myself. I took a moment to gather my thoughts. 'Mike and I... bought that bed in my room together,' I whispered.

I let that sit for a bit.

'So, we sleep in my room,' he said, swinging his legs onto the floor and sitting up.

'Oh, it's your room now, is it?' I said with a smile.

He put his hand out for me to take. 'It's my fuck pad,' he said in that lowered tone that made my insides spark. 'And besides, I'm known for leaving great tips.'

I laughed, and he picked up his bag and began pulling me toward the door.

When we got upstairs, Will had a quick shower, and I raced into my bedroom to get some sexier underwear on. I slipped into his bed, pulling the covers up high and waited for him.

We had covered some ground that evening. All the things that had been playing on my mind had all been categorised and filed into the correct folders, and for the first time since I met Will, everything seemed... right. Perfect.

Will came back in, his lower half wrapped in a towel. His eyes swept over my covered body as he walked into the room, and he put his things down at the end of the bed. He turned, his dark gaze finding mine, a ghost of a smile passing across his features before he suddenly whipped the duvet off me.

A small shriek escaped me as I recoiled, crossing one arm over my face to cover my blushes and the other over my tummy in case of any wobbly bits on show. Will immediately closed the distance between us and gently lifted my arms away, placing them by my side. He used his thumb at the base of my chin to bring my eyes in line with his.

'Don't shy away from me, Lucy. I don't want you to feel awkward around me. I want you to feel confident. Free. If you don't feel like that, I'm doing something seriously wrong.'

'I don't feel awkward... It's just... I'm not used to...'

As per usual, I couldn't seem to articulate myself, but Will made the decision to park the conversation by planting a kiss on my lips. He pushed up a little to take a leisurely look down my body. I could see the large bulge below his towel, and when our eyes met again, he smiled.

'Don't move.'

He slowly lifted away, moving back down to the end of the bed, and then I had to really concentrate on not moving my arms, fighting against my natural reaction.

'Beautiful.'

He took a firm hold of each of my ankles and suddenly yanked me down the bed. I gasped as my arms lifted above my head in the process, my hair fanning out above me and my feet landing on the floor.

'Don't move,' he reminded me.

I was so far out of my comfort zone that I jumped when Will put his hands on my thighs.

'Relax, baby,' he said as he slid his hands up, hooking my knickers over his thumbs and slowly removing them. He placed his hands on my knees and tried to part them, but I couldn't help resisting.

'Lucy,' he admonished. 'Come on, relax. It's just me.'

He bent and peppered kisses up my thigh, and while I was distracted, he pushed my knees apart. Glancing up at me, he grinned before dropping down to kneel. His hands worked their way around to the back of my hips before swiftly hoisting me up and landing his lips right on my centre.

I gasped, immediately looking at the door, worried I'd been too loud. When I looked back at Will, I could see the smile in his eyes before he made a show of rolling his eyes into the back of his head as if he was passing out with pure pleasure, and I giggled.

Will handled my body with such confidence, moving, moulding, and adjusting to his needs but, most of all, mine. He knew exactly how to please me and always made sure I was sated before he considered himself. Like now, alternating from small fluttery licks to wide, firm strokes, attending to every layer with exquisite precision.

'Jesus, Lucy, I can't seem to lap you up fast enough.'

That did it. I turned my face to the side, squeezing my eyes shut. At least this way, I could hide half my heated cheeks. Once again, Will was in my face in seconds, lying on his side, and when I opened my eyes, he was grinning and covered in my arousal. I went to wipe it off, but he grabbed my hand, directing my fingers to brush over his jaw and then placed them in my gaping mouth.

'Oh, I have some work to do,' he said.

I looked down, and he grabbed my hip, pulling me against him and kissing me. He'd purposefully made me taste myself but then, just as quickly, he was gone, rummaging around in his bag.

'I… I started taking the pill,' I whispered, rolling onto my back, guessing he was looking for condoms.

He whipped back around and crawled back up over me, removing his towel as he did so. I glanced down to see his thick hard dick bobbing between us, pre-cum beading at the crown.

'What? You didn't say.'

'I started taking them last weekend, but because I'm mid cycle, I had to wait seven days.'

'And you want me bare?' he asked, disbelief lacing across his face. 'I mean, I'm clean... b-but I totally get it if you want me to get tested again,' he added, stumbling over his words.

'Tested?' I asked. Was that an American thing? Not using condoms was the norm for me. Prior to Mike having the snip, I'd had a coil fitted, so it wasn't something I'd had to consider for a while. Not that I was about to tell him that. But testing, was that what couples did these days? To prove they weren't carrying anything. It seemed so clinical.

'I trust you,' I said honestly.

It was his turn for his mouth to gape. I hadn't realised this was such a big thing for him. His face was a picture.

'I um... fuck,' he said hoarsely.

And then suddenly, I wondered if he wanted *me* to get tested.

'If you don't want to, that's fine. I can...'

'No!' he said a little too sharply, and I smiled.

A sigh of delight left his mouth as he lifted my knee up and then looked down while he coated the tip of his now throbbing cock, mixing our arousals together. When he looked back up, I could see the prominent veins in his neck pulsing. His eyes... were so dark only a trace of pine green remained.

I took a quick unsettling breath in at this sudden change of mood. His eyes bore into mine, and without warning, he shunted his hips forward, plunging in deep.

My cry was muffled as he immediately captured my lips with his.

The groan he emitted was so guttural it added to the sensation. After several hard deep thrusts, taking a moment with each to seat himself fully, his pace became intemperate. The silky taught skin of his cock was the perfect texture for me, and I closed my eyes momentarily, relishing in the feel of him.

'So fucking tight,' he murmured, 'So fucking perfect... So. Fucking. Incredible.'

The words were whispered through gritted teeth between thrusts as he began to lose himself, fucking me, each slam so forceful I was being jolted up the bed. Moving me physically higher in every sense of the word. He closed his eyes. I couldn't work out if he was completely lost in the moment or whether he was trying to regain some control, but seconds later, they had sprung back open.

In one swift movement, he lifted my leg over his shoulder and yanked the cup of my bra down. He seized my boob in his hand, my nipple in his mouth, sucking until its hardened length became painful. I whimpered, a little shocked, the pain dissipating as he gently kneaded and licked me. My focus returned to the deep ache building inside me from his torturous pace.

And then he did it again.

'Will!' I cried out with pain.

The ache heightened. I looked down. Will's fingertips were pressed into the flesh of my breast, and his mouth was wide over my nipple. He looked up, and I gasped, his eyes ablaze with determination and... was that anger I could detect? Shit. I began to squirm, panic seeping in, but he pinned me down, unlatching his mouth from my nipple.

'Lucy,' he said soothingly in a low rumbling voice, one that I'd not heard before. 'Don't fight this.' His gentle voice was a contrast to the grip he had on me and the fire in his eyes. His gaze didn't falter as his lips landed back on my nipple, and he slowly sucked the flesh back into his mouth. The sensation morphed from pleasurable, to intense, to unbearable as my chest rose of its own accord to counteract the pain, and just as I was about to scream, he released it. 'Feel it, baby,' he murmured.

And the ache inside ratcheted up once more. Suddenly my mind and soul were joining the dots. The pain he was inflicting was causing a pleasurable ache within, and just as I figured this out, the mortifying confusion hit me. I shouldn't be enjoying this. I looked down at myself, my nipple red and swollen, erect and pebbled. But the need deep inside me was escalating.

'Christ, baby, don't cry.'

I wasn't crying. I think a few tears escaped when I was trying to curb the pain.

'I'm sorry,' he said, alarmed, 'I thought... it's too soon.'

But his voice seemed distant, my brain struggling to make sense of the warring sensations. Will was gently kissing my tears away and was about to pull out when it all clicked into place.

'Do it again,' I said in desperation, and he stilled. 'Don't stop, do it again,' I panted.

'Fuck. Yes.'

Slamming back into me, he clamped his lips over my breast again, pulling his head back, lifting my boob up with it as the suction fought against gravity. The carnal, ravaging move caused something to snap inside, and for the first time, I opened up to him. Something I didn't realise I'd been holding back from him, something I'd been holding back my entire life.

Somehow my hips widened, my insides dilated, and my back arched. Will thrust himself in again, and the cry that left me sounded foreign to my ears. The connection was so much deeper than before.

'Holy fuck, Lucy, I'm gonna come,' he choked out, having released my now burning chest.

But I couldn't speak as the move had set me spiralling into my own orgasm. One so intense I didn't know whether to push him away or ask for more. Will was staring at me in awe, cradling the nape of my neck and watching me fall to pieces. I felt the hot pumps of his release shoot deep inside me while he whispered, 'fuck, fuck, fuck,' over and over, in pure hedonism, until all I could hear was our ragged breathing.

Will was still hovering over me, staring at me in disbelief as I came back down to earth like I was some kind of enigma. The contagious smile that slowly crept over his face as our breathing normalised made me laugh with embarrassment.

'Don't you dare be embarrassed. That was mind-blowing. What happened? For a second there, I thought I'd seriously fucked up. I guess you haven't played with pain before.'

I shook my head, still unable to speak.

'Are you okay?'

I looked down at my chest, five fingerprint-sized purple bruises around the edge of my boob, indentations of bite marks in line with my areola, and my nipple, raw. Will was looking down, too and sunk his teeth into his lower lip before looking back up at me with concern.

'I liked it,' I said, frowning.

'Mmm hmm,' Will responded, nodding, encouraging me to elaborate.

'I thought what you were doing was wrong...'

'But?'

'But it felt good,' I whispered, not wanting to admit it.

'Good?' he questioned.

'Amazing,' I clarified.

He smiled, not in a patronising way, in a proud way. As he gently lifted the cup of my bra back over my sensitive skin, I lowered my leg, and he carefully pulled out before wrapping his arms around me.

'I take it what you had with Mike wasn't like this.'

I shook my head and looked away from him. I really didn't want to think about Mike right now.

'Hey, don't be ashamed. I'd far rather this than know you'd done these things with other people.'

I looked at him with a serious appraisal. I was sure he'd done every sexual act known to man with many women. He shook his head, knowing exactly what I was thinking.

'It's never felt like this. I'm not saying I've never played with pain before...'

That stung, despite me knowing how experienced he was. He cupped my cheek tenderly.

'But I've never loved anyone before either,' he said with complete sincerity.

I exhaled, any thoughts of jealousy or envy leaving me along with the breath.

'Not even Alysa?'

'No,' he said, shaking his head. 'I think at the time I thought I was, but it doesn't even compare, Lucy. I've never met someone I can't bear to be apart from. Someone that sends me so goddamn crazy. And someone that's opened up to me like that.'

A light flush warmed my cheeks at the thought of what we just did, and Will smiled at me, adoration in his eyes.

'I love you, Lucy.'

'I love you too.'

Chapter 3

Following the exposure in the press, the requests for appointments for my physio business were off the scale. Appointments were being requested on all social media platforms, including email, text, and calls. I was thankful that Frankie had taken it upon himself to sort through the inquiries, knowing that my non-techy brain would probably blow a fuse.

Frankie had also found a free online booking system and was populating the link onto all the socials and autoreply messages so that all future enquiries other than calls were directed to one place. We had spent an evening together while he patiently gave me a training session on how to use the system. My need for step-by-step tutoring caused Frankie and Will to exchange amused expressions, which was not helping.

Needless to say, I was super busy for the next few weeks. Each morning Will and I would get up early and walk the dogs. It was fast becoming my favourite part of the day because it was quiet, and we were able to walk and talk without getting stopped by fans or papped unexpectedly.

I was concerned that Will would want to go home, but a large package arrived after a couple of days. It was a guitar. A guitar for the UK, he'd announced. Whenever I had a small break, I would find him scribbling lines in his notebook, strumming out chords, or humming melodies.

After a few failed attempts at going out in the evening and spending more time stopping for selfies with fans than talking, we decided it was easier to stay in. I'd cook, and Will would tell me stories about his touring days, the places he'd visited, the places he wanted to take me to, and then we'd eat and either watch a film or play cards or he'd ask me silly questions like, if you were a biscuit, which biscuit would you be and why.

We were in a perfect Will and Lucy bubble.

A *Wucy*.

How pathetic!

'WOULD YOU STOP DISTRACTING me? I need to set my treatment room up before my early client arrives,' I said, trying to keep the stress out of my tone.

I had agreed to take an extra booking first thing because I was completely full until we went to New York, and this guy was insistent that he'd been trying to book, and the new system wasn't working.

'But you look so fuckable in the mornings, your hair all messy and...'

'Will!' I whisper shouted, batting his hand away, effectively putting a stop to his attempt at pulling my knickers back down.

He chuckled, his hand disappearing back under the duvet.

'I'm gonna be lonely on the dog walk,' he whined, and I rolled my eyes as I hovered over him to kiss him goodbye.

He was wrong. *He* was the one that looked fuckable in the mornings, his lean torso and toned arms on display. His green eyes were bright with enthusiasm for another day of writing and creating.

'I'm sure you'll manage,' I said, not allowing him to lead me into another conversation.

I kissed him chastely and darted out of the room before he could do or say any more.

'So, what can I help you with today?'

My client seemed taken aback by the question, which was odd as he was so desperate for an appointment.

'Erm. It's my back,' he snapped.

'Okay, and what appears to be the problem?'

He was an older guy, probably in his early sixties. He was fairly ordinary looking, of average build, had grey hair, and wore chinos and a loose shirt.

'Well, it's sore.'

God, this was like getting blood out of a stone.

'And the pain that you're experiencing is an ache? A shooting pain? Stiffness?'

'An ache.'

'And whereabouts is the ache?'

'All over.'

An all-over backache. Hmmm. Normally if someone had pulled something, it would be in a particular area, so the fact it was all over was possibly pointing toward an autoimmune disease or something more sinister.

'And when did the pain start?'

'Look, I just need a back massage,' he said curtly.

I frowned.

'You do realise I'm a physiotherapist, not a massage therapist.'

'It says on your website that you offer massage.'

'Yes, as part of a treatment...'

'Well, in that case, I want a massage.'

I bit my tongue. I knew I was tired, so I thought it would be best to swallow my pride and just go along with it.

'Okay, well, if you'd like to take your top off and lie on your front on the couch, here's a towel, and I'll be back in a moment.'

I left him to it for a few minutes before knocking and re-entering. He was lying on the couch as I'd instructed, but when I went to tuck the towel into the waistline of his briefs, I realised he was naked. I quickly glanced at the clock, I really didn't have time to delay before my next client, so I ignored it and began to massage his back.

'So, when did you qualify as a physio?'

Now he wanted to make small talk. This guy was odd. I just couldn't put my finger on it, and it was making me wary. I answered his questions with as little information as possible. He kept shifting around as if he was uncomfortable, and at one point, I swore he readjusted himself.

He moaned as I moved my hands down the length of his spine with a slow, firm pressure. I closed my eyes for a second. It wasn't the first time someone had moaned during treatment, I'd had people fall asleep before now, but it wasn't a moan of pain or relaxation. It was as if he was getting off on it.

'Are you enjoying that?' he asked in a husky voice.

Oh my God.

'Pardon me? I assume you mean my job?'

He coughed and shifted around again.

Alarm bells were ringing, and I didn't feel comfortable anymore. There were another five minutes left of his treatment, but I wanted him out. Out of my treatment room and out of my house.

'Do you know what? I can't seem to find anything wrong. I'm going to leave you now to put your clothes back on.'

He didn't say anything, so I left the room. I paced up and down for a few minutes before knocking, and I was thankful to discover that he was dressed. Normally I'd ask if he'd like to rebook, but instead, I just asked for payment.

When he put his hand in his pocket to get his wallet out, his hand lingered there as he subtly moved his hips back and forth, and when I looked up at him, he was staring at my chest.

Christ.

'I think you should leave.'

I opened the door, ushering him out, and I was so thankful to see Frankie making a drink in the kitchen. The man clocked him immediately and swiftly left.

As soon as he'd gone, I shut the door and rushed back into the treatment room, gathering the couch roll up and forcefully scrunching it into a ball before throwing it in the bin.

'Mum, are you all right?'

I looked up at Frankie standing in the doorway, feeling confused about what had just happened.

'That man, he was... I don't know... I think he was getting himself off,' I said as I was wiping my hands down my top to try to get rid of the feeling of his skin on my hands.

'What? Mum! What did he do?'

Frankie had already retrieved his mobile from his pocket and was ringing the police before I could explain. He wrapped his arm around me, and tears sprung to my eyes at the realisation of what had happened and, more importantly, what could have happened.

I leapt out of my skin as the door suddenly reopened, fear racing through my body and numbing my lower spine. The dogs came bounding in followed by Will. He took one look at my face.

'What happened?' he asked, chucking the dog leads on the dining table as Frankie let go of me, Will immediately taking his place.

'Police, please,' Frankie requested.

I could feel Will's body tense, drawing back slightly. He looked at me, searching my eyes.

'He, he was... getting himself off,' I managed.

'Er, yes, my Mum has just been sexually assaulted.'

Will suddenly pulled away from me.

'That man?' he asked, rage scolding his features, gesturing towards the door.

I tried to respond, but as I took a breath in, I choked on a sob, and Will's whole face contorted. He lunged toward the door.

'No!' I shouted, but he'd disappeared before I could stop him.

As Frankie continued to explain what had happened to the police, I went to follow Will, but Frankie grabbed me around the waist. Before I'd managed to break free, Frankie thanked the person on the other end and hung up the call.

'Mum!' he said, exasperated. 'Stop.'

I slumped into his arms.

'The police are on their way, okay?'

Will came flying back into the kitchen, using the doorframe to assist with the sudden change of direction. He was completely out of breath.

'Can't see him,' he managed between gasps.

Turning the tap on, he drank straight from the flow.

The doorbell went, and I jumped again, staring at the closed door as if the devil himself were standing behind it before realising it would likely be my next client.

Frankie went off to deal with them while Will wiped his mouth with the back of his hand, leading me into the lounge with his other and turning to face me.

'Are you okay?' he asked and immediately followed it up with, 'What did he do?'

An hour and a half later, I was sat in the lounge with two female police officers, having explained the entire ordeal to them again.

Frankie had contacted my remaining clients due in that day to say I'd been taken ill and was now raking through my social media accounts, emails, and messages with a fine-tooth comb.

'Well, I think we've got everything we need, but if you happen to remember something after we've left, you can contact us on this number.'

I picked up my phone, ready to save the details, but once I'd brought the phone to my face to unlock the screen, bile rose in my throat before the phone slipped through my fingers as if it was covered in slime.

The wallpaper on my phone, which once had a picture of the boys standing smiling side by side, had been replaced with a picture of an erect penis.

If I hadn't felt violated before, I did now.

'What the fuck?' Will said.

Standing, Will went to pick the phone up, but the police officer stopped him. She pulled out a glove and an evidence bag from one of the pockets on her stab vest and proceeded to carefully place my mobile inside.

I began to tremble, the enormity of the situation embedding itself into my very being. All the what ifs rolling around in my head. I was vaguely aware of Will seeing the officers out and having a hushed conversation with Frankie as he continued his research into the booking before sitting beside me.

'How are you feeling?' he asked, placing a blanket over my shoulders despite the warm evening.

'Just... really unsettled.'

An involuntary shiver passed through me.

'Hey,' he said, putting his arm over my shoulder. 'He's not gonna come back here. The security company is checking the footage, and they're sending someone to watch over the house. You're safe.'

Silence fell between us.

It wasn't that I didn't feel safe. Anxious maybe. I frowned as I deciphered my true feelings, surprising myself that anger was one of them.

Will let out a frustrated sigh.

'I'm sorry,' he said.

Silence fell between us again, and I realised he'd figured out why I was feeling angry before I had.

The press coverage of our relationship had put my job in jeopardy.

'I'll pay,' he announced.

I exhaled a short laugh.

'My wages? What, like a kept woman?'

'No,' he said, disgusted at the notion. 'I'll pay your losses.'

'Well, that could be a hefty bill over the next twenty-odd years.'

He remained silent.

'It's not just the money, Will. It's what I trained for. It's what I want to do. I like helping people. I can't just give it up.'

Although I was looking at the floor, I could hear the anger in Will's breath.

'Lucy,' he said through gritted teeth. 'What if he'd done something else? What if he'd raped you? It's not worth the risk. I know this is a tough decision, but I don't want you putting yourself in a dangerous situation.'

'But it's all I know!' I said in exasperation.

'Now is not the fucking time to be stubborn, Lucy,' he said with a stern voice.

I looked at him, furious that *he* was getting angry with *me*. He was being so flippant. How would he feel if he had to give up his job? The tension in the room was growing, and I wasn't prepared to stay in its chokehold even though it was my house.

'I'm going to Steph's,' I announced, standing.

'What!? Lucy, no!' Will stood too.

'What, are you gonna stop me from seeing my friends now?'

That shut him up. He took a breath in to say something and thought better of it. Stepping back to let me by.

AFTER SPENDING A COUPLE of hours with Steph, discussing the ordeal in minute detail as only a woman could, I had a plan. I would continue working but only see patients who I'd seen before. I had enough regulars to keep me afloat, and I would lay off taking new bookings unless they were related to my patients.

I arrived back at the house to a raft of paparazzi. Why on earth were they there? Maybe the police car on the driveway had instigated their arrival. Or maybe they had some secret alert about police reports?

Either way, I was very thankful for the additional security measures that Will had put in place, even though my trusty old run-of-the-mill family car looked ridiculous with tinted windows. It looked like a boy racers car without the lowered suspension. A security guard waved me in, and as soon as the new gates were shut, I got out and headed back into the house.

'Mum!' Frankie said as he and Paddy, my youngest boy, lifted their gaze from his laptop. 'Will's security cameras managed to capture an image of the man, and they sent it to the police. Paddy and I then looked through all the social media accounts of people that had started following you since you met Will, and we found a picture of a guy that looked similar, so I rang that number that they left and gave them his handle.'

I just stood there staring at them both, amazed that my son had managed to track him down so quickly.

'And we just had a call to say that the man has been found and is in custody,' Paddy added quickly at the end, as Frankie gave him a look of annoyance at him finishing the story.

'Wow! I'm so grateful to you. Thank you.'

I gave them both a hug, giving Frankie an extra squeeze.

'Where's Will?' I asked.

'Dunno, in his room, maybe?' Frankie suggested.

I slowly walked up the stairs, and I couldn't help the feeling that I was holding my tail between my legs. I kind of flew off the handle, and it wasn't really his fault. Not personally, anyway. I hesitated outside his bedroom door. It had been pushed to but wasn't shut. Giving it a nudge, I let it swing open.

Will was lying on his side on top of the bed, wearing just his jeans. Christ, how was I supposed to concentrate on the conversation we needed to have? He looked up from his phone with a placid expression.

'I'm sorry,' I said.

He closed his eyes for a moment.

'No, I'm sorry. This is all my fault.'

'It really isn't. But I'm sorry I shot off,' I said, pinching the bridge of my nose. I took a deep breath. 'I'm not going to give up work,' I declared.

Will's face became pensive, but he remained silent.

'I will, however, only see patients that have had treatments from me previously. I'll ask Frankie to cancel all the other bookings.'

Will pushed himself up and came to stand in front of me. I watched as his deltoids rippled and his pecs contracted while he moved.

'I think you have yourself a deal, ma'am.'

It took me a second to return my gaze to his, and he smirked at me.

'But I'm not going to accept any compensation,' I blurted out to cover up my blatant gawping.

'No?' he said, smiling. 'Not even if I repay you in another way?' he asked in a lowered voice.

He brushed the back of his knuckles across my already-hardened nipple, his hand running up and over my shoulder.

I jumped as the door slammed behind me, and Will grabbed hold of my hips, pulling my body flush to his.

God, this man will be the death of me.

THREE WEEKS LATER, I sat on my white wooden chair on the deck above the sand, a couple of rows back from Will, who was on best man duty with Jake for Paul. I looked out beyond the beautiful pergola, wrapped in pretty blush roses, to the Atlantic Ocean and reflected on the last few weeks.

Will stayed at my house until it was time to leave for the wedding. Not only had the new security system been installed, but I finished work one day to find a brand-new bed and mattress set up in my bedroom, the old one nowhere to be seen.

The press eventually stopped camping outside the house after Will had gone out and made a statement. The media had begun to report me as being some kind of home wrecker following the G.A.M. Awards. There had also been some crazy allegations that Will was abusing me and after numerous calls with his PR agency, Will had set the press straight.

He had explained that although he and Alysa had been in a relationship previously, it had been over for a couple of years, but they remained friends. He'd also officially confirmed that we were an item which had led to many more questions about me that he had refused to answer. He didn't even address the abuse claim.

I had finally started the process of filing for divorce, and I'd also managed to secure an agreement in principle for a mortgage that would sever my ties to Mike financially too.

I had managed to arrange four weeks of holiday. My client list was always lighter in the summer holidays, so there were only a few disgruntled customers. The boys were on holiday with Mike. He had used some of his redundancy money to take them on a trip of a lifetime around Canada. I was reluctant to leave the dogs in kennels for an entire month, so Will had organised for a dog sitter to stay at the house.

I was going to miss them all terribly.

I hadn't seen Will since we arrived yesterday. He had dropped me off at the wedding venue into Hannah's arms and left immediately to catch up with Paul for his stag do. Once I'd checked in, I hoped to take a walk on the beach and rest before the big day tomorrow until I discovered the bridal party schedule left in my room. I had been waxed, plucked, and primped, my nails had been painted, and I'd received a facial before I practically fell into bed.

I looked at Will in his dark royal blue suit and stripy tie, whispering something to Paul, probably trying to calm his nerves before his bride arrived, and my heart sang. He had walked into my life unexpectedly and taken my heart on a roller coaster ride like no other. But, since the award ceremony and the dust had settled, we were finally managing to enjoy each other's company without too many external constraints.

I looked up the aisle. She couldn't be long now, I thought. My new phone buzzed in my hand. I couldn't stand to use the old one so Will had ordered me a new one. It was Golf Buggy Guy.

Yo, Leia! Hope you're having the best time in NY. See you in Spain, Han.

We had kept in touch, and by a wonderful coincidence, he was organising the festival in Spain that The 'king Band was due to headline for next month, and I couldn't wait. So, I quickly tapped back a response.

At the wedding right now. Can't wait to see you. I love you.

I know.

I smiled, knowing he'd use the famous line from Star Wars.

The music suddenly started, and I quickly stuffed my phone in my bag and stood up with everyone else. I glanced over at Will, who was looking at me, and he signalled to ask if I was okay, which caused several people to look around and stare. I smiled in response before looking at the ground, embarrassed, and when I glanced back, he was relaying the moment to Paul, so I turned to watch as Hannah started to make her way down the aisle, hoping my cheeks were not too red.

She looked beautiful in a scoop neck lacy vintage number, a curvy, long-sleeved, floor-length dress, which wrapped around her, and as she walked by, I could see the material crossed over behind her, revealing a section of her toned, tanned back. Her bouquet was beautiful too. All the flowers looked like they'd been picked in a meadow. She had two little bridesmaids who were scattering petals onto the sand. They wore tiny flower crowns and cute satin dresses in the same cream colour as Hannah.

The ceremony was shorter than I had imagined, and everyone had been given petals to scatter over the happy couple as they walked back up the aisle, and then we all cheered and clapped. They looked so happy together.

I looked down, smoothing the creases out of my dress, and admired my pretty pedicured toes through my dark red high-heeled sandals. My dress was fitted and stopped just above the knee with a slight split up the back. It also had a shallow scooped neckline and capped sleeves with a bold floral design on an off-white background.

I felt a hand on the small of my back, the heat making my legs go a bit jelly-like.

'Hey, beautiful. You look stunning,' Will whispered.

'Thank you, you look rather dapper yourself,' I said, turning and fondling his buttonhole flower.

'And who were you texting before the ceremony?' he asked.

'Do you watch me all the time?'

'I try to,' he said, looking straight at me with a wry smile.

'It was my other boyfriend, Han Solo. He's so much more famous than you.'

I waved my hand at him with an air of nonchalance, and Will laughed.

'Oh yeah, he's doing Spain, isn't he?'

'He is. Did he message you?'

'No, but I like to keep tabs on your other boyfriends.' I rolled my eyes. 'No, it came up on the schedule the other day.'

A waitress went by with a tray of fizz, and Will grabbed two glasses. 'Hold these. I think I'm needed for some photos.'

I quickly put my clutch under my arm and took the glasses, sipping out of one of them.

'And don't drink too much. I have plans for you later.'

I nearly spat the drink back out as he had said it slightly too loudly. But instead, I turned to face the sea, hoping the breeze would cool me down. Did he just enjoy embarrassing me?

'You must be Lucy,' a man said who had stepped up beside me to enjoy the view.

He was around the same age as Will, tall with blond hair, wearing a dark grey suit and the required uniform All-stars.

'Yes, are you a friend of Will's?' I asked, scrabbling for a light topic. I was rubbish at small talk.

'Yeah, we went to school together. I'm Drew. It's good to meet you.'

He put his hand out, but I just held up the drinks.

'It's good to meet you too. So, do you know Paul through Will?'

'Yeah, we all used to hang out together, mainly in Will's garage, listening to tunes and stuff. His mom would always make us cookies, so it was the place to be.'

I laughed nervously.

'I'm due to meet his mum in a couple of days.'

'Ah, she's awesome, I expect she'll be really pleased to see Will too.'

'Hey Drew, how you doin', man?' Will asked.

Oh, thank God, he was back. I smiled brightly and passed Will his drink, and then, thankfully, another waitress went by, so I put my empty glass on her tray.

While they were catching up, I wondered how his mum felt about him spending so much time in the UK, and all his friends for that matter. I was the one that had taken him away from them. I was about to sit in a room with a bunch of strangers who thought I had plucked Will from their lives, with Will sitting on the head table doing his best man thing. I had a horrible day nightmare of people throwing food at me.

'Are you okay?' Will asked. 'You have the weirdest expression on your face.'

'Mmm hmm,' I nodded.

Now was not the time to address this. It was Paul and Hannah's day, so I would have to push the thoughts to the back of my mind until tomorrow, when I would be sensible and tell Will what I was thinking.

'Okay, well, I have some people I'd like you to meet.'

Oh God...

'AND THIS IS STRYKER. Stryker is in The Deck. We tour with them a lot,' Will explained as he introduced me to yet another person.

He was about the same height as Will, with messy wavy blond hair casually tucked behind one ear, blue eyes, and a stubble beard. He had a golden tan, and if I didn't already know he was in a band, I'd have him pegged as a surfer.

'Lucy Daniels,' Stryker said slowly with a cheeky grin while he scanned me from head to toe. His gaze lingered a millisecond too long on my chest before he stepped in, and rather than shaking my hand, he lifted it up and kissed the back of it. He looked directly into my eyes, and I looked away, embarrassed, and he diverted his gaze to Will, giving him a wicked smile.

'Behave,' Will said with seriousness to Stryker, but there was a hint of amusement in his voice. 'You promised you'd look after her for me.'

I frowned slightly, wondering what Will meant.

'Of course, I'll look after her,' Stryker replied, grinning at me, pulling me into his side and wrapping an arm around my waist as I looked at Will, alarmed.

'You'll be sitting with Stryker during the wedding breakfast,' Will explained just as the Master of Ceremonies announced that we should all be seated.

'Which gives me at least an hour to sway her,' Stryker said, giving me a wink.

He pulled me towards our table, leaving Will looking up to the ceiling and shaking his head in mock annoyance before he made his way to the head table. I wasn't quite sure what to think. It felt strange having another man's arm around me, but if Will was happy with the arrangement, he must trust this guy.

Within a few minutes of sitting at our table, he introduced me to everyone as Will's girlfriend. I noticed they were all used to his relaxed, witty charm. Turning his attention back to me, he asked me about Frankie and Paddy, so Will had obviously given him the low-down, and I began to relax.

Chapter 4

Two hours later, I was introduced to so many people. All their names and faces seemed to merge into one. Having eaten, I felt exhausted and went to the restroom for just that. I needed to hear a friendly voice.

'And then I had to say hello to a whole bunch of people who all think I kidnapped him,' I whined.

'Babe, I'm sure they don't think that you've stolen him away from them,' Steph tried to assure me.

'One guy actually asked me what it was that I had that meant he didn't return.'

'I hope you told him it was your tits.' She laughed, but I didn't say anything. 'He has not stayed in the UK because of your tits,' she said sternly.

I sighed audibly.

'Anyway, babe, I'm gonna go, it's eleven-thirty over here, and I want to go for a run in the morning. It will be fine, just enjoy yourself, you're in the Hamptons daarling, and don't drink anymore. Bye, babe.'

What was she talking about? I wasn't even drunk, but I felt exhausted.

I came out of the ladies to find the party had moved on. Everyone had left their tables in the marquee and were either on or sitting around the dance floor. I was feeling unsteady on my feet, so I decided to get some water. I finally reached the bar after negotiating several tables and chairs and found a bar stool to sit on.

'Just a glass of water, please,' I said to the barman.

I rubbed my forehead, trying to massage some energy into me.

'There you are!' Will said.

There he was! He looked so sexy. He'd taken his tie off and undone the top button of his shirt. The barman put the glass of water down for me, and I took it and sipped, looking up at Will.

'Are you feeling all right?' he asked.

'Well, this is the thing... I feel really tipsy, but I haven't had much to drink,' I said, vaguely pointing at my water.

'Okay,' he said, laughing a little. 'I think you might be a bit jet-lagged. Come on, let me get you up to our room.'

'We have a room here?'

'Yeah, come on.'

He practically pushed me off the stool and took my arm to guide me through the party towards the lifts. Once inside, I looked at him and then at the floor.

'What?' he asked.

'You look hot,' I whispered as if someone other than him might hear my admission, or was it just because I lacked confidence when telling him how I felt?

He smiled as the lift doors opened, and he took my hand as we walked down the corridor. He swiped the key in the door, pulled me inside, and then immediately pushed me up against the back of the door and kissed me.

I would never get bored with this. On the outside, people saw a kind and considerate Will, but behind closed doors, he became quite demanding and masterful, and I loved it. He pulled away and spun me around, unzipping my dress, gently pushing it off my shoulders, and letting it fall to the floor. He wolf-whistled, and I smiled shyly. I had purposefully bought and worn a new set of underwear. He stepped back.

'Turn around, Daniels.'

I turned and tried to look at him seductively before chickening out and looking at the floor. He stepped in, catching my chin and lifting it so our lips met.

'I love that you're still so shy. It's cute.'

We kissed, and I started to undo the buttons of his shirt, pulling it out of his trousers with haste. He fiddled with his cuff links and then shrugged the shirt off. He took my hand and walked me over to the bed.

The room was huge, and the bed was high. I could hear the ocean outside the floor-to-ceiling window, and there was a lovely breeze coming in, making the curtains ripple and dance in the wind.

He sat me on the edge of the bed while he took his trousers and shoes off, and I bent down to undo one of the buckles on my heels, but before I'd managed to get hold of the tiny strap, he took my hand and pushed me back on to the bed.

'Leave the shoes.'

Oh.

He crawled up the bed and looked at me.

'What?' I asked.

'Everyone loved you. I knew they would. Stryker especially,' he said smiling.

'They don't think I've taken you away from them then?'

'Is that what you've been thinking this whole time?' he asked, shaking his head.

'Well, I guess that's how I'd feel?'

'They're happy for me and were super pleased to meet you... stop overthinking everything. And besides, they'd know why if they could see your tits right now.'

'Will!'

I went to smack him, but he grabbed both my arms, laughing, and after a short wrestle, he pushed them down onto the bed and held them there. He swooped in and kissed me before I could say anything else, and then slowly, as I was falling under his spell, he let me go when he was confident I wouldn't retaliate.

I wrapped my hands around him, pushing my fingers into his hair. His kisses slowly descended my neck, and as I ran my fingers over the contour of his shoulders, I wrapped my legs around him. His kisses continued past my boobs, onto my waist, and to the top of my briefs. He then pushed himself up to standing, pulling my knickers down my legs and over my shoes.

'This bed gives me a great vantage point,' he said.

I looked down, and he just stood at the end of the bed, looking at me. I immediately felt exposed and closed my legs, pushing myself onto my elbows, and he laughed.

'Will, what are you doing? Would you stop it?'

I looked to see if there was a spare cushion I could lob at him, but they were miles away at the top of the bed.

'Why are you so shy? You seriously have nothing to be shy about,' he said, watching me. After a moment of consideration, he said, 'Bend your knees.'

'Will,' I whined.

I dropped my shoulders, trying to convey that I did not feel comfortable doing that. He waited, his expression serious, and I reluctantly lifted them, putting my heels on the edge of the bed.

'Now open your legs.'

'Will, I...'

'Just stop thinking and open your legs,' he said with authority.

He knelt, and despairingly I lay back, flat on the bed so I couldn't see him, and looked at the ceiling. I slowly opened my legs.

'Great view,' he said in a gruff voice.

I rolled my eyes and held the bridge of my nose, wondering how long I could keep them there before I actually kicked him. He took hold of my knees and pushed them a little wider, I was about to wriggle out of his grip, and then he kissed me, right there, causing me to force my head back into the mattress. And then he began circling his tongue, and I looked down at him. I could just see his eyes watching me. I could tell he was smiling, and I shook my head, looking up to the ceiling again.

He was constantly testing me. Testing my ability to hold on, testing how far I'd go doing something I was uncomfortable with or simply testing my patience. Despite being insanely embarrassing at times, it was always exciting.

He began dipping his tongue inside me, but continued the circling with his thumb, I wasn't going to be able to hold on for much longer, and I could feel myself building. I held my breath, I knew he was watching me, but I wouldn't give him the satisfaction of looking at him.

Without breaking the circling, he said, 'hold on, Lucy.'

I was so close, and then he slowed to a stop. I knew he would, he always preferred me to come with him. It was like he was orchestrating a perfectly timed dance.

He took his boxers off as I lay there while my imminent climax ebbed away, and I wondered what he would do next.

He crawled up to look me in the eye, 'You okay?'

'Yes,' I assured him.

He kissed me, softly at first, but it became persistent, and he ground his erection against me. I was about to take him in my hand, but he pulled away, and then standing again, he forcefully pushed me onto my right side so that I was in the foetal position. Swiftly positioning himself, he entered me with a sudden thrust, and I moaned. The height of the bed allowing him to stand as he drove into me.

'God, I missed you last night,' he said breathlessly.

He took my arm out to the side and then pushed my shoulder into the bed, so my top half was twisted to face him. He delicately brushed his fingers down my shoulder onto my chest and then pulled the cup of my bra down, completely exposing my boob. I watched as his eyes danced, and then looking at me, he took my nipple in his mouth.

He hadn't done this since the night he came back and although he wasn't biting me, the thought of that night sent a bolt of energy right into my most sensitive area. I closed my eyes, desperately trying to concentrate on something else.

'Lucy,' he chided.

I opened my eyes, and he was shaking his head.

'Don't come.'

I started to pant, and he pulled out, releasing me. I took a deep, steadying breath. He crawled up again, searching my eyes to check I was okay and smiled, kissing me again. My whole body was alive, the slightest touch, kiss or stroke sending tingles across my skin.

He stood again and pulled me up to standing. I wobbled slightly on my heels, but he took me in his arms, kissing me. He leaned back and pulled the other cup down and gently teased and twisted my nipple. I took him in my hand, but he pulled away.

'Why won't you let me touch you?'

'Because you turn me on too much.'

He spun me around and pushed me onto the bed.

'Lift your knees, keep them on the edge.'

Even though he wasn't tall enough to reach me there, I wondered what he would do, and then he licked me, dipping his tongue into me again. I was not going to last, but he didn't stay there for long. He continued to lick me all the way up to my lower back, and I automatically contracted. A strip of wetness cooled as the air hit. He hadn't licked me there before. It felt positively weird but kind of nice.

'Crawl forward.'

I crawled up the bed, allowing him room to kneel behind me, but he didn't move.

'Fuck, you're dripping.'

'Will!' I said again, my voice coming as a needy plea, and I looked round to see he was stroking himself.

He moved up behind me, chuckling to himself as he came into position, the tip of his dick nestled at my opening, and I tried really hard to stay still, but I wanted him. I went to move my hips, but he stilled me with his other hand and then slowly, torturously moved inside me, starting a slow rhythm, and then I felt something in that untouched place again, was it his finger, his thumb? He gently massaged it, and it felt really odd. I tried to pull away, but he grabbed my hip.

'Relax, Lucy, try to relax.'

I took a steadying breath in, really trying my hardest to relax, and as I exhaled, he pushed his thumb past the ring of muscle, and I squirmed.

'Stay still,' he demanded.

Oh my God! I took a sharp breath in, and I couldn't help the mewl that passed my lips on the out-breath. I'm not naïve, I knew people did anal play, but I never thought I'd be one of those people. Was it dirty? Yes. Did I like it? I wasn't sure.

'Are you okay?' he asked.

'I think so?'

'Just go with it.'

He found a gentle rhythm, but the sensations I was feeling were sort of clashing. One felt amazing, and the other felt wrong, yet they were both in harmony. His pace began to speed up. I couldn't work out which sensation to concentrate on.

'Are you close?'

'I... don't know,' I said between breaths.

Then, using his other hand, he started to circle me with his fingers. Jesus. It was too much, there were too many sensations, and I wasn't sure if I liked it. I was about to ask him to stop when suddenly, out of nowhere, I started to build, and it was like I was building in three different ways.

'Ahhh, Will!' I scrunched the sheets up in my hands.

'Let go, Lucy. Let go.'

And I did, and it was like nothing I'd ever experienced. Everything pulsated and contracted at different times, yet in unison, and I screamed my release. I knew he was coming too because the rhythm had become erratic as he lost control. My insides, outsides, and every sinew were a wash of pure pleasure, lapping over me before the final wave slowly retreated.

He gently removed his thumb before pulling out, and I closed my eyes, trying to absorb what had just happened, but I was so exhausted. He turned me over onto my back and crawled up to check in on me, but I could barely focus. He kissed me gently, stroking my arm and shoulder, slowly bringing me back to reality.

'Lucy... say something.'

I looked into his eyes sleepily.

'There are no words.'

He smiled with pure satisfaction. He knew he'd outdone himself, raising the bar again.

Chapter 5

I blinked a few times, letting the light flutter in. I had hardly moved. The bed was still made, and I was naked, but a blanket had been placed over me. I heard a shower on, but it sounded like it was miles away. Then, as I came to and had a good look around the room, I realised it was actually a suite. There was a lounge area I hadn't noticed when we got back last night, and beyond that must have been the bathroom.

I slowly sat up and slid off the end of the bed, frowning when I saw my shoes and bra on the floor. My legs quivered as flashbacks from last night gradually filtered through my mind. I wrapped the blanket around me, the fresh morning air gently blowing through the window. The view caught my eye. It was stunning, with a blue sea and white sand.

I padded over to the bathroom, the door was open, so I snuck in. A pillar in the middle of the room separated the most oversized bath I'd ever seen, and the enormous walk-in shower. I leaned against the post and watched Will for a few moments before he sensed someone was present and pushed his hair out of his face. He looked at me, his eyes darkening before he signalled for me to join him.

There were two shower heads the size of dinner plates, and he flipped the other lever on for me, but what came out was freezing, and I screamed as he dragged me over to his side. Trying not to laugh.

'Sorry about that. Good morning, beautiful. Are you okay?'

'Yes, why wouldn't I be?'

'No reason,' he replied with a little glint in his eye, and then he kissed me chastely before dipping back under his stream to rinse his hair.

I checked the temperature before stepping under my own flow of luscious rejuvenating water. I washed my hair and made full use of the hotel toiletries, which smelt divine. Will was watching me, he was always watching me, and I would occasionally meet his gaze.

I switched off my shower, wrapped a towel around me, and stepped over to the enormous sink to brush my teeth. It was super long with two sets of taps. Will joined me, coming to brush his teeth alongside me, and he kept glancing over at me.

'What?' I asked after spitting out.

'Just checking you're okay... after last night.'

He came up behind me, looking at my reflection in the mirror above the sink.

'I am,' I replied, but I couldn't hold his gaze and looked down.

He smiled, kissing my neck.

'Good,' he said, palming my arse cheek, "cause I'm gonna enjoy exploring you,' he said, giving me a firm squeeze before he strode into the bedroom. I shook my head and couldn't help but smile at myself in the mirror, and then I shivered, wondering how far he wanted me to go.

Gathering my toiletries back into my sponge bag, I quickly popped my contraceptive pill before heading back out to the bedroom.

'This is a very extravagant bedroom for a wedding guest to stay in for one night. Did you get an upgrade?'

He laughed a little.

'Err, I dunno, Paul organised the rooms,' he said vaguely as he busied himself by fetching his clothes from his bag.

'You look pretty,' he said, changing the subject.

I'd dressed in another set of new white underwear and pulled a white maxi dress over the top. It was fitted around the waist, long and flowing. My sky-blue sandals completed the look. I may have been on a rather elaborate shopping trip before this holiday.

'Thanks.'

Will dressed in a pair of dark blue skinny tapered trousers, rolled up slightly with another shirt which he tucked in and rolled the sleeves up as well. It was weird seeing him in different clothes, he even had flip-flops.

'Are we going somewhere?' I asked.

'Yes, down to breakfast.'

'Oh, is it an organised event with the rest of the wedding guests? Should I wear something else?'

'It's not organised as such, but the rest of the wedding party will be there, I'd imagine, and no, you look beautiful. You always look beautiful.'

We stepped out of the lifts, Will took my hand and walked towards the marquee. The twinkling lights had been removed, and the sides had been rolled up, allowing an uninterrupted ocean view. We sat at a table for two and were immediately served coffee.

I couldn't help but notice the whispering. I had gotten used to people's reactions when Will walked into a pub or restaurant, but surely these people knew who Will was. There was really no need to whisper unless I had a massive stain on my dress or something. We were served with smoked salmon, a selection of charcuterie and a beautiful display of fruit.

Paul and Hannah entered the room, and everyone clapped as they made their way to a table with both sets of parents. Will started to pile food on his plate, and I opted for some melon slices, a bit of Parma ham and a few grapes.

As the breakfast went on, it became more informal, and guests were swapping tables and catching up with things they'd missed the night before, lots of people wishing Paul and Hannah a wonderful life together.

'So, what's the itinerary for the rest of the trip?' I asked.

It had been pretty prescriptive up until that point because of the wedding, but we had just over three weeks! I had never been on holiday for so long, an entire month to do as we pleased, and I couldn't wait to see Will's home.

'Well, when we've checked out of here, I thought we'd head over to my apartment. Then we're seeing Mom tomorrow. I've booked the three of us somewhere for lunch.'

I nodded, chewing on the delicious melon.

'But the rest of the time is ours to do what you want. Got any particular things you wanna hit up?'

'I don't think we have long enough for me to list them... the Statue of Liberty, the Flatiron, Empire State & Chrysler buildings....'

He smiled, but I didn't get the chance to finish my list because just then, Paul wandered over to the table. Will stood, and they shook hands and shoulder bumped.

'Thanks so much for yesterday, man. I was so nervous. I'm kind of glad it's over.'

He then turned his attention to me.

'And thank you for sparing him, I imagine it was pretty daunting in a different country with a whole bunch of strangers.'

'Don't mention it,' I said, waving the comment away. 'I hope you're very happy together.'

Somebody tapped a microphone just then, and the Master of Ceremonies announced that Paul and Hannah were about to leave. Paul quickly pulled Will in to whisper something in his ear. Looking at the table, Will slowly lifted his gaze to meet mine. I couldn't determine whether he was angry or found the exchange funny, but I stood, along with everyone else, ready to wave the bride and groom off on their honeymoon.

Once they had gone, Will and I went back to the room to pack. When we checked out, the valet handed Will some keys and parked outside was a shiny red 67 Chevi Camaro.

'Is that your car?' I asked, my mouth slightly open.

'Nope, I hired it.'

'Oh my God, it's amazing.'

He opened the door for me to slide in and then hopped in after me.

'This is just like the movies,' I said, beaming.

He started up the engine and put his arm around me, but just then, Stryker leapt in beside me, making me jump.

'Nice wheels, Reynolds. Someone's trying to make a good impression. Where are we going?' Stryker asked, putting his arm around me as well.

'Fuck off, Stryker. Nowhere with you,' Will replied, humour in his voice.

'Shame, I was hoping you could re-enact your performance last night,' he said, trailing his fingers across my shoulder with his free hand.

Performance? I was confused because they didn't play last night, it was the wedding, and then we went to... I slowly turned to look at Will, realisation dawning on me and he had closed his eyes, his jaw set.

'Fuck off, Stryker,' he said again with a touch of anger in his voice.

I realised then what Paul had told Will at breakfast, deliberately keeping it from me to save my embarrassment. Stryker chuckled, realising he'd pissed Will off, and climbed out to leave, just as someone approached and asked Will for a selfie.

In the few moments, while Will politely obliged, Stryker leaned back in to kiss my cheek and whispered, 'Sounded fucking amazing, I wish I'd been spectating.'

I gasped as he winked and walked away.

'Come on, let's get out of here before anyone else discusses our sex life over their morning coffee.'

He looked at me and shook his head. Turns out our bedroom had been over-looking the terrace and half the guests had heard us. I was mortified.

An hour and a half later, we pulled into a car park underneath a large building. Will lifted his sunglasses onto his head. He looked nervous.

'Are you alright?' I asked.

'Yeah... I just can't recall the last time I brought a new person back,' he mused.

'A new person!?' I asked with a chuckle, not really understanding what he meant.

He bit his lip.

'As in someone, I didn't know... before.'

Before when? Before he got famous or before he bought the place? Either way, I didn't have time to ask because he'd already got out and started gathering our luggage. The doors slid open after entering a code on the lift panel, and we stepped in.

I couldn't make out what Will was thinking. He was looking at the floor, his long fringe covering his face, so I interlaced my fingers with his for reassurance. Was he embarrassed? Was his place going to be really messy?

The lift doors opened, and Will took a deep breath in and picked up our cases. Then, looking at me for the first time and using his chin to signal for me to move forward, I stepped into the marble foyer. I initially assumed it was a shared space, but as I got my bearings and my eyes followed the corridor line to the window at the back, I wasn't quite sure.

Will gently pushed the small of my back, encouraging me to move forwards, and as I did, my eyes were moving from one side of the space to the other, my mouth slowly opening. We walked past several doors to our left and right, and then I stopped, unable to walk any further until I'd had a chance to absorb the room.

A huge open plan room lay before us, a kitchen to the right with an enormous breakfast bar in contrasting marble to the floor, six stools lined up along one side. Beyond that was a gorgeous round dining table that could seat maybe twelve people. On the left was a sunken lounge area with a bespoke curved sofa facing the TV.

And the view.

The view out of the floor-to-ceiling windows that stretched across the entire back wall of the room looked across the water to New York. I mean, you could see all the buildings and Brooklyn Bridge. There was a seating area outside with another table, chairs, and sun loungers.

I couldn't believe it.

I had guessed that Will was wealthy, I just hadn't asked or thought about *how* wealthy. My initial search of *Will Reynolds* had brought up reports of extravagant purchases in swish locations, but I wasn't sure how much of that to believe.

We had stayed in some fancy hotels, but I had just figured that was all to do with the band. My mind bounced over the events that had occurred over the last few weeks. The tip he'd left for staying at my house. The necklace. The bespoke security. The bed. The first-class tickets over there.

And now the apartment. It must have at least five bedrooms.

'What do you think?' Will asked, disrupting my train of thought.

I glanced at him, finally remembering to shut my mouth and swallowed. Then looking back at the view, I slowly edged forwards until I was level with the glass and rested my fingers gently on the huge pane. I heard Will pull a drawer open, and then I jumped as the glass started to move to my right. The panes concertinaing as they went. I stepped out, walking over to the wall to take in the full view. Will followed, but he let me look out uninterrupted.

'Oh my...' I couldn't even finish my sentence. 'It's... amazing... incredible... sooo much... space.' I managed, and then I turned back to look at him.

He just stood there looking at me, slowly rubbing his chin with a slight smile on his face. I looked back at him with the apartment laid out behind him. On second thoughts, it wasn't very him, it was... like a show home, and I frowned.

'What?' he asked, his eyes trying to read my thoughts.

I walked past him and back in. I walked right into the centre of the room and put my hands on my hips. There were no pictures, the soft furnishings were... bland, and despite knowing that it had been empty for a few months, it didn't feel... homely. I turned back to face him.

'It's... not very... you. Where is all your stuff?' I asked.

He smiled, a big smile that he couldn't seem to shift. He pulled the drawer of the breakfast bar open, replaced the remote and then walked over to the fridge, which was empty apart from not one but several bottles of champagne. Was he renting?

'This place is kind of an investment. I keep it on because mom and my friends are here, but my house, my home is in LA. I'm gonna take you there next week, but I knew you wanted to see New York.'

I shook my head a little, trying to compute everything. This was *just* an investment? His *actual* house was in LA?

He took two champagne flutes out of one of the cupboards.

'Do you have any other places you wanna tell me about?' I asked.

It was meant as a joke, but then I realised how rude that probably sounded.

'You don't have to answer that,' I said, suddenly colouring up.

'I've just sold my brother's place, and I'm... investing in something else,' he verified, opening the champagne and pouring me a glass. 'I also have a holiday apartment in Paris.'

I took it and took a long sip before he'd even had the chance to pour his own, and he half-smiled before lifting his glass.

'To holidays?'

I smiled because I knew he'd said that for my benefit.

'To vacations,' I amended as we clinked. 'Although this is more of a coming home after a long working holiday for you, I guess!'

'Working? Is that what you call it?'

He laughed, feeding his free hand around my waist, drawing me in for a kiss, and then placing his forehead on mine.

'So, you're cool? I was a bit nervous. I should have said something before. It just never seemed to be the right time.'

'Well, I'm afraid I don't have any secret properties to tell you about. It's just the house... and Billie the camper-van!' I smiled.

'They weren't secret... you're making me feel bad,' he said seriously.

'Well, don't,' I kissed him chastely, not wanting to ruin the moment, but a strange feeling was creeping over me. I couldn't work out if it was excitement, shock or panic, but Will took my glass, put it down, and kissed me again.

Chapter 6

The next morning, I woke feeling decidedly fuzzy-headed. Will was still asleep beside me. We ended up drinking several more glasses of fizz and then ordering in a pizza. Recollections of the evening slowly washed over me. More fizz in the bath together, sex in the shower and then, I thought maybe more sex when we went to bed.

Oh God.

I slowly sat up, allowing my head to adjust to the new level I was holding it up at, before lowering my feet onto the floor.

'There's some Advil in the kitchen drawer,' Will mumbled without moving, obviously feeling as bad as I was. 'What's the time?'

I reached over and looked at my phone.

'Um, twenty-five past eleven,' I confirmed, squinting.

'Shit!' Will said, sitting up, suddenly alert. 'We're meeting my Mom in just over an hour!'

'Oh my God,' I said, putting my head in my hands. 'This is not good.'

Will was in front of me far too quickly for someone as hungover as I was, he dragged me up to standing, and I dry heaved. Will looked at me sympathetically.

'Let's get you in the shower.'

He literally turned the shower on, pushed me under it and then disappeared. When he came back, I was still standing there.

'Lucy, come on!!' he said seriously.

He got in with me and washed my hair. In any normal circumstance, it would have been a luxury, but I was feeling increasingly sick by the second. Then, flicking the lever off, he grabbed a towel, wrapped it around me and moved me towards the basin.

'Where are your things?'

'Erm, in my suitcase,' I said as I sat down on the side of the bath.

He went off to search for it, but I couldn't hold it in any longer. I shot over to the loo and threw up. Oh, thank God, I sat back down on the edge of the bath to collect my thoughts. I actually felt a bit better.

'Do I need to cancel?' Will asked sceptically, appearing behind me.

'No. I think I can do this.'

He smiled, relieved, and I took my sponge bag out of his hands.

I'm not sure how, but we descended in the lift half an hour later. I was wearing a beige knee-length silky shirt dress that tied at the waist and kitten heels. Will had even made an effort, wearing a jacket and some boots that kind of had a cowboy vibe to them. I bit my lip. I was nervous. I was about to meet Will's Mum.

'She'll love you,' Will said, reading my mind and the lift doors opened.

'Terry!' I said, flinging my arms around him. He was taken aback, and I suddenly felt awkward as he stood there like cardboard. Will pursed his lips together, but I could see a smile in his eyes.

'Lucy,' he said formally, shaking me off and trying not to smile.

Will shook his head, waiting for me to get in the car. I looked at Will as he got in and mouthed 'sorry' as he tried not to laugh. I was just happy to see him. I couldn't see what the problem was.

We pulled up outside The River Café, which was tucked right under Brooklyn Bridge.

'Do you want me to come in?' Terry asked.

'Nah, it should be fine, stay close though, yeah?' Will said.

'Sir,' Terry said, confirming he understood.

The car door was opened, and Will got out, putting his hand out for me.

'Good afternoon, Mr Reynolds, your Mother has already arrived,' said the doorman and ushered us towards the door.

'Of course she has,' Will said under his breath.

Was he nervous too? Will did not let go of my hand, despite the fact I had sweaty palms. We were led across the restaurant to a table looking out across the river, it was a beautiful setting. There were the usual hushed whispers as we passed the other diners, and as we reached the table, Will's Mom stood.

'Mom, this is Lucy, Lucy, my Mom, Iris.'

I hadn't even thought to ask Will what his mum's name was.

'Iris, that is such a pretty name. It's lovely to meet you,' I said, shaking her hand.

She was shorter than I had imagined. Grey long hair that hit below the shoulders, and she had clasped the front sections back at the nape of her neck with a few Kirby grips. It struck me as the sort of thing an old ballet dancer would do. She was slim for her age and wore simple, classic clothes, a blouse and pencil skirt, and her make-up was light.

'And it's lovely to meet you too, Lucy. I've heard a lot about you.'

Will kissed his mum on the cheek, and then we all sat down. The table was set with a thick white linen tablecloth, plates with a sage green rim and neatly folded linen napkins.

'I assume you are trying to impress Lucy by booking a table here,' she said to Will. 'It's a tremendously long way to walk in the heat for an old lady like me.'

Will closed his eyes.

'Mom, why didn't you get a cab?' he scolded, shaking his head at her, looking into her eyes.

'I like to walk, you know that!' she explained, puckering her lips in mock annoyance, then turned her attention to me.

I was trying not to smile.

'So, Lucy, tell me all about your boys.'

Will's mum was so sweet. She was grounded and loving, recalling stories of when Will was growing up. I wasn't sure how much she knew about Ben, Will's brother, and the fact he was in rehab now, but thankfully, I wasn't put in any awkward situations.

From what I could gather, life had been tough when Ben and Will were little, but I had a feeling Will played a huge part in looking after her now. She must be so proud of him and everything he'd achieved.

The food was something else. I had scallop with celeriac puree to start, it looked like a piece of art when it arrived, with tiny leaves and edible flowers. The scallop was enormous and tasted amazing. For main, I had steak, and it was melt-in-the-mouth good.

'Do you ladies want dessert?' Will asked but before we could reply, a member of staff sidled up beside Will.

'Pardon me for interrupting, Mr Reynolds. May I have a word?'

'Oh dear,' Iris said. 'Our time is up.'

The waiter leaned in and said something into Will's ear as he simultaneously pulled his phone out of his pocket. She knew as well as I did that the press, or some fans were gathering outside. Terry had to meet us out back, but we had to walk through the main kitchen to get there.

The staff member opened the double doors and whistled, and every Chef, Sous Chef and Kitchen Porter stopped what they were doing and turned to face us with their arms by their sides, like they were working for some sort of militant leader.

'Sorry about this, folks,' Will said as he led his mum out by her arm with me in their wake.

'Good afternoon, Iris,' Terry said warmly, opening the car door.

'Lucy,' he said, addressing me and I glanced at him apologetically for our earlier encounter, but he gave me a warm smile too, and all was forgiven.

Iris and I got in the back, and Will sat next to Terry. We managed to bypass the small group of photographers without them noticing, and Iris struck up an easy conversation with Terry. So, it was acceptable to speak to him about non-related work things. They clearly knew each other well.

'I would invite you in...' Iris said, clasping my hand on my knee as we pulled up outside her house. 'But I am in need of a little lie down after that long walk and all the drama.'

I laughed a little. 'It's fine. It was so wonderful to meet you at long last,' I said, squeezing her hand.

Will opened the door and held his hand out.

'Come on, let's get you in, Mom.'

He walked her up the little garden path and the steps on the wooden veranda to her front door before hugging her. She whispered something in his ear, patting him on the back and then putting her key in the lock. Will looked so lanky stood by her, it was almost comical.

A few moments later and Will jumped in the back with me.

'Jeez, that was intense. Have you got any Advil?' he asked, looking at Terry.

Terry was chuckling to himself as he rifled around in the glove box before producing a blister pack.

'Intense?' I asked. 'I thought it went okay?' I said, feeling a bit defeated.

Had I read it wrong? Will turned his attention to me.

'Lucy, she loved you! I just mean the banging headache I had the entire time we were there.'

Oh.

I bit my lip and looked at him.

'What do you wanna do now?' he asked.

'I think I'm in need of a little lie-down,' I replied with a smile. Terry and Will laughed.

'Did you pack a swimsuit?' Will asked out of the blue as Terry pulled onto the main road.

'I did... why do you own a spa retreat too?' I said flippantly.

He glanced at Terry, who had returned to looking straight ahead and then shot a glance back at me.

I felt a bit sheepish. I was still coming to terms with the surprise of the enormity of his wealth. Not because I had a problem with it as such, but despite me joking about it yesterday, I did feel he had kept it from me. When I had been redoing the mortgage agreement on my house, I had discussed it openly with him, and he had had plenty of *ins* to talk about his... homes—plural.

'Nooo,' he said slowly. 'It's just that there's a pool on the top of my building, I could see if it's free,' he said, but he sounded a bit pissed off, and I looked into the footwell feeling awkward.

He pulled his phone out, I assume to check availability, and I looked out the window until we arrived back.

In the elevator, the awkwardness bloomed in the small space.

'I'm sorry,' I said, not being able to stand the tension any longer.

'No, I'm sorry I didn't tell you before. I guess I've just had to be a bit... protective?'

The lift doors opened, we walked through to the kitchen, and he lifted me onto the counter, standing between my legs and putting his forehead against mine.

'I've been stung in the past,' he said, tucking my hair behind my ear. 'I've told you before that I struggle to meet people, and it's because sometimes people just want to know me because of who I am, and what I earn.'

'So, have I passed the gold digger test?' I asked, moving my head back and raising my eyebrows.

I felt like an employee having my three-month review. Will closed his eyes tightly, realising he had offended me.

'Lucy... please forgive me. I knew you were different, but I... I don't know, it was stupid. *I* was being stupid, and then it became a thing, and... now I've fucked up.'

Apart from that initial night in my lounge, when I looked up to see who *Will Reynolds* was, I had tried hard not to look at stuff online. Especially after all the rubbish they'd printed about me.

'Say something.'

'I searched you up... the night after our first date. I wanted to see who you were. Who The 'king Band were... but that was all. I didn't search up *Will Reynolds's wealth*, and then make a plan to seduce you.'

Will looked down at the counter, embarrassed, and so he should be.

'Is there anything else?' I asked.

Will looked back up, confused.

'Anything you haven't told me,' I clarified.

'No, there's nothing. This is it. This is me,' he said with boyish playfulness in his eyes. I tried to suppress a smile but failed.

'Okay,' I said, sighing and rolling my eyes.

I couldn't stay cross with him for long, and as he looked at me, his eyes started to darken as he pressed his lips to mine. He slid his hand up my inner thigh.

'Did I tell you, you look mighty fine in this dress?' he said as his fingers reached my knickers.

'No, but then we didn't have much time this morning.'

'My mom loved you,' he said, looking into my eyes as I took a breath in.

'I'm not sure we should be talking about your mum while you have your thumb inside me,' I said, and he smiled.

'I won't tell you I was mentally undressing you at lunch then.'

Using his other hand to undo the buttons on the top of the dress and failing. I laughed, and instead, he kissed my collar bone. Sliding his thumb back out, he lifted me back onto the floor.

'Get your swimsuit. We've got an appointment with the pool,' he said, and I sighed.

I was now wet, and he wanted to go to the bloody pool, ironic, really. I couldn't help but notice that the bed had been made when I went back into the bedroom to collect my things.

Okay, so the pool was pretty epic. It was adjacent to Brooklyn Bridge to the point where I wondered if people could see us if they happened to have a pair of binoculars.

'What other facilities does your building have?' I asked.

'A gym, an indoor pool, a tennis court and a creche, I think,' he replied.

We were both leaning on the side, looking at the view.

'And you've booked this out?'

'Yeah, we have it for an hour.'

'And what's your actual home like?' I asked.

'What is this? An interview? You'll see it next week.'

Will was obviously getting fed up with all my questioning, and I looked at him, resting my head on my arm. He looked across at me and laughed through his nose.

'I know it's a lot to take on, but you'll get used to it. Come on, I'll race you to the end.'

And suddenly, he started to swim off.

'That wasn't fair,' I said breathlessly as I caught up with him. 'You had a head start.'

He was grinning like a Cheshire cat, and then he grabbed me and kissed me.

'So, you wanna see a whole bunch of buildings which, may I add, you can see from here? What else?' he asked. 'It's a shame Hannah isn't here,' he added.

'Why? Because you don't wanna come with me?'

'Not that I don't want to, it's just that tourist destinations are tricky,' he said.

I looked up at the sky and sighed.

'Are you trying to tell me, you've brought me to New York, and you're going to make me go and see all the tourist attractions on my own?' I asked, putting my hands on my hips under the water, which was far less effective.

'Terry will take you,' he informed me. I put my head to one side. 'Look, if there's one thing you reeeally wanna do, I could probably organise it with the team. It would need to be managed, the venue would need to know in advance, and we'd probably have to go after closing....'

'Okay, okay, I get the picture... forget it,' I said rolling my eyes comically.

'I'm sorry, Lucy.'

It was fair to say he did look pretty sorry.

'There's a whole bunch of stuff I need to do while we're here, so why don't you have a couple of days to yourself? I reckon you can tick everything off your list in forty-eight hours. Besides, you don't want a loser like me attracting unnecessary attention.'

I chewed the inside of my cheek, thinking. I guess Will wouldn't want to go to Bloomingdales anyway, or the Magnolia Bakery come to think of it.

'Alright...' I said, only allowing a little disappointment to show. 'What is it that you need to do, anyway?' I asked.

'Well, I need to pop into the studio and do some retakes on a couple of tracks, meet with my manager, and Paul suggested we do a gig when he gets back from his honeymoon, so I thought I'd set the wheels in motion for that....'

I frowned at him.

'...and I've got a whole bunch of paperwork I need to sort, but that might have to wait until we get to LA. What?' he asked, realising I was frowning.

'None of that sounds very... holiday-ey.'

'That's why I thought I'd get it done while you're doing the holiday-ey things. Are you gonna take your hands off your hips now?' he asked as he pulled the elastic of my bikini bottoms towards him.

Chapter 7

Will advised me to get up early, partly because it would be quieter and partly because it would get hot. He wanted Terry to take me, but I wanted to walk over the bridge. It was well signposted, but I was still convinced I was travelling the wrong way on the subway. Thankfully when I came out, I was pleased to see the sign for the High Street, Brooklyn Bridge station. So, I walked up the steps and took signs to the Brooklyn Bridge walkway.

There were so many people on the bridge, and you had to stay on the correct side and kind of fall into step with everyone else, but thankfully no one seemed to be in a rush, and I was able to soak up the sights along the way.

I'd walked over Clifton Suspension Bridge many times, but this was something else. The architecture alone was stunning. The harbour was vast, and I just had to stop and take a picture of the New York skyline. I looked back for Will's rooftop pool, but I couldn't make it out. It took me about twenty minutes to reach Manhattan, and the general walking speed began to increase.

I picked up a can of soda from one of the little kiosks and meandered along with no real purpose. I had booked a ticket to go up the Empire State, but that wasn't until the afternoon, so I had the morning to get my bearings. There was so much to take in and so many people.

I turned a corner and looked up.

Oh wow, it must be Times Square. When I thought of New York, it was not the Statue of Liberty or the Empire State. It was the billboards that came to mind. And there I was. It was so colourful. Maybe that was why they made the taxis and the traffic signals yellow, to put a bit of happy into the tall, grey concrete city.

As I stood there taking it in, I felt something vibrate in my bag. It was my phone, a text from Will.

Good morning, Beautiful, you left without saying good-bye. We're going out tonight, buy a new outfit X

I loved that men thought that saying 'we're going out' was enough information to determine what sort of outfit to wear.

Good morning, and goodbye. Where are we going?

I could see he was texting back, so I waited.

We're going to a bar with a few of my friends, it's classy. My card is in your purse X

What the hell?

I scrabbled around in my bag while moving to the side to get out of everyone's way, and my mouth fell open when I saw his black credit card. I felt uncomfortable about it, but I didn't want to make him feel bad.

I'm sure I've packed something that would be suitable X

My phone started ringing.

'Will, it's a lovely thought, but I....' I said as I started walking along again, but he interrupted before I could finish.

'I want to buy you something. I feel bad about not being with you so please, buy an outfit, a complete outfit,' he said seductively, which made my heart skip a beat.

'Will...' I said, sounding a little whiny.

'If I haven't received a notification on my account that you've spent some money before coming back, I'm not gonna let you in!'

I slumped my shoulders and breathed out angrily.

'It's fifty-fifty.'

'What is?'

'The code, dopey,' he said.

'You realise how stupid that is?'

But he'd hung up. Grrrr, he could be so damn annoying sometimes. That gorgeous, rockstar, rich boyfriend of mine. I rolled my eyes, but a small smile appeared on my face. Fifty-fifty was the name of one of their tunes, if only everyone knew!

I could have gone crazy, literally crazy and gone to all the posh shops but a) I didn't feel worthy, and b) I didn't want to take the piss. Bloomingdales it was. It took me a while to get my eye in, but eventually, I spotted a beautiful dress.

It was black, embellished with sparkly beads and fitted at the waist. It had a round neck which I would typically shy away from due to my boobs, but the main body of the dress was a V neck, and then there was a semi-sheer covering, with the round neck and three-quarter-length sleeves, ideal for the cooler evenings. It hit just below the knee, and it was by a designer who I'd never heard of, but as I had the time, I decided to try it on.

It was so beautiful and fitted perfectly, but it was soooo expensive. As I was looking at myself in the communal mirror in the changing room, another lady came out of her cubicle.

'Oh my, that looks stunning on you,' she said, beaming at me with big white teeth. 'Going anywhere nice?'

'Oh, um, the description was a classy bar, that's all I could get out of him.'

She assessed me for a moment, I wasn't sure what to do with myself, so I began to fiddle with the sleeve of the dress.

'You're not... Will's girlfriend, are you?' she asked, and I glanced at her. Shit. What should I say? Should I confirm that to a stranger? 'Sorry, it's just that you're English, and I'd heard that Will was bringing his girlfriend over from the UK... I'm not explaining myself very well. I'm Cara, by the way,' she said, putting her hand out for me to shake.

I tentatively took her hand and shook it. She was of African origin, utterly striking, tall with the darkest skin, huge round white eyes and the biggest smile.

'My boyfriend, Thomas, works with one of Will's friends, and I overheard them talking about it. I'm a music journalist and... well, I've seen your picture before,' she admitted.

I immediately looked around, wondering if this was some kind of set up. A journalist? Christ, I needed to get out of here.

'Don't panic. I'm not paparazzi,' she clarified, sensing my anxiety. 'I work for Rolling Stone.'

'Oh, I see,' I said, dropping my shoulders in relief. 'Sorry, I'm a bit on edge, new city and all... I'm Lucy.'

'Right,' she said, beaming at me. Her smile was so radiant I couldn't help but smile back.

Just then, a store assistant walked in and stopped in front of me.

'Oh, wow, that looks fantastic on you,' she said.

'That's what I said,' Cara chipped in.

'I have the perfect clutch to go with that. Wait there,' the assistant added, and before I could say anything, she'd disappeared.

I glanced at Cara, wide-eyed, and she was pursing her lips in amusement. 'I can guarantee she'll be coming back with more than a clutch,' she said, laughing.

Half an hour later, I stared at myself in the mirror, biting my lip. Not only did I have a clutch, but I also had underwear, shoes, a jacket and a cool wrap-around bracelet that tied everything together. Cara stayed with me to help with the decision-making.

Whereas I was being typically British and polite about everything the assistant brought in for me to try, Cara was cut-throat. Too trashy, not classy enough, wrong colour, too high, too short, not practical. She had the assistant wrapped around her little finger, not in a demeaning way. She just had a way with people, being direct without being insulting.

'Well, I think we've cracked the classy bar outfit!' Cara said, giving me a wink, 'and I've managed to find something to wear to Thomas' gig tonight.'

I smiled at her, 'Thank you for all your help. I really appreciate it. I'm a bit unaccustomed to the sorts of... establishments that Will tends to go to.'

'It's my pleasure. And honey, I know what it's like. I was the same when I first met Thomas. Everywhere and everyone appeared so… cliquey, but actually, when I got to know them, particularly those in the music industry, I discovered they were just like us and, on the whole, came from humble backgrounds. It's just that most don't like being papped, so they tend to keep themselves to themselves.'

I nodded.

She had hit the nail on the head. It did seem cliquey, that's how I'd felt at the G.A.M. awards, but it was nice to know I wasn't alone. Cara had obviously been in a similar situation to me, and she seemed like a nice woman. One that hadn't got caught up in the glitz and glamour.

'Mind you, I'm normally working nowadays,' she said, laughing. 'Speaking of work, I should really get back. It's been lovely to meet you, Lucy. I can't wait to tell Thomas!'

She hugged me quickly and left me with the sales assistant, who patiently waited while I got changed and took my items to the counter.

My eyeballs nearly popped out of their sockets when she rang everything up, but I quickly composed myself and tried to look confident as I handed over Will's card. A small smile appeared on the shop assistant's face as her suspicions of which *Will*, Cara and I had been referring to had been confirmed on the card.

I picked up all my bags and walked out of the shop, biting back a huge grin. It had been strangely liberating to spend someone else's money. I hadn't incurred any buyer's remorse, and I happily swayed the bags back and forth until I got outside, and the oppressive heat hit me.

It was so hot, and I was kicking myself for doing the shopping before my tourist fix that afternoon. I was also hungry, I hadn't had breakfast, and it must've been around lunchtime by then.

An eatery on the ground floor looked good, so I found a spare table and chose a salad. It was ginormous, it could have fed several people, and I couldn't help but wonder why their portions were so insane. Even the salads would make anyone gain weight.

I had not realised how art déco the Empire State building was. It wasn't until I was queueing and reading about its history that I discovered it was built in 1931. The nineteen-thirties were my favourite era. I loved the style and the glamour it portrayed. I didn't know much about fashion, but I had done Art at school and did a whole project about Erté.

I had to admit that the view didn't blow me away as much as I thought it would. Maybe I was spoiled by the views from Will's apartment. Still, it had been something I'd wanted to do for such a long time, and it was one to tell the boys about. Thinking about the boys, I was beginning to miss them and my friends, for that matter. It was so rare for me to be away, and it had only been a few days.

By the time I got back down, I was parched, and my feet were killing me, so I ducked into the next available coffee shop and managed to find a stool to perch on. I checked my phone and noticed a missed call from Steph. I called her back.

'Hey, Sister, how's it going?' she asked.

It was so good to hear her voice.

'Really good, thank you, I have so much to tell you! Will's apartment is amazing. He doesn't even live there, it's just an investment, and he has another place in LA that we're visiting next week. So, thanks to Will and his credit card, I went to Bloomingdales this morning, and I've just been up the Empire State—'

'Woah, woah, woah, Lady!! Stop right there, waaaaaaay too much information to absorb in one phone call. So, Will doesn't live in Brooklyn? I thought his family were from there.'

'They are, but he moved to LA, well, I don't know when but yeah, the apartment here is like... I dunno, he keeps it on to visit his friends and family,' I confirmed, remembering how he had explained it to me.

'Have you actually googled his net worth?' Steph asked.

'No, why would I do that?'

'Curiosity!' she said with excitement, and I could hear her typing.

'I don't want to know! Don't tell me!'

She did a high-pitched whistle like a deranged owl, and I closed my eyes.

'Babe, you need to hang on to that one.'

'Can we talk about something else?' I asked, eager to change the subject.

'Well, we can, but I have absolutely nothing to tell you, Clevedon is still here, and quite frankly, it's boring without you. Don't you dare come back and tell me you're moving to Brooklyn... or LA, for that matter.'

'Ha! I won't. I was only thinking earlier how much I was missing you all.'

'Well, we'll obviously miss your amazing general knowledge at the quiz on Thursday,' she said, and I pouted.

'I know full well that Claire will have spilt a glass of wine on the quiz sheet before the end of the night, so general knowledge or otherwise, you'll come last, like always. In fact, we should get a prize for coming last every week. At least we're consistent,' I mused out loud, and Steph laughed.

'Well, call me in a few days when you can bombard me with more mind-blowing information,' she said.

'I will. Speak soon, babe.'

I drained the last dregs of my coffee and decided to head back across the bridge.

When I eventually got to the elevator, I realised I didn't know the code. I tried fifty-fifty, and the doors opened. Honestly, did his team not give him advice on thinking of a more secure code?

Will was sitting at the breakfast bar on the phone to someone, his laptop in front of him which he closed as I approached. He lifted his index finger to indicate he'd only be a minute, so I headed into the bedroom. I sat on the bed, placing all my shopping bags on the floor and it felt so lovely to be off my feet that I lay back and stared up at the ceiling. I sighed to myself. How had I got here exactly? I shook the thought from my mind and decided to have a shower.

It wasn't long before I sensed I was being watched, Will stood by the bathtub, and he smiled.

'Good day?' he asked.

'Yes, thank you, you?'

He took his t-shirt off and walked over to the sink so that he could have a shave.

'I did. It was productive,' he said, looking at me in the mirror.

I flicked the shower off, but I could hear a humming.

'What's that noise?'

Will looked at me seductively.

'It's the hot tub,' he confirmed, and I frowned, wrapping a towel around me.

'I didn't think you had a hot tub?'

Will splashed his face, dried it off and swiftly did away with his trousers and boxers, replacing them with a towel. He pressed a button beside the window.

'Well, I do.'

He tilted his head. The window slid across, revealing a hot tub bubbling away. It was below floor level. It had glass panels allowing for a beautiful view across to Manhattan, yet complete privacy at the same time.

'After you.'

There were hooks just outside the door, so I hung my towel up, feeling overly naked all of a sudden, and I quickly stepped in. Will did the same.

'No one can see us, it's completely private unless we have guests.'

He pressed another button below the towel hooks, and a section of the fencing separating the hot tub from the rest of the balcony moved to the side. That's why I hadn't spotted it before. He pressed the button again, and the panel slid back into place.

'Drink?'

I spied the champagne bucket as he settled opposite me, stretching his arms out either side of him around the edge of the tub. He looked hot. Hot in a hot tub.

'I'm not sure that's a good idea if we're going to meet your friends. I haven't had dinner yet.'

Will's fringe was dripping onto his pecs, and I couldn't help but look.

'We're not going out until later, much later, so we can order something in now if you like?' he suggested, but I wasn't really listening.

Before I knew it, I had closed the space between us and straddled him. I kissed him, and he wrapped his arms around me and smiled.

'Miss me?' he chuckled.

'Maybe,' I said, suddenly embarrassed.

I started to well up for some reason. I swallowed hard, trying to hide my random emotion, but I could feel a tear on my lower lid, and before I had the chance to shake it away, Will cupped my face.

'What's wrong?' he asked, concerned, and I shook my head, but I felt overwhelmed suddenly.

'I don't know, sorry, I guess it's just... all a bit much.' I stroked his cheek and sniffed a little. 'I love you,' I sighed.

'Hey, I love you too. Don't freak out. Nothing's changed.'

I took a deep, cleansing breath in and slowly breathed out.

'Lucy, it's all good, we're all good.' He kissed me and then searched my eyes again. 'Okay?'

'Okay,' I said, more to convince myself than him.

He kissed me again, and I deepened the kiss because I needed him, really, really needed him. I wanted to forget about everything and lose myself in him. I think Will knew where my head was at because suddenly, there was an urgency between us. I could feel him waking up beneath me, and his kisses descended to my neck. I tipped my head back and closed my eyes, enjoying the feel of his lips against my skin.

'Lucy...' he said breathlessly.

I looked back at him.

'I don't want to make love to you out here, I want to see you,' he said, looking straight into my eyes.

I moved back, allowing him room to stand, and he took my hand, stepping out of the hot tub and, in turn, pulling me out after him. We part walked, part skipped, and partly ran into the bedroom. Stopping by the bed, he dropped to his knees and kissed me without hesitation. I held on to his shoulder to steady myself and took a fist full of his hair in my hand as he licked me.

He lifted my leg and placed my foot on his shoulder to allow him more access, and he slowly eased his fingers inside me. I looked down at him, and he was looking straight back at me.

'Will, don't, I want you.'

He stood up but kept his fingers in place and kissed my lips, my arousal sliding between us.

'Lie down,' he said.

Slowly easing his fingers out of me, and licking them before climbing on top of me, taking one of my nipples in his mouth. His fingers were back circling me again, and I found him, moving my hand up and down in a slow, methodical rhythm. His kisses ascended to my mouth, and his breathing was becoming laboured.

'Stop,' he said.

He lifted my leg right up so that my knee was by my shoulder and, taking hold of himself, he slowly pushed into me, inch by inch, until he filled me, and our foreheads were touching.

'It's just you and me. Everything else is hearsay,' he said, trying to reassure me.

He had said that on purpose. It's what he had told me when we were first together, and the press had got hold of some pictures of us. Our kissing was wet and feverish, and it seemed that just as we were finding our stride, I was climbing.

'Will!' I pined and closed my eyes, shamelessly admitting I was close, but instead of stopping and changing positions, he picked up his pace.

'Look at me,' he whispered demandingly.

I opened my eyes, and he was watching me, pushing me higher, and as I panted, he lifted my knee further still, sinking in deeper. Right there, our climaxes aligned, and my heart bloomed. He really did make me whole. Letting go of my knee, he began to kiss me again, and I wrapped my legs around him. We stayed close and carried on kissing for the longest time, neither of us wanting to break the spell or move away from each other.

'WILL? WILBA! ...WILL, are you up here, man?'

What was that? I thought sleepily... Who was that, I thought, suddenly alert and sitting up.

Will stirred.

'Will, there's someone in the apartment,' I said, shaking him.

'Huh?' He rubbed his face. 'Fuck, shit... Jake?' he called, suddenly sitting up and grabbing a pair of boxers out of the drawer.

'Will? Are you in the hot tub?' Jake called.

I could hear him walking out onto the balcony. Will opened the door a crack as I pulled the sheets around me.

'Jake, man, I'm sorry, we fell asleep. Grab yourself a beer. We'll be five minutes.'

'Dude! You're such an old man. Get your glad rags on. We're gonna get lit tonight.'

Will shut the door and looked over at me, dragging a hand through his hair.

'Arrgghh, totally lost track of time.'

He walked back over to me and knelt on the bed.

'Are you okay?' he asked, holding my chin up gently with his hand.

'I am, but there is no way I will be ready in five minutes!'

He kissed me chastely and then pushed himself back up.

'Take as long as you want.'

He pulled his jeans on, sprayed some deodorant and found a fresh t-shirt. I marvelled at how quickly he could be ready, and I smiled. He leaned back over to kiss me again.

'Do you want something to drink now?'

'As long as it comes with a water chaser,' I said, knowing I'd need to pace myself.

'Coming up.'

He slipped out of the door.

Chapter 8

Standing there in all of my new clothes, I felt nervous. I could hear more voices in the kitchen and on the balcony, but they all seemed to be male. I hoped Will hadn't invited me to a lad's night out. I was wiping some errant mascara from my eyelid when Will came in with my fizz and water.

'Wow, you look incredible.'

'Is it too much? You said classy, but if you're wearing that....'

He came and stood behind me and kissed my neck, his eyes travelling down me in the reflection and stopping at the shoes. They were higher than I'd typically wear, but Cara had made me do several practice walks up and down the changing room, and they were reasonably comfortable.

'It's perfect. We're going to a jazz club.'

Stroking his hand from my hip to my knee, and as he smoothed his fingers up my inner thigh, he took the hem of the dress with it so he could take a sneaky peek at my underwear. His eyes met mine in the mirror.

'I wish I hadn't looked.'

What? Did he not like them?

'Now I know, and I have to wait.'

Oh.

I turned to face him.

'I'm really nervous,' I admitted.

'Don't be. They can't wait to meet you, and besides, you've already met half of them.' He took my hand. 'Come on.'

I didn't have time to think, he just dragged me out of the bedroom.

Jake and Drew stood at the breakfast bar, and I was thankful to see some familiar faces. Jake immediately put his arm around my shoulders, pulling me away from Will and planted a big wet kiss on my cheek.

'Hey, Lucy,' he said in greeting.

I immediately coloured up, and Will smiled at me mischievously.

'I hope you're rejuvenated after your *sleep*,' Jake said, using air quotes for the last word.

'Jake, man, we were asleep, I swear,' Will said, holding his hands up, and then he gently pulled me back towards him and put his arm around my waist. 'Will you make an effort to make her feel comfortable,' he said, shaking his head and then kissing my temple.

'Sorry Lucy, I'm only winding you up.'

'It's fine. I'm sorry we weren't ready,' I replied as one of the women I'd spotted on the sofa sidled up to Drew.

'Lucy, can I introduce you to my wife. This is Clem,' said Drew.

'Hi, Clem, good to meet you,' I said, shaking her hand.

She was shorter than me, with long auburn hair which had been blow-dried into soft curls that tumbled around her back and shoulders. She wore a dark green body-con dress which accentuated her curves.

'You too,' she said, smiling.

'So, what have you been up to since the wedding?' Drew asked.

I looked up at Will to see if he was going to answer, but he looked at me and raised an eyebrow. Okay, so the floor was mine. Damn.

'Um, I met Wills Mum... and I've done a few touristy things... been shopping... that's about it!' I said, looking back up at Will.

'Yeah, we nearly got mobbed at the River Café, Terry had to take Mom home.'

'Ah, man, you'd think they'd have some respect,' said Drew.

'Zero respect,' Jake confirmed.

'Let me introduce you to the others,' Will suggested

He took my hand, leading me out to the balcony.

'Guys, this is Lucy, this is Leo and Milly.'

He gestured to the couple who stood on the left, and I shook their hands.

'This is Bo, and you know Stryker.'

I shook Bo's hand too, hesitating when I turned to Stryker as it seemed silly shaking his hand, I wasn't expecting to see him again and I hadn't told Will what he'd said outside the wedding venue.

'It's really great to meet you all,' I said as Stryker looked at me with a twinkle in his eye.

'Milly plays keys, and she's doing a stint at the jazz club tonight, hence we're all going to cheer her on,' Will explained, as I diverted my gaze back to Milly.

'Oh, I see. Are you nervous?' I asked.

'Noo, it's just a turn-up and play kinda thing, very relaxed,' she said.

'Don't play it down,' Leo chimed in. 'You have to be invited. It's not an open mic night.'

She looked at him batting her false eyelashes at him. She had a sleek dark brown bob and black flapper dress and patted his cheek while puckering her lips.

'I'll keep you,' she said, and everyone laughed.

I'm glad the women were wearing dresses. The men had all made an effort, too, apart from Will. It was almost as if he didn't need to because he'd be recognised or simply that he didn't care.

There was a buzz, and Will piped up, 'That'll be the cars.'

Everyone knocked their drinks back, and I slipped away quickly to go to the loo and grab my clutch. When I returned, everyone had gone apart from Will.

'Ready?'

I nodded, and he took my hand. Terry was waiting for us, and Will and I slipped in the back.

'You okay?'

'Yes, I'm fine... I promise.'

He seemed overly attentive, not that I had a problem with that, but I didn't want him to think I would burst into tears at any moment.

There was a long line of people waiting outside the club when we arrived, but Terry pulled right up outside the entrance. He got out and opened the door, Will got out first, and before I'd even stepped out, people were calling his name. Will pulled me in behind him, and we ducked straight in, he didn't stop to wave, and we headed down the steps.

Will seemed to know exactly where he was going, and as we entered the main bar, I saw Jake on the left lifting a red rope to one of the booths, and letting us quickly step in. There were drinks already on the table, champagne, vodka, gin, whisky and wine. Will poured me a glass of champagne without asking what I wanted and handed it to me.

'We didn't eat, did we,' he remembered shaking his head.

I grabbed his shoulder, pulling his ear down to me and said, 'You did.' I looked at him and bit my lip.

'Lucy Daniels,' he scolded as Drew passed us both a shot.

'Oh, God,' I said under my breath as I knocked it back.

I looked out at the bar. It was just how I'd imagined it, small round tables with chairs facing the stage. I tried to picture it in its heyday. It had that Gatsby vibe. Milly had styled herself perfectly to fit in. I imagined women standing about with their long cigarette holders and fake beauty spots, men in flat caps and shiny shoes.

We had been there for a good hour by the time Milly got up on stage. She was joined by a singer, a double bass player, a trumpet player and a drummer with those funny drumsticks that looked like they had a hairdo. There was a polite hush amongst the crowd as they all checked in with each other, and then they started to play, 'I Feel Foolish' by Caity Gyorgy.

Everyone started clapping and whistling before allowing the song to be heard. I couldn't believe how fast the singer was singing the words. I was amazed. And Milly sat there happily and easily bouncing along on the keys. I glanced at Leo, who was clearly proud and smiled.

'She's good, huh?' whispered Will.

I hadn't realised he'd sneaked up behind me. I nodded, not wanting to interrupt, but as the song went on, everyone slowly resumed their conversations which I thought was a shame, but I guess socialising was the whole idea.

I excused myself to go to the ladies, Will nodded to someone, and I realised Terry was waiting in the shadows. He followed me, but I didn't speak to him. I was too conscious of all the eyes watching my movements.

As I came out of my cubicle, someone else came out of theirs simultaneously, and I took a double take. 'Cara?' She looked over at me, and then realisation hit.

'Lucy!! What a coincidence!'

'Unbelievable! Is this the gig that your boyfriend's playing at tonight?'

'Yes, he's up next. Funnily enough, when I saw Milly, I wondered whether you guys would be here.'

'Milly the pianist?' I asked.

'Yeah, she works with Thomas sometimes,' she explained, shaking her hands in an attempt to dry them.

'Huh, small world.'

'Oh, the music industry's like that, everyone knows everyone.'

'It would appear so,' I said, still staggered we'd happened upon each other again.

We walked back out into the bar and as we approached the seating area I added, 'Well, wish Thomas good luck.' I gave her a little hug to say goodbye.

'Thank you,' she said, hugging me back. 'Oh, your boyfriend's coming,' she said as she pulled back, looking over my shoulder.

'Lucy? Who's this?' Will said as he reached us, looking at me quizzically.

'Oh, this is Cara. Cara, Will.'

Will shook her hand, and Cara shook it back, smiling shyly.

'Cara's boyfriend knows Milly, he's up next,' I explained to Will.

'Ah, so you must be Thomas Lorenzo's girlfriend.'

'That's right,' Cara confirmed.

'Awesome, you guys must come and join us afterwards,' Will suggested.

'That would be lovely, we'll try, although I've got a couple of people to interview this evening,' she said.

'Well, if you can, we're sat over there. Come and find us,' I said.

She headed off in the direction of the stage, and we wandered back to the booth.

'I can't believe you made a friend in the restroom!' Will said when we got back, and I laughed.

'I didn't even meet her there. We met in Bloomingdales earlier.'

His jaw dropped.

'I know, right?' I said, lifting my shoulders. I found it even more bizarre that Will knew her boyfriend, more than a coincidence.

Milly's set was coming to an end, and as they all stood and bowed, we all clapped, whistled and cheered. She nodded gratefully and bowed to the crowd again. Leo made his way down to the front to welcome her off-stage. He took her in his arms and dipped her low before kissing her.

'Ah, he's so God damn smooth,' Drew said, appearing at my side.

I spotted Will chatting to Stryker on the other side of the booth, Stryker was laughing heartily but Will looked stern.

'Oh, it's sweet. Have they been together long?' I asked, trying not to be distracted, but I couldn't help wondering what Will and Stryker were talking about.

'A few years now, I guess. Between you and me, I think he needs to lock it down. I don't know why he's delaying. She's hot,' he said.

That grated on me, the last comment. Why did some men think it was okay to wander about commenting on how they felt about other women when a) they were taken, and b) they had women of their own?

'Maybe he's waiting for her to ask!?' I suggested.

He laughed out of his nose and nodded slowly.

'I can see why Will likes you.'

I drew my eyebrows together, wondering why my comment would have an impact on the reasons why Will liked me.

'Don't get me wrong, we were all pretty chuffed when he found someone after all that shit with Alysa.'

I didn't want to hear about Alysa, but I got the feeling I didn't have a choice.

'God, I never thought those two would ever split,' he mused, as I spotted Cara by the stage. 'They'd been on and off for years, but she screwed him over big time.'

I didn't say anything in the hope he'd eventually shut up. He wasn't telling me anything I didn't know already.

'And when they lost the baby....'

Okay, *that* I didn't need to hear.

'Will was totally cut up.'

I looked at the ceiling and then looked Drew straight in the eye.

'Have you finished?' I asked a little abruptly.

He moved his head back like I'd slapped him. He really was a dick. I turned and lifted the red rope and walked down to the stage to catch up with Cara, taking a few deep breaths as I did so.

I wasn't cross about the news. I was upset that Will hadn't told me. Maybe he couldn't bring himself to tell me. Maybe it was too painful, but that in itself was hurtful. I thought our relationship was deeper than that.

'Oh, Thomas! Thomas, this is Lucy,' Cara said when she saw me, but he was just about to go on stage.

'Good luck,' I said, nodding to him and smiling at Cara, who was fizzing with excitement.

I noticed Terry was propped up against the wall nearby, but he was distracted by something happening in the booth. I could tell he was torn, but then he took a call on his phone. I quickly looked behind me, but too many people were gathering for me to see. The band began, and what a classic to kick off with, St James Infirmary by Louis Armstrong.

If you had seen a picture of Thomas, you would not believe he was capable of singing with such a gravelly voice. He sounded about forty years older than he looked. Everyone was mesmerised.

'Wow!' I mouthed to Cara, and she smiled with delight.

After the first number, everyone had settled back into their conversations again. I leaned towards Cara.

'What are you doing tomorrow?' I asked.

'I have the day off,' she confirmed.

'I don't suppose you fancy doing the tourist thing with me. All I've managed so far is Brooklyn Bridge and the Empire State.'

It was a long shot. She was probably ten years younger than me and didn't need some random woman pushing forty to entertain on her day off.

'I'd love to!' She immediately took her phone out. 'What's your number?' she whisper shouted.

I took the phone and typed it in, ringing mine so that I had hers.

'I'm sorry to interrupt Lucy, but can I escort you back to the booth.'

It was Terry, and I could tell by his tone that it wasn't really a question. I looked at Cara, wholly mortified and then smiled, but my eyes didn't join the party.

'I'll call you. I'd better go.'

I hugged her and followed Terry back to the booth like I was some kind of puppy on a lead being taken back to its crate.

I saw Jake first. He pushed Will's shoulder.

'She's there, dude, don't sweat.'

Will turned, relief evident on his face, and he grabbed my hand and pulled me into the booth, into him.

'Where the fuck did you go?' he asked, clearly pissed that I had left without telling him.

I looked up at him with my jaw set. He looked around and pulled me further into the booth, finding a section of the bench for us to sit on. He sighed, pulling me in close, sideways on his lap.

'Please don't wander off,' he said, trying to temper his voice. 'I'm not always in a position to be able to follow you.'

I realised then, that Will needed Terry to guard him, but he was guarding me instead, so he couldn't leave the booth. I felt sorry for him. It was like he had to wear a ball and chain whenever he came out. I was beginning to understand the enormity of his need to live a normal life. When he realised the anger had left me, he lifted my chin and kissed me.

'What did you say to Drew?'

I tensed up and glanced across the room to see where he was, but Will's fringe obstructed my view.

'He's gone.'

Oh. Well, that was awkward, I didn't want to drive a wedge between them, and it was not the time or the place to discuss what he'd told me.

'Erm, he just made a couple of comments that I didn't... think was very appropriate.'

There, that should do it. Will didn't even flinch.

'Lucy, I don't wanna hear the watered-down version.'

Pants.

'He said that Milly was hot, and that Leo should get on with locking her down,' I said mimicking his accent.

Will laughed.

'He shouldn't be saying stuff like that. It's disrespectful.'

Will was nodding slowly.

'And what did he say about Alysa and me?' he asked.

Damn him, he knew all along. I rolled my eyes. Could I keep anything from this man?

'That's not a conversation for tonight,' I said honestly.

He knew by my reply what Drew had divulged. I could see it in his eyes. It hadn't come as a surprise if I'm honest. When Will and I had the baby conversation a few weeks ago, a few stones were left unturned, but it didn't seem relevant at the time.

I knew that Alysa had done some horrible things that had made him turn against her, and the thought of them losing a baby had crossed my mind. That would be enough to break anyone. I looked into his eyes and smiled sorrowfully.

Suddenly, Will took in a long breath and looked up at the ceiling, breaking our trusty fringe cocoon, and I sat up a bit, allowing reality to flood back in.

'Shots?' Will suggested out of the blue.

I looked at him. He seemed distant, and I hesitated, but we needed to do something to get the night back on track. So, I turned, looking to see what was available on the table. I got up and poured us both a shot of black Sambuca.

'Good choice,' Bo said.

Jake turned and started nodding his head too. So, I poured everyone a shot, and we all clinked and drank together. Milly and I struck up a conversation about our top five films, and Will seemed to relax with the lads, drinking and chatting.

A couple of hours later, I was feeling tired, so I checked my phone and realised it was nearly three-thirty. What time did the place close? I thought Cara and Thomas would have joined us by now, but I couldn't see either of them when I looked over. Come to think of it, I couldn't see Will either, but then I heard him coming back from the direction of the loos, his arm draped over Jake.

'Yeah, well... Drew is an ass,' Will slurred.

Jake shot Terry a look and guided Will back to the booth. He was wasted, and I realised I had never seen him this drunk. He looked at me but couldn't focus and then put his arm around me, nearly pushing me over as he lost his balance.

'Okay, dude, shall I get Terry to take you guys back?' Jake suggested.

'Yess!' he said, perching on the edge of the table, knocking a few bottles over.

He wrapped his arm around my waist and forcefully pulled me into him. I nearly stumbled, tripping over my heels.

'This girl... I... I... I make her whole,' he announced.

It wasn't to anyone in particular, but he always had an audience, and I looked at the floor with embarrassment.

'Buuut, does she make me whole?' he asked questioningly.

I closed my eyes. If I could have picked up a chance card and was told to return to go, I would have done. How could he put so much doubt in our relationship with one small sentence?

Jake stepped up with Terry, and they each took one of Will's arms. I moved out of the way, and someone took hold of my hand, it was Milly. She looked at me, and I could tell she'd heard what he'd said. My mind was reeling, and I didn't know what to do. I suddenly felt very alone. I was in an unfamiliar city with a man I had only known for a few months.

Suddenly I felt nauseous. I rushed towards the toilets and made it just in time to throw up in one of the sinks. As I washed the sink down and patted water on my face to cool off, I heard a scuffle outside. It was Jake and Milly.

'You can't go in there,' Milly said.

'Terry told me to come and get her,' Jake replied.

'She might not want to go back,' Milly insisted.

'She doesn't have a choice,' Jake said, incensed.

There was more scuffling, and in the end, I opened the door, and they both stared at me. I walked past the pair of them, pulling my phone out of my clutch. I booked the next cab on the app and headed out of the club. Terry spotted me, and I think he thought I was going to get in the car, but my taxi pulled up just in time, and I got in.

'Um, I need a hotel for the night. Where do you recommend?'

He turned, looked me up and down, and then pulled away, Jake and Milly emerging from the club as he did so.

The William Vale hotel was somewhat corporate but super swanky. I was thankful that it was so early in the morning because there was hardly anyone to witness my tear-stained face when I arrived.

There was just a Receptionist, who had probably had to deal with this situation many times before. As I pulled my credit card out of my purse, I realised I still had Will's card and I moved it to a different part of my purse, so I didn't use it by mistake.

After taking payment for the room, the receptionist directed me to the lifts, and as I walked across the lobby, trying to avoid eye contact with a couple of late-night stragglers, I heard someone call my name.

'Lucy? Wait here a sec... Lucy, are you okay?'

I picked up my pace. I just wanted to get to my room, I didn't want anyone to see me like this, but the person caught my hand and whipped me around.

'Lucy, I thought it was you. What are you doing here?'

It was Stryker.

'I... we...'

I took a shaky breath in, and he pulled me in for a hug. It was surprisingly comforting, and I couldn't help a couple of sobs escape. My head was fuzzy with booze, and I was so tired, but Stryker held me there for a few moments, and I was thankful for it. I felt lost, a tiny ant in the big wide world and a long way from home.

'Just give me a moment,' he said, pulling away and heading back over to the woman he was with.

I don't know what he said to her, but she nodded and headed over to the bar before Stryker turned back to me.

'Are you staying here?' he asked and spotted the key in my hand. 'I'll take you to your room.'

He guided me to the lift with his hand on the small of my back.

The elevator lights were less than flattering, and I peered at myself in the mirrored wall. My face was a mess, and I looked at the floor. I could feel Stryker watching me from the opposite side, a weird tension began to build in the tiny space, and a sudden wave of consciousness came over me.

I barely knew this man, who admitted he wanted to watch Will and me having sex, and I was letting him walk me to my hotel room. What the fuck was I doing? As the lift doors opened, I quickly exited.

'I think I'll be okay from here,' I said quickly, avoiding his gaze.

'Lucy, I'm not gonna try anything. You're Will's girl. He's made that perfectly clear. I just wanna make sure you get to your room safely.'

I looked up at him.

'Will would expect me to.'

'Would he expect you to say what you said to me outside the wedding venue?' I asked without thinking.

Stryker stepped out of the lift and gave me what appeared to be a sympathetic smile.

'I told him what I said to you earlier tonight. He was cross with me.' He paused, and a smile spread across his face. 'It's how I know that you're the one,' he said, looking me straight in the eye.

'What do you mean?' I asked, how would he have come to that conclusion?

'He won't share you,' Stryker stated matter-of-factly.

What?

'Share me? Why, has he shared women with you in the past?'

I was confused, did he mean Will had had open relationships before or did he mean...

Stryker was still smiling and shook his head a little.

'Let me walk you to your room, and I promise I will leave you at the door.'

My mind was reeling, and I absentmindedly let him escort me to my room. I felt so stupid, I had tried to talk to Will about his past, but he had shut me down. I know that my previous relationship was pretty conservative to say the least. Still, it wasn't as if I didn't know what other people got up to.

'I'm not naïve,' I blurted out as we got to my room.

Stryker lifted his eyebrows. I wasn't sure whether he did that because he was surprised by my sudden outburst or whether he thought exactly *that* of me.

Naïve Lucy.

'I know you probably think I'm some silly woman from Great Britain who hasn't lived because she lives in a sleepy seaside village but...'

'Goodnight, Lucy,' he said, interrupting my ramblings.

He nodded as if to bid me farewell without having to make contact, stepped back and began to walk back down the corridor. I wanted to tell him I knew people had threesomes, foursomes, polyamory, whatever... I wasn't against it, I just hadn't done it personally, but instead, I simply swiped my key and stepped into my room.

Chapter 9

Had Will turned on the hot tub? I blinked my eyes open and then sat up suddenly. No, the noise I could hear was my phone vibrating in my clutch. I looked around the unfamiliar room and slowly lay back down, the events of last night dawning on me.

If I was completely honest with myself, I was cross for believing that I made him whole. He'd never actually said it back to me, I had just assumed. Was I the rebound? Was I just the plaster for the wound he was still trying to heal after Alysa? Had he stayed in the UK to get over her?

My phone was still vibrating.

On the one hand, I could just put Will's behaviour and mini speech down to alcohol, and desperately try to believe that I was enough. But, on the other hand, I couldn't help but think that the instigator of the heavy drinking was because he was still grieving the loss of a baby, and just how sad that was.

And then I remembered about Stryker. Where did he spring from? Was he staying at this hotel too? And who was that woman he was with? And how did I feel about the whole sharing thing? Sharing... in a sexual way? Together at the same time or separately? Had Will slept with Stryker?

'He's a rock star, Lucy... he's probably done *everything*,' I said to myself.

I slowly rolled over and reached for my bag, my mobile constantly buzzing away. I had twenty-nine missed calls from Will, and as I held it, it started ringing again. He was obviously frantic, and I wasn't about to block him again.

'Hello.'

'Lucy, thank God. Where are you?'

'In a hotel,' I replied flatly.

'Which one? I can send Terry to come and get you.'

I could hear he was pacing, his footsteps echoing through the phone.

'I don't want Terry to come and get me... I want... I need a bit of time.'

'Lucy, please don't do this. We need to talk... about Alysa and the baby.'

That was true, but that wasn't the only thing bothering me.

'It's not just about that.'

'Well, what is it?'

I massaged my temple with my free hand. It was so many things. I hadn't formulated them all in my head.

'I just need some time, please. Can you give me some time?' I asked.

'Lucy,' he pleaded. 'I wanna see you. I wanna make you whole.'

I closed my eyes and hung up.

That was our thing, what he said to me in private, and he'd made a mockery of it last night. After all the pictures and made-up stories about us, the ones I knew about at least, there were probably many more. This was worse. Like he'd exposed us. I hadn't realised, but I'd clung to the little things that meant something to us that no one else would understand, because it was all we had that was sacred.

I scrolled through my phone, conscious that my battery wouldn't last the day. So, I text the boys to see what they were up to and told them I was okay, just in case anything was reported in the media after last night. I text Steph to let her know Will and I had fallen out, but I was alright. And then I saw a missed call from a number I didn't recognise. That must be Cara, and I was supposed to be calling her today.

'Lucy?'

'Hi, yes, it's me.'

'I'm so sorry we didn't come over last night. Thomas was exhausted, and by the time I finished, it was late.'

'Oh, don't worry, the night turned sour, and Will and I had a bit of a falling out,' I admitted.

'Oh no, are you okay?'

'Yes, I checked into the William Vale because I needed some space, but now I realise I am a bit stuck as all I have with me is what I wore last night.'

'Oh my God, I'm literally five minutes from there! I can bring you some clothes, would that help?'

'That would be amazing. I'm sorry to put you out.'

'Not at all. I'll be with you in like, half an hour.'

I jumped in the shower, and after a quick phone call to reception, a staff member arrived with a little mini toothpaste and brush. It wasn't long before there was another knock at the door. Cara came with a carrier bag of clothes and two coffees.

'I tried to think of everything you might need, but I can't really help you with foundation.'

She smiled, her big white teeth beaming at me, and I laughed.

'Thank you so much, you're a life saver.'

She had brought jeans, a couple of tees, a sweatshirt and flip-flops. The jeans were way too long for me, but I rolled them up. I popped a bit of mascara on to wake my eyes up and some blusher. Done.

'Right, let's get out of here,' I said, stuffing last night's clothes in the same carrier bag Cara had brought with her. 'I need to buy you some breakfast... well, lunch actually.'

I was so hungry. I hadn't eaten for nearly twenty-four hours. I checked my phone quickly. Will had a text.

Please come back X

That's all it said. He was going to have to wait. I hadn't even begun to gather my thoughts.

We headed out. Walking with someone who knew where they were going was so lovely. Cara knew all the little shortcuts, and before I knew it, we sat down in an Italian place called Fragole on Carroll Street.

'So, did Thomas enjoy the gig?' I asked.

'He had the best time, he's been invited back, which is high praise for that venue, so he must have made a good impression. You can't just be famous to perform there. You have to actually be good.'

'That's fantastic! He is so good. You do not expect that voice to come out when you look at him!'

'I know, everyone says that,' she admitted with a shy smile.

'So, who were you interviewing last night?'

I was blatantly avoiding the obvious topic, but Cara could tell I wasn't ready.

'Oh, it was just a couple of quotes to go with the gig review... that's mainly what I do, it's how I met Thomas,' she confirmed.

'No way! So, what sort of gigs and are you as cut-throat in your reviews as you are with shop assistants?'

She laughed at that.

'Any sort of music, I love music... well, mainly funk and soul... and I love writing. It started as a hobby, but then a friend of mine got a job at The Alternative, and he put a couple of things my way. It kind of blossomed from there and yes, I'm honest, but I think that's how you gain respect, otherwise people don't take you seriously.'

'You're right, honesty is the best policy,' I said, looking out of the window, my mind drifting to Will for a moment.

'You sound like my mom,' she said, laughing.

'That's because I am a mum,' I admitted.

'You are?'

She seemed surprised.

'Yeah, I have two teenage boys.'

'Shut. Up! You do not look old enough,' she said, pushing my arm.

Just then, our food arrived. I had ordered the bolognaise, and it looked amazing. I started tucking in and was pleased to discover it tasted as good as it looked. I finished half the plate before I spoke again.

'I'm so hungry, I didn't have dinner last night,' I said before shovelling another fork full in.

'So, what happened last night?' she asked tentatively.

I finished my mouthful slowly, wondering how much to tell her.

'You don't have to talk about it,' she added.

'No, it's fine. It's good to talk. I don't really have anyone here to talk to. Last night was the first time I was out with his friends. He's been staying in the UK for a few weeks,' I explained. 'And one of his friends... told me something that... was a bitter pill to swallow.'

I didn't want to tell her. I barely knew her.

'It was about his ex-girlfriend... and then later, he was drunk and said some stuff that upset me.'

I was going to leave it there, but there was so much more.

'And I'm struggling with the reality of having security and press around us. He doesn't seem to notice or care but...'

'But it's weird, right?' she said, finishing my sentence for me.

'Yeah, like intrusive but... not. I don't think I'll ever get used to having a private conversation when it's not actually private.'

'Well, you end up having two versions of yourself.'

I frowned, not really understanding what she meant.

'A bit like when you're having a really shitty day, but you work in a coffee shop, and you have to smile at all the customers.'

A small smile lifted at the corner of my mouth.

'When you step outside, the public and the press are your customers, you plaster on a smile and save those private conversations for when you're alone.'

I guess that's why I was so cross with Will because he hadn't stuck to those rules.

'Security is a different kettle of fish. You have to trust them, and I think it's best if you get along with them because they're going to see some shit!' she said, smiling and lifting her brows knowingly.

I thought back to all the encounters between Will and me that Terry had witnessed, and I flushed.

'You know what I'm talking about,' she added with a wink.

I looked out of the window again, conscious that she was doing all the talking.

She leaned in.

'If it's any consolation, I thought his ex-girlfriend was a bitch.'

I laughed. She was doing her best to make me feel better.

'Seriously. I had a run-in with her once. I was trying to grab the attention of someone in a group who was supporting The 'king Band at a show a while back. I had my press pass on, and despite other press being allowed backstage, she took an instant dislike to me and maintained that there were too many people backstage already. I could see through the little window in the door that there was plenty of room, but she had some sort of superiority complex and wouldn't let me through.'

'Hmm, I've only met her a couple of times, but that doesn't surprise me for some reason.'

There was a long pause in conversation as we both took the opportunity to finish our meals.

'Did you wanna come back to mine?' Cara asked, eventually.

It was such a lovely offer considering she didn't know much about me.

'That sounds lovely, but can I ask one more favour?'

'Shoot,' she said without hesitation.

'I need to see the Lady Liberty,' I said, and she smiled.

'Of course, do you like boats?'

It was the easiest way to see the statue and free. The Staten Island ferry. Why would anyone pay? I got some great pictures, and it was cooler out on the water. Cara was the perfect travel guide, pointing out all sorts of little gems I wouldn't have spotted had I been alone.

We got on well, considering our age difference. She was ten years younger than me but we both enjoyed yoga, despite the fact I had hardly practised in the last few months. She'd done Sports Science at school and had considered training as a Physio herself, but it would have meant her moving away from her mum, who was unwell at the time.

My phone started buzzing again as I tried to take another picture. It was Will, and I sighed. Cara clocked it and looked at me with concern.

'I expect he's getting worried about you.'

I felt guilty, admittedly. Knowing him, he was probably going insane.

'I suppose I should get back... although I've been having the best time,' I said, and I really had. It was so nice, just... being.

'Well, I'm glad I took your mind off it if nothing else, and you know, when I first met Thomas, it took me a while to adjust. It's a different way of living, for sure... but it can be fun, and you'll make new friends who understand. Like me!' she said, flashing me her beautiful grin again, and I couldn't help smiling back. It was contagious.

'Whatever happens, I need to return these clothes, so we'll definitely see each other again before I go.'

'You're gonna leave him?' she asked, shocked.

'No! I don't think so. I meant leaving New York. We're going to LA in a few days.'

'Oh,' she said, looking out at the harbour.

'It would be great to stay in touch though.'

FIFTY-FIFTY. I STILL couldn't believe it. I took a deep, mind-clearing breath in as the lift went up. Where do we even start? I was about to step out of the lift when I looked up along the corridor and saw everyone staring at me.

'What the...' I said under my breath.

Terry, Jake, Bo, Milly, Stryker and Will all stood or sat around the breakfast bar. I was not expecting an audience, and before my feet would do anything, the lift doors pinged, and I had to quickly hop out before they shut again.

'Okay, guys, let's leave them to it,' I heard Jake say, and they all started gathering their things as I stepped to the side of the entrance hall.

'Lucy.'

Terry nodded as he passed me to get into the lift, Jake and Bo following suit. Stryker gave my shoulder a squeeze. Milly gave me a knowing smile and then pressed the button, waving before the lift doors closed.

I took another breath in, readying myself to face Will, and as I looked up, Will rounded the corner with his hands in his pockets, head down. I had a sudden flashback to when he had walked in on Steph and me having an argument once, and I was reminded of those feelings inside me that bloomed every time I saw him. A mix of lust, worship and desire. It hadn't changed. If anything, it had become more evident.

I looked at him, and he looked at me. He looked awful. Unshaven, tired... sad. I took a breath in to say something, but he closed his eyes, and I detected the slightest shake of his head. He didn't want me to talk? He didn't want to talk? I was confused, and I knitted my eyebrows together, searching his eyes for some kind of explanation.

'Lucy, I'm so, so sorry,' he said thickly.

Gosh, he was really upset. I couldn't bear it. I wanted to say 'not to worry' because that's what I always did in these situations, but he held his hand up.

'Let me finish. I'm not done.'

He pressed his fisted knuckles into his teeth for a moment before continuing.

'Alysa and I... we were expecting a baby, she was maybe eleven weeks and um....'

He coughed, trying to rid himself of the constriction in his voice, but holding a hand out, signalling for me to wait.

I started to well up.

'We were getting ready to tell everyone.'

He couldn't look at me. All I wanted him to do was look at me.

'It was the same time I found out she had been sleeping with Ben, and as you know, we had a massive bust-up.'

I closed my eyes, and the tears fell. I knew what he was going to say.

'She aborted it.' He sniffed. 'She texted to tell me she'd done it.'

I shook my head. I couldn't believe how insensitive someone could be. I wasn't against abortion by any means, but aborting a baby without so much as a thought for the other person? And then a dark thought crossed my mind. Could it have been Ben's?

'And if you're wondering if it was Ben's....'

How did he do that?

'He can't father a child. He had a motorbike accident years ago.'

I stepped closer. I wanted to hold him and let him cry on my shoulder. But he shook his head again and took half a step back. It was killing me.

'Seriously, Lucy, I haven't finished.'

He wiped his face with his hands before pushing his fingers through his hair.

'I really fucking wanted that baby. Never have I wanted something so much in my life, and it nearly killed me... I nearly killed myself.'

He put his hands on his hips and looked down as if he was embarrassed.

Oh my God... he'd tried to commit suicide?

'I turned to drink. I was a complete asshole to my friends. I slept with whoever the fuck would sleep with me. I was on self-destruct.' He sniffed again, wiping his nose with the back of his hand. 'It was Paul who sorted me out. He put me through therapy, got me counselling, got me playing again....'

I guessed that was when he walked into my life, and I figured he was done. I took the smallest step toward him.

'Lucy, last night....'

I shook my head as if to implore him not to worry. It seemed so irrelevant in light of the circumstances.

'What I said....'

He'd remembered?

'Milly told me.'

I looked at the ceiling in disbelief at his ability to read my mind.

'That was just me, protecting myself... and being really fucking drunk. It was selfish. It was private. And I'm really fucking sorry. Of course, you make me whole. You are my... total... my everything, my love... my life.'

There were no gaps between my tears, just two streams tracking down my cheeks. I was at risk of creating a snot bubble. I took a big sniff, but it was less embarrassing than the alternative, and I blinked enough of my tears away to look at him. Stepping in, I pulled his forehead down to mine.

'I'm really sorry for your loss,' I said, and he kind of laughed and sobbed simultaneously, putting his head on my shoulder and feeding his arms around me, pulling me in close.

I could feel him silently keening, his broad shoulders juddering, and I let him weep. I felt so sorry for him. This global star was expected to be rock and roll and perform in front of thousands of people. This man, who had more money than anyone could ever wish for, was so... vulnerable and broken with grief because of someone, something entirely out of his control.

I thought about Alysa and the turmoil she must have been in after Will had discovered that she had been sleeping with his brother, but nothing should have stopped her from allowing Will to be part of the decision about the life they had created. A hatred I didn't know I had was spawning inside me, and I had to take a few calming breaths to stop myself from screaming.

Eventually, Will lifted his head back up, his eyes were completely bloodshot, and he looked exhausted.

'I really fucking love you, Lucy. I'm sorry I kept that from you. I just find it really hard to talk about.'

I cupped his face with my hands.

'I love you too,' I sighed.

Staring deep into his eyes, I grazed my fingers across his stubble. 'How about I run you a bath, and then we can order in your favourite pizza?'

A smile began to appear on his face.

'You sound like my mom,' he said, dipping his head down again.

'Really? You're the second person to have said that to me today. I'm beginning to get a complex.'

Will laughed and frowned as I took his hand and led him to the bathroom. I flicked the tap on and turned back to Will. He was struggling with the concept of someone looking after him, and he looked awkward.

'Will, I'm glad you told me. I don't want us to have any secrets anymore. I can't cope with finding them out through other people,' I said, waving my hand around as if to include all the elements of his life in my comment. 'When I asked if there was anything else the other day, I meant *anything*.'

I took his t-shirt off and then bent down to undo his shoelaces.

'Would secrets include you acting like my mom and me having a boner?'

I stood straight back up and put my hands on my hips, desperately trying to keep a straight face. He was laughing.

'Will!'

He grabbed me, kissing me forcefully, and I kissed him back. We had spent one night apart, and it was too long. He still smelt faintly of alcohol, but I didn't care. He pulled my sweatshirt off.

'Whose clothes are these? They don't smell of you,' he detected.

'They're Cara's. She came to rescue me today.'

Pulling my tee off next, he said, 'That's my job.'

He lifted my chin and kissed me lovingly.

'Come, let's shower first.'

Chapter 10

Sitting at the corner of the breakfast bar in our bathrobes, tucking into a pizza, Will seemed like a new man. The anguish from his face was gone, and he seemed relaxed and carefree, as if a huge weight had been lifted from his shoulders.

I felt a deeper connection with him, too, like the post-coital bond, but all the time. Even sitting there, sharing food and talking, we had seamless fluidity. That buzz I felt if he brushed my arm to reach for a slice of pizza had been replaced with a warm caress of my soul.

'Was Drew pissed off with me?' I asked suddenly, conscious that I didn't want to cause any issues among his friends.

'What because a woman stood up to him? Probably, but I really don't care. He's spent most of his life trying to hook up with women that are way out of his league, and despite marrying Clem, that hasn't seemed to have stopped him. Leo thinks he's a jerk, as does Bo, but I guess because we've known him since school, he's just always been there.'

'Milly's lovely,' I mused.

'Milly is ace! I knew you two would get on. I met her when we were touring back in the early days. We were both striving for the same thing... recognition. She couldn't handle the rejection, of which there was a lot back then, so she went travelling for a bit and then came back here and started to teach piano. I didn't see her for years. We'd kind of lost touch, but then I was out with Leo one night, and we caught a show, and she was playing.'

'Is that when she and Leo got together?' I asked, and he laughed.

'Yeah... well, it was the start of it. She's a tough cookie to crack.' He tore another piece of pizza off and added, 'Like you.'

'Hardly,' I said, but before Will could disagree. 'How about we invite them here for dinner tomorrow... and I was thinking maybe, I could invite Cara and Thomas too?'

Will smiled.

'Sure, I could organise a chef,' Will said as a matter of course.

'You will do no such thing. I'll cook!'

Will laughed and raised his eyebrows.

'Tough cookie...' he repeated, and I shook my head.

'Is there anyone else you'd like to invite?' I asked.

'Maybe Jake. He'll probably decline, though.'

'Does he not have a significant other?' I asked, licking the grease off my fingers.

'Plenty of others, none of whom are significant.'

'Oh, shame, I kind of like him.' I thought out loud, between licks, and he looked at me intently. 'What?'

'And do you like Stryker?' he asked.

I looked back at him and picked up a napkin to finish wiping my fingers, his expression was placid, but the question was loaded.

Did he know that Stryker was at the hotel last night? Stryker had admitted that he had told Will what he had said to me in the car, so I'd have to assume he had mentioned it because he was here when I got back. I replied with another question.

'What does Stryker mean by sharing?'

Will's gaze didn't falter, but did I detect a smile appearing at the corners of his mouth? And then he bit down on his lower lip, obviously contemplating his answer.

'Stryker and I go way back. We've done lots of touring together, and when you're touring in a van or a bus, you're kind of living on top of each other... you don't get much privacy,' he said, sliding off his stool, placing himself between my legs and looking down at me with darkening eyes.

'You didn't answer my question,' I said.

'You didn't answer mine,' he batted back at me.

'Yes,' I replied simply, and he laughed through his nose.

I wanted an answer.

'Lucy...' he said, shaking his head, but I lifted my eyebrows as if to mean business. 'Fuck,' he whispered under his breath, closing his eyes for a second. 'Sometimes we'd end up bringing girls back at the same time... one thing would lead to another... there was a lot of alcohol... and drugs involved back then—of which I don't do anymore,' he added hastily. 'Occasionally, if the girls were willing, we'd swap... share, whatever.'

I let that wash over me for a moment, concentrating on not changing my expression in any way. Will still looking straight into my eyes, trying to read me.

'And Stryker wanted to do that with me?' I asked to clarify, and Will smiled, biting his lip again, a little glint in his eye. 'He told me that he told you... he was at the hotel I stayed at last night.'

'I know. And yes, he finds you very attractive, but I told him to back off. I don't want you feeling awkward around him, he's a good friend, and I trust him implicitly.'

Again, I let that information sit there for a bit while I processed it.

'Are you done?' he asked, standing tall and pointing to the pizza as if the conversation was over.

'But what if I *was* willing?' I asked suddenly.

It was out before I'd had the chance to actually think about it, but as I said it, I felt like I should own it, so I readjusted my shoulders, sitting up straight.

Will closed his eyes and set his jaw to the side, taken aback by my question. When he looked back at me, he narrowed his eyes a little, almost like he was trying to scan my brain for answers.

'Those girls back then were...' he hesitated, looking up as if searching for the right answer.

'One-night stands? Prostitutes?' I suggested, but he was struggling with his answer, and I bit my lip while I patiently waited for him to confirm.

'Girls... I didn't care for,' he said finally, and then he coughed a small laugh. 'Why? Do you wanna threesome with Stryker?'

His question took me aback.

'Umm.'

It was my turn to squirm.

'I've never really thought about it. I've never been in a situation where it would be possible, but then... I didn't really know what sex could be like until I met you,' I admitted honestly.

Will smiled and resumed his position to cup my face. He took a breath in and then sighed.

'Look, I love that you're willing to try new things, but can we take one step at a time? There's so much more I wanna do with you, and if I'm honest, I don't know if *I'm* willing to share you. I'm not sure how I feel about another person touching you. I guess as circumstances changed for us, the band, I mean, the more private I've become.' He moved his head back and looked down his nose at me. 'Is the interrogation over because I fucking hate talking about my past sex life?'

I smiled and bit my lip.

'Mmm hmm,' I said, slipping off my stool to put our glasses in the dishwasher.

Will was watching me with a little smile on his face.

'What?' I asked.

'You. I blatantly would have left those for the cleaner.'

'Well, if we ever live together, you'd better get used to putting glasses away yourself!' I said, tilting my head at the end of the sentence as if to make a point.

'Or, you'd better get used to not having to do it.'

I swallowed then and looked at the floor, unable to fathom the possibility. Will sighed.

'I'll put the glasses away if it makes you feel better.'

He held his hand out to me, I took it, and he drew me in.

'We'll work it out, okay?'

I looked up at him.

'It might just take time... for me to remember.' He lifted his eyebrows up. 'Oh, come on, I'm trying to be funny.'

'I know, it's just... it's like I'm living in a dream,' I said wistfully.

I hadn't meant to say that out loud, but a great big goofy smile appeared on Will's face.

'Let's watch a film,' Will suggested changing the subject.

We started watching The Joker, I never got to see it at the cinema, and it seemed like the perfect opportunity because Will's TV screen was the size of a cinema screen. It felt like we were doing something normal. It wasn't easy to find things to do that were normal, and I wondered how long it would take for everything to feel... normal. The Joker should have been the perfect distraction, but I couldn't put my thoughts to bed. I got up to get some water.

'You know...' I jumped, not realising Will had followed me to the sink, 'I have a better idea to distract you from whatever it is you're overthinking.'

He kissed my neck, moving his hands down the contour of my torso, hips, and thighs. He pulled on the knot of my bathrobe, allowing it to fall open and took my breasts in his hands, kneading them gently. I could feel him getting hard, and I closed my eyes, lolling my head back onto his shoulder as I undid his robe and massaged him. As his breathing began to get heavier, he moved his hands down to my hips and turned me to face him.

Kissing me, he pushed my robe off my shoulders, it fell to the floor, and I immediately looked over at the windows.

He chuckled. 'No one can see in. It's privacy glass.'

He lifted me onto the kitchen counter, it was freezing, and my skin responded particularly my nipples.

'But what if they have those special cameras?' I murmured.

He pushed my legs apart and began kissing my collarbone.

'What special cameras?' he asked between kisses as he still descended over my tits.

'The ones that can see through privacy glass?' I said breathlessly as he reached my hips.

'I'll let you know when they've invented them,' he said as he reached his goal, pushing my chest back to give himself more room.

I had to quickly put my arms out behind me to stop myself from falling back onto the marble surface before he covered me completely with his mouth and began to gently suck. My head fell backwards as I simultaneously pushed my pelvis into him. I had to quickly pull my thoughts away from what he was doing to stop myself from building.

'You know, I don't think it's fair that you're still wearing your robe,' I said.

He skilfully shrugged his robe off without breaking contact and slipped his thumb inside me. I took a sharp intake of breath, and I tried hard to think about something else.

'And I don't think it's fair that I have to sit on this cold, hard surface.'

He stopped what he was doing, took his thumb out and slowly lifted his head, wiping the residue from his mouth as he did so. When his eyes finally came level with mine, I bit my lip, trying to disguise my smile. His jaw was set, and he had fire in his eyes.

Suddenly, he picked me up and plonked me on the floor in front of him. He stood there for a moment with his hands on his hips, his penis fully erect, clearly wondering what his next move would be. And then he bent down, grabbed hold of my legs and lifted me on his shoulder.

I yelped with delight.

I thought he was going to take me into the bedroom, but instead, he walked back over to the lounge area and pretty much threw me down onto the sofa. He crawled on top of me, so our eyes were in line again.

'One more peep out of you, young lady, and I will fuck that mouth of yours.'

I gasped in mock horror, and he kissed me, devouring me, and I fed my arms around him, holding him close, smoothing my hand down his back and over his butt.

'You know, when you don't think you're ever gonna get the opportunity to do this again, it always feels so much more amazing when you do,' he said with hooded eyes.

'Did you really think I wasn't going to come back?' I asked.

'I thought it would have been a good opportunity for an out after my drunken behaviour.'

'And you think I'm looking for an out?'

'I think you overthink stuff.'

I looked away toward the coffee table, and he chose that moment to slowly slide himself inside me, forcing me to look back at him. My insides contracted to accept him, and my breath caught as he did so.

'I just need time,' I said as he withdrew almost entirely before slamming himself back into me. 'Ahh'

'I hope so,' he said, and he did it again, and again, and again, before settling into a steady pace.

He knelt up, pulling me with him, so I could straddle him. I kissed him, weaving my hands into his hair as I rode him. His hands were caressing my back, his teeth nipping my neck, his lips kissing my jaw, and his tongue licking between every kiss and nip.

'How do you feel about sex toys?' he asked suddenly, and I stopped riding him.

What? This was a slap in the face. Was I not doing enough for him? He put his head to one side as the confidence I had built with him dripped off me like snow.

'Lucy, you look horrified. Tell me what you're thinking.'

'Um...' I eased off him. 'I'm thinking people use sex toys if they... need them?'

I used the back of the sofa and pushed myself up to standing, Will stood too and lifted my face to his. This was super awkward. How long had he been thinking about using them? Mike and I had never used sex toys, and we probably should have done, but Will and I... I thought everything was good. It was the one aspect of our relationship that I felt didn't need addressing.

'I'm not horrified... I'm mortified,' I whispered.

'What? Lucy, don't read too much into this. It was just an idea. I'm sure some couples use them because they need them, but I was thinking more for fun.'

He kissed me, but I was feeling more and more aware that I was naked, standing in his vast lounge with floor-to-ceiling windows, privacy glass or otherwise.

Will could tell I was recoiling, and in an attempt to make me feel more secure, he leant down and flicked a button on the remote, and some curtains began to track along the entire length of the windows. The material alone was probably enough to cover one side of my house at home. He grabbed a blanket from the arm of the sofa, wrapped it around me and then picked me up. I clung to his neck, and he carried me through to the bedroom.

Placing me in the middle of the bed, he did the same thing with the curtains in the bedroom, lowered the lights so that they were almost out and then put some music on to fill the space. I was slowly starting to relax a little.

'Would you like a drink?' he asked.

It was pretty late, and as I had woken most mornings with a hangover since we'd arrived, I declined.

He crawled up the bed until our foreheads met.

'Our sex life is amazing, you are amazing, and the whole toys thing was just a suggestion. But, if I'm honest, it was more for me.'

I closed my eyes and sighed, but he continued.

'Not because I need more stimulation, the opposite in fact. I was going to suggest using a cock ring.'

He pushed my long fringe out of my eyes. I'd heard of cock rings, but I had no idea what they did.

'They help suppress ejaculation... and there have been a few times when I could have done with one,' he smiled.

'Really?' I asked.

'Really,' he repeated. 'You really fucking turn me on... like no other, your body, your smell, it does something to me.'

'I smell?' I asked, and Will laughed.

'Not a bad smell, just your smell, your pheromones. They make me hard.' He glanced down, and I laughed because he was fully standing to attention. 'But Lucy, we may not need them, but they're fun... and I want to restrain you.'

'What!' I said, suddenly feeling uneasy again, and he laughed. 'It's just a fantasy of mine, and maybe, if I can keep your hands out of the way, I might last longer.'

I thought about that for a moment, looking at the structure of his modern four-poster bed.

'Tying me up?' I clarified.

'Possibly... just keeping your hands out of the picture for a while.'

'But I like touching you.'

And I trailed my fingers down his torso towards his more than impressive manhood. Dancing my fingers over his soft, silky skin as his cock jumped around like it had a mind of its own, and then I grabbed it.

'Fuck!' he said as I did so, and then I began slowly smoothing him up and down.

'And I like turning you on, it turns me on,' I said as his breathing became heavier.

'Okay, but just....' He breathed out a ragged breath. 'Think about it.'

And then he enveloped me, our bodies responding to each other's movements with their own language. We didn't need to talk, we had done so much talking today. He slowly pushed himself back inside me and began to move, but he took a much slower approach.

I think he felt he needed to be gentle with me. I had to admit I was feeling pretty fragile. There seemed to be new challenges every day, but we'd deal with them one by one, overcome them and be stronger for it.

'Lucy, look at me,' Will said, pulling me back into the here and now.

I looked into his eyes.

'I lost you for a second,' he said.

He lifted my knee, pushing in deeper still, then rolled us both over so that I was on top. He immediately put his thumb in his mouth.

'Sit up. I need you to come. I'm not gonna last.'

He began circling me with his thumb. I had spent so much time playing tricks with my mind to stop myself from coming, thinking he needed longer, that I realised I had checked out. It took me no time to check back in, and I began to build, moving my hips back and forth.

He suddenly sat up, supporting himself by placing his arm behind him and using his other to tease my nipple. I adjusted myself and wrapped my legs around him, not realising how deep that would cause him to go.

'Ahh, jeez!' I choked.

'Christ, Lucy, I'm gonna come, don't fucking move.'

His release was so deep, I could feel the shudders as his cock pumped into me. I had been so close, but I hadn't come, and he knew it. I pulled my legs back around and eased off him, but he was not finished with me. He pushed me back onto the bed, simultaneously pushing my legs apart and immediately put his tongue where I needed him to.

I couldn't quite believe what he was doing, his load was dripping out of me, but he didn't seem to care. He pushed his fingers inside me, and that was enough to spark my orgasm. He sucked every last contraction out of me until my quivering knees stilled.

His green eyes were back staring into mine, his chin glistening with a mix of our arousals. I wiped his face with my hand, and he smiled wickedly.

'So, about that cock ring.' I rolled my eyes before he kissed me. 'I love you.'

'You can't say that in the same sentence.'

'I love you,' he said again.

'I love you too.'

Chapter 11

The following day I woke feeling refreshed. I had to check that it was morning because the curtains were like blackout blinds. Will was still asleep, so I quickly showered, grabbed my phone and set myself up at the breakfast bar with a pen and pad I'd found in one of the drawers. I was chuffed to have received a text from Cara to confirm that she and Thomas were able to come.

By the time Will emerged in his boxers, hair completely dishevelled and a semi on the go, I had created a menu.

'Morning, Beautiful. Busy?'

'Aha, where's the nearest supermarket?' he came up behind me and peered over my shoulder at my list.

'Hmmm, that's quite a list.'

He kissed my shoulder.

'That's because all you have in your apartment is booze.'

Will looked up suddenly. The lift light was on.

'Who's that?'

'Probably the cleaner. I'm gonna jump in the shower.'

I bloody well hoped it was because he shot back into the bedroom before the doors opened. Sure enough, an older, rounded lady clutching a holdall of products appeared in a smock.

'Hi,' I said so as not to surprise her.

'Humph,' she said, assessing me with pursed lips.

I looked around because that wasn't the welcome I had expected.

'You must be Lucy,' she said with a strong New York accent.

Oh, she knew who I was.

'Yes, hello.'

I put my hand out to shake hers, but she just looked at it. How had I offended her? All I'd said was hi and hello.

'Um, well, I'm just about to go food shopping. Can you recommend anywhere?'

'Wegmans,' she said, then she turned on her heel and wandered into the lounge area to plump the cushions.

Will was still in the shower, so I grabbed the two shopping bags I'd found while looking for the pad and pen and headed out, searching up Wegmans as I headed down in the lift. It was a bit of a trek, but I figured I could get a taxi back. I had been gone less than three minutes when Will called.

'Where are you?'

'On my way to Wegmans? Well, I was. I'm now talking to you and can't see where I'm supposed to be going.'

'Okay, well, I'll send Terry to collect you.'

'I can get a cab,' I confirmed.

'You could, but we have Terry at our disposal. This is what I pay him for, so getting a cab would be excessive.'

I rolled my eyes.

'Fine.'

'Oh, and Milly & Leo can come tonight. Jake is still scratching his balls... Stryker has also confirmed.'

He said the last part hesitantly. I wondered if he was having second thoughts following our conversation yesterday, but I ignored it.

'Okay, I'll buy for eight, and then they'll be leftovers if Jake can't make it.'

'Cool, you still have my card, right?' he asked.

Shit, I did still have his card.

'Oh my God, sorry, yes, I'll give it back when I get back.'

'I wasn't asking for it back. Use it, please. It's the least I can do with everything that's happened with your job.'

I rolled my eyes. He had literally been paying for everything since the incident, and although the man had been arrested, Will obviously felt guilty that I'd had to put the brakes on growing my business.

'I'm going now. Otherwise, I'll get lost,' I said, not confirming or denying the use of his card, and I hung up.

The supermarket was immense. It took me ages to find everything but find everything I did. Kir Royale's for arrival drinks, salmon blinis to start, herb-crusted chicken for main, and lemon torte for dessert. I even bought flowers and napkins for the table and some nibbles to put out to have with drinks.

Terry was waiting for me outside, and I hoped he hadn't been there long. He immediately hopped out and helped me load everything into the boot before holding the back door open. I realised once I'd gotten in that I hadn't seen him since returning to Wills. I wondered how often he had dealt with a drunk Will.

It didn't take us long to get back. Terry leapt out of the car once we had pulled up by the lifts and grabbed every single bag out of the boot before I'd had a chance to walk to the back of the car. I went to say something, but he nodded towards the lift as if to tell me to enter the code.

As we ascended, I felt useless and thought it was ridiculous that Terry was carrying everything. The further up we went, the more cross I became. I wasn't happy about the situation. It felt sexist and elitist. I strode straight into the apartment. Will was sitting at the breakfast bar.

'Hey, did you get everything you needed?'

I was so livid by the time I reached him that I slapped his card, the pen and the pad down on the counter in front of him and stomped off to the bathroom to cool off.

Splashing my face did not work, so I began pacing around, trying to get a hold of my breathing.

'See you later, Terry,' I heard Will call as he opened the bedroom door.

I frowned before hearing a soft knock.

'Are you okay?'

I breathed out audibly.

'Can I come in?'

I unlocked the door without saying anything and leaned against the vanity unit with my arms crossed. Will opened the door and was in front of me within two strides.

'What did I miss?'

He tried to pick my chin up, but I moved it away.

'Did Terry do something?' he asked disbelievingly.

'Yes! He did everything,' I stated pointedly. 'I did nothing,' I said, slapping my chest. 'I just rode up in the lift! And

Terry carried every single bag.' I huffed out of my nose, shaking my head.

With the slightest smile in his eyes, Will stood there, his mouth open. I looked at him, stony-faced. He slowly gathered his bottom lip with his thumb and forefinger and squished it into a mini heart shape, looking at me and wondering how to deal with my outburst.

He was about to say something when I asked, 'And why did you just say that you'd see Terry later?'

There was a pause.

'Because... I asked him to come over tonight.'

'To dinner?' I asked to confirm.

'No... to be on hand.'

I could tell he was choosing his words carefully.

'For what? He wasn't on hand the other night when everyone was here.'

'That's true, but I didn't have any guests coming that I didn't know.'

'So, he's coming because Cara and Thomas are coming?'

'Yes. He'll be discreet.'

'Can you imagine how that is going to make them feel?'

Will looked at the floor.

'It's just a precaution. They'll understand.'

'Well, Terry can either be *precautionary* at the dinner table as our guest, or we cancel, and you can eat all that food yourself.'

I walked back out of the bathroom to go and unpack the shopping, leaving Will open-mouthed again.

A while later, he stalked into the kitchen. I was busy preparing the lemon torte, ready to put in the fridge to set before getting on with the salmon blinis. As I turned with the torte, Will opened the refrigerator for me and waved his hand like he was welcoming royalty.

'Nice apron,' he said as he closed the fridge.

I glared at him.

'Nice... jeans.'

Will laughed, knowing that our rut was over, and fed a hand around my waist, brushing some flour from my cheek with his thumb.

'I called Terry off,' he confirmed.

'Thank you.' I swallowed.

'I'm sorry, I have a way of doing things here, and it's just habit.'

'No, *I'm* sorry, I'm just not used to having people do everything for me.'

'Can you not just enjoy it while you're here?' he said, lifting his eyebrows.

I pursed my lips, 'Fine, I'll try.'

'Good girl,' he said with a devilish grin but before I could reply he pushed me up against the fridge and kissed me. Pushing my chin up, he kissed my neck.

'Will, I still have a ton of things to do,' I said breathlessly.

'Hmmm,' he growled into my ear and then glanced at all the ingredients out on the breakfast bar. 'I might be more of a hindrance, but is there anything I can do?'

'Yes, could you wash those blackberries, please? I need to prepare the cocktails.'

'Wash them with what?'

I looked at him thinking he was joking, but he looked straight back at me.

'Okay... can you find me eight champagne flutes. In fact, you could set the table.'

I smiled to myself because that was the boy's job at home. I finished assembling the blinis, put the herb crust together, and prepared the new potatoes and green beans so they were ready to go on. Will finished what he classed as setting the table and then took a call. I think it was Paul. Why was Paul calling from his honeymoon?

I folded the napkins into this cool abstract lily pad that a friend had taught me to do once and adjusted pretty much the whole table setting. Using the flowers I'd bought, I cut the heads off the Gerberas, found a shallow pasta bowl for them to float in for a simple centrepiece, and then used some of the rose petals to scatter over the rest of the table.

As I was looking for somewhere to store the remaining napkins, I discovered a bag of tea lights and, using saucers as holders, I put them around and about the place. I finally worked out how to use the remote and lowered the lights around the dining area.

I just needed to prepare the cocktails and put the nibbles out, but I would do that after a shower. I walked into the bedroom, and Will was standing looking out of the window, still on his phone.

'...crazy because I arranged for Terry to come over.'

I coughed, and Will spun around.

'Paul, I'm gonna have to go.'

'Don't mind me, I'm just getting in the shower. Hi Paul.'

Will smiled.

'He says hi,' Will relayed.

I headed into the bathroom and flicked the shower on so they could talk. Will was obviously filling Paul in on my petulant behaviour earlier. I was beginning to feel a bit silly about it, and I thought about my conversation with Cara. Hopefully, she was right, and I just needed some time to adjust. Maybe *I* needed to download. I was missing the girls.

I showered quickly. I was excited and a bit nervous. I wanted to ensure everything was ready before anyone arrived. I wore the silky shirt dress that Will said he liked when we went to lunch with his mum. I kept my makeup light. I was going to put my pretty new shoes on, but my feet were still sore from wearing them the other night, so I decided to stay barefoot.

'That's an excellent idea, man, anyway, you need to get back to your wife and I....'

Will looked at me as I came back into the bedroom.

'Wow, you look gorgeous....'

I blushed.

'Not you, douchebag. See you, man.'

He hung up.

'Hey.'

He grabbed my hand as I walked by to put my eye brush back in my sponge bag.

'I didn't mean to be talking about you when you came in earlier. It's just I value Paul's advice.'

'It's fine. I think that's what I need to do. Maybe I'll call Steph tomorrow.'

'Good idea. But you know, it's natural for you to feel overwhelmed,' he stated, and I frowned.

It was an unusual turn of phrase for him.

'Did you get that line from Paul?' I asked.

'Yeah, was it obvious?'

I laughed, and he gave me a cheeky smile as we walked out into the kitchen. Will stopped in his tracks.

'Woah!'

I smiled. It did look pretty cool. The evening Manhattan skyline added to the atmosphere.

'You like it?' I asked while getting the chilled champagne flutes out of the fridge, ready to pour the crème de cassis and champagne.

'I love it.'

He kissed me on the nose, not wanting to ruin my makeup and then tried to swipe a blackberry, but I smacked his hand.

'They're for the cocktails. Pour those bags of nuts in here, would you?' I said, passing him some bowls.

'Yes, ma'am,' he saluted like a boy scout.

An hour later, everyone had arrived. I loved hosting dinner parties. I just didn't get the opportunity to do it very often at home.

Jake had come, after all, despite being unable to find a date. Thomas was happily chatting with Leo and Milly about music. Will was talking to Cara about her job. Jake was telling Stryker about a film he'd watched the night before, and I was preparing the chicken ready to go in the oven. I could feel Stryker's eyes following me around the kitchen. As I turned to wash my hands, Milly sidled up to me.

'Everything okay after the other night?' she asked, keeping her voice low.

'Yeah... thanks. I'm sorry I took off. I just needed some headspace.'

'Honey, you do not need to explain. I can't imagine what you must be going through. When you meet someone, you don't expect... this!' she said, waving her free hand around.

'I get the feeling you can probably imagine better than most.'

'It'll just take time,' she said as Will stepped up beside me, weaving his arm around my waist, and I quickly looked to see if Cara was alone, but she'd joined Thomas and Leo.

'Yeah... time,' I sighed.

Will squeezed me into him, knowing what we were talking about and then peered into my champagne flute and swiped the blackberry out of my glass. I shook my head, and Milly laughed.

'I could do with everyone sitting up now,' I whispered to Will, and he grabbed a knife from the counter and tapped his glass.

'Could everyone make their way to the dining table now, please,' he announced like he was a master of ceremonies.

I coloured up and rolled my eyes. I hadn't had a chance to speak to Cara, so I was pleased to see the last remaining empty seat was next to her. I brought over the starters, made sure everyone had a drink and then sat down.

'I have a bag of clean clothes for you to take home with you when you go, don't let me forget.'

'Oh, you didn't need to wash them, thank you. I take it everything's okay now?'

'I'm getting there. I see Thomas and Milly have been chatting.'

'Yes, I think they're going to do some sort of collaboration... aaaand,' she said, lowering her voice, 'Will has asked if I'd like to review their private gig in a few weeks and do an exclusive interview,' she added, beaming.

'Oh wow, that's such a great idea. Why didn't I think of that?'

I looked over at Will, but he was deep in conversation with Leo.

'I mean, a review of The 'king Band at a private show *and* an exclusive interview, he *never* does interviews, that's huge,' she said, and I smiled at her, realising the enormity of the offer and then I heard the oven beeping.

'One second.'

I returned to the kitchen to check on the chicken, it needed a few more minutes. The potatoes were nearly there, and I popped the green beans in the microwave.

'Everything okay?' Will asked as he stepped up beside me, having cleared the starters away.

I smiled and bit my lip. 'Perfect, thank you.'

He scooped me up and kissed me.

'Stop mackin' on your girl,' Jake said as he came over, and Will shook his head in disbelief. 'Is it okay to smoke a tab on the balcony?'

'Sure,' Will said, and Jake took himself off. 'He can talk,' he said and then kissed me again. The microwave started beeping, but Will wouldn't let me go until everyone at the table was wondering what the incessant noise was, drawing their attention to us. Stryker wolf whistled. For Christ's sake! Will's kiss turned into a smile as he finally let me go, and I whacked his arm. Was he purposefully making a show in front of Stryker or just everyone in general?

'You are so embarrassing sometimes.'

He grinned and then wandered back to the table to see if anyone needed topping up as I prepared the mains. Despite the embarrassment, I couldn't help but smile to myself. This kind of felt normal, I suppose. Will was the perfect host, and I was enjoying myself.

I started to bring the mains over, everyone had shuffled about, and I was between Will and Stryker. Will was chatting to Milly and Jake.

I topped my water up, and Stryker nudged my arm.

'This is amazing,' he said, pointing to his half-mouthful.

I laughed.

'Couldn't wait to finish your mouthful to tell me that,' I said in a teacher kind of way.

He swallowed.

'I like occupying my mouth,' he replied, looking straight at me.

I looked straight back and concentrated on not flinching. He'd said it on purpose to gain a reaction, and I wasn't going to give him the satisfaction.

'Where did you learn to cook?' he asked, changing the subject.

'Oh, just at home.'

'They must have real good cookery schools in the UK.'

'No, I meant... never mind. So, what do you do while you're not talking with your mouthful?'

'Haha, well, obviously there's the band, but when I'm not working, I travel. I don't have a fixed abode. I just move from place to place as I please, either staying with friends or book a B&B.'

I was surprised. I thought he'd have some swanky apartment somewhere.

'So, what have you surmised from all your travelling?'

It was quite an open question, but I was avoiding it getting too personal.

'That whatever country you're in, the more north you go, the crazier the people are... as in open. Willing to explore new things, you know?'

I thought about my friends who lived up north and smiled. He was right. I hadn't really noticed it before. Will's hand was suddenly between my legs. I glanced at him, but he was still engrossed in his conversation with Milly and Jake.

'I'm right, right?' Stryker asked.

'I guess so,' I said, tensing up.

I couldn't believe what Will was doing while talking to someone else. I lowered my hand and tried to move him away, but he firmly grabbed my thigh and moved his hand closer to my pelvis. I was desperately trying to think of something else to ask Stryker.

'So... what are you doing in New York at the moment?' I asked finally.

'I'm having dinner with my friends,' he replied, looking straight at me with a wry smile as Will's fingers reached their destination. 'I live for the moment. I don't do much planning outside work. Go with the flow, you know?'

'Aha,' I said in a higher-pitched voice than I had hoped.

Was Will purposefully making me feel awkward? Just as his fingers were about to slip inside, I suddenly stood up and excused myself to go to the loo, giving Will a glare. On the way back, I crossed paths with Cara, who was looking for the loo too.

'There's one just through there,' I said. 'You okay?'

'Yes, the food is delicious, and your friends are all lovely. Thank you for inviting us,' she gushed.

'Oh, don't be silly. It's the least I could do after all you've done for me.' I squeezed her hand. 'I'd better get on with dessert.'

Milly and Will joined me in the kitchen with all the plates.

'Thanks, just leave them there. I'll sort them.' I was searching through the kitchen cupboards. 'Do you have a sieve?'

'Erm...' Will said as Milly pointed towards the bathroom to signal she was headed that way.

'Don't worry, I'll just sprinkle the sugar rather than dredge.' I thought out loud as I checked the last cupboard.

Will perched on a stool with his wine while I took the dessert out of the fridge. Resting one of his elbows on the breakfast bar, he placed his chin on his hand as if setting up camp to watch as I finished sprinkling the sugar, ready to cut the torte into slices. His eyes were glazed, and before I started cutting, I poured a glass of water and carefully placed it in front of him. I didn't want a repeat performance of the other night.

'You look so fucking hot in that dress,' he said as he picked up the water and drained half of it.

'I wore it for you.'

I smiled as I started placing the slices onto the plates. I glanced at the table, everyone was happy chatting, so I stole the opportunity to put some dirty dishes in the dishwasher. Will came round to my side of the breakfast bar, I thought he was going to help, but he took the fork out of my hand and lobbed it into the sink, allowing it to clatter around.

'Leave those, come and socialise... that's the point, right?'

He was right, it was rude to do them while they were here, and I picked up four of the slices to take them over. Will tried to work out how I'd picked them all up and then gave up and picked up two, running back for the others.

'Mmm, super tangy and melt in the mouth,' Thomas said. 'Praise to the Chef.'

I flushed, smiling, and everyone cheered and clapped. Will put his hand on my thigh again and squeezed, and I noticed he'd switched his wine for water.

As the evening ended, I nipped into the bedroom to collect Cara's things.

'Here you are. Thanks again, and thank you for coming. It's been nice to meet you properly, Thomas.'

'Thank you and you,' he said.

'He totally thought you'd ordered in until I told him you had cooked,' Cara admitted, and I laughed.

'Well, listen, the great thing is, is that we'll see you in a couple of weeks.'

'Yes, I can't wait. This could be the break I need,' Cara admitted as Will joined us.

'You deserve it. You've worked so hard,' Thomas said, looking at her adoringly.

I had discovered this evening that Will knew of Thomas through the music industry, Milly and Stryker did too. He'd written several hit records for some well-known pop artists and was famous and wealthy in his own right.

He was such a gentleman, and I marvelled at their interaction. They were grounded and obviously in love. I knew Cara had come from a modest background so she gave me hope that I would eventually get used to this different way of living.

'You should come out to LA,' Will suggested to them, witnessing how well we'd gotten on over dinner.

'That could work,' Thomas said.

'Bye, guys,' I said as they disappeared into the lifts, just as Milly and Leo headed over with their coats to say their goodbyes. Stryker and Jake were next.

'That was epic,' Jake said, giving me a friendly hug and as he drew back, he shook Will's hand, pulling him in. 'You lucky fucker,' he said to Will loud enough for us all to hear.

'Hear, hear,' Stryker said as he pulled me in for a hug too, his hands skating dangerously close to my arse. He brushed his lips across my ear, 'I loved watching the look in your eyes while Will was touching you,' he whispered, and I gasped.

'Hands off, Stryker,' Will said sternly and pulled me away from him.

'For fuck's sake, Stryker,' Jake said. 'I hope he's not up to his old tricks again,' he added, looking at me.

He gave Stryker a shove. Was Jake in on this previous arrangement too? Was it just one massive orgy back in the day? Will moved in behind me and wrapped his arms around me protectively.

'Goodnight, guys,' Will said as his lips landed on my neck, and Jake pushed Stryker towards the lift.

As the lift doors were closing, Will's hand disappeared up my dress, Stryker and Jake witnessing the move before the lift began to descend. I pushed his hand away as I turned to look at him with a furrowed brow, and Will licked his lips, amusement in his expression.

As per usual, the second everyone left, I was immediately shattered. It must be something to do with putting on a show. I don't know how Will did it.

'I know everyone else kept saying so, but that food was out of this world. Stryker thought you were a trained cook.'

I smiled shyly.

'And everyone you meet loves you.'

I couldn't cope with all the compliments, so I opened the dishwasher.

'Nah ah ah,' Will said, waggling his finger in front of my face. 'We're going to bed.'

'But I hate going to bed when the kitchen is untidy. It makes the hangover so much worse the following morning.'

Will took my hand, pulling me towards the bedroom, switching lights off as he went.

'Well, you'll be pleased to know that by morning, the cleaning fairies will have been and done it for you.'

I closed my eyes, realising now why Will had been so reluctant for me to load the dishwasher. Did the cleaner come in every day?

Chapter 12

Not a single rose petal was in sight. It was back to its pristine, show-home glory, and I hadn't heard a thing. The only thing that remained was a faint smell of wine and stale cigarette smoke, and I was suddenly transported back to my Mum and Dad's parties back in the day. That smell the following morning was the sign of a good night.

I made myself a coffee and headed outside to admire the view. It felt weird not clearing up. This coffee I had in my hand would normally be the reward for filling the dishwasher, wiping down the sides and doing all the recycling. It almost didn't taste as good, but I'd told Will I'd try to enjoy it, and besides, I was on holiday.

The door slid open behind me.

'Why is it whenever I wake up, you're not there?' Will asked, stopping behind me and feeding his arms around my waist. He rested his chin on my shoulder and looked out.

'Because I'm an early riser,' I said.

'So am I,' he replied, pushing his hips into me. 'Come back to bed,' he said in a low gruff voice.

I turned to face him, he was only wearing his boxers, and I put my coffee on the table. Before I could say anything, he was kissing me, pulling my blouse out of my waistband to gain access to my tits. Our kissing quickly became heated, and he began to undo the fly on my jeans.

Then, as if suddenly remembering where we were, he pulled me back into the apartment.

Half an hour or so later, we were both sat up in bed, I was replying to Steph's text, and Will was looking at his laptop.

'I don't know what she means by, *at least you're dressed*. Maybe she's sent it to the wrong person.'

Will didn't reply, so I looked over my shoulder to see if he was listening. Instead, he was shaking his head at his laptop, which was never a good sign.

'I'm such an idiot,' he sighed.

I was about to ask why, but he simply turned the screen for me to see. Several pictures of us standing on his balcony lay before me, like a comic strip. One of Will stood behind me looking over my shoulder, the next one of us kissing, then one of my loose blouse, and the last one of Will pulling me into the apartment.

They'd carefully taken the shots to make it look like Will was naked, and the caption read, *Will uses his final weapon to lure Lucy into his arms*.

I tried to keep a straight face, but a small titter escaped, and I clasped my hand over my mouth.

'Oh, you think that's funny, do you?' Will said, smiling as I started giggling. He slapped his laptop shut and pounced on me, and I shrieked. 'You're becoming quite a household name.'

'What do you mean?' I laughed.

'The media, they love you.'

I stopped laughing and looked at him, waiting for him to clarify what he meant.

'I'm being portrayed as the mean, drunken rock and roller but you... you can do no wrong. You're the girl next door.'

This was news to me. Last I'd heard, I was a home wrecker, but Will had put a stop to those rumours. I just assumed the media had got bored and moved onto someone else... or so I thought. I sat up suddenly, and Will flopped back onto the bed, looking up to the ceiling.

He let out an audible sigh.

'For fuck's sake,' he said under his breath.

'What?' I snapped.

I was flummoxed that *he* was in a piss.

'You! I can't get a handle on what you're thinking. You were laughing about this a minute a go,' he said, looking at me perplexed.

We were interrupted by his phone vibrating. He looked at the screen and ignored it.

'Well, you're making it sound like they always write about us,' I said, and he sat up and stared at me dumbfounded.

'Lucy... they do. Are you seriously trying to tell me you didn't know?'

I sat there, astounded at this revelation. Why hadn't he said something before? How would I have known?

'You told me not to look,' I whispered.

The back of my neck felt hot. Was I going to be... I leapt up and ran into the bathroom, but after heaving a couple of times, the heat in my neck dissipated, and I leaned back against the shower's glass wall and slid to the floor. Will arrived with some water. He came and sat down next to me.

'I know I told you not to look, but everyone looks... right?... Fuck!'

He was shaking his head in disbelief. His phone started to vibrate again.

'They want to know your side of the story. They want to know how you stay so level-headed, and how you manage an alcoholic boyfriend. They want to know what fucking recipes you use.'

His phone started up again.

'Daisy, I'll call you back.' He hung up, and I took a few sips of water.

'Recipes?' I said eventually. 'That's a bit random, isn't it?'

'They ran some pictures of you at Wegmans yesterday.'

'But I wasn't with you in Weg... mans.'

The penny began to drop. The press had been following *me*.

'I thought Cara might have mentioned it last night. She was in a couple of the pictures. They'd reported something about you becoming best friends with Thomas Lorenzo's girlfriend.'

He took hold of my hand, interlacing our fingers.

'How long has this been going on?' I asked.

'There's been bits and pieces since we got together, but it's kind of intensified since we got over here. That's partly why I spoke to Paul yesterday. It seems someone at the wedding leaked some pictures... I think it might have been Drew.'

'Oh, my God. That's awful. He's your friend,' I said, squeezing his hand.

'I must admit that stung. It's been a while.'

There was disappointment in his tone. I draped my arm over him, and he returned the gesture.

'Can we move back into the bedroom? My ass is going to sleep.'

He didn't wait for me to respond, he stood up, dragging me with him.

'I need to call Daisy back,' he said, lifting his phone to his ear.

'Who's Daisy?'

'PR... Daisy, hi.'

I slipped a bathrobe on and found my own phone.

'I wasn't naked. I had briefs on,' Will explained, and I looked up at him and then at his dick. If only Daisy knew she was talking to a naked Will! He headed out to the kitchen.

I replied to Steph.

Hadn't realised the media were following me, could really do with a chat, can we FaceTime soon?

I sent it just as Will came back in finishing up his conversation with Daisy, but just as he hung up his phone began to ring again, and he rolled his eyes.

'Mat,' he said in greeting as he flopped onto the bed.

Mat was their new tour manager. I heard them discussing the pictures, and Will was filling him in on what Daisy had suggested, so I left them to it and went off to make more coffees.

I sat at the breakfast bar and looked over at the window again and across to the view. Someone was out there, taking pictures of us, invading our privacy, and making money out of it. It was unnerving, and I felt imprisoned, trapped, and unable to move without being followed.

And yet I was sat on an oak stool in a pure silk dressing gown, with my elbows propped up on a marble breakfast bar, drinking a coffee from a machine fit for a barista. These were the luxuries that Will had worked for, but at what cost?

Curiosity got the better of me, and I searched up the report about Will on his balcony. The insinuation was that the bad boy of rock was seducing me into his debauched lifestyle. My name was in blue.

I had been made into a search engine link.

I hovered over it for a moment and then clicked on my name. My eyes widened as I took in the sight. There were so many pictures. Not so many articles, but it seemed that every time I'd left the house since the G.A.M. awards, there was an image to remind me of the occasion.

The pictures that were attached to the articles were ludicrous.

Will's girlfriend, Lucy Daniels, meets mom-in-law-to-be.

Lucy Daniels moves to New York.

Lucy flees after Will shows his true colors.

Lucy leaves kids with father to build a new life with Will.

Stories were created purely on assumption and speculation. I felt powerless and annoyed that they were allowed to write this shit without proof, and I could not correct them. I was just here on holiday, for God's sake. I wish I hadn't looked. It was making me feel worse. I was at their mercy. Prey. Someone who can be spoken about but not heard.

The lift whirred into action, someone was coming, and it wasn't the cleaner. She had been. I leapt off my stool, dropping my cup in the process, and raced back into the bedroom.

'Someone's coming. Someone's in the lift,' I said, panicked, as I ran over to Will, who was pulling his jeans on with his phone still wedged under his ear.

He grabbed me. I was shaking. My breathing was erratic.

'Lucy, it's just Mat.'

He ended the call and chucked his phone on the bed, hugging me tight and pressing the side of my face into his chest.

'It's just Mat, baby,' he said again with a sigh, kissing the top of my head. 'Sorry, I should have said.'

I closed my eyes and listened to his heartbeat while I tried to bring my breathing under control, but I couldn't. What the hell was wrong with me? I was really on edge.

'Will?' I heard Mat call.

'Won't be a sec, man,' Will called back. 'I invited him over. Our call was taking longer than expected, and he was nearby, so I suggested he pop in.'

He pulled me in, tighter still.

'I feel like a goldfish,' I said between breaths, and my voice sounded shrill.

'A goldfish?' Will repeated with a laugh in his voice.

'Yeah, in a bowl... stuck on a shelf for everyone to watch.'

I turned to put my hands around his neck, but my hands were trembling. So, I switched to place them around

Will's torso instead in an attempt for Will not to see them, but it was too late.

'Lucy...' he said with compassion and lifted me up. 'I think you're having an anxiety attack.'

He walked over to the bed and placed me down, and as soon as he did, I wrapped the duvet around me as if to shut everything out, even Will. Will slid down the bed so that our faces were aligned.

'Do you want me to call a doctor?'

I shook my head.

'Okay. I'm just gonna go get you some more water. Will you be okay for a minute?'

I blinked my eyelids instead of nodding, and he pulled a t-shirt on, grabbed his laptop and phone, and slipped through the door.

I could hear Will saying something to Mat about me and picking up broken crockery as I slid further still under the duvet.

If I could just teleport myself back home.

I lifted my hand back up to look at it, and it was still shaking. It was weird, I didn't feel like I was having an anxiety attack in my brain, but it was as if my body had other ideas.

I thought about the boys, and I thought about the dogs, and I even thought about Mike... not in a sexual way, but they all made me feel safe. I pulled my knees up to my chest and hugged myself. This wasn't what I imagined our holiday to be like. Me hiding under a duvet, shaking like a leaf, and Will having a meeting with his tour manager.

I heard Will return, and the mattress give.

'Hey, you awake in there?'

I replied, but it was all muffled with the duvet.

'I made you some tea, and Mat bought some pastries.'

I didn't move, I was beginning to feel a bit numb, and you'd think if I were having an anxiety attack, I would be feeling all sorts of emotions. But, instead, it was as if someone had swooped in and cleared out my inbox, hit reset, and all that was left was space, a vast cavernous space.

'I'll put them on the side,' Will said eventually.

I could sense Will was hovering, and then I thought he left the room. I lay there for a while. I didn't know how long. My mind was blank. Nothing. I was just staring at the folds in the sheets. I pinched the sheets together, and then with the heat from my fingers, the crease would return to normal.

I remembered the tea and was worried it might have gone cold, so I slowly unfurled. Pushing myself up onto all fours and crawled my way to the edge of my soft cave, peeking out, squinting, and then swinging my legs around to sit.

'Hey.'

I looked up, and Will was perched on the armchair at the side of the room with his laptop.

How long had he been there?

'Hi,' I replied and took several long sips of water.

'How are you feeling?' he asked.

'I don't really know,' I admitted.

'Can I sit with you?'

I wasn't quite sure why he was asking. Had I missed something?

'Of course,' I said, confused.

'I've witnessed a few anxiety attacks over the years. I just wanna make sure you're comfortable.'

I nodded slowly.

'Is Mat still here?'

'No, I sent him home. He sends his regards.' He adjusted his seating position so that he was facing me. 'I've made some arrangements. I hope you don't mind.'

'What do you mean, arrangements?'

'A friend of mine has a villa in The Hamptons.'

I didn't know what he was about to say, but despite feeling trapped, the thought of leaving this apartment was not something I wanted to do any time soon.

'I know you're probably feeling a bit daunted about going out right now, but you need to get some fresh air. This place is fully secure, and it has its own private beach. So, we can chill out there.' He took my hands in both of his and then added. 'I've also organised for someone to come and see you, a professional experienced in this... situation.'

'A counsellor?' I asked.

'Kind of... a psychiatrist who specialises in dealing with the media, she knows her stuff.'

Woah. A shrink. Was I that bad? I thought this was supposed to be a holiday.

'Because you think I had an anxiety attack?' I asked while he moved closer and rested his hand on my cheek.

'Because I thought that you might like to talk to someone about... what you're feeling and what your options are, and maybe she can teach you some coping mechanisms... if this all gets... too much.'

I could tell he was choosing his words carefully.

'It's just an option. There's no pressure... it's just... I'm worried about you.'

The concern in his eyes was sobering. I must have really scared him.

'A private beach?' I asked him to clarify.

He smiled and nodded.

'Private... it's a no-drone zone. You can knock out as many sandcastles as you like, and no one will ever know,' he confirmed.

A small smile tugged at the corners of my lips. Will stood up and gently pulled me to standing.

'You don't strike me as the kinda guy that has a bucket and spade,' I said.

'I won a sandcastle competition once, I'll have you know!' he said as he lifted me and began walking towards the bathroom, and I laughed.

'Please tell me there is photographic evidence of that.'

'Probably, you'll have to ask Mom.'

He set me down and flicked the shower on, kissing me tenderly. He pulled the bow on my bathrobe, smoothing it off my shoulders and allowing it to billow to the floor.

'Take a shower. You'll feel better.'

Chapter 13

The smell of the sea air hit me the second Terry opened the car door. It was a sunny day but quite breezy by the sea. I stood for a second, pointing my face to the sun and allowing the wind to flow through my hair as Will said goodbye to Terry.

When Will said villa, I assumed he meant a ground-floor apartment with a pool, but this was something else. It was modern, a light grey mushroom colour with anthracite window frames, clean lines, and huge angular roof lights.

It wasn't until we headed up the stone steps that I could gauge the enormity of the place. We stepped onto the balcony and walked around the side of the building, and I realised we had been at the back of the property, and we were several floors up.

The view was breath-taking. Looking down, there was a pool, the centrepiece of a beautifully manicured garden, and beyond that was, as promised, a beach and, of course, the Atlantic ocean. The sun was low in the sky, making the sea look shimmery.

Suddenly, blocking my view was Will.

'I really hope those are tears of happiness,' he said as he put the bags down and brushed them away with his thumbs.

I hadn't even realised I was crying.

'Sorry,' I said, wiping my face with my own hands. 'I guess it's just been a bit of a whirlwind since we arrived.'

'I know, it's kind of hit all at the same time, huh.' He lifted my face with the crook of his hand. 'Shall we go and find our room?'

We could have chosen several. There were thirteen bedrooms with en-suites and a sea view.

'This is ridiculously excessive just for the two of us,' I said as we were wandering around. 'Who owns it?'

'Just a friend,' Will said with a strange look in his eye.

I was about to ask more questions, surely someone who owned a place like this would be fairly well known, but Will carried on.

'If you want, we can stay in the pool house. There's a bedroom there, too,' Will suggested.

In the end, I chose the room on the apex of the building. It wasn't the biggest, but the dual aspect meant you had an uninterrupted view of the sea. The bed was positioned in the corner, taking full advantage of the seascape and the wrap-around balcony, which had a hot tub and an outside bar and BBQ area. Will put the bags on the ottoman at the foot of the bed.

'Come on.' Will took my hand and led me back out of the room. 'Let's take a walk, and then we can come back and have dinner.'

'Don't we need to go shopping first?' I asked, more to remind him.

'No...' He seemed to be hesitating. 'We're on holiday, right?'

'We are...' I said slowly, wrinkling my nose at the thought of more take-outs.

'Well... this place comes with a live-in chef,' he said in a flurry as if he was trying to slip it into the conversation without me noticing and pulled me outside to distract me.

I shook my head, smiling. I love that he was trying to hide that we had our own private chef, despite the fact we were walking through a villa that could house the population of a small town.

Never had I felt so alive and free as we walked along the beach. It was lovely to walk outside without the constant possibility of someone stopping Will for a selfie or someone taking an unwanted picture. I hadn't realised how much weight it held over us. I could tell Will was feeling it, too. There was a certain confidence about him that I hadn't seen since we had left the UK.

We walked down to the shore's edge, and I took my sandals off to walk in the shallows. Will sat down on the sand and leaned back on his elbows, looking out to sea while I picked up the tiny shells that caught my eye in the sparkly water.

A boat was anchored in the distance, it looked majestic as it bobbed on the horizon. It felt like it had been so long since we had had the opportunity to simply be in an open space, and I looked over at Will. He looked straight back at me and beckoned me over with his index finger. As I neared, he put his hand out for me, and I joined him on the sand, propping myself up.

'Have you seen the boat?' I asked.

'I have, I believe it belongs to the villa. We could go out on her tomorrow if you like.'

'You can sail?' I asked, astounded, and he laughed.

'No, we'd need a skipper.'

We lay there in comfortable silence for a while.

'Are you feeling okay?'

It was about the fifth time he'd asked me.

'Will...' I said, closing my eyes and slowly shaking my head.

He turned to face me.

'What? I'm worried about you, Lucy. I feel awful. It's heart-breaking to watch you in such turmoil. If I had the power to make it stop....'

'Will, it's not your fault,' I said, turning to him, 'stop blaming yourself.'

'I'm just worried that it's all going to get too much and you're gonna want out.'

'I'm not looking for an out, Will,' I tried to assure him.

I put my hand on his cheek and looked into his eyes.

'I promise you.'

I kissed him gently, but as soon as our lips connected, he pushed me back onto the sand and deepened the kiss. It was as if he'd been waiting for me to make the first move all day. His kissing was persistent, and his fingers were making light work of the buttons on my sundress. He immediately pulled the fabric of my bra cup down and devoured my nipple, simultaneously pushing his leg between mine so that his fingers could travel between my legs.

'Will, slow down.' I managed between kisses.

'But I want you, Lucy.' He kissed me again. 'I need you.'

He slipped his fingers inside me, and I automatically looked around to see if anyone was watching. I mean, did this private beach have a fence? Surely there was a chance someone could just walk along the shoreline and not know where the private section of the beach started or stopped.

'Lucy, stop overthinking everything. We're alone,' he said as he undid his fly.

'It's too risky,' I said, and he sighed.

Then, jumping up suddenly, he grabbed my sandals and took my hand, pulling me up and dragging me back up the beach. As soon as we were in the confines of the property, he led me up the steps to the lawn and dropped my sandals, ordering me to lie down.

'Here?' I asked, a little shocked that we weren't going back to the house.

'Here,' he demanded with intent in his eyes.

He pulled the zip on his jeans down before climbing on top of me. I couldn't help but smile, and as he came level with me, I lifted my eyebrows.

'Keen?' I asked, and he looked down as he laughed out of his nose.

'Just shut up and let me make you whole. Make me whole.'

And with that, he pulled my knickers aside and lined himself up.

'Okay?'

Despite being all masterful, I loved that he just had to double-check.

'Okay,' I confirmed.

He eased his way in. I bit my lip to absorb the pain as my insides adjusted around him.

'Sorry... not sorry,' he said, and I laughed.

He knew I wasn't wet enough, and he gave me a moment.

'Lift your arms.'

A frown passed across my face.

'I want your hands out of the way.'

I did as I was told, and by doing so, my boobs lifted, and Will pulled both of my cups down. I felt so exposed outside, and I couldn't help but look around.

'We're alone, Lucy, I promise. I would not be doing this if I was in any doubt.'

He began to move, and my heart was racing. It felt so risqué being outside. Will's pace was faster than usual, and with every jolt, my tits were being jostled around, and Will was looking at them with a salacious grin.

'Will!' I admonished and went to pull my cups back up, but he grabbed my hands, forcing my arms back up and pushing my wrists into the ground.

'No hands,' he ordered, looking at me with an overly serious expression. 'Otherwise, I'll tie you up,' he said, lifting his eyebrows slightly as if he was pushing me to challenge him.

I inhaled abruptly. This dominant side of him was causing a small frisson of fear inside me, but that fear was somehow turning me on. An added thrill as the atmosphere around us became ominous.

He kissed me, still holding my wrists and squeezing my nipple hard. It burned, sending a zing of pleasure straight to my core. All I could do was moan into his mouth, which seemed to spur him on. His pace picked up, and he squeezed my nipple harder still. I moaned again.

Propping himself up on his elbow, still gripping my wrists with his free hand, he suddenly bit down on my breast. I yelped, looking down at the source of pain as he eased his jaw slightly to allow his teeth to scrape along the flesh, the skin stretching, pulling me taut until my nipple was between his teeth.

I was panting, concerned that it would be too much, but the pressure of his teeth was just firm enough to keep hold of my nipple. The heat intensified, and he began flicking his tongue over the tip. The sensations mainlined straight to my clit. He may as well have been flicking his tongue over that instead.

My orgasm suddenly gripped me with such force that I practically went rigid. Will released my wrists and my nipple simultaneously, breaking the dam, and the blood that had been surging to move freely, rushed through me, taking my orgasm to a level I'd never experienced.

Will grabbed my jaw as I whimpered and moaned so that he could look into my eyes. His jaw was slack, and his breathing staggered as hot bursts of his own orgasm pounded every last contraction out of me. The look of satisfaction on his face as he did so was one of pure triumph.

As I lay there, my chest heaving, Will looked at me with a demonic grin.

'Lucy Daniels,' he said as if he was chastising me. 'Who'd have thought you'd be so compliant for me.' He grinned, looking down at me while I was still trying to compose myself. 'You know, compliance is the first rule of submission.'

'But you didn't ask me to do any... I'm not a...'

'I'm not labelling you, Lucy. I'm just making you aware of it. People label themselves too quickly, and then they're not willing to experiment.' He gently brushed his knuckles across my cheekbone. 'I didn't need to ask you to do anything, but your body?' He looked down at me again, pulling his lower lip through his teeth, mimicking what he had done with my nipple. 'Your body likes to obey. It's instinctive, and fuck, if it doesn't turn me on.'

I took a moment to think about what he was saying. He was discovering things about me that I didn't even know about myself. I'm so consumed with the sensations when we're in the moment. It's all I'm aware of.

'It just feels like I lose control,' I said eventually.

'Of your thoughts, maybe, but in turn, you're allowing your body to take the lead. Watching you... it's awe-inspiring, and the fact that you trust me with your body, that means everything to me.'

I looked down at the pair of us and giggled.

'We're still fully dressed.'

He grinned before pushing himself up to standing and put a hand out for me. I readjusted my bra and did a couple of buttons back up before taking it and turning to head up to the house.

Chapter 14

The next day Will arranged for the *professional* to come and see me. I wasn't sure how I felt about it, but I figured it couldn't do any harm.

Will was acting weird. Just before she arrived, he'd asked the chef to make up a tray of English tea and biscuits and assured me that he would head out for a walk and make some calls to give me complete privacy.

'Do you think I'm going to talk about you?' I asked.

'Being that I'm the problem, I kinda figured you would.'

'My problem boyfriend,' I said, catching his hand.

He turned to face me.

'My girl next door.'

The bell went, and he kissed my nose.

Once we'd introduced ourselves and settled on the veranda with our tea and biscuits, she asked me to explain what had been happening.

I found it interesting that nearly all people in this profession always had mental issues of their own. She was part beautiful, part plastic. Beyond her glasses, she had fillers everywhere, perfect teeth but receding gums which suggested a poor diet. I wondered what she looked like before all the work.

'And you weren't aware of the media coverage until that point?' Roxy asked.

'No, I think Will had assumed I had looked... it was a bit of a shock.'

'I'm sure it was,' she said as she sipped on her tea.

I had a feeling she didn't like it, but I was surprised how good the tea was. All the tea I had been served with so far had been watery to say the least, but this was really good.

'So, from what I can gather, a couple of things are at play here. There's the adjustment to a more affluent life and dealing with the media. And when I say media, I mean everything that comes with it, the feelings of entrapment and the hounding of the press.'

I nodded.

We spent the next ten minutes going through several breathing exercises that I could use to help calm my nerves during high-pressure situations. She wanted to spend the rest of the session getting to know me and talking about the positives of being in the spotlight. I was beginning to switch off, I wasn't sure I'd experienced any positives, but she was insistent that I heard her out.

'So, what I'm trying to say is that you could harness your newfound popularity and put it to good use. Maybe there is a charity close to your heart or a project you'd like to fund? I'm sure Will has charities that he supports and a media or PR team that guides him when the going gets tough.'

I sighed, remembering that first meeting in the hotel room and how daunting it was.

'Well, they will be able to coach you and maybe create the *Lucy Daniels* brand.'

I frowned, and she smiled, realising I was struggling with the concept.

'I just wanted to open your eyes a bit. Being in the limelight is not all bad, and if you're clever, stay focused, and grounded, which I can see you already are, you can steer this in whatever direction you want.'

I looked at the floor.

'You have the power. Our time is up for today, but may I recommend we have another chat once you've had a chance to absorb what we've discussed?'

'Sure, I'll get Will to contact you,' I said automatically.

'Will is not my client. You are. Here's my card,' she said, handing it to me.

'Enjoy your time here. It's a beautiful villa, but be aware that the circus is still out there, and once you've recharged the batteries, you need to have some coping mechanisms in place. Even if that is shouting at Will.'

She winked, and I laughed.

'I like you, Lucy, and I can see why the media does too.'

Oh God.

Will wasn't back by the time she had gone, so I decided to go for a swim. After swimming a few lengths and realising just how unfit I was, I propped myself up at the end of the pool to soak up the view. I could just about make out the boat, and I wondered if Will had looked into taking her out.

I could hear my phone vibrating, so I hauled myself out and was pleased to see it was Frankie.

'Hi, how are you? Are you having the best time?'

'Aww, it's amazing, Mum. Paddy and I have just been on one of those super long zip-wire things. It was so cool. And yesterday we went to this amazing water park, the slides were really steep, I nearly left my balls behind!'

I laughed and flopped down on a sun lounger. It was so lovely to hear his voice.

'What have you been up to? Apart from kissing Will on his balcony.' I closed my eyes. 'Was he actually naked? Dad thinks they air-brushed him.'

My stomach turned as I thought about Mike looking at the pictures and wondered how I would feel if it had been the other way round.

'No, he wasn't, it was just the angle of the pictures. Anyway, why are you even looking? Please don't search this stuff up.'

I'd lost count of how many times I'd told them not to.

'Mum, we didn't need to look. They're everywhere. I even overheard a couple of women talking about the article at the pool yesterday. They couldn't believe you'd taken him back.'

What the hell? We hadn't even split up. It was just so strange to think that a pair of women in Canada who I didn't even know were talking about me.

'Anyway, Will's apartment looks amazing.'

'It is amazing, but we're not there at the moment. We're staying at a villa in The Hamptons, and then we're heading to LA,' I explained.

'LA? Why LA?' Frankie asked.

I went on to explain about Will's house and that we would stay there for a bit before returning to Brooklyn for the gig. Paddy and I had a chat too. His favourite part of the holiday so far had been swimming with dolphins. I had a sudden pang of sadness that I was missing out on all these exciting things they were doing and felt strangely jealous of Mike being able to experience them together.

'I really miss you boys, but it sounds like you're having the best time. Say hi to Dad.'

'Will do,' Paddy said.

'Love you, Mum, bye,' they both said in chorus.

'Love you too,' I said thickly, and I had to blink my tears away.

A pang of homesickness made my heart lurch and I decided to ring Mum and Dad.

'Three-four-three-eight-one-eight,' my Dad said in greeting.

Why did that generation always answer the phone with their phone number?

'Hi Dad, it's me.'

'Lucy! Alison,' he called. 'Our famous daughter is on the phone.'

I rolled my eyes, not just for the comment, more for the fact that he was immediately handing me over to Mum.

'Lucy how are you, dear?' she asked. 'And how is that boyfriend of yours?' I was silently thanking my lucky stars that she hadn't seen the pictures. 'His arms are so sculpted... and his bottom is very pert.'

'Mum!' I said in dismay.

Okay so she had seen the photos, in fact it sounded like she was staring at them.

'He's fine, thank you.'

'Attaboy,' I heard my Dad call.

Oh my God, they were so embarrassing sometimes.

'He's very polite though,' Mum continued.

'Polite?' I asked, confused.

'Yes, he called yesterday.'

'He did?' I said, sitting up on the lounger.

'He wanted to apologise for embarrassing you and we had a nice chat about what you'd been up to. We heard all about the wedding and the dinner party. It sounds like you're having an amazing time.'

Had he indeed. I was surprised he hadn't told them he wanted to use sex toys and tie me up so that he could fuck me.

I sighed.

'Oh, Lucy, we thought it was very thoughtful.'

She went on to tell me about the song they were working on in choir that week and that Philip, her best friend's son was getting married in May, and that they'd been invited to the reception. I told her about the house we were staying in, the private beach and the sight-seeing I'd done. She seemed impressed.

After finishing the call, I felt content that I had caught up with my family. I rolled over and pulled the straps of my bikini down to avoid any tan lines. I could hear the sea, the birds, and the pool water trickle as it went through the filter system. I took a deep breath in and sighed the release.

Could I *harness* all this attention and put it to good use? I had a feeling it would take up a lot of time. What impact would it have on the boys? And my business? I wondered what people thought about me, those women in

Canada. Did they think I was foolish? The silly girl next door.

I could hear running and opened my eyes, wondering what was going on before I heard an almighty splash. I turned to see Will had dive-bombed into the pool, showering me with cold water, and I sat up.

'Will!' I shouted as he returned to the surface and pushed his hair out of his face.

'Hi!' he said, grinning, and I couldn't help but laugh. 'Are you good?'

'Well, I was until someone showered me with cold water.'

Then, he hauled himself out of the pool and came over to kiss me, drenching me in the process before scooping me up.

'Do you feel better?' he asked.

'I do, actually,' I said, clinging to his neck. 'What have you been up to?'

'Throwing my girlfriend in the pool.'

'What? Nooooo.'

But it was too late, he leapt into the pool with me in his arms, and we both completely submerged. I came back up spluttering, and while pushing my hair out of my eyes, Will swam up behind me and undid my bikini top.

'Will,' I shouted again.

I turned to smack him, but he was too quick, and he grabbed my arm and pulled me towards him, lifting me in the process so he could wedge his head between my boobs, and I couldn't help but laugh. He slowly lowered me and kissed me, and I kissed him back.

'What's this about you calling my parents?' I asked.

He looked at me to gauge my mood. I raised my eyebrows.

'I just felt I should check in and apologise for shaming their daughter in the press.'

I was about to disagree, but I realised someone was standing by the pool.

'Lunch, Mr and Mrs Reynolds,' the chef announced.

He half bowed, and half nodded before turning and walking back to the house.

Will looked at me and tried to suppress a laugh. I wasn't sure whether it was because the Chef had caught us canoodling, because I was half-naked, or because he'd referred to me as Mrs Reynolds, but we both got out of the pool to dry off. I was starving.

Will had taken full advantage of his time that morning and had made many phone calls.

He had spoken to Paul, Jake, and Mat to set the wheels in motion for the gig. I was sure Hannah was delighted to have her honeymoon interrupted with band stuff. They were due to return the next day. I thought they'd take longer, but it was Paul's Mom's seventieth in a few days, so they had decided to take a couple of weeks later in the year.

The boat was sadly unavailable. It had something wrong with it and was booked in at the Chandler in a few days. It was a shame. I had kind of been looking forward to it. The ultimate escape, but then I guess we were *staying* in the ultimate escape.

Will didn't ask about my session. Maybe he thought I wanted to keep it private, or he didn't want to put any pressure on me. There wasn't much to say because I hadn't come to any conclusions. To be honest, I had more to think about now than I had done before. Roxy's proposal was interesting, but by agreeing to do it, I was also agreeing to be seen in the public eye willingly, and surely that in itself would open a whole can of worms.

Will took another call, it was about the gig, something to do with the promotion, and I finished the last of my fish cakes. The chef was excellent, and he had chosen a lovely bottle of wine to accompany our lunch. I sensed that the conversation was getting a little awkward, and I looked over at Will, but he stood up and started heading back up to the house. There were some beautiful petit fours on the tray, and I tried one. Oh, my goodness, strawberries, and cream, wow.

'Do you wanna go out tomorrow evening?' Will asked as he strode back down to the pool.

An involuntary shiver went through me.

'Um... where?' I enquired, shielding my eyes to look up at him.

'Paul and Hannah are having a do at their place.' He sat down on my sun lounger, leaning across me. 'Like a post-wedding party, so no need to worry about the press,' he explained.

Being able to socialise without the paparazzi sounded wonderful. I couldn't help but smile.

'Yes... yes, please,' I said.

'Yes, please? You gettin' bored with me, Daniels?' he said, leaning in.

'No, but it would be nice to see some other people,' I admitted. 'It's amazing here. I love that we're not having to look over our shoulders all the time, but it's pretty isolated.'

'Take a walk with me,' he said, standing up.

'I just need to pop some clothes on,' I said, gathering my things to go up to the house.

'No, you don't.'

He was right, I didn't need to, but he was wearing jeans and a t-shirt, so I grabbed one of the Turkish towels and fashioned it into a sarong. He laughed, and we headed out. Walking down to the shore again, I immediately started looking for shells.

'You love a shell, don't you?'

'I do... my grandmother took me to a place when I was little, not far from where we went in Exmouth, called A la Ronde. Two sisters had decorated the entire place with shells, and I've loved them ever since.'

I picked one up.

'This one is a King's Crown.'

Will took it from me to take a good look.

'Hmm, I can see why,' he said, inspecting it.

'And this one is an Alphabet Cone.'

He took that one too.

'Looks more like an ice cream cone.'

I chuckled, and then he bent down and picked something up.

'What's this one then?' he asked, testing my knowledge.

I smiled because he had picked up a special one, and I stopped walking, slowly closing his hand around it, and I looked up at him.

'That one is called an Angel Wing.'

I looked down to where he'd found it, and as if by chance, its pair was nestled by his shoe. I picked it up and gave it to him. His eyes looked glassy, realising the symbolism they held. I smiled at him dolefully, leaned up and kissed him. He pulled back and cleared his throat.

'God, I love you,' he said.

'I love you too.' I replied.

He slipped the shells into his pocket, and we wandered along some more.

Chapter 15

The following twenty-four hours were just heaven. I found a yoga mat in the pool house and spent forty-five minutes or so trying to remember as many poses as possible. Will played his guitar and did some writing. We swam in the sea. The chef made us the most fantastic Paella, and we chilled by the pool.

It wasn't until a couple of hours before we were due to leave to go to Paul and Hannah's that I started to become anxious. Will came up to the bedroom with a glass of fizz as I was about to get in the shower.

'Terry is picking us up, and he'll take us straight there,' he said, sensing my nerves.

'Do you think this is how people start to get agoraphobia?' I asked as I took a long sip.

'It'll be fine,' he assured me. 'I won't leave your side.'

I opted for jeans with a dark grey boat neck top with batwings. I wore it off the shoulder, and my bra strap was visible, so I put a camisole over it and dressed the look up with my gold strappy heels. Will wore some smart blue, nearly black jeans, and a t-shirt with a blazer.

'Blue jeans!' I said with mock horror. 'I didn't know blue jeans were allowed in your wardrobe.'

'Hey, leave my blue jeans alone, and besides, I don't have a wardrobe.'

He came up behind me and kissed my neck as I did my make-up at the dressing table. I was wearing the *becoming his girlfriend* necklace he'd given me a few weeks ago. He clocked it and smiled.

'I'm glad you're wearing that tonight because I got you this.'

He had another Stephen Webster box in his hand and placed it on the dressing table. It was longer than the previous box, maybe a pen?

'Will, it's not my birthday,' I admonished him.

'I know, but I wanted to buy you something. It's been... a tough week.'

He picked the box back up and handed it to me.

'Just open it, would you?'

I took it from him and pushed the box from its sleeve. I lifted the lid, and my jaw dropped. It was a striking bracelet in a similar style to my necklace. A row of chevrons, each one encrusted with sparkly black pave stones. It was beautiful, and I ran my finger delicately along the chain.

'Wow, Will... it's stunning.'

He pulled the bracelet out of the box and attached it to my wrist. I turned my hand a few times to let the stones catch the light. He smiled, stood up and then presented me with a shot. I frowned and looked at him in the reflection of the mirror.

'Are you trying to get me drunk before we leave?'

'No, just trying to help you calm your nerves. Drink.'

He clinked his glass with mine, and we both took them back. Hmmm, peachy, I thought, licking my lips.

'It's a Woo Woo,' Will confirmed, and I laughed.

'I don't think you need to woo me. I'm already yours.'

'Good to know.'

He held his hand out. 'Come on, Terry's here.'

Paul and Hannah's house was like all those houses you see in American films where a house party takes place. It was detached, with, I'm guessing, about four or five bedrooms, an open-plan kitchen-diner that opened onto a terrace with a pool.

Nearly everyone was outside, sitting or standing around the pool. Will clearly knew his way around the kitchen because he grabbed two champagne flutes from one of the cupboards and helped himself to the bottle sitting in an ice bucket on the island.

Paul emerged from the terrace with a fantastic tan.

'Hey, man,' he said, and he and Will shook hands, shoulder bumped, and then hugged, patting each other on the back.

I couldn't help but smile.

'Luuucy,' he said, moving towards me with his arms outstretched. 'Some week, huh?'

I had no idea how much Will told him, but I figured quite a bit. He gave me the biggest squeeze, which I wasn't expecting, and then, pulling back, he held onto my shoulders.

'We're gonna have a great night, and you'll be pleased to know that prick Drew isn't here.'

He winked before releasing me.

I hadn't actually thought about him, but before I could say anything, Will fed his arm around my waist, passing me a glass.

'Did you have a good honeymoon?' I asked to change the subject.

He gave us the highlights. It sounded like there had been a lot of sightseeing, eating, and drinking.

'I hear we missed out on some amazing food at your place, though,' Paul said. 'Jake was blown away.'

I smiled, a little embarrassed, and then, out of the corner of my eye, I saw Milly and Leo by the pool, and she beckoned me over. Will saw the exchange.

'You go. I'll be two minutes, I promise,' Will said, and he ushered me towards the door.

I won't leave your side.

My arse, I thought, and I rolled my eyes as I nervously headed out, feeling like everyone was staring at me.

'Hi,' I almost whispered as I got to her.

'Lucy, how are you? Glad to see Will's got his pants on today.'

My cheeks flushed, and I looked over at him. He and Paul were in deep discussion.

'The paps loved that, huh? I bet they're crawling all over you.'

'Actually, we escaped. We're hiding out in a villa on the coast,' I admitted.

'Oh my God, I don't blame you,' she said, and Leo leaned in.

'Lucy, can I introduce you to Paige?' he asked, gesturing to the woman he was standing beside. 'Paige, this is Will's girlfriend, Lucy. Paige is the singer from The Words but runs her own agency now.'

Oh, my goodness, my parents loved The Words. We shook hands.

'Great to meet you. I understand I need to tap you up for your lemon torte recipe,' she said as Leo grinned, nodding next to her.

Laughing, I explained that my mum had to take the credit for everything I knew. Paige was older than most of the people there, with grey hair styled into a sharp bob. She had an authoritative aura about her but super hip with leather trousers, loads of bangles, and bright red lipstick.

'I didn't need the introduction. I've seen enough pictures to know who you are.'

'Oh, Paige, she probably already feels like a spectacle,' Milly interjected, nudging her as I looked over for Will again.

Another couple of guys had joined him and Paul, but he caught my eye, and I could see him trying to make his excuses. Christ, I thought this would be easy. I thought about Steph and the girls back home. I was yearning for them.

'Well, she's gonna have to get used to it if she stays with that rogue.'

Why did people insist on talking about me as if I wasn't there? And why did people keep talking about us as if we weren't going to be together for long?

'Lucy!' Hannah called, she was by my side in a flash, and it was lovely to see another friendly face.

'Hannah, how are you? Look at your tan!' I said as I hugged her.

'Look at you more like, you look stunning.'

I gave her an odd smile, being that I was just wearing jeans and a top.

'Huh?' she gasped in delight and lifted my wrist to look at my bracelet. 'Is that Stephen Webster?'

She turned round to look at Will, still holding my arm in the air, pointing at it. Will locked her gaze for a second, despite chatting to one of the guys, and smiled wickedly. Could she be causing any more of a scene?

'Wow, he sure is smitten.' She leaned in. 'twen'y thousand dollars smitten,' she said, dropping my arm, as it nearly fell off, and my jaw went with it. I immediately covered it up with my other hand.

'Oh honey, don't cover it up,' Paige said. 'It's too beautiful to hide.'

My mouth was parched. I was about to make my excuses when Will arrived, slipping his arm around my waist.

'Sorry about that,' he whispered before addressing the group. 'Ladies, Leo... Paige, it's been a while.' He leaned over to kiss her on the cheek.

'I'm glad to see you picked well this time. try to keep your pants on, though, dear.'

Everyone laughed.

'I keep them on when it's necessary,' he said, a little too seriously for the situation, and I think everyone realised the joke was over.

Paul turned up with another bottle of fizz for refills, and Will pulled me to one side, putting his forehead to mine.

'Are you okay?'

'I am now,' I said, trying not to sound too pissy.

'I'm sorry, I got caught up.'

He turned back to the group just as Paul reached us to top us up.

'Everything all right?' Paul asked, looking at each of us in turn.

'Less limelight required,' Will said, reading the situation well.

'Oh, I can fix that,' Paul said, and he tapped his glass, pulling Hannah into his side.

Will and I stepped back to give them some space.

'Thanks all for coming, we've had the best time on our honeymoon, but while we've got you all together, we wanted to let you know that we're expecting a baby in February!'

I looked at Will with a massive grin on my face while everyone whooped and cheered, and he winked. He clearly knew already.

'And before you do the math, yes, we knew before the wedding. I've never been that good at planning.'

Everyone laughed.

'Anyway, enjoy the rest of your evening.'

He kissed Hannah while everyone clapped before she was swamped with about five women who wanted to know the entire story.

Paul turned back to us.

'That should do the trick.'

'Congratulations.' I said. 'When's the due date?'

'February nineteenth,' he confirmed.

'Really lovely news.'

'I'm afraid it's gonna make life pretty busy over the next few weeks. We've somehow got to record, launch, and tour the next album before the little one arrives, so apologies in advance,' he said, looking at me.

'That's fine. I could do without this one hanging around and getting my face in any more pictures.'

I gave Will a nudge with my elbow, and they laughed. Paul topped us up again and headed off to do the rounds.

Before Will and I had had a moment to talk, Jake appeared.

'Thank God for that. I swear I was gonna slip up before they announced it.'

Will laughed. He obviously knew, too. I guess they were all work colleagues, after all.

'I nearly said something to Milly at yours the other night,' he said, shaking his head.

All the little private chats with Paul and the phone calls were starting to make sense. I imagined the entire team had been on this for weeks, trying to line everything up. I marvelled at how discreet Will had been.

'Do you know who that is?' Jake asked as he nodded to a woman wearing a striking burnt orange dress across the pool.

'No man, sorry,' Will said.

But that didn't deter him. He wandered off to the other side of the pool to introduce himself. Will shook his head, looking back at me.

'That poor woman,' he said, and I smiled. 'You're not mad at me about the bracelet then?' he asked.

'I don't know. It depends on whether you'll be mad at me when I put it up for auction to raise money for the starving children in Ukraine.'

He smiled and closed his eyes.

'Please don't do that. It was a gift. Just accept it. Besides, I'm sure you can think of other ways of raising the money.'

Did he know what Roxy had suggested? Surely, she wasn't allowed to discuss what we had spoken about with him.

'Lucy,' Will whispered.

I looked up, realising I'd just been staring at the pool. He kissed me, bringing me back into reality.

'Sorry,' I said, and then I finished my drink as if to signify I was all party.

'Well, you kept that under wraps!' Stryker said, his head appearing between us on Will's shoulder, and he wrapped his arms around both our shoulders, his long fingers dangling dangerously close to my boob.

'Not my news to tell,' Will said as Stryker gave me a big wet kiss on my cheek.

Will shook his head in disbelief at his brazenness. Stryker moved positions so that he was standing on the opposite side of me to Will, trailing his fingers down my back as he did so before resting his hand on my waist. Paige came to join us.

'I hope you're behaving yourself, Stryker,' she said, clearly having witnessed his over-friendliness.

Stryker broke away and stepped forward to give her a kiss on the cheek.

'Impeccably, as always, Paige,' he replied, giving her a little bow. 'How the devil are you?'

'Do you need me to have another word?' Will whispered in my ear.

'I can handle it,' I whispered back.

I felt more confident knowing that he had my back and clearly didn't miss a trick.

'Okay, I'm gonna go and get more drinks.'

He took my glass and headed back in. Stryker didn't miss a beat and wrapped his arm around my waist while Paige looked at me and raised one of her eyebrows. Did she know what he was like?

'Have you met this little beauty yet?' Stryker asked Paige as he gave me a squeeze.

'Yes, I've already had the pleasure,' she said, assessing us.

I plastered a smile on my face for her benefit and hoped Will wouldn't be too much longer.

'Isn't she gorgeous? I'm actually quite jealous.'

His hand tracked further down, his fingers splayed, taking my whole arse cheek in his big hand and gently squeezing it.

'I'm sure you are,' Paige replied flatly and then turned her attention to me. 'I'm actually very pleased to have met your acquaintance as I have a proposal for you. Do you have a moment?'

Stryker realised he was being dismissed and slowly released me, leaving Paige and me alone. I smiled at her cautiously, wondering what on earth she was about to say.

'Have you heard of Over the Wire?' she asked.

I frowned. I was a bit taken aback. Why on earth would she be asking if I'd heard of a lingerie company? I automatically looked down at my cleavage to check I didn't have a four-boob situation on the go.

'Um, yes... the lingerie company?' I asked, just to make sure.

'Correct. They're a client of mine and they're looking for a suitable model for their next collection.'

'Okay,' I said with a laugh, wondering why she was telling me this.

'Their next collection is to be aimed at the more mature woman, not that I'm suggesting you're old by any stretch of the imagination. However, they look for models slightly younger than their intended market.'

She paused.

'I'm sorry, I'm not following.'

'I think you'd be perfect.'

'What?'

I looked at her, completely dumbfounded, and she smiled.

'You have the figure they're looking for, you're the right age, you're new on the scene, and well, everyone loves a girl next door.'

I laughed again.

'You want me to model for them?' I asked disbelievingly.

I could see Will making his way back around the pool. Paige clocked him too.

'Think about it,' she said, slipping a card in my hand.

I looked at her, and she lifted a single brow before suddenly asking what we planned on doing while we were there. I got the distinct impression she wanted to keep the conversation between us. Did she think that Will wouldn't approve?

After a beat, I found my voice again and was about to reply.

'Well, we came back for the wedding and for Lucy to meet my mom,' Will replied for me. 'We're heading over to mine in a couple of days.'

'Nice, sounds like you've got it all planned out,' she said as Paul joined us.

'Well, we had until this one threw a spanner in the works,' Will said, winking at Paul. 'I have a feeling I'm gonna be needed back here sooner than I thought.'

Oh. That was news to me. I knew Paul had said that Will would be busy, but I hadn't realised it would impact our time in LA.

'You know we're doing a show in a couple of weeks,' Will said to Paige.

The band had decided to do a small show to try out some of the new material. They weren't going to advertise it, it would be for friends, family, and industry types, and they would play at their favourite venue, The Pound. I laughed when they mentioned the name, and they all looked at me quizzically. I felt the need to explain.

'The Pound is where you would take a stray dog if you found one on the street or if you had lost your dog, you'd go to the pound to collect it.'

They all looked at each other and started laughing.

'I will never think of that venue in the same way,' Paul said.

Hannah joined us with another bottle of fizz.

'I can't believe I'm dishing this stuff out, and I can't drink any myself,' she said as she began to top everyone up.

'Aww, congratulations. I wasn't bothered about being unable to drink when I was pregnant. I was more gutted about the lack of brie,' I admitted.

'What? I can't have brie either?' she said, rolling her eyes.

'So, you've got kids already?' Paige asked.

'Yeah, two boys, they're amazing, but my childbearing days are over,' I said, and Paul glanced at Will.

'Wait, so, you're not thinking of having kids?' Hannah asked outright, looking incredulously at Will.

Will looked at her in surprise and then shot a glance at Paul.

'Honey, not everyone has to have kids,' Paul said to Hannah.

'Well, I know that...' she said, looking from me to Will, and then she took a sip from her water, looking across the pool a little embarrassed.

I bit my lip. This was awkward. Hannah suddenly turned.

'I'm just going to use the restroom,' and she headed off.

'I'm so sorry, guys, she's just got babies on the brain all the time at the moment. It's all we ever talk about.' Paul apologised.

'It's fine,' I said reassuringly, waving the awkwardness away with my hand and then taking a long sip of my drink.

'Don't worry about it, man,' Will said, backing me up, and there was a knowing look between them.

Had they discussed this before? I never imagined men talking to their mates about stuff like that. I thought it was just women.

An hour or so later, I was sitting with Will on a sun lounger opposite Stryker and Jake. They were reminiscing about their early touring days. Stryker recounted hilarious stories. He reminded me a bit of Steph. He loved to hold court and be the centre of attention. I could see why women found him attractive. He was charming and funny. I was pretty wasted by that point and had taken my shoes off for fear of tripping and falling into the pool.

Hannah caught my eye from across the pool and waved me over. I leaned into Will. 'I'm just gonna go over and see Hannah.' I stood up, having to lean on his shoulder to steady myself.

'Waaay,' he said like he was a donkey neighing, grabbing hold of my hips. 'You all right?'

'Mmm hmm, glad I'm not wearing those,' I said, vaguely pointing at my shoes. He stood up and decided it was best to escort me around the pool.

'You'll have to put them back on later,' he whispered in my ear, and my lips parted at his admission. 'Delivering a slightly wasted Lucy for you,' he said to Hannah and Milly as we arrived, and I rolled my eyes as he walked back.

Hannah was incredibly sober and made me feel even more drunk than I was, but thankfully Milly was on my wavelength. I decided to switch to water all the same.

'You have to tell me what happened with Drew,' Hannah said. 'And then you need to tell me what else I can't eat because I'm clueless. None of my friends have started having babies yet, so you are gonna be my living and breathing search engine.'

'Oh God, you might wanna wait until I'm sober for those questions,' I said honestly.

'No, this is the perfect time to ask. I don't wanna hear the sugar-coated version.'

I told her what happened with Drew with the help of Milly because I didn't actually know what had happened once I'd gone off to speak to Cara. And then she was straight in with the baby questions.

'Did you have natural births?' she asked first.

'Yes, as natural as can be, dosed up to the eyeballs with every drug they offered me.' They both laughed. 'Do you have any kids, Milly?' I asked suddenly.

'No.' She leaned in. 'I was pregnant once, in my early twenties. I was on tour and was seeing... this guy, nothing serious, but obviously, when I found out, it got serious pretty quick, and he turned into a complete jerk, so I ended up getting an abortion.'

'Wow, that's brave... I don't think I could. Not that I'm against it, just me personally,' I said.

'It was the toughest decision of my life, and there is still a part of me that regrets it,' she admitted, and I smiled at her sympathetically. 'But he had done a runner, and I wasn't earning enough to support a baby, so I didn't have a choice.'

I thought about Alysa and the choice that she had made. How cruel she had been because that baby would have had... everything. And then I thought about what Will had said about Milly coming back there to teach piano and wondered if that had been the underlying reason.

'I'm sorry about my comment earlier,' Hannah said out of the blue.

'It's fine. We had the baby talk when we met. My boys are nearly ready to leave home, and I couldn't imagine starting all over.'

Neither of them said anything, and despite being drunk, their silence seemed to speak louder than words. And then Hannah fired another question at me, and I made them laugh with anecdotes about my pregnancies.

'SO BASICALLY, IF IT'S not happening and you want baby out, you need to have sex because there's something in the sperm that kind of kicks it all off.'

Hannah coughed, and I sensed someone was behind me. I shut one eye and said, 'Is Paul standing behind me?' Milly scrunched her nose up and nodded. 'Fuck,' I said, and Milly started pissing herself laughing as Hannah stood up, and I turned to see Paul, Will, and Stryker.

I wondered how many people had heard. Stryker clearly had because he was stifling his laughter, and Will was just shaking his head with a massive grin. I bit my bottom lip to stop any more words from escaping.

'Do you want me to call Terry?' Will asked, which made me feel even worse.

Milly stood up, and I thought I should too, but I had moved quicker than my brain could compute, and I stumbled. Stryker caught me, righting me, and then put his arm around me.

'Hey Will, can I take this one home? She's fun.'

'No, you fucking can't,' he replied, but he was still smiling. 'I'm gonna call Terry,' he stated as if he'd decided the night should end.

'Hell no! This party is just getting started,' Stryker responded and leant across the table to crank the music up.

I looked at Will, concerned that I had offended the hosts and trying to gauge how he felt about Stryker, who still had his arm wrapped around me. Will took my hand and tugged me towards him, pulling me in close as the music started pumping.

'Tell me if you wanna go,' Will said.

He was worried I was uncomfortable.

I looked over his shoulder and spotted Milly and Hannah chatting in the corner, lifting their hands to their mouths each time they spoke and occasionally nodding in our direction. They were clearly talking about us.

'I'm just worried I've offended Paul and Hannah,' I admitted as the music was switched to a funky beat, the sort of music I loved to dance to.

'You haven't offended them, no way. I just sensed you were feeling uneasy around Stryker.'

Was I? I didn't think so. I was kind of getting used to his touchy, feely persona.

'I can handle it,' I repeated. 'As long as *you're* not feeling uneasy?'

He laughed through his nose, and his hands began snaking around me.

'I'm used to it, and I know he wouldn't do anything I'd be unhappy about unless he had my consent, but you let me know if you want out.'

I wasn't sure whether he meant out from the party or out from Stryker.

'Consent? What are you, like a pimp or something?' I giggled.

'Not at all, but boy, am I gonna wind him up.' And with that, he began to move his hips to the music, and I went with the flow, moving with him.

Chapter 16

Half an hour later, a large dance area had been created. Paul had moved some of the pool seating out of the way, and the group was half in the kitchen, half by the pool. Nearly everyone was dancing, and the vibe was chilled. There was no antsy attitude like you get in the clubs sometimes because everyone knew each other.

I was having fun, and although I had switched to water, I had just enough alcohol running through my veins to lose my inhibitions on the dancefloor. Will was such a good dancer, I hadn't danced with him like this since the festival, and it didn't matter that I wasn't as good as him because he was leading, and his strong arms were keeping me secure in the movements. Despite the cooler evenings, I was pretty warm. All the dancing and warm bodies were making my cheeks flush.

'Take your top off,' Will said as he pulled me in close.

'What? No!'

I only had a bra and camisole on underneath. Admittedly it was quite a nice champagne silky camisole with lacy edges, but still.

'Take it off,' he repeated, more seductively, and he looked at me with warm glazed eyes.

Oh, fuck it, these people were our friends, and there was no press there. It wasn't as if I was going to offend anyone. I slowly peeled it off and chucked it over by my shoes and purse. Will took a second to drink me in, the cami showing a bit of cleavage with its plunging neckline. He took my hand, lifted it up and spun me around slowly, getting a bloody good look before pulling me back in close.

'You're beautiful, Lucy,' he said, holding me tight, swaying to the music.

I could feel his heart thumping next to mine, and then, as the beat dropped, he swiftly placed his leg between mine and securely held on to my torso, and he dipped me down. My arms loosely followed, falling lower than my head, before pulling me back up and making my head rush.

I giggled.

'Do it again,' I said, biting my lip, and he did, but this time it was lower, and when he pulled me back up, he turned me around, facing me away and moved me back in close.

His hand briefly cupped one of my tits as he pulled my pelvis back into his. This was turning him on, I could feel him hard against me, and he kissed my neck all the way up to my ear.

'Are we winding him up yet?' Will asked.

I frowned, but my eyes scanned the room, and there, sat on one of the pool chairs, was Stryker. He was leaning his elbows on his knees, a bottle of beer in one hand, and making no attempt to hide the fact that he was watching us.

Our eyes locked for a moment, and he just sat there and then leant back in the chair, placing his arms on the armrests, showing me the bulge in his pants that his jeans were doing little to hide.

What the fuck?

My lips parted, and I took a breath in, turning back to face Will, who was chuckling.

'Will, what are you doing?'

There was mischievousness in his eyes, and I couldn't help but smile.

'Stryker wants to fuck you.'

I looked straight at Will.

'But he knows he can't have you, so I'm just making damn sure he knows what he's missing.'

'How do you know that?'

'Because he asked me if he could.'

'He asked you if he could fuck me?'

I couldn't believe it, the nerve of the guy.

'Yeah,' Will said matter-of-factly.

'Is that how it goes around here? You see someone else's girl you like the look of, and then ask their boyfriend if it's okay to fuck them?'

All the while, we're swaying to the music, Will's thigh between my legs and his hands slowly gliding over my body.

'No, it's just Stryker, he can't fucking help himself, and he usually gets what he wants because the ladies flock to him, but God, it pisses him off when he can't get it.'

I shook my head, feeling a bit like some kind of show-girl but utterly flattered by the fact that Will found me attractive enough to show me off in that way.

'Dance with him.'

'What? Why would I do that?' I asked.

'Well, you can see how turned-on Stryker is. I want to watch you.'

He let that sit between us for a bit, and I looked at him for a long moment. A small smile appeared on his face, and then he turned me away from him again.

'Let me watch you, and then I'll take you home and fuck you.'

My insides contracted, and my pulse began to quicken as his hand headed south between my thighs. I could feel the heat of his hand through my jeans as he slowly brought it back up. I glanced around the room, but no-one was looking, apart from Stryker. We locked eyes again, and he put his beer bottle down.

'He's a good dancer,' Will encouraged. 'Better than me,' he admitted.

He really wanted me to do this. I could tell.

'I promise he'll look after you, and as soon as you want out, we'll go.'

'Okay,' I whispered.

I was still a bit unsure, but as soon as I'd said it, he looked up at Stryker and flicked him the slightest of nods. Stryker stood immediately and made his way across the dancefloor, his eyes fixed on me.

My heart was pounding.

'May I take this dance?' he asked Will politely, a seductive tone underlying his question, and Will kissed my neck once more.

'Enjoy,' he whispered in my ear. With that, Stryker took my hand and yanked me towards him, our chests thrashing together as he took hold of my waist and placed his thigh between mine, just as Will had done moments before.

He dipped me low, swooping me around and rolling me back up his body, pretty much making me grind into his leg.

'Fuck, your tits look good at that angle.'

I gasped as he pressed his forehead to mine, and we began to move. Will was right. He was a phenomenal dancer and so strong. Our bodies moved together as one, but mainly because he was holding onto me so tight, there was no room for me to falter. Will was casually watching from the side-lines, and every now and again, he would catch my eye, and I could see his desire.

After a couple of tunes, I was becoming breathless, and he slowed the pace.

'You are so sexy, Lucy. You make my dick twitch every time I see you.'

I looked across to Will, who had been momentarily distracted by Milly and Paige, but he glanced over their shoulders, making sure I knew he was still watching.

'I'm not sure you should be saying those things to someone else's girlfriend,' I replied, licking the corner of my mouth slowly. I'd done it on purpose, and his dick responded.

'Why do I get the feeling that you're not quite the girl next door once Will gets you into the bedroom?'

He looked at me, assessing me.

'The media created that persona, not me,' I replied, not confirming or denying his suspicions.

He smirked and glanced over my shoulder, I assume at Will.

'Did he tell you?' Stryker asked.

'What? That you want to fuck me?'

I asked him straight, and my boldness caught him off guard. I didn't break eye contact with him. Instead, I wetted my lips and slowly sunk my teeth into my bottom lip, and he couldn't help but look. I wouldn't normally act like that, but Will had somehow given me a newfound confidence. And because he was clearly a bit of a ladies' man and was used to getting what he wanted, I couldn't help but wind him up because I had zero interest in him.

'Fuck. That man is so God damn lucky,' he said, still staring at my mouth.

'The man that I love?'

He looked back at my eyes, a big grin appearing on his face, and then he bit his lip and shook his head.

'Wilba! Get your ass back over here,' Stryker called.

Will excused himself immediately from Milly and Paige, and as he approached, Stryker released me.

'Thank you for the dance, Lucy Daniels.'

Will looked at Stryker with his eyebrows high and curled his arm around me, sending shivers all the way up my spine.

'Are you okay?' Will asked me, a little perplexed.

'I am now,' I said honestly, looking straight into his eyes, and he smiled, the electricity between us almost palpable.

I looked back at Stryker. 'Thanks for the dance, Stryker.'

He grinned, looking from me to Will, and then put his hand out to shake Will's hand. Will shook it. The unspoken bet between them had been won by Will. Stryker walked away as Will turned, wrapping me in his arms and kissed me.

'I am dying to know what you said to him,' Will said.

It struck me then how much Will trusted me. He had basically offered me up to Stryker, knowing that I wouldn't take his advances any further.

I smiled.

'My feet are tired,' I declared.

I'd tell him another time.

'Well, in that case, it's time for me to take you home and fuck you.'

I giggled, and he took my hand, leading me back to where my shoes, top and bag were. Stryker was nowhere to be seen, but Milly spotted we were leaving and came over to say goodbye. She pulled me in for a hug.

'That is the first time I have ever seen Stryker leave a party without a woman or two. Good on ya, Sister.'

She smiled at me, giving me a knowing look, and it occurred to me that she was probably hanging out with the bands when all this sharing was happening. She'd probably heard and seen a lot, maybe participated. Stryker was definitely not her favourite person. Her demeanour soured whenever he was around. It suddenly occurred to me that maybe Stryker was the one that bolted when she found out she was pregnant.

I smiled back just as Paul turned up.

'You guys off?'

'Yeah, where's Hannah?' I asked.

'Oh, she went to bed hours ago. Thanks for coming, guys,' he said, shaking Will's hand and kissing me on the cheek.

'Congratulations again,' I said.

Will took my hand again, and we left to find Terry ready and waiting outside.

He opened the door for us, and I said, 'Not hugging the driver,' as I got in, and Will laughed.

Will followed and immediately pinned me down on the back seat.

'You're lucky you're wearing jeans,' he said as he kissed me.

'Jeans or otherwise, there is no way I'd allow you to fuck me with Terry there,' I said, probably a bit too loud because Will chuckled at my choice of words, knowing that Terry had perhaps heard.

By the time we arrived, I was very sleepy, and Will had to prop me up as we walked up the steps to the villa.

'Don't go to sleep on me, Daniels. I've got plans for you,' Will reminded me as we headed into the kitchen.

He poured me a big glass of water.

'Are they sleeping plans because I'm pretty tired,' I said.

'Sleeping with you, plans,' he said, grinning as I drained half the glass in one hit.

He took my hand and led me up to our bedroom, and I went straight into the bathroom because I was desperate for a wee. I brushed my teeth and undressed. I was about to put my dressing gown on when Will came in.

'You won't be needing that,' he said, taking my hand.

Back in the bedroom, I could see my shoes on the bed, and he sat me down and started putting them on my feet.

'What is this, a re-enactment of Cinderella?' I asked, flopping back onto the bed as he laughed.

Once he'd finished with the shoes, he hopped onto the bed and looked straight into my eyes.

'I don't recall Cinderella being tied up, but we can act out a new scene if you're happy with that?'

Oh.

I went to say something, but I couldn't form the words.

'Are you happy with that?' he asked.

I wasn't *not* happy about it, so I just nodded.

Will disappeared out of sight for a second and returned with the sash of my dressing gown. I looked at him, a little fearful. He put his hand out, and I took it as he pulled me up to sit.

'Give me your hands.'

My breathing had shallowed, and I slowly lifted my hands as I stared into his eyes. Will smiled and gently wrapped the sash around my wrists, it wasn't tight, just secure, and I was unsure of his intentions. I was watching him like a hawk.

'What are you going to do?' I whispered.

'Nothing you don't wanna do,' he said, smiling with a half frown. 'This is supposed to be fun, relax.'

He pulled me up to stand and walked me to the side of the bed.

'Shimmy into the middle. I'm gonna tie your hands to the headboard.'

'I'm not sure it's possible to shimmy with your hands tied,' I said.

'Come on, appease me,' he encouraged, shooing me onto the bed, and I moved into position.

He tied the ends of the sash around one of the headboard bars.

'Convenient,' I said, and he grinned, suddenly pulling my legs down, forcing my arms to straighten above my head.

I gasped.

'Not quite the girl next door, are you now?' he said and proceeded to get undressed.

He was clearly turned on already. I lifted my eyebrows and swallowed. He laughed through his nose and shook his head.

'Two seconds.'

He disappeared into the bathroom but came straight back carrying what looked like a hairband.

'What are you gonna do with that?' I asked, intrigued as he knelt beside me.

'Wear it... it's a cock ring.'

And he rolled it down himself until it was secured at the base of his penis. My nipples were hardening with anticipation, but I couldn't cover myself up.

'Are you gonna turn the lights out?' I asked, becoming more and more aware.

'No,' he said straight. 'I want to watch you come.'

My insides spasmed, and my mouth was beginning to go dry.

'Bend your knees,' he ordered, and I did as I was told.

He pushed them apart. My breathing was already becoming laboured.

'I'm gonna go down on you, and I want you to come.'

'But I... you....'

It was too late, he was already there, and I was powerless to stop him. This was going to be over with so quickly. I thought he wanted it to last longer. He didn't use his fingers, just his tongue and his lips. He was gentle, with the softest licks and the most delicate kisses, but I began to climb all the same.

He didn't move any faster or harder for me, in fact, he pinned my hips down so that I couldn't move them, and it was really frustrating, and when I came, it was so concentrated. I pulled on the sash, desperately wanting to free my hands because I could feel my insides contracting, my clitoral orgasm peaking, but in desperate need of some friction within. I felt bereft.

'Ahhhh, Will, you're not playing fair,' I said as he slowly rose, wiping his mouth with the back of his hand.

'I'm not done, Lucy, far from it,' he said and kissed me.

I wanted to touch him, and in an attempt to have some control, I wrapped my legs around him, pulling him in, but he pulled back, and I couldn't help but sigh. He levelled with me.

'Can you taste yourself?'

'Yes,' I admitted and shook my head.

'It's sweet, huh? I love tasting you,' and he slowly moved down. 'And I love your tits,' he said, taking one in his mouth and sucking while slipping his fingers inside me. 'You are so wet,' he laughed.

'Will!' I said, becoming impatient.

I needed him inside me. I had just come, but not in the way I wanted to. I wanted him to fuck me. That's what I wanted. He had somehow made me come without hitting the spot, and I couldn't help but think he was toying with me.

'What do you want, Lucy?' he asked, smiling.

I looked at him with my jaw set. He was going to make me beg, and I shook my head.

'No?... You don't want me to do anything?'

I looked up at my hands, trying to work out how I could free myself. And then I looked down at the heels of my shoes and then back up at him, a dark thought crossing my mind for a split second. I could use them as a weapon.

'Woah,' he said, the same idea crossing his mind, scrambling back on top of me. 'What the fuck?'

He looked me straight in the eye.

'I want you to fuck me,' I said seriously, staring at him intently.

He let his breath go, and I think he was shocked that he'd seen a side of me he'd not seen before. To be honest, I was pretty surprised myself, but he was driving me crazy.

'Lift your knees,' he said, regaining control, and I quickly followed his instruction.

He swiftly thrust himself inside me, not giving me the time to adjust before he began to move, but I didn't care. I wanted him so badly. He knelt, lifting my hips with him and pushing my ankles up, so my shoes were crowning his head like some kind of God. My God. I was starting to climb again, and I looked up at my hands, trying to think of something else, anything else.

'Will, I can't hold on.'

He stopped straight away and broke our connection.

'Turn over.'

I turned, and he lifted my hips, forcing me onto my knees, pulling my arms taut and thrust himself inside me again.

'If I think you're gonna come, I'm gonna fuck this pretty pink ass of yours.'

What?

I didn't know if I was ready for that. He set a pace, it wasn't particularly fast or slow, but he kept it simple, he didn't touch me, and I didn't want him to because that would definitely make me come.

'You look so damn good,' he said, and then I heard him flip the lid off something before feeling some cold liquid running down me.

'Will, what are you doing?'

'Making sure you're comfortable, this is lube,' he explained as he began to massage my arse.

Oh my God. He was actually gonna do it.

'Don't worry, I won't do anything until you're ready.'

'I don't know when I'll ever be ready,' I admitted.

'Just relax,' he said as he slowly slid his thumb inside me.

'That's easy for you to say,' I replied.

Ignoring me, he scooped some of the lube up with his fingers and began circling me, my insides immediately starting to wake up. As he twisted his thumb, I started to build, and I was desperately trying to think of anything that would take my mind off it.

'Lucy, are you gonna come?'

'No!' I said, shaking my head, but I was lying. I was so goddamn close.

'Are you lying to me?' he asked with humour in his tone.

I couldn't speak because I was holding my breath, but my body betrayed me, and an involuntary groan resonated from deep within me.

'You naughty girl,' he said, but I could hear the smile.

I was literally on the brink, and he pulled out, slowly pulling his thumb out too, and then I could feel him pressed against me.

Everything seized up.

'Breathe in, baby,' he said, gently increasing the pressure. 'Now, slowly breathe out.'

I followed his instruction, and as I let my breath go, he managed to push his tip past the muscle obstructing him, and I whimpered. I stayed as still as a statue.

'Fuck, Lucy!' he said.

I could hear his jaw was clenched, and he was panting though his nose, trying to restrain himself.

'Are you okay, baby? Is it burning?'

How did he know it would be burning? I hated that he was so knowledgeable sometimes.

'Mmm hmm,' I managed.

His fingers began circling my clit again, and my muscles immediately relaxed, the burn easing.

'You good?'

'Aha,' I said, and he pushed a little further. 'Oh, God.'

'try to relax. Breathe steady.'

I closed my eyes, concentrating on the delicious feeling on my clit. He pushed in some more.

'Holy fuck, you're so tight, so perfect.'

He withdrew slightly and drizzled more lube over us before pushing back in, but this time he went further. Before I could object, he pulled back and waited. He groaned. I think he was struggling to keep himself under control, and he steadied himself by placing his hands on my hips.

'Lucy, I'm gonna hold still. I want you to move. I don't wanna hurt you, so just move as much or as little as you want.'

He couldn't trust himself. He wanted me to lead. I carefully, delicately moved forward and slowly glided back. His hiss was so feral a wave of pleasure passed through me. I did it again.

'Fuuuck,' he gritted out. 'So, fucking good,' he said, trembling.

The fact he was enjoying it was turning me on so much. I moved forward again, and this time it felt slicker, easier. As I moved back, Will's fingers sunk into my hips.

'Nearly there, baby,' he panted.

Moving away with ease now, I felt empty, so I quickly thrust my pelvis back, and I felt Will's hips meet mine.

'Yes, Lucy. Fuck!'

Will held my hips, stilling them as he tilted his, and the depth of the motion sparked a feeling deep inside that was so rich, so full, I couldn't contain the moan. He pulled back.

'No,' I cried, the emptiness acute.

He slammed back in, grunting as he did so, and I moaned again. I could feel his balls slap against my pussy and then his fingers returned to my clit, and it was my undoing.

'Aggghhh!'

I screamed into the pillows as my climax tore through me, and he began riding me fervently, milking every wave as I squeezed the bathrobe sash tightly in my hands.

'Fucking... phenomenal,' he said.

And he suddenly pulled out, and I could feel his release spray over my back, grunting with each spurt. What the hell did he do that for? I collapsed onto my side, and Will made quick work of removing the cock ring before undoing the sash.

'Come on,' he said, pulling me up.

'I am not moving,' I mumbled.

He hoisted me up and carried me into the bathroom, knocking the shower lever on with his elbow.

'Will, I just wanna go to sleep now.'

'Believe me, you'll thank me in the morning.'

He held my body under the warm water, being careful not to get my hair wet and then set me down. Then, grabbing some shower gel, he quickly washed himself and then washed me.

'Okay, that's just weird. Stop it now,' I said, pushing his hands away sleepily.

I actually had my eyes closed. He grabbed a towel and wrapped it around me, and I walked back into the bedroom like my body was a magnet to the bed and got in with the towel still around me. Will was chuckling to himself, and it was around then that I passed out.

Chapter 17

As I came to, I gently rubbed my fingers over my eyes and thoughts of the previous night washed over me. I slowly sat up and looked over at Will. He was still asleep, and then I looked down. Why was I wearing a towel?

Oh my God.

'Good morning, Beautiful,' Will mumbled.

'Why did you come over my back?' I asked without thinking... maybe I should have saved that one for later.

Will laughed a little, shaking his head.

'Because otherwise, my grain would be leaking out of your ass right now,' he said sleepily, and I grimaced. 'And you would be whinging at me.'

'Did you wash me last night?'

'Mmm hmm, I didn't want you waking up feeling dirty,' he said, rubbing his face with his hands. 'Come here.'

I lay back down, and he pulled me in, slowly blinking his eyes. 'You were amazing last night. Did you enjoy it?'

With my cheek resting on his chest, I thought long and hard about how I felt. I was surprised at how much I enjoyed the restraining part. It added an element of risk because I allowed him to take control, but it also enhanced our trust. I screwed my nose up at the thought of the burning, but if I was honest with myself, the orgasm had outweighed the short period of discomfort.

I'd obviously been thinking about my answer for too long because Will suddenly rolled me onto my back and peered down at me with concern.

'Talk to me.'

His intense gaze made me colour up, and I couldn't stop my face from forming an embarrassed smile. His furrowed brows turned into a smile.

'It won't always burn,' he said, knowing what I was thinking, but I had to look away. 'Was it worth it?' he asked, gently bringing my face in line with his, but I was doing everything not to catch his line of sight, desperate to avoid his questioning.

He dusted kisses all the way along my jawline as he fed his fingers into the hair at the nape of my neck. Suddenly he scrunched my hair into a fist, causing my head to snap back, nipping my earlobe at the same time.

I yelped.

'If you don't tell me that you enjoyed it, I will *never* do it again.'

'I enjoyed it,' I whimpered.

A great big grin formed on his face as he let go of my hair.

'Music to my ears,' he said before kissing me passionately.

An hour or so later, I was sitting in my bathrobe on the balcony, and Will appeared with a tray laden with everything you might want after a very late night. Cans of ice-cold cola, tea, coffee, water, crusty toast dripping with butter, chocolate and pastries. My eyes hungrily scanned over the tray of goodies, and I took a can of cola.

'How are you feeling now?' Will asked, sitting on the chair beside me.

'About last night? I'm okay about it... like I said, I enjoyed it,' I assured him, looking out to the ocean, still unable to look him in the eye.

'Good to know, but I meant in general.'

Oh.

'Um, good. I like it here because we're alone, but I get the feeling the longer we stay here, the less I will want to go back to the apartment,' I said honestly.

'How do you feel about going to LA?'

'I don't know because I haven't been.'

'Okay... well, it's as secure as this place... Fuck it. Look, I really wanna take you there, it's my home, and I've been putting it off because I want you to feel comfortable, and I don't want you to have another anxiety attack, but it's...'

I stood up and plonked myself on his lap.

'I'd love to go. I just needed some time to absorb everything that's happened.' I stroked his face. 'I'm ready.'

He grinned.

'Okay, I'll make the arrangements.'

And he patted me off his lap, springing into action to go and get his phone, calling back over his shoulder.

'We'll need to pop back to the apartment, though, because I've left some stuff there that I need.'

I looked back out to sea. The last few days had been amazing. I didn't really want to leave, but if Will's place was as secure, then at least we wouldn't have to worry about being photographed.

I found it weird that Will's home was in LA when his friends and his mum were in Brooklyn. Why didn't he set up a home there? Maybe he had another set of friends in LA. Or perhaps he preferred the location. I was intrigued, but I thought I'd save my questions until we arrived.

I also wanted to talk to Will about my options regarding my conversations with Roxy and Paige. I wanted to know how it would work. What charities he supported, assuming he did and how much time he invested in the work he did for them.

I was also conscious that Roxy had told me I needed to strike while the iron was hot. Apparently, there was a window with the media, and you had to either take the bait or leave it to go mouldy during that window. The latter could mean that they turn against you. I didn't like that idea, especially after the home wrecker accusations. At the same time, I kind of felt like I was being bullied into making a quick decision.

'Thanks, Miranda, and I'm sorry for mucking you around. Yep, see you this evening.'

He ended the call.

'This evening?' I asked.

'Yeah, we need to pack up.'

'What, now?' I said, standing up, and Will cupped my face.

'Yes, now... our flight is in three hours, and it'll take about five and a half hours to get there.' He explained. I looked back at the view, and Will smiled. 'Hey, I have a pretty cool view too, it's just a different ocean.'

I pursed my lips, he was always second-guessing my thoughts.

'It's so beautiful here, thank you for bringing me.'

'I'll let Daniel know,' he said before turning toward the stairs.

'Wait... what? As in Daniel that I met at the G.A.M. awards?'

He looked back over his shoulder and grinned.

Oh my God. We had been staying in James Bond's house!

I WAITED IN THE CAR while Will nipped back into the apartment, and I smiled when I realised he'd picked up another guitar.

'Two guitars?' I said as Will slipped back in, and he smiled.

I was not expecting a chartered flight. I don't know whether Will didn't mention it because he thought I'd question it or whether he didn't even think about it, either way, I slept most of the way because I was still feeling tired. Never had I slept on a flight without getting a cricked neck. Will spent the entirety on his laptop. Every time I stirred, I could hear him tapping away.

It was dark when we arrived, but it was warm, much warmer than New York. Will lived in the hills of Pacific Palisades. I'd never heard of it, geography was not my strong point, but it was adjacent to Santa Monica, which I had heard of.

The driver, who went by the name of Fletch, pulled up alongside a few cars. I wasn't sure whether there was more than one residence or whether the other vehicles belonged to Will. Will hopped out, clearly excited to show me his home and helped Fletch with the luggage as we walked down some steps.

From what I could see, the house was modern, sort of set into the hill. The road was above us, and the driver had come down a reasonably steep driveway flanked by many trees. The walls were a light stone colour, quite square as if there were cubes that connected at different levels, with warm dark wood features to soften the stark shape.

'Thanks, Fletch,' Will said to the driver before ushering me through the doorway.

Once inside, I smiled because if you knew Will, you would know this was his house. The interior design was modern, mirroring the outside. Although, everywhere you looked, there was memorabilia from tours, musical instruments and pieces of art that he'd picked up on his travels.

It was far more colourful than I'd imagined. Oranges, teals, yellows and purples came through in a rug, cushion, or picture.

We walked through the hallway and stepped down into the kitchen, which had an industrial, rustic vibe. Stainless steel worktops and plain wooden kitchen cabinets that looked like they hadn't been finished.

Hanging from the ceiling was every size copper pan you could ever wish for, which I thought was funny because Will didn't cook, but their colour matched the orangey tones throughout the kitchen and the dining area that I could see on the far side.

The island was concrete with wooden stools along two sides to break up the sharp lines. And there was an enormous painting of David Bowie in pop art colours. At first glance, it looked like Bowie was doing the 'shhh' sign with his index finger but actually, he was doing the sign for the devil's horns, but sideways.

Will stood in front of me and put his hands on my shoulders, tipping his head to one side.

'I mean, I'm guessing you're happy because you haven't stopped smiling since we arrived.'

I looked at the floor and bit my lip. I was super happy, my tummy was doing flips, and my heart was fluttering. Why had I put this off for so long? This was Will's home, and I loved it.

'Say something!'

I lifted my hand to my mouth because I was almost embarrassing myself with my goofy smile, and I looked at him and started nodding.

'I love it. I really love it,' I said, and Will laughed a kind of thankful laugh and then looked over my shoulder.

'Miranda! Hey, how are you?'

I turned to see a woman similar in age to me, with wavy dark brown hair and brown eyes, average build. She smiled warmly.

'Good, did you have a good journey?' she asked.

'We did. Miranda, this is Lucy.'

We shook hands.

'Hi.'

I didn't know what else to say. Who the hell was she?

'Miranda looks after the house,' Will confirmed.

What, like a house sitter?

'Oh well, it's lovely to meet you, the house is wonderful.'

Is that what you said to someone who looks after a house.

'It's good to meet you too, Lucy,' she said, tucking her hair behind her ear. 'Well, I'll be on my way. Just call if you need me.'

'Thanks, Miranda,' Will said, and she picked up her bag from the hallway and left.

'Looks after the house?' I said, looking at Will quizzically.

'Yeah, you know, does the housework, checks in on it when I'm not here, organises the gardeners... I don't know, just stuff,' he said, brushing it off and opening the fridge.

He pulled out a bottle of champagne, and my face fell.

'Okay, no champagne. What would you like?'

'Tea?' I asked tentatively, screwing my nose up, realising it was unlikely.

Will started opening cupboards, looking around, finding some Chamomile tea, and holding it up.

'Perfect,' I said.

I perched on a stool as I watched Will work around the kitchen.

'It's weird being back here. It's been ages. I can't wait to show you around. I can't believe you're here! After last week, I never thought we'd make it, and I was kicking myself for not bringing you here first.'

'I'm sorry... I'm not normally like this. My head has just been a bit all over the place.'

Will walked round to my side of the island, placing my steaming mug in front of me.

'Thank you.'

'Lucy, please don't apologise. It's entirely my fault. I should have primed you about the media a bit more. Told you what to expect,' he said, pulling a beer out of the fridge and taking a deep pull.

'Why LA?' I asked suddenly, and Will looked a little taken aback. 'I mean, the house is beautiful, but... the location? Do you have friends here?'

'I have a few friends in LA, but that's not why I came here.' He looked across to the windows as if contemplating his answer. 'This place came to market just after everything went down with Alysa, and I happened to be in the area, so I took a look around and made an offer there and then.'

'So, it was an impulse buy?' I asked with my eyebrows raised.

He smirked.

'What can I say? I'm an impulsive guy.'

I pursed my lips, and Will gave me a quick kiss on my temple before taking our bags into the bedroom while I finished my tea. I walked over to the other side of the island and looked across to the dining area. It was such a cool space. The kitchen was asking to be cooked in. It was a shame Will didn't. It was wasted on him.

When he returned, he showed me around the various reception rooms. There was the lounge with two big low Chesterfield-style sofas facing each other. No TV, I noticed. It was just a social space. There were a few framed platinum discs to the side, not in direct eye-line but there all the same. Like he was proud of his achievements but didn't want to ram it down your throat.

We then headed down another couple of steps, and I smiled again, as did Will. There was a pool table, a dart board and some stools around the edge with shelves at the perfect height for drinks. Then, further down still, we came into a cosy lounge with a TV.

Each of the spaces or cubes was similar in size, and I could see that you could either block them off or have all the doors open to have a flowing, rambling, larger space.

We passed through a sort of secondary hallway with doors leading off in all directions. We took the door opposite. 'This is our room,' he said.

'Your room,' I corrected him without thinking.

He paused, and I felt like I'd said something out of turn, but he just nodded slowly. It was bigger than the reception rooms but smaller than the master bedroom in the apartment. The bedroom was similar in style to the one in Brooklyn, with a modern four-poster bed, a large chest of drawers and some built-in wardrobes covering an entire wall. I could see it had an ensuite, but we didn't go in.

'I'll show you around the rest of the place, but unless I've got people staying, I don't use it, so it's pretty basic,' he explained.

There were a further six bedrooms, and they were all similarly decorated in muted tones, and each had an ensuite. They reminded me of hotel rooms. At the end of one of the corridors, I was pretty lost by this point, there was an external door. I assumed it was the back door, but Will opened it, and there was a short bridge leading to yet more cubes. We walked across it, and I tried to see what the outside space was like, but it was too dark.

Will opened the door opposite, it was a thick-set door, and I guessed what was inside. It was his studio, he flicked all the lights on, and I could see we had walked into a sort of office space with a computer and several screens. A huge, thick glass panel separated the office and the main studio space. It was a bit of a mess with a few microphones, leads, several guitars, a drum kit and a separate booth with a microphone.

Will opened another door leading to what I can only describe as a studio apartment. There was a bed, a sofa, a little kitchenette and an ensuite.

'Do you sleep in here?'

'I've been known to,' he admitted. 'Or Paul and Jake have.'

'Together?' I laughed.

'Yeah... sometimes we just work until all we can do is sleep,' he said. 'Speaking of sleep, it's pretty late. Are you tired?'

'I should be... I guess I slept quite a bit on the flight.'

'Okay, let me rephrase that. Will you come to bed with me?' Will asked, and his question caught me off guard.

'I don't think you've ever asked me that,' I said, smiling.

'Well, I'm asking.'

'Always,' I replied, and he looked at me, took my hand and pulled me in close.

'Sometimes you say things, and I don't know where I stand, and then other times you make me feel like... like I'm the one.'

Woah, the conversation had suddenly gotten pretty heavy.

'Do you think I have other *ones* to choose from?' I said, trying to lighten the mood.

'You know what I mean, Lucy. Earlier, you said our bedroom was mine, but if I'm not mistaken, we called the room at the villa our room.'

He was right, I hadn't thought about it, but I think I still called my room at home, *my* room. And besides... that was before we came out here, and now... it didn't feel very fair. How was I going to explain that?

'Yeah... I um... it's not very...' I looked down.

'It's not very what?' he pushed.

'Equal,' I said quietly.

He looked up at the ceiling.

'Lucy, when we got together, your heart was open, you were happy to share everything with me, and you share the one thing that is most precious to you, your family, and that is so much more than this.'

'That's not the same,' I protested.

'They are part of your life, and this is part of mine. You're gonna have to accept that if we're gonna make this work.'

Wow, it really had got heavy. I started chewing the side of my cheek.

'Sorry,' he said, stepping back a little and dragging his fingers through his hair.

'Gosh, this is hard,' I said, breathing out.

'Is it? It doesn't need to be. Lucy, this is me. I wouldn't have brought you here if I didn't want to share it with you.'

He searched my eyes for answers, but suddenly I felt tired. I always felt tired when I was stressed or anxious.

'Can we talk about this in the morning?'

I felt under pressure. I wanted to talk it out. Speak to Steph. My mum, maybe?

'Yeah,' he sighed, defeated and holding the bridge of his nose. 'No!' he said suddenly, and I looked at him with surprise. 'This whole week has been so fucked up, I wanted it to be special, and I kept thinking you were gonna want out, that you were gonna leave me and run back home. I can't go on like this,' he said.

I hadn't realised he was so on edge.

'I'm sorry... I've been so wrapped up in my own thoughts I... I guess I just haven't had to think about someone else's for a while....'

'I'm trying to be patient. I'm trying to give you time, but I love you, Lucy, and it's killing me.'

It was as if we were back in the hotel room when he wanted to make our relationship official and what that would entail, but I had no idea back then that he was... this wealthy, and I couldn't help but feel like I was living in a dream and that I'd wake up, eventually. The bubble would burst. I didn't want to risk accepting it in case it all fell apart. Was I holding out? Maybe I'd wrapped a metaphorical security blanket around me. And that blanket was more obvious to Will than it had been to me.

As I stood there warring with my own feelings, Will waiting for me to respond, his shoulders dropped, like he was giving up.

'Fine, you're right. Let's wait until morning to have this conversation.'

And he turned the lights out in the studio, leading back across the little bridge to the main house.

Back in the bedroom, I went into the bathroom to prepare for bed and was surprised again at the size. It wasn't small by any stretch of the imagination and had all you would need, but it was smaller than the one in the apartment. I thought that if I had lots of money, I would make my main home the most opulent, but he had said he wasn't here much. Maybe he felt it was excessive.

'Have you got everything you need?' Will asked as I was brushing my teeth, and I nodded.

Chapter 18

I woke naturally, and when I opened my eyes, I sat up straight away, and my mouth dropped open. I got out of bed and walked straight over to the window. The view was so beautiful, and it went on for miles. It was so... green. The landscape fell away down the hill, and at the very foot of the picturesque scene was the Pacific, glistening away in the distance. Palm trees, rooftops, and pools dotted around breaking up the greenery, but I couldn't get over the blue of the water.

Wow.

Only then did I realise why I had thought the bedroom was small. It wasn't small at all. It was just that half of it had been closed off last night, and the other half was outside. A huge single pane of glass separated the two. Outside were two wooden reclining chairs and a table between them. There was a hot tub to the left, which you could access from the bathroom too.

Looking at the structure, it was clear that one of the cubes above sort of overhung the room and the outside section was partially shaded from the sun. At the very end of the room, basking in sunlight, there were another couple of chairs to the side with a BBQ. Again, the green spilling in with lots of pot plants and trailing plants from above, giving it a tropical feel.

Standing there, I remembered our conversation last night and tensed up a bit. We hadn't had sex. It was the first time in a while, but there was no awkwardness. We just fell asleep, both aware that we needed to talk.

I was desperate to get a handle on it because it upset Will, but it was bothering me. I imagined it was similar to finding love and winning the lottery at the same time. I knew Will had worked for his money. He hadn't been handed it on a silver plate, so he knew the value of it. Maybe that was the problem. Maybe *I* felt like I hadn't earnt it, and how could I justify so much wealth when people were homeless, starving or dying?

I slowly turned and realised Will had been watching me from the bed the entire time. He hadn't said anything. He just let me experience the view in my own time. I was a bit embarrassed. I must have looked like I was gawking. I then realised a tray with some coffee and fruit was on his bedside table. He'd obviously been up and got back into bed before I woke. Will smiled at me but was frowning at the same time, obviously unable to read what I was thinking for once.

'Do you want some coffee?' he asked as he plumped my cushions up next to him, enticing me back into bed.

'Please,' I replied as I climbed back in, and he passed a mug over to me.

I sat back, staring out at the view while sipping. It was like someone had painted a picture and hung it in replacement of a window. It was perfect.

'I knew you'd love that view, but I want you to look at this for a second.'

He produced his laptop. 'I want to be completely open with you.' He opened it up to reveal a spreadsheet. 'Here is a list of the charities I support, the percentage of what I earn that goes to them and how much they get,' he said.

I put my coffee down, taking the laptop from him to take a closer look.

'I'm an ambassador for that charity,' he explained, pointing. 'I lost a couple of relatives to the fires in northern California and wanted to do something to help. This one is just a small organisation in Brooklyn. It's for the rejuvenation of a skatepark I used to hang out in when I was younger, so I've funded a new half-pipe, and I pay the wages of a guy who teaches the kids to skate safely. And this one is for struggling musicians. It's a charity that provides space for musicians to practice and play together and organise gigs and stuff. The others are just charities to which I have given one-off payments this year, ones that I've come across and decided I want to support.'

'What does DV stand for?' I asked, pointing at the screen.

Will paused for a fraction of a second.

'Domestic Violence.'

I looked up at him and was about to ask why he'd chosen that charity, but he continued.

'My Mom... I was too young to remember, but she admitted it when I asked her about my Dad's disappearance.'

He moved the cursor and flicked to another page. He obviously didn't want to talk about it. There was a pie chart showing his income and where his money was going, and I could see that a large portion of it was for charities.

'What's M O M?' I asked, and he laughed.

'My mom,' he confirmed.

'Oh,' I replied, feeling a bit silly, and then I stiffened when I saw the name, Ben.

Will sensed it, and he shifted round to face me, sorrow in his eyes.

'It's payment for his rehab. When it's settled, that will be it. He'll be on his own.'

A flashback of Ben's dark eyes, millimetres from mine as he threatened my life, caught me off guard, and a shiver passed through me.

Will leaned across, feeding his hand around the back of my neck, searching my eyes.

'I'm fine,' I said before he could say anything.

He kissed me chastely and then returned his attention to the laptop.

'I just assumed you knew some of this as it's fairly well publicised, but I keep forgetting that you don't look. I know there are a ton of charities out there that could probably do with my support, but you have to draw the line somewhere. And the charities I've chosen all mean something to me. And we'll find charities that mean something to you, and we can support them too.'

I quietly thought about that for a moment, letting it all sink in. And then I remembered my conversation with Paige. I had all but forgotten about it, what with coming out there. Maybe I could earn some money for charity. This is what Roxy was talking about, how I could help and the control I had over that. Modelling though? I didn't know the first thing about modelling.

'Roxy said there was a window, and I needed to act before the media did a one-eighty,' I said.

'What, so you can get massively stressed out and overthink everything?' He put the laptop to one side. 'Lucy, we have no control over the media. They will write whatever the fuck they like. One minute I'm the drunken deadbeat that rock and roll was created for. The next, I'm a global heart throb because I've written a love song, and tomorrow I'll be... a noble gentleman who's funded the next big charity drive. So, Roxy was probably saying that if you want the girl next door persona as your thing, then maybe now is the right time to go for it.'

Will took my empty coffee cup, put it on the bedside table and turned to face me.

'Daisy tells me that she's been approached about you doing a couple of interviews.'

My mouth popped open.

'Just some live women's lunchtime panel-show thing. Apparently, people wanna know how we found each other, what happened with my brother and how you're dealing with the press.'

I shook my head. How embarrassing would that be? And surely that was just feeding into people's morbid curiosity.

'You shake your head, but if I told you how much you'd get paid for that, it might make you think twice.'

He took a big breath in and out and then moved closer to me.

'Has any of this made you feel any better about equality?' he asked as I pushed the pillows back and wriggled down to a lying position.

'A bit,' I admitted. 'I'm still struggling with the fact that I earn, what?' I looked down to the end of the bed, trying to work out the maths. 'Two percent of what you earn.'

'They're just numbers, Lucy. When I was younger, my mom earned way less than you, and my Dad had left. It was tough. I can't deny that when the money started rolling in, I did some crazy shit. It was fun, and then I realised I had so much money, I needed someone to tell me what to do with it.'

He rolled across me until our eyes were level.

'I know it's a cliche, but money doesn't buy you love.'

'Well, that's lucky because I can't afford you... well, maybe your index finger,' I said thoughtfully as I smiled, and he laughed. 'Or an ear... or possibly a toe.'

'A toe! You'd buy my toe?' he asked, pinning me to the mattress with his body. 'What if my toes weren't for sale?'

'I would buy your fringe,' I said, brushing it away from his face. 'I expect it would be cheaper because you could grow it back, and I could auction it, strand by strand.'

'You've really thought about this.'

'I think about a lot of things,' I said with an air of nonchalance.

'You really do,' he said before kissing me between my eyebrows. Then, lifting his head, he said, 'Accept it, and I'll give you my fringe,' He offered as he pushed himself up and swiftly pulled my knickers off.

'I'll accept it if you make me come twice again,' I said cheekily.

'Lucy Daniels,' he chastised me. 'You wait until you see how much money I get when I tell The Star what the girl next door just said.'

I giggled.

An hour later, we were sitting having breakfast at the island in the kitchen. The light that came into the house was beautiful. Basically, the side of each cube that faced the view was a window so you could enjoy it wherever you were in the house. I couldn't help but look.

Once we'd finished, Will showed me around outside. The games room led out to the swimming pool, but you could also access it from the kitchen and dining space by coming down a couple of external steps. There was another cube which housed a changing room, shower and loo, along with the mechanics for the pool's pump.

At the end of the pool, there were several steps down to the main lawn, but from there, although the garden was well-established with shrubs and trees, it was pretty sprawling. When we eventually got to the bottom of the garden and looked back up at the house, it almost looked like a building made of Lego.

All the cubes were joined at different levels. There were only two cubes that didn't have windows, one was the hallway, and the other was the TV room. That room had a half window on the other side, so the view didn't interfere with the screen. I could see the little footbridge to the studio, but behind the footbridge were three more cubes in a line.

'Did we go in there?' I asked, pointing.

'No, that's just the garage,' Will confirmed. 'Come on, let's get back up to the house.'

When we walked back up, I noticed another car on the drive, it had been there yesterday, so I guessed Miranda was back. Sure enough, when we reached the kitchen, all of our breakfast things had been cleared away.

I slowly walked along the length of the island. Will hopped up on a stool. I couldn't say anything, I had accepted, but it made me feel uneasy. I looked back at Will, sitting with one elbow on the island, biting his thumb and watching me. He was trying to cover up a smile. He knew what I was thinking.

'We could have done that,' I said quietly.

'Yes, we could have done.'

He left it there, hanging between us. I turned and looked back out to the view. He came up behind me, feeding his arms around my waist.

'What would you like to do this afternoon?'

WE SPENT THE NEXT FEW days chilling by the pool, doing as we pleased. We played pool one evening, Will was far better than me, but I hadn't played for about twenty years. He ordered me a yoga mat as a surprise and rigged his laptop up to the TV so that I could cast an online session.

Will played his guitar a lot and wrote lines down that came to him as and when. We caught up with the boys via FaceTime. He tried to teach me how to play darts one night, but I was rubbish. We talked a lot, sunbathed a lot, and had sex a lot. It was amazing, but I was beginning to feel like we were trapped again. We hadn't left the house in nearly four days.

'I wanna go out,' I said all of a sudden, swinging my legs over the side of the sun lounger to face him.

'Okay... where?' Will asked, putting his guitar down.

'Anywhere, the beach, a café, a restaurant... all the above.'

'The beach we can probably do, a café or restaurant would need to be... organised. And there could be press, and if there is, they'll know we're here.'

'So, it's kind of like, letting the cat out of the bag?'

'Yeah... it's up to you.'

'But if we don't go, they're winning, right?'

'They're winning if we do go,' he said, and I sighed. 'Why don't we just go to the beach? That might fix your itchy feet.'

We set out in a sporty black sedan. I'd never been in an electric car before and couldn't believe how quiet it was.

'This is so much quieter than Billie,' I said as we swept down the windy road.

'Oh, she can be noisy if you want.'

As we glided round the next corner, we came to a straight, and Will floored it. The engine roared, and I was flung back into my seat as I shrieked with delight. Will looked over at me grinning.

'If that doesn't do it for you,' he shouted, 'we have other options.'

I thought about the large garage and wondered how many cars he had as he slowed back down.

'I figured this would be least showy,' he added.

We arrived at Topanga beach within about twenty minutes. Apparently, Santa Monica and Will Rogers State beaches would be too busy. The sand was white, and the sea was blue. It was perfect, and Will and I walked hand in hand along the shoreline. He was sporting a baseball cap and sunnies in an attempt to disguise himself a little. It was so good to be out. It wasn't busy, the occasional runner and a few surfers.

'This is the first public space I've been to since I went shopping in Wegmans.' I announced.

'It's something you'll get used to.'

'Do you think if I went to Wegmans every day, they'd get bored with taking pictures of me in there?' I asked, and Will laughed.

'Are you planning on going to Wegmans every day?'

'Well, no, but I plan on going to the supermarket fairly regularly when we get home.'

'Yeah, so about that....' Will started.

My heart suddenly dropped.

'You're not coming back to the UK?'

'No, it's not that, it's just we haven't talked about my work commitments over the next few weeks.'

There was a pause as if he was getting ready to drop a bomb.

'I've pretty much finished the writing, but we haven't even started rehearsals yet, and that is gonna take time. So, it kind of makes sense that we get started on that while we're all together because it'll need to be recorded, mixed and mastered after that.'

'So, you want me to go home?'

'No... I just don't want you to get bored.'

I thought about all the work I'd done to plan this trip and the clients I'd to let down.

'I'm sorry. Obviously, I didn't plan on Paul having a baby when we organised this trip.'

'So do I need to lose weight, get a string bikini, and take up smoking so I can lie by the pool wearing my big sunglasses and getting a tan while I wait for you to finish work?'

'And I can emerge from the studio, pasty white and fuck you whenever I like? I'm all over that.'

We both laughed despite my feeling a little bit aggrieved about the situation.

'So, when do rehearsals start?'

'Well, we've got the gig at The Pound, and we need to rehearse a bit before that because we'll be playing the new tunes to create a buzz for the new album, so....'

'Tomorrow?' I finished the sentence for him.

'Well, maybe not tomorrow, but in the next couple of days.' He looked across at me and winced. 'Hey, how about I book you in at a spa?'

'Will, you pretty much live in a spa!'

He stopped and sighed, putting his forehead against mine.

'We,' he said, and I rolled my eyes.

'If you died tomorrow, that house would not become mine, so it's yours. We may have a room there, but the house belongs to you. I have accepted that you live between two places, and I am accepting of the fact that you have *the help* in the form of Miranda, Fletch and Terry, but I'm not about to start calling your hilltop mansion or your apartments ours.'

Will pursed his lips.

'Baby steps,' I added, and he shook his head.

'The help... really?' Will said, smiling.

'Really.' I deadpanned, and we carried on walking.

Chapter 19

As soon as we returned to the house, Will had a newfound energy. He made phone call after phone call. He was excited.

I ended up taking myself out to the pool. After scrolling through my phone for a while, I realised boredom would kick in quickly, so I ordered an eBook reader. Will had quite a few books. In fact, one wall of the lounge was filled top to bottom with books, but they were all music-related or complicated mysteries. Suddenly realising I didn't know what Will's address was, I headed back into the house, and as I entered, Will hastily finished his call.

'What's the address here? I need to order something.'

'What are you ordering?' he said, coming over for a cuddle.

'An eBook reader. I feel I'm going to need something to occupy myself.'

'I'm doing my best to organise everything so we get this down as soon as possible.'

'It's fine. I will make full use of this amazing kitchen you never use. I might even use one of those copper pans you use for decoration,' I said, looking up at them.

'Well, there's a food order coming tomorrow, so you can make a list for Miranda, and she can add everything to it. I'm just gonna head over to the studio and make sure we've got everything we need,' he said, tucking my hair behind my ear and kissing me chastely before digging out an envelope from the sideboard which had the address on. He bounded off along the corridor.

As I plugged the address details into my phone, it rang. It was a number I didn't recognise.

'Hello?'

'Lucy, it's Paige. I hope you don't mind. I got your number from Hannah.'

'Oh, hi Paige.'

'I was wondering if you'd had a moment to consider my proposal.'

'Um, well, sort of, although there's one major issue... I've never done any modelling.'

'That won't be a concern, I can assure you. However, Nikki from Over the Wire is very keen to touch base with you. She'd just like to have a chat at this stage. Would you mind if I forwarded your contact details to her?'

I hadn't spoken to Will about Paige's suggestion, but if it was just for a chat, I guess it wouldn't hurt.

'Sure, no problem.'

'Great, well, I hope you're enjoying LA. I'll catch up with you soon.'

The line went dead, and I blinked at my phone a couple of times before resuming my order.

The next couple of days seemed to go so quickly. I knew my time with Will would come to an abrupt end when Paul and Jake arrived, so I was keen to make the most of it, but he seemed to be on his phone or his laptop all the time. Whenever I asked if he wanted to do something, he needed to check on an arrangement or reply to a message.

The thought of taking up smoking was becoming more and more appealing.

I was also aware that I was slowly turning into a caged animal, so I made a snap decision and I called Fletch to take me to the beach. Will was in the studio, so I texted him to tell him where I was going. I walked along the beach for a while. It wasn't until I switched directions twenty minutes later that I realised Fletch was shadowing me.

Had Will asked him to do that? As soon as I was aware that he was there, I felt a bit stupid walking along aimlessly with Fletch trailing behind me, plus the beach wasn't scratching the itch. I needed civilisation and to be amongst other humans. It was like a gravitational pull. So, I walked up to the road, and while putting my sandals back on, I spotted a café that looked nice.

'Hi, could I have a flat white, please?'

'Sure, honey, you here on vacation?'

I guess the accent gave it away.

'I am, actually,' I smiled.

'Oh nice, where ya stayin'?' she asked.

'Um, at my boyfriend's place.'

'Four dollars seventy-five,' she said, and although it was brief, as I waved my card over the scanner, there was a look, and she glanced over my shoulder toward Fletch. 'Take a seat. I'll bring it over,' she said, smiling.

Shit.

Did she recognise me? If she did, would she tell anyone? I looked over at her, and she looked at her phone while the coffee was pouring. I was about to suggest she put it in a takeout cup, but my phone started buzzing.

'Hey, where are you?' Will asked. He sounded a bit worried.

'I'm just getting a coffee. Don't worry, Fletch is with me,' I explained, spying Fletch loitering outside the entrance.

'Where?'

'Just in the beachside café at Topanga. I figured you'd be busy, so...' I trailed off because I didn't know why I didn't ask him to join me. I guess I just didn't want another rejection.

'I'm sorry I've been so busy, but I'm free now. Do you want me to come and meet you? We could go for a drive together?' he suggested, and I smiled.

'I'd love that.'

The waitress brought my coffee over.

'Thank you,' I said, looking up at her, and she smiled.

'You don't have to thank me,' Will said, and I laughed.

'I was talking to the waitress.'

'Okay, I'm on my way.'

'See you in a bit.'

But he was gone. I looked back to thank the waitress properly, but she'd disappeared out back. I stared out at the view, and everyone was just going about their day. Walking dogs, a couple taking a selfie and a few others sitting in the café catching up. It was so lovely to people-watch. It was one of my favourite pastimes.

My phone started buzzing again, it was a UK number, so I answered straight away.

'Hello?'

'Lucy Daniels?'

'Uh-huh.'

'My name is Nikki from Over the Wire. I just wanted to have a chat with you, explain what we're all about and answer any questions you might have.'

I looked over my shoulder to check I couldn't be overheard, but she launched into her pitch before I'd had a moment to respond.

Body positivity was their primary focus. Celebrating women of every shape, size, age, ability and skin tone. Their goal was to empower women and to make them feel confident. Nikki felt that I would be ideal because their up-and-coming collection was aimed at women around my age looking for comfort yet still wanting to feel sexy.

I had to admit, it sounded like a company I'd be happy to work with, they had a great image, and it wasn't seedy at all. And they were a British brand, not that I was particularly patriotic by any stretch, but if I was going to do this, I'd prefer to support a company that was UK based.

That aside, I was still unsure. I'd never done any modelling before, and not only that, but it felt like they were making a huge mistake. I was just Lucy Daniels from Clevedon.

'And did Paige tell you that I don't have any experience?'

'Our team are extremely skilled. This really won't pose a problem—pardon the pun.'

'But why me?'

'You have just bagged one of the world's biggest rock Gods, so for all of us single, middle-aged women out there, you are giving us hope, if nothing else.'

I laughed disbelievingly.

'Plus, you have a great figure, one that represents a healthy lifestyle, an achievable goal for our target market.'

My figure was a goal. I scoffed a little.

'You really don't get it, do you?' she said, laughing, and I drew my eyebrows together. 'Paige told me you were down-to-earth, but I didn't believe her. All agents say that about their clients, but you're the first person I've come across that actually lives up to their reputation. It's rare in this industry, and if anything, it makes me want you even more.'

'Well, I certainly like the company's principles, and it would be lovely to work with you, but...'

'But you need to have a serious chat with your boyfriend?'

'Right,' I answered, allowing my smile to be heard.

'I understand. However, the shoot is only a few weeks away, it's in London, and Will would be more than welcome to join you if that helps to sway things.'

'Okay, that sounds possible.'

'Well, you have my number, if there's *anything* we can do to help, you know where to find me, and in the meantime, I'll email over some samples for you to look at.'

'Thank you, Nikki. It's been lovely chatting with you. I'll be in touch.'

'Great! You too, Lucy.'

I was just finishing my coffee and about to gather my things when a car screeched up outside the café. They had obviously been driving way too fast to stop so suddenly. A guy jumped out, and then I spotted a camera just as Fletch strode through the entrance.

Oh fuck.

I looked back at the waitress, and she looked at the floor. I couldn't believe it.

'Ma'am,' Fletch said, putting his arm out to escort me out.

'Lucy,' a man called, drawing everyone's attention to me.

I grabbed my phone just as a text came through.

GET IN THE CAR

It was from Will, and I saw his car pull up in front of the other one. At the same time, another vehicle pulled up behind the first.

I threw my phone into my bag and grabbed my cardigan. More camera crew got out of the other car. Everyone in the café was turning and getting out of their seats. People running along the beach stopped to see the commotion as I rushed towards the car, Fletch guarding my every move.

'Lucy, what do you think of LA?'

Then, as if he was timing it perfectly, Will got out of the driver's seat, diverting all cameras towards him as I slipped into the passenger seat.

'Will, is it good to be home?'

'How's Lucy finding it?'

'When are you gonna lock her down?'

'Are you moving back?'

As soon as Will heard my car door shut, he slid back in, closing all the flashes and shouting out and pulled away at speed. I looked behind me, and they all jumped back into their cars.

'Are you all right?' Will asked, glancing over at me.

'I'm sorry.'

'It's fine, as long as you're okay. I was travelling behind them. I had a hunch they were paps. I could tell by the speed they were going.'

'I just wanted to get a coffee and... people-watch.'

'Lucy, if you want to go somewhere, just say. It just needs a bit of organising,' he sighed. 'And we need to be prepared.'

'Okay.'

That was all I had to say. I felt like Will was trying hard not to tell me off. I had no idea what I would have done if Fletch hadn't been there or if Will hadn't arrived when he did. I looked behind me again, but I think Will had managed to lose them.

'Where do you wanna go?' Will asked.

'Will, I don't even know where we are, let alone where I want to go.'

We were driving along a fairly busy road, palm trees on either side, and it kind of looked familiar.

'We're on Sunset Strip,' he revealed.

'We are?' I had no idea we were so close. 'Wait, are we near the Hollywood sign?' I asked, and Will rolled his eyes.

'I can't believe we're doing this,' he said, shaking his head, and he changed lanes.

We drove past so many landmarks that I'd seen in films and clubs that I'd heard of. Whisky a Go Go had a giant poster of The 'king Band.

'Don't you find that weird?' I asked as we pulled up to some lights, and he looked over to see what I was looking at. 'I mean, your face is four times its normal size up there.'

He laughed.

'I guess I'm used to it. It's a brand. It's no different to seeing a company logo. Although, I can remember texting Mom to tell her that our album cover was being advertised in Times Square. I thought that was pretty cool... at the time,' he mused.

'What did your mom say?'

'I dunno, she probably didn't reply.'

'Aww, you were obviously really proud of yourself. Surely, she said something.'

'Maybe... anyway, there you go.'

He nodded his head forwards, and there it was, the Hollywood sign, nestled in the hills. I leaned forward and bit my lip.

'You wanna take a picture, don't you,' he said, and I nodded, grinning.

'Of course, I do,' I said excitedly.

'Okay, well, we can't get too close.'

A few minutes later, he pulled into a car park for a huge DIY depot.

'Be quick,' he warned, and I hopped out and quickly zoomed in, snapping a few pictures before climbing back in. 'Happy now?'

'Yes, thank you.'

'Are you hungry?' he asked as he pulled away.

'Why, have you organised for us to go somewhere?' I enquired.

'No... maybe another night.' He pulled into a fast-food drive-through.

'Oh, you know how to treat a girl,' I said, and he laughed.

We ordered two Double-Double burgers, fries, a can of lemonade and a strawberry shake, and then we drove back along the strip towards the coast. I had to admit it was pretty good. They certainly knew how to do burgers in the US. When Will finished, he checked his phone and then looked at me.

'The boys have arrived,' he confirmed, and I nodded.

Our time was up.

'Hey, we won't start rehearsals until tomorrow. Tonight, we drink.'

'Oh God, I don't know what's worse!'

IT WAS GOOD TO SEE Paul and Jake. They were clearly familiar with the place because they'd already taken their stuff to their bedrooms and all their equipment into the studio. I found it funny that they treated each other's places like theirs. I loved Steph, but she didn't have a key to my place... I mean, she may as well, but she didn't.

I'd headed back to the kitchen to find some more crisps or chips, as they call them. I looked back to where we were playing doubles on the pool table, and Will looked so happy. He had his best friends with him, brothers almost, and they were all about to embark on a creative journey together. I could practically feel the energy between them. Will caught me looking and smiled back before taking his shot.

'Come on, Lu, you're up,' Jake called.

I grabbed another bag and some more beers and headed back down.

'Oh, she brings supplies,' Paul said and took two of the beers off me, passing one to Jake.

Somehow, I managed to pot two balls in a row, it was a pure fluke, and I think the alcohol was helping.

'Yes, girl,' Jake said as he nudged me with his hips in celebration.

Will and Paul looked at each other as if they meant business, and Paul took his shot. He potted one, but the white followed, giving two shots to Jake.

'Oh, what an error,' Jake said to Paul as Jake winked at me and proceeded to pot three more balls.

It was Will's turn, he was under pressure to catch up, and I bit my lip, trying to stop myself from smiling. He potted a ball and then missed the next, so it was back to me. We had two balls left, but they were both hiding behind the opposing balls.

Will sucked a breath through his teeth and said, 'Oh, tricky.'

He lifted his eyebrows, staring straight at me.

'Come on, girl, you can do this,' Jake said encouragingly.

I was trying to work out if I could at least touch one of our balls so that Will and Paul didn't get two shots. Oh, sod it, I hit the white ball off the cushion, and it came shooting back, thankfully hitting our ball first. Phew, I thought, but then it rolled along the cushion and slowly plopped into the hole. I couldn't believe it. My mouth popped open, and Jake jumped up and punched the air before giving me a massive hug. I was laughing.

'What? That was rigged,' Paul said, and Will stood there, leaning on his cue and shaking his head.

'You get another shot,' Will said to me.

Jake leaned into Will and said, 'Good cook, a good judge of character, good at pool... I wonder what else she's good at?'

Will pushed him away, shaking his head. I looked away from the exchange, a tad embarrassed and back to the table. Unfortunately, I was again in a position where I couldn't hit our ball directly. I tried the cushion trick again, but the shot fell short by a couple of centimetres.

'Aww, shame, two shots, Paul,' Will said, smiling wickedly at me.

Paul landed two more balls, and then Jake managed to pot our last ball, we high-fived, and it was just the black left.

'Oh, pressure... just if he was a slightly better drummer,' Paul said, and Jake glared at him in jest.

He took the shot, and the ball went down.

'Ah!' I shouted, running around the table to hug him, and Jake lifted me up. 'Well played.'

'You too, girl.'

He held me there for a second too long before letting me down and then smacked my arse.

'Jake,' Will said in a warning tone, and I looked at the floor.

Paul looked at the ceiling.

'Come on, let's get some more drinks,' Paul said, glossing over the awkward air that was suddenly hanging between Jake and Will and headed up to the kitchen, taking Jake with him.

I went to follow, but Will whipped me round to face him and kissed me, pulling me in. I pulled back and looked into his eyes.

'I love you,' I mouthed.

Will was staring at me with intent, and I held my breath because I thought he was cross with me about Jake.

'I love you,' he mouthed back before taking my hand and leading me up to the kitchen to join the others.

We headed out to the pool, Will sat on one of the chairs and pulled me onto his lap. I got the feeling he was being a little possessive, and although it was subtle, the arm he placed around me was protective, as if he was shielding me from the others.

'So, what were you up to earlier?' Paul asked. 'Hannah said you got papped at Topanga.'

'That was my fault,' I admitted. 'I went to get a coffee,' I said flatly.

'No! Not a coffee,' Paul said in mock horror, and I laughed. 'Well, you're doing well,' he nodded. 'Lucy Daniels was taking a walk to consider her options. Where will she choose to live?'

I rolled my eyes.

'Actually, I saw a lovely picture of the two of you walking along that beach the other day. You were both laughing,' Jake added.

'Really?' I said, and I spotted Will lifting his hand as if to shut him up.

I thought back to that day, we'd been talking about the logistics of the album launch, and I hadn't seen any photographers. I sighed, and Will twisted me around.

'It was just a candid shot, probably taken on a cell phone,' Will said.

I didn't want to think about people taking pictures of us, violating our privacy and souring a perfectly nice evening, and I could tell Paul and Jake were sensing a bit of tension. I was desperately trying to think of something else to talk about, but Paul beat me to it.

'What did Paige want? Hannah said she asked for your number.'

Shit.

Will's eyebrows furrowed as he looked at me quizzically, and I realised in that very moment that I had been kind of... not putting it off, but... trying to find the right time to speak to Will about it. Why did I get the impression that Will wouldn't be too impressed? Was it because of Paige's sudden change of topic when he approached us at the party?

'Umm... she thought I might be interested in doing some modelling for one of her clients.'

'Really?' they all said in tandem, Paul and Jake with a touch of excitement in their voices and Will with an edge of concern in his.

'Yeah,' I said, treading carefully. 'It's for Over the Wire, but I don't know, I haven't got any experience.'

Will's eyebrows were still furrowed when Paul and Jake congratulated me. I got the impression that Will's smile was a little forced, so I made light of it by moving the conversation on.

'How's Hannah doing?' I asked Paul.

'Yeah, really well. Our second scan is coming up soon, so she's excited about that.'

'She?' I questioned, eyeballing him.

'Yeah... it's all we talk about,' he said, and I laughed.

'Oh, she'll get bored in about...' I looked up at the sky, 'seventeen, eighteen years.'

Everyone laughed, and Jake headed off down to the end of the garden for a cigarette.

'Seriously though, it's like all other topics are inconsequential. So, I'm kind of glad to have a break.'

'It's a testing time for any relationship, especially with crazy hormones thrown in,' I empathised.

'Yeah... that!' he said, and I guessed there had been some disagreements between them.

I turned back to Will, who was unusually quiet. He was just looking out across the hills, and I wondered if he was finding the conversation difficult. I sensed there was boy chat on the horizon, so I stood up.

'I'm gonna head to bed,' I said, and Will snapped out of his reverie and stood up too. 'You stay.'

'No, it's cool, it's late, and we've got a long day tomorrow,' Will said. 'See you at ten,' he said to Paul. 'Night, Jake,' he called.

I looked at Paul, annoyed with myself for ending the night so abruptly, but he just wished me goodnight too. We headed into the bedroom.

'I honestly don't mind if you wanna stay up,' I said as I walked into the bathroom.

'I do wanna stay up, just not with them,' he replied, following me in. 'I'm gonna be spending way too much time with them over the next few weeks, and I'd much rather be with you.'

He turned me round to face him, despite the fact I was doing my teeth.

'Promise me you won't suddenly shoot off, though. If you start getting itchy feet, tell me.'

I nodded and then turned back to spit out. I shooed him back out so I could use the loo, and then we swapped, and I climbed into bed.

'What have you got planned for tomorrow?' he asked, getting in next to me.

'I have a full day of baking and cooking planned. I can't wait to use that kitchen,' I admitted, and he smiled.

'Cool, so you'll be around at two? It's just that Mat and some of the team are arriving for a meeting,' he explained.

'What, and they're staying here?' I asked.

'No, they're staying in a hotel, but they'll be hanging out.'

'Okay, sure.'

He smiled and kissed me chastely.

'Once we go into that studio, I don't know when we'll come out,' he admitted. 'But I promise that I'll sleep with you... I might even do things to you while you're asleep.'

I laughed.

'What things?' I enquired.

'Well, I can demonstrate...' and he rolled on top of me and kissed my neck.

'I might be a bit cross if you wake me up just for that.'

Then he began to move down.

Chapter 20

I woke bleary-eyed. I turned, but Will wasn't in bed. Instead, there was a note on his pillow that simply said, *I love you*. It was ten forty-five, and I was gutted that Will hadn't woken me before heading to the studio, but he'd kept me up until the early hours. In fact, he fully took me through my paces, and I hoped that the walls were soundproofed because, otherwise, Paul and Jake would have heard us.

This whole tying me up thing was driving me crazy, and Will was enjoying it a little too much. He kept taking me to the edge and making me beg, and I was not doing it in the most ladylike of manners, which Will thought was hilarious.

Once I'd torn myself away from the view, I got ready and set about getting all the ingredients I needed to bake. Unfortunately, I couldn't find any weighing scales, so I had to use measuring cups which I was not used to, and I kept having to convert all my trusty recipes, which was a ball-ache.

It also took me ages to work out how to use Will's oven. I don't think it had ever been used because it stank, and I had to slide open the doors to the garden. However, by lunchtime, I had made shortbread, scones and biscotti, and the smell of baking had taken over the bad smell.

I allowed myself a warm scone with butter before starting the preparation for my afternoon of cooking. I was just browning off some mince when the doorbell went. I'd forgotten Mat was arriving. Mat and no less than five other people were standing on the doorstep.

'Lucy? I'm Mat, it's good to finally meet you.'

Mat shook my hand and then introduced me to the rest of the group.

'This is Tom, Olaf, Penny, Kieron and Sally.'

'Hi! I'm rubbish at remembering names, so apologies in advance,' I said as they all filed in.

'It's great to meet the girl next door finally,' Kieron said, and I rolled my eyes. 'Maybe that's something we can discuss later. I have a few proposals for you.'

'Kieron.' Mat said scoldingly, and Kieron lifted his hands as if to say he was finished. 'Are you okay to show us through, Lucy?'

'Of course, sorry, I thought you knew where you were going.'

As I led them along the corridor, past the bedrooms, I could hear Paul.

'It smells amazing out here,' he said before seeing us. 'Mat! They're here,' he called back to the others.

I left them to it, remembering the mince was still on the hob. I had just started to chop an onion when the whole entourage of people came back into the kitchen. They were all talking at once, and Will scooted around the island before cupping my face to kiss me.

'Erm, the smell is kind of making us all hungry, so we decided to take a coffee break,' he said, lifting an eyebrow and then casting his eye over the sugary goodies on the cooling racks. I couldn't help but laugh.

'Help yourself,' I said.

'Awesome!' he replied, picking up a piece of shortbread.

I put all the bakes on plates and placed them in the middle of the island while Paul was on coffee machine duty. Will perched on a stool, watching me as I carried on chopping up the onion.

'What are you making?'

'Cornish pasties,' I confirmed, and he looked impressed. 'Do you have HP sauce over here?'

'I'm gonna say no because I don't know what that is.'

I started chopping the carrots, wondering how I could replicate HP sauce. You couldn't have pasties without it. Maybe there would be an end-of-aisle in the supermarket dedicated to UK brands like there was in France. Using the knife to slide the carrots into the mixture, I pulled out a couple of potatoes ready to chop. Will had clearly gotten bored with waiting and came up behind me, placing his hands on my hips.

'You were amazing last night,' he whispered before kissing my neck. 'Sorry, I didn't wake you this morning. You looked so peaceful.'

His hand travelled down the front of my thigh, and I looked over to the group to ensure no one was watching.

'I thought you'd be smoking by the pool by now, but baking is so much better.'

'Maybe I'll do that tomorrow,' I whispered as his hand changed direction up my inner thigh.

I put the knife down, and Will spun me around, catching my lips with his.

'Ah, man, we'll never get him back in there now,' Jake said, drawing everyone's attention to us.

'Hey, this is supposed to be our holiday,' Will protested.

'Fair point,' Paul said, obviously feeling responsible.

Olaf looked at his watch. I thought he might be the producer.

'On a more serious note, we really should get on,' Olaf said, and everyone finished their drinks and started stacking them up, thanking me for the cakes before heading back towards the studio.

Will kissed me once more and joined the others, and I didn't see them again for the rest of the day.

I finished the pasties, made another batch of shortbread, and once everything was cooled, I packaged them all up.

I poured myself a glass of wine and sat by the pool, my thoughts returning to the modelling contract. Will hadn't brought it up again, so I figured he was cool with it. The fact that the shoot was in London in a few weeks almost felt like it was meant to be as we'd be back in the UK by then. A flutter of excitement ran through me as I imagined standing in front of a camera while someone like Austin Powers shouted various commands at me.

I was just starting to get creeped out by the quiet of the night when I heard one of the sliding doors open by the studio. Jake, Mat and Kieron piled onto the balcony for a cigarette break.

'The new stuff sounds mint,' Mat said to Jake.

'Yeah, well, Will's in a really good place. I've never seen him write like this before. It's just pouring out of him,' Jake said.

I was about to go in, but then I heard Kieron say, 'It's the girl next door. We need to hone in on that one. We could use her.'

I froze. Use me. What the hell?

'Kieron, you need to give her time. She was losing it when I visited Will at his apartment,' Mat said.

I closed my eyes. I'd happily forgotten that Mat had been at Will's place when I'd had my anxiety attack.

'Lu is ace, and Will will go nuclear if anything happens to her,' Jake warned.

It was fair to say that Kieron had been put in his place, but what did he mean by using me? Using me for what? They all headed back in, and I decided it was bedtime. It was only nine-thirty, but I was knackered after the previous night.

I was vaguely aware that Will had climbed into bed, I had no idea what time it was, but when I woke, he was fast asleep. I quietly slipped out of bed and got in the shower. I shrieked when I felt a hand on my hip before Will covered my mouth with his. I kissed him back vehemently, having only spent half an hour or so with him yesterday. It felt like forever since I'd seen him. His hands were all over me, like he wanted to feel every inch of me, and his lips were insistent, nipping and sucking.

'Come back to bed. I haven't got long,' he said, lifting me without waiting for my reply and carrying me back into the bedroom. We were both completely soaked, but

I didn't care. He entered me the second I was lying down. Looking into my eyes, he gave me a few moments before kissing me again.

My God, I needed this man. I wrapped my legs around him tightly, pushing him into me, tilting my hips to accept him further. My eyes rolled into the back of my head as I pressed it back into the mattress. Will nipped my collarbone, and I dug my fingernails into his back.

It was as if we needed to cause each other pain to express how powerful our feelings were. The fusion between us seemed to blend in every way, from the literal connection to our thoughts and souls. I wanted to be him. Crawl inside him. Be as one. Our movements were in perfect unison. Pure bliss.

'Lucy,' Will said in the distance.

I could barely hear him. I was so lost in him. I blinked a few times to focus. Our bodies were moving of their own accord, like they were meant to move together.

'Fuck, Will, I love you so much. I can't even explain what level I'm on.'

I was panting, crying, and I realised I needed him more than air.

'Lucy, you are my life, my whole life,' he brushed the tears away, kissing where they were. 'You are my light, my energy.'

It was as if he was reading his vows to me. I was desperately searching for something to say, something poetic and meaningful that would explain to him how I was feeling. Saying I love you wasn't enough, and then it came to me.

'Will... you are my view, my sun and my sea.'

He kind of laughed, and I thought he'd found it funny, but a single tear dripped onto my face, and he kissed me, burying himself into me, pushing deeper still. It was almost biblical. Suddenly I was on the precipice, and my orgasm teetered there. I couldn't speak, my body was his, and our souls fused as my release became audible. It was like no other. I didn't even know what I was doing. He could have done anything to me. I was in euphoria.

I was aware that he had climaxed, and he was kissing and nipping my lips, trying to bring me back into the present. It was like I was coming around from passing out, becoming aware of my breath, heart, and body.

'Lucy, that was incredible. Are you with me?' he asked, pushing my damp hair off my forehead.

I had to physically feel my face to check back in with myself.

'I don't know what happened. That was... something else.'

I couldn't even string a sentence together.

'I think *they* might know what just happened,' he said, smiling, and as I came to, I could hear voices in the kitchen. I was suddenly alert.

'Oh my God, was I loud?' I asked, panicking, and Will bit his lip, obviously not wanting to cause further concern. 'Oh no.'

'I think the neighbours may have heard.' He laughed, and he kissed my gaping mouth. 'Don't worry about it. I don't care. This is our house.'

I shook my head at his comment, especially the last one, while Will stood up, pulling me up with him. He led me back into the shower, which was still on, and we showered together before he quickly got dressed.

'I'll see you later. Oh, some more people are arriving this afternoon. Will you be here to let them in?'

'I'm not planning on getting a coffee out, if that's what you mean.'

I was about to ask if we'd be able to talk about the modelling thing later, but he stepped toward me.

'I love you,' he said, kissing my forehead, and before I could reply, he was gone. Seconds later, I could hear Jake whistling and a few cheers that only men could offer another man in appreciation of his prowess. I rolled my eyes and then smiled to myself. I didn't care. I loved that man, it was scary.

Biscuits and a goat's cheese frittata were going to be my mornings work, and then I needed to find a book to get into. One that I could lose myself in... like Will, I thought. Now that I knew where everything was in the kitchen, I enjoyed using it. It had a lot to do with the amount of worktop space and the view.

'Are you purposefully baking to lure us out of the studio?' Paul asked as he came up the steps to the kitchen.

'I'm sorry, is it disrupting your creative flow?' I asked in a sarcastic way, and then added. 'But no, I'm baking to stop myself from going insane and feeling like a prisoner while on holiday.'

He looked down at the floor, and I felt awful for making him feel bad. 'I mean... I felt like that before you arrived... I didn't mean the holiday part necessarily.'

'Lucy, you're doing just fine. We all get it. We've had the privilege of dealing with this level of intrusion on a steady increase, and you've just been blasted with it in one hit.'

I hadn't thought about it like that before. He was right. It's like those people who go on reality TV shows. When they enter, they're normal, and when they come out, they're celebrities.

Paul was already making coffee, so I got all the biscuits back out on the island, but before the rest of the team rocked up, I headed out to the garden. I was sure I saw some herbs growing when Will showed me around initially, and I could do with some for the frittata, maybe some chives. I was in luck. I picked some chives and grabbed some mint while there too.

As I walked back up to the house, Will was striding down.

'There you are. You not joining us for coffee?'

'Um, well, I can. I just don't wanna be the clingy girlfriend.'

Although, if I was honest with myself, I was avoiding Kieron after overhearing his comments yesterday. At least Paul, Jake and Mat seemed to have my back.

'Well, you're not, don't ever think that,' he said, grabbing my hand and taking me back up to the house.

'Will,' I began, wondering if now would be the right time to speak to him about my conversation with Nikki from Over the Wire.

'Hey, Lu,' Jake called. 'What are these called?'

'Oh, they're just spice biscuits.'

'I've had spice biscuits before, and they sure as shit didn't taste as good as this,' he said, laughing.

'They're delicious,' one of the team added.

'Thank you.'

They were so appreciative, I wondered how many of them lived on a similar diet to Will, constant take outs. It was a nice feeling. I think I was missing being a mum.

They all filed back into the studio once they'd had their fill, and I began to prepare the frittata, kicking myself that I hadn't spoken to Will about the modelling. I placed it in the oven and went back to the bedroom to get into my bikini.

I decided on a swim before lunch. Maybe I should swim each day and try to do as many lengths as possible. I was already struggling to find things to do, and the novelty of baking would wear off, eventually.

But before I'd had a chance to think about it, I heard the doorbell. Bloody hell, that must be some more of the team arriving. I quickly tied the sash of my robe and raced to the front door. I didn't even have time to check the camera and heaved the door open.

I stood there staring for a good few seconds, my jaw nearly on the floor and then I started crying. There, standing in front of me, was Steph, Claire and Zara.

'Oh, babe,' Steph said, pulling me in for a hug.

'Oh, my fucking God, get out of the way,' Claire said, pushing us to one side and striding into the house. 'Look at that bloody view!' she said as I hugged Zara, ushering them both in and heaving the door shut.

'Have you just travelled from London? You must be knackered,' I said while they dumped their things and made their way into the kitchen.

'I slept for a good seven hours on the flight,' Zara said. 'I hope we get to fly back on that plane. It was amazing, it was just the three of us, and we all had a bed.'

It was slowly dawning on me that Will had been planning this for a while.

'He managed to keep it quiet then?' Steph asked, giving me another squeeze as I brushed the last of my tears away.

He so had. I couldn't believe it. My friends were there, in Will's kitchen.

'This place is amazing,' she said as she let go and walked down into the games room and then up into the lounge before returning to the kitchen.

'What would you like to drink?' I asked, opening the fridge. 'Fizz?'

I heard a resounding yes, so I pulled a bottle out and grabbed four flutes. The girls busied themselves, looking around and taking turns to use the bathroom while I prepared the drinks.

'Did she cry?' I heard Will ask as he strode in, hugging me.

'Of course she did!' Steph said, accepting a kiss on the cheek from him before he said hi to Zara and Claire.

Paul and Jake followed, and there was a round of kisses and hugs and hellos before Will rallied the boys to be on luggage duty and showed the girls where they were staying. Will jogged back to the kitchen to give me another hug.

'You okay?' he asked.

'I am now,' I beamed.

'Well, I can see you're already sorted for drinks, but we'd better get back in there. We just popped out to say hi.'

I was a bit gutted but also kind of pleased because we probably had so much girl talk to catch up on.

'We'll try to finish earlier tonight, but I can't promise anything.'

He kissed me and then went to go, but I pulled him back.

'Thank you,' I said earnestly.

He cupped my face and kissed my nose before striding off in the direction of the studio.

'Just how many rooms has this place got?' Claire asked as she swiped a glass off the island and headed out to the pool, clearly not needing an answer.

I noticed she was wearing her bikini underneath her dress. Steph and Zara padded in, copying my attire like it was the done thing while on holiday. Before taking mine, I handed them their glasses, and we headed out to join Claire.

'So amazing,' Steph crooned, not really to anyone in particular.

'It's beautiful, isn't it? I haven't tired of it yet,' I confessed.

'And this is just one of Will's places?' Zara asked, standing at the end of the pool and looking back at the house.

'He has an apartment in Brooklyn and one in Paris,' I confirmed. 'And apparently, he's about to invest in another property because he's just sold Ben's place, but I don't know anything about that one.'

They all oohed and aahed before each staking a sun lounger, but I didn't want to dwell on his assets.

'So, what have you been doing since you got out here?' Zara asked. 'I bet you've got tons of pictures.'

I was lying on my front, looking into the pool, and I didn't know how to respond.

'I've got a few of the New York skyline, and... oh, I've got a picture of the Hollywood sign. We're not that far from it, actually.'

I pushed myself onto my elbows, pleased that I'd come up with something, but the girls were all looking at each other. I knew they could sense something wasn't right, and I started to well up. They had gathered around me in less than a second. Steph put her arm around me, and Claire clutched my hand. I took a long breath in to try to explain, but all that came out was a sob, and I buried my face in my hands.

'Oh Lu, what's wrong?' Steph asked. 'Will said you needed cheering up, but I figured you were just homesick.'

I pushed myself up to kneeling and sniffed a very unladylike sniff.

'It's the press mainly. I don't know how much you've seen, but it's been a bit relentless since we arrived. We've hardly been out, and when we do, they catch us, even when we think they haven't. And I know I haven't got a right to complain....' I said, waving my hand around at the space we were sitting in, 'but I feel completely trapped. I can't even go for a walk on the beach.'

The tears were tracking silently down my cheeks.

'Surely Will can do something?' Claire said as she got up to fetch another bottle of fizz.

'Trips out have to be organised like a military procedure,' I said, using air quotes for the word organised. 'Will thinks I'll get used to it with time but... oh, I don't know.' I smoothed my hands over my face, wiping the tears away. 'I had an anxiety attack at his apartment, so we stayed at a villa in The Hamptons to escape the media for a bit. And I ended up seeing a shrink.'

'Fuck!' Claire said, arriving back.

'And what did the shrink say?' Steph asked.

I moved my legs into a cross-legged position, and the girls shifted around to make themselves more comfortable.

'Roxy, the lady that came to see me, said that if I was clever, I could use my position in the media to my advantage. And, I've just had a call from a lady called Nikki about the possibility of doing some modelling for Over the Wire.'

'Oh my God, that's so cool,' Zara said. 'Over the Wire are all about body positivity. I really like their ethos.'

'And apparently, Will's PR team want to talk to me about doing some interviews,' I continued.

'Well, that sounds positive,' Steph said with an empathetic smile.

'But can you imagine me being interviewed by, I dunno, Julie White from The Packed Lunch? I'd be so tortured with nerves. I wouldn't be able to speak.'

The girls all started giggling.

'What?'

'It's Wright,' Claire said.

'Oh.' I couldn't find any humour in it.

'I could do it on your behalf!' Claire suggested, and that made me smile.

'Babe, I wish you'd phoned. We could have done a joint FaceTime,' Steph said, stroking my back.

I didn't want to make her feel bad by telling her I had tried, so I made light of the subject.

'Well, I guess that would have been a damn sight cheaper than Will flying you all out here,' I said with a laugh.

'And to New York,' Zara said.

'What? You're coming to New York too?'

'Hell yeah, baby,' Claire confirmed.

'Will's got it all planned out. We're coming to the gig. I think we're on a spa day tomorrow,' Steph said. 'That was my idea.'

'Oh my God! I thought I would be baking, swimming and reading for a week.'

'Cheers to...' Steph was trying to think of an appropriate topic.

'Best friends,' I finished, and we all clinked. 'Are you hungry? I made a frittata earlier.'

A couple of hours later, we had all had lunch, and several more glasses of fizz, and we were all chilling back by the pool.

'Do those boys ever come out?' Claire asked.

'I don't even know when Will came to bed last night, they just keep going until they drop. It's not just them. There's a whole team of them in there.'

'Wow, how big is it?' Zara asked.

'Oh, it's like a separate dwelling. It has a kitchen area and a bedroom, everything you might need,' I explained.

Chapter 21

I headed back up to the kitchen to get a glass of water, making sure I was pacing myself. I was hosting, after all.

'Pour me one, babe,' Steph nudged me as she glided up to the island, plonking herself on a stool. 'So, now that you've talked it out, do you feel a bit better?'

'A bit,' I said, passing her a water. 'I haven't had the chance to speak to Will about Over the Wire, but we've discussed the possibility of me doing these interviews, and he left the decision with me. His team, however, there's a guy called Kieron...' I glanced down the corridor and lowered my voice. 'I overheard them talking, and he wants to use me somehow, and I don't know what he means.'

'Use you?' She frowned. 'To make money for them?'

'I don't know, maybe promotion? I haven't told Will. Jake seems to have my back, that's who Kieron was talking to, but I don't want to upset the apple cart.'

'Hmm, sounds like you've had it all going on.' She took several long sips of water. 'I've seen all the articles. At least the press like you. Can you imagine what it would be like if they hated you?'

'I dread to think, it was bad enough with the home wrecker label,' I said, refilling my glass. 'I was in a café the other day, and all these people with cameras just started turning up in cars, it was scary. I'm frightened to go out.'

'You've lost weight,' she stated, eyeballing me.

'Have I?' I said, maybe I had. 'Well, it's not like I haven't been eating.'

'You're clearly having way too much sex,' she said, lifting her eyebrows, and I stifled a smile. She grinned. 'Things are good with Will then, yeah?'

'Amazing,' I said, almost embarrassed at my quick response and closed my eyes, trying to squeeze the flush from my face. 'I love him so much, I don't actually know how to express it properly.' She smiled a knowing smile. 'What Mike and I had pales into insignificance.' I rubbed my forehead. 'I just wish... I wish it was easier.'

'It will just take a bit of time to adjust,' she said, and I looked at her, trying not to sigh. 'Heard that one too many times?' I nodded. 'Another drink?' She grinned, and I laughed. 'Come on, whatever happens, we're going out tomorrow, even if we have to put a bag over your head.'

Claire stumbled in from the pool. 'She's only bloody fallen asleep! I was having a conversation with her, and she bloody fell asleep!'

Steph and I laughed. I heard voices coming down the corridor, and I checked the time, it was ten past ten. Had they finished for the day? A little frisson of excitement fluttered through me.

'Thanks ever so much, guys, sorry for another late finish,' Olaf said to the team as Mat ushered Kieron and some of the others out of the door. I gave them all a half-wave. Mat shut the door, looked at the ceiling and then turned to us.

'Long day?' I asked, offering him a glass.

'Those guys are relentless,' he said, pointing towards the studio. 'It's like they hit play, and it's on repeat, I heard your song about twenty-six times today.'

'My song?' I said, frowning.

'Ah.' His face fell. 'It's probably a working title, forget I mentioned it,' he said, waving it off.

'Oh my God, he's written you a song,' Claire said, and Mat scrunched his eyes.

'Mat, this is Claire, and this is Steph,' I said to save his embarrassment and change the subject. 'Mat is their new tour manager.'

They all shook hands.

'Here he is, a glass of champagne in his hand already,' Jake said. 'Oh! Ladies,' he said with a little bow. I turned and got another glass out, pouring one for Jake. 'Thanks, Lucy.'

'Are you done for the night?' I asked.

'I fucking hope so, those two are still stroking their strings in there,' he said, and I felt a little deflated.

'Shall we go and get that one to bed?' I asked Steph, nodding towards the pool.

'Good idea,' she replied.

Once Zara was safely tucked up in bed, we joined the others back in the kitchen, but Claire had obviously taken herself off to bed as she was nowhere to be seen. Jake and Mat were talking about Kieron.

'He's just a typical PR guy, brand and image-focused,' Mat said.

'He's a dick,' Jake said, 'I've no idea why Daisy sent him.'

I don't know whether it was the alcohol or whether she thought she was looking out for me, but Steph suddenly said, 'So, what is it that Kieron wants to use Lucy for?'

I closed my eyes because they would know I had listened to their conversation.

'Oh, has Will asked you about it already?' Mat asked, looking at me, but before I could answer, Steph cut in.

'That's by the by. We want to know what you think.'

Oh, she was good.

'Personally, I think it's a good idea,' Mat said.

'You do?' Steph asked, and I could see Jake looking from him to her and then to me.

I looked straight back at him, expressionless, but the penny dropped, and he was about to protest when Mat said, 'Niall O'Brien's the perfect fit, he's British, and he'll make—Ow!'

Jake had clearly kicked him and was now giving him the evils.

'Wait, what?'

'The Night Show,' Steph guessed, looking at me, nodding, and I shook my head gently.

The Night Show was a chat show, famous for interviewing all the big celebrities and they often did interviews on location as well as in the studio.

'I'm just gonna go to the loo,' I announced and a few minutes later, I was splashing my face with water and looking at myself in the mirror.

Had I lost weight? I turned to one side, looking at my profile. I didn't think so. Niall O'Brien... I shook my head again. I quite liked him, or at least I liked him for how the media portrayed him. Just as I was about to leave, there was a frantic knock at the door.

'Lucy! Open up!'

It was Will, I opened the door straight away, and he barged in, immediately grabbing me and putting his forehead to mine.

'It's totally up to you what you do, no one is going to make you do anything, and if you want, I'll get rid of Kieron.'

He was really concerned, and his eyes were searching mine.

'Will, I'm okay. I just came to use the loo.'

I ran my thumb along his jaw.

'They want to interview us as a couple, it'll give me an opportunity to promote the new album but if you're not into it, I'll decline and do it on my own.'

'I'd kind of guessed Kieron wanted me to do something like that. It was just the way he'd phrased it. I don't want to be used. I want it to be worthwhile.'

'So, what, you're thinking of doing it?' he asked.

Was I?

'I'm still thinking about it... more to the point, what's this about *my* song?' I asked, and his expression softened, he looked bashful and maybe a little coy. 'Will?'

'I wrote something... it's not ready,' he said, not committing or confirming it had anything to do with me, but he clearly didn't want to talk about it.

'Okay... leaving it there,' I said, lifting my hands as if to create a barrier, and he kissed me, pushing me back up against the sink.

'I can't stop thinking about you from this morning,' he said between kisses. 'I've never seen you like that before.'

I pulled his t-shirt off.

I needed to touch his skin.

'You were... sentient, alive,' he continued.

I started kissing his chest.

'Yet, not there,' he added.

I began to undo his fly.

'I wanted to be you,' I breathed, kissing his abdomen.

That sounded stupid.

'I meant. I wanted us to be... one.'

I moved down onto my knees, and Will glanced at the door. I looked up at him, uncertain if he wanted me to continue.

'No?' I asked, questioning my own actions.

He reached over and flicked the lock.

'I am never gonna say no to this,' he said with a laugh, and I pulled his jeans and boxers down together before quickly taking him in my mouth.

Will hissed.

'You should drink champagne more often,' he said, and I could hear everyone chatting in the kitchen as Will braced himself on the mirror and closed his eyes.

I opened wider for him as I licked and sucked the crown of his cock.

'I really hope Lucy is okay.' I heard Mat say, and I looked up at Will seductively, and he smiled back at me, biting his lip.

They thought Will was in here checking I was alright. He closed his eyes again, and I could see him holding his breath, trying not to make any noise. I took hold of his balls and massaged them, and Will placed his hand at the nape of my neck. I opened wider and allowed him to hold my head as he pushed in deeper.

Watching him try to contain himself made me smile, and Will looked down at me with a slight reprimand.

'For fuck's sake Lucy,' he whispered with warmth in his eyes, and he held my head in place.

I began to massage the area just behind his balls, and he obviously liked it because before I knew it, he was thrusting his release straight down my throat while he desperately tried to suppress his groans, and I began to giggle.

He dragged me back up to standing, kissing my giggles away and pulled his jeans and boxers back up. Then, pinning me up against the vanity with his hips, he said, 'Are you gonna go and smoke by the pool now?'

And I realised our joke had almost become a reality, and it wiped the smile straight off my face.

'You are not *that* girlfriend,' Will said quickly, realising I'd taken offence, and he kissed me again. 'Don't ever think that.'

Five minutes later, we were back in the kitchen with the others, all checking if I was okay. It was quite sweet that they were all so concerned, but I assured them I was alright.

Mat was a bit pissed, not in the American way, in the English way, and when we all decided to head back out to the pool, he put his arm around me.

'If I've lost my job over what I said earlier, just tell me now,' he slurred.

Even though he tried to say it quietly, because he was drunk, it was pretty loud, and Will heard. I looked at Will, astonished that he thought I had so much influence over his employment, but he smiled and looked at the ceiling as if to signify he didn't care, despite now realising Mat was the one who had spilt the beans about the song.

'I think you're fine, as long as you can sneak me a copy,' I teased.

Mat looked at me with a pained expression, not realising I was winding him up.

'Do you really think I would make you do that?'

'If you do, I will kill you,' Will interjected a little too seriously. 'You'll have to be patient, Daniels,' he said, pulling me onto a sun lounger with him.

Poor Mat, he was fairly new to the fold, and I could tell he didn't feel settled. He didn't actually need to be here for the recording process, but Will's manager had suggested he hang out with the band for a few days before the tour so that they could all get to know each other properly.

'Do you have a significant other?' I asked him.

'I do... it's kinda new, so it's early days,' he said, looking out across to the view. 'She lives in Brooklyn, so I won't be seeing her again until this lot finish.'

'You should have said, you could have brought her with you,' Will said.

'Ah, it's too early for that,' he admitted, 'thanks though.'

'Well, you'll bring her to the gig, right?' Will said, asking but also confirming an invitation.

'Sure, I'll ask her if she's free,' he said, feeling a little more relaxed. 'How long have you guys been together?'

Will and I looked at each other, both of us checking to see who would respond, and he gestured with his hand for me to answer.

'A couple of months now, it's been... an unconventional start,' I said, looking at Will.

'We're getting there, though,' he replied, looking back with a slight frown.

'It must be tough, but you guys seem rock solid,' Mat said, finishing his fizz, swiftly being topped up by Steph who was doing the rounds. 'I mean, how do you even go about meeting someone genuine?' he asked, aiming the question at Will, and Will laughed.

'You find someone who doesn't know who the fuck you are, and then you don't tell her until it massively backfires,' he said, and I smiled, looking down at myself.

'You can say that again,' Steph said, sitting down next to Mat. I noticed that Paul had joined Jake for a cigarette, and I turned to Will.

'I didn't know....' I began, but Will put his index finger up to my lips, and I realised that this was not something I'd be sharing with Hannah any time soon.

'This one totally put her through the mill,' Steph said, pointing the bottle of champagne she was still holding at Will. 'She went MIA at a festival and had the whole site looking for her.'

I closed my eyes at the memory, and Will pulled me in close.

'Hey, I read about that, that was just before I landed this job. I totally thought it was made up.' He took another sip of his drink and then added. 'Niall would love that story.'

'Niall who?' I asked, assuming he was talking about a friend.

'Niall O'Brien... we've hung out a couple of times, that's why I had him in mind when Kieron....' He trailed off, and I wasn't sure if Will had given him a look, but then he said, 'Do you know who Niall O'Brien is?'

I laughed.

'Of course, she bloody does, we had him before you!' Steph said. 'I bet you haven't even seen an episode of the sitcom he was in.'

'You've lost me,' Mat confirmed.

'You haven't lived,' she said, and I laughed with her, having a little private British joke. It was so good having my friends around me. It wasn't until they arrived that I realised I'd been missing an appendage. Paul and Jake came back to join us, and the conversation moved on.

Steph and I got chatting about Zara, and she filled me in on the latest with her divorce. It had become very messy as I'd predicted, but I was pleased to hear that she was standing firm and had a fantastic lawyer.

'Well, I hope she rinses him for all he's worth. Is he still with that woman in Cornwall?' I asked.

'She left him!' Steph confirmed, and my jaw dropped.

'So, Will, what do you think about *hot stuff* here landing a modelling contract? She could be the next Eva Herzigova,' she said, looking down at herself and adding, 'Hello Boys,' quoting a famous ad campaign from our teens.

I began to giggle until I saw Will's stony expression.

'Over the Wire are a lingerie company?' Will said questioningly but before I could answer Jake shoved his shoulder.

'Where have you been? Living under a rock!' Jake asked, standing and picking up a few empty glasses, but Will's eyes did not leave mine.

'I... assumed you knew that,' I added.

'No. I did not. And no, I am not happy about it.'

The group grew silent, and all eyes were on Will.

'Come on, man, it's not as if she's gonna be naked,' Jake said, trying to ease the tension Will had suddenly created, but instead, Will stood up, facing up to Jake.

'How would you like it if your girlfriend was strutting around in her underwear in front of a camera,' he sneered, poking his index finger into Jake's chest. 'So that some sleaze can sit in their living room, jerking off to her.'

What the hell! Is that what he honestly thought? This was supposed to be about empowering women to feel comfortable in their own skin. The thought of men looking at me hadn't even crossed my mind.

'Dude, chill the fuck out,' Jake said, shoving him back with his free hand. 'We all know Lucy is yours. Stop being so possessive.'

Steph shot me a glance with her eyebrows raised, clearly waiting for me to step in. Paul shook his head, demonstrating his annoyance that the atmosphere had taken a turn, and Jake turned on his heel with an aggravated sigh, heading back up to the house with the empties.

Will looked down at me, his tongue in his cheek, but I wasn't about to poke the bear. It wasn't the time or the place.

'Shall we talk about this later?' I suggested.

'Fine,' Will said flatly, sitting down but not willing to make eye contact with anyone.

Jake reappeared with a tray of shots, and as he handed them out, the tension began to dissipate.

Mat was already wasted, but they encouraged him to drink more.

I pulled on Will's arm and frowned at him.

He leaned in.

'It's his initiation night.'

I realised this was the first time Mat had been invited to join them after work.

'He's gonna stay in the studio tonight if that's okay?'

'You don't need to ask me that. This is your place,' I whispered back, and he pouted.

'You're gonna have to get used to it sometime,' he replied, and then he kissed me chastely.

I was doing my best to get used to everything, but this was never going to be my place. My place was in Clevedon.

Poor Mat looked like he was going to pass out. Steph was practically holding him up.

'Do you not think it would be a good idea to get him to bed?' I asked Will.

'No! He either has to pass out or spew first!'

I shook my head but couldn't help smiling at his boyish behaviour.

'And tomorrow, he has to sit through Jake laying his drums down,' Paul added.

'You guys are so cruel,' I complained, and they all agreed, grinning at each other.

'So, what is the process from creation to release?' Steph asked.

Just then, Mat heaved, and in her haste to find a suitable vessel to contain the puke, Steph passed him a champagne flute. Will and I quickly lifted our feet onto the sun lounger as Mat puked into the glass, all over his hand and onto the floor while Jake took a picture.

'Eww, you just puked on my feet,' Steph said as Will, Jake and Paul started clapping and cheering.

'For crying out loud, you lot act like children sometimes,' I said, trying not to smile as I started to get up to find some kitchen roll.

'Sorry, Mom,' Jake said like a toddler with a wolfish grin.

'Where are you going?' Will asked.

'To clean that up!' I replied, and Will grabbed me.

'Oh no, you don't,' and he lifted me and started carrying me into the house, avoiding the sick.

'You can't leave that for Miranda. It's not fair,' I protested.

'Watch me,' he said, increasing his grip around me, and he took me all the way into the bedroom and placed me on the bed.

'That's awful, Will, poor Miranda,' I said, feeling irresponsible, but Will was already pulling my bikini bottoms off.

Chapter 22

Even though Will was in the studio again the following day, he was doing a marvellous job of embarrassing me at every given opportunity. He had sent a Limousine to collect us and take us to the spa, not a modern Limo, a 1980s retro Limo. It was actually quite funny. Steph thought it was hilarious, but Claire and Zara were a little perplexed.

Upon arriving at the spa, we discovered that Will had arranged for us all to have the full works. The *Ultimate Retreat* included a massage, facial, manicure and pedicure. I had also been booked in for a haircut, and I quickly figured out that the place had been booked out exclusively. We were greeted with healthy smoothies, and I was handed a gift bag.

'Aww, so romantic,' Zara said.

There was a note which I now recognised to be in Will's handwriting.

Don't be mad at me. I want you to relax without worrying about getting papped. I hope you like the gift. I love you X

I was going to wait to open it in private, but Claire had other ideas.

'What is it, what is it?' she said, jumping up and down on the spot.

'Oh my God,' I said, covering my face with my hands when I saw the Stephen Webster box inside. Surely the spa day was enough. He really shouldn't have. I carefully slid the box out of its sleeve and opened it. It was a pair of black pavé butterfly stud earrings.

'Aww, to match the necklace,' Steph said and put her hand on her heart.

'And the bracelet,' I whispered.

'Wait. He's got you a necklace, a bracelet and a pair of earrings?' Claire asked.

'I know, totally over the top,' I said.

'Oh my God, you know what this means, girls... the ring is next!!' she said, clapping her hands with glee.

'No,' I said, shaking my head as if to make the word more poignant. 'We haven't even discussed that. We've only been together a couple of months.'

'Oh, come on, if he asked you tomorrow, you're not going to say no,' Claire said.

I looked down at the box and wondered what I would say. By agreeing to marry him, his place would be mine, and mine his. I'd be agreeing to a life of organised trips and the constant dread of the paparazzi. Is that what I wanted? Would it always be like this?

'Ohhh, are things not as rosy as they seem?' Claire asked.

'It's not that, he's amazing. I just don't know if I will ever get used to being so... restricted,' I tried to explain.

'If by this...' she said, twirling her finger in the air, 'you feel restricted, I think I could put up with it,' she said.

I glanced at Steph, who gave me a sympathetic smile. I think she got it, even if the others didn't. It was hard to explain, and from the outside, I was living the life of Riley. I put it to the back of my mind, it's not something I needed to think about anyway, and I carefully put the earrings back in the bag.

As we were being assigned our therapists, I sent a quick text to Will.

I can't imagine how much you've spent to avoid a picture being taken but thank you and thank you for my gift. I love you. X

By four-thirty, we had all been suitably pampered, and I'd had my hair cut. I'd only had a trim as I was enjoying being able to put it up in the warmer weather, and it was now sitting neatly above my shoulders.

On the way home, I looked at everyone's nails and smiled to myself. It was funny that we had each chosen colours that represented our characters. Zara had gone for a classic pink, Steph had gone for a neon orange, Claire had a tortoiseshell design, and I had gone for neutral.

'What are we going to do tonight?' Zara asked.

'I was thinking of a BBQ by the pool?' I suggested.

'Sounds perfect. I'll try not to pass out tonight.'

'And then we could go clubbing,' Claire added, and I scrunched my nose up. 'Oh, come on! We're in LA.'

'We're here to see Lu,' Steph reminded her.

'What, we're just gonna sit around the pool for the next few days?' Claire asked.

'Let me speak to Will. It won't be until tomorrow, though, as he might not finish until late.'

Claire rolled her eyes, and I felt terrible. It was like I had to check with my Dad.

When we returned, Mat was sat at the island with his laptop, and the girls went off to pop their things away.

'Are you all right?' I asked.

'I've had better days, sorry, I'll head back to the studio now. I just couldn't handle the noise,' he said, and the poor guy looked awful.

'Oh, don't leave on our account. You're welcome to stay.'

I automatically got him a glass of water.

'Actually, I'm glad I caught you,' he said, turning to face me. 'I spoke to Niall today. He happens to be back in Brentwood tomorrow. If you want, I can ask Kieron to speak to the guys at The Night Show and organise something?'

I just looked at him wide-eyed.

'It might just give the public what they need, and the press might lay off you guys a bit. Have a chat with Will and let me know.'

Tomorrow was... tomorrow. I took a deep breath in.

'Um... yeah, I'll speak to Will.'

'They'll make you feel super relaxed, and Kieron will brief them on what they can and can't ask. Niall is a nice guy.'

'Okay, leave it with me,' I said and headed off to the bedroom, bumping into Steph on the way.

'We don't have to go out, babe.'

I looked past her to check Claire wasn't around and then ushered her into the bedroom.

'Oh wow, this is gorgeous,' she said, looking around Will's room... our room.

'The thing is, I'd love to go out, but if I get spotted, who knows what will happen? They can turn up like a swarm of locusts,' I explained.

'Maybe we could all go out? Safety in numbers?'

'Maybe...'

We both looked out at the view.

'Worth moving here for,' Steph said, and I looked at her. 'Are you not considering it? This place is amazing.'

'It is, and if it were in the UK, ideally Clevedon, it would be perfect. You're not here for a start!'

'But I could visit, the boys have got rooms already, and you could be a kept woman,' she winked.

'Can you imagine how bloody boring that would be?'

'You'd have to fill all those rooms with more babies to keep you busy,' she said, and I slapped her arm. We both heard someone clear their throat and looked round to see Will was standing in the doorway.

'Oh, hi, I wasn't expecting to see you until later,' I said.

'We finished early. Jake is like a machine,' he replied.

'I'm gonna go and catch up with the girls,' Steph said, squeezing my arm, excusing herself.

Will held the door open for her.

'Thanks so much for today, it was amazing,' she said.

'My pleasure.'

He strode into the room, cupping my face and kissing me gently.

'Your hair looks glossy.'

'My boyfriend arranged for me to have it cut,' I said, swishing it from side to side, 'and he also bought me some beautiful earrings.'

'This guy sounds amazing, but you don't appear to be wearing them,' he said.

'It wasn't the place to wear them.'

'Well, you can wear them tonight, I think the guys could do with a break, and I bumped into Claire in the hall. I think she wants to get lit.'

Trust that girl to get straight to the point. He kissed me more sensually this time, and I would have happily taken it further, but he pulled back.

'One of these days, I'm gonna give you something I'll expect you to wear every day.'

A surge of warmth charged through me as my breath quickly expelled. Was Claire right? Was he alluding to the fact that he was thinking of proposing?

'Will... I...'

He kissed me again. Surely this was something we would talk about.

'Let's take a shower,' he said, pulling me towards the bathroom.

Okay, maybe he didn't mean a proposal. Perhaps he just meant he'd buy me something for everyday wear.

An hour later, we headed out to the kitchen. I wore a green pleated calf-length satin skirt, a simple black boat neck tee tucked into it, and my gold strappy heels. I was also wearing the earrings and bracelet. I thought the necklace would have been overkill. The plan was to get some food and then head to a club. Everyone was already standing around the island drinking champagne.

'Aww, you look gorgeous,' Steph said, putting her arm around me.

'Thanks, babe. I love the colour of your blouse. Did you have that in mind when choosing the colour for your nails?' I asked, and she nodded.

'Right, we've got Tao's and then Tramp Stamp Granny's,' Mat announced.

'Aww, what? I wanted to go to Avalons,' Claire whined. 'Not some tramps place.'

I looked at Steph. Claire was beginning to piss me off.

'Sorry sweetheart, Avalons is off the menu, too risky,' Mat said.

'Thanks, man. Everything else sorted?' Will asked, and Mat nodded.

Zara passed me a glass of fizz. She'd been pretty quiet since she'd arrived, and I wondered if she was okay.

'Thanks, babe, you look stunning,' I said, and she smiled.

I couldn't help but notice that she glanced fleetingly at Jake.

Oh! Did she like him?

I took a packet of nuts out of the cupboard and filled two ramekin bowls. Will and Mat were chatting by the pool table, and signalled for me to come over, Will feeding his arm around my waist.

'So, we've got two cars coming, one with security, so I need you and Will in that car. One of us will travel with the girls,' Mat said, waving his hand towards Paul and Jake. 'We have a private area at Tao, but we have to walk through the main restaurant to get to it, so by the time we leave, there could be press. We'll just have to make a sharp exit and follow security signals. I've reserved a table at TSG's, but it's not separate from the rest of the venue, so we'll just have to see how we go. You and Lucy place yourselves along the back wall, okay?'

Will nodded, and he looked at me.

'Okay?' Will checked.

'Okay,' I said, and we all joined the rest of the group.

'Security briefing?' Steph whispered in my ear. She didn't miss a trick that one.

'Have you had a chance to speak to Will about The Night Show?' Mat asked me.

'What about it?' Will asked.

'Let's talk in the car,' Mat suggested.

I leaned over to Mat and whispered in his ear.

'Can you send Jake with the girls?'

He frowned, then smiled, then nodded. Will looked at me quizzically, and I looked straight back at him and shook my head, hoping that he'd understand that I'd fill him in later. Mat gave two loud claps and announced that the transport had arrived.

I felt a little torn that I wasn't travelling with the girls, but very happy that I was spending some time with Will.

'So, Kieron emailed to say he'd spoken to the team, and they would be stoked to have an interview with you guys tomorrow,' Mat said, and Will looked at me.

We still hadn't had the opportunity to discuss it, and I think he was concerned it was too much, too soon. It was strange, since the girls had arrived, I felt a bit more confident and safer, I suppose. Safety in numbers. Steph was right. I was coming round to the idea, and if it meant the press would lay off us, surely that would make life easier.

'Where?' I whispered, almost not wanting to know.

I don't know why that was important, but I had an image in my mind of sitting in an expressionless hotel room. Each on one of those easy chairs that hotels always had, facing each other with a coffee table and a fruit bowl between us, sipping on water, and it all being very prim and proper. Very British.

'I'm sure they'll come up with some suggestions, but I think they're pretty keen, so you could probably call the shots. They could do it at the house if you feel most comfortable there?' Mat said, looking at Will to check he hadn't suggested something out of turn.

'If you want to do this, you choose. If the house is right, do it there,' Will said, squeezing my hand.

'Can we talk about this later?' I asked Will, suddenly feeling like I was being put on the spot and I needed to speak to him about Over the Wire too.

He put his arm around me. Not that I was bothered about Mat or Paul being there, but I wanted Will's opinion.

'Sure,' he replied, and Mat nodded. He was very perceptive, and I liked that about him.

Tao was amazing. We managed to get in and seated without too much ado. The private seating area was on a mezzanine level overlooking the main restaurant. It was all very symmetrical, with an identical private room opposite on the other side of the open-plan restaurant.

Despite being so open, the restaurant itself felt quite cosy, and I'm sure the wooden beams and flooring helped warm the place. A vast electric blue Buddha sat at the back of the room, and the lampshades were magenta pink, adding a pop of colour to the otherwise plain brown backdrop.

The table was long and rectangular, it could have easily seated more than eight of us, but it meant we had plenty of room. I sat next to Will, who had placed himself with his back to the restaurant, I wasn't sure whether that was a purposeful move or not.

Steph plopped herself down next to me with Paul on her other side. I was pleased to see that Zara had sat next to Jake, and I caught her eye and smiled. She immediately looked down at the menu, obviously not wanting to draw attention. Claire almost fell off her seat as she sat between Jake and Mat, and I realised she was already drunk.

'Don't worry about choosing,' Mat announced. 'I've asked them to provide a selection.'

A waiter suddenly appeared with a tray of cocktails. It was called Tao-tini, a vodka-based drink with rum, cranberry and lime. It was delicious, and I looked over at Claire, who was already guzzling hers like it was going out of fashion. I was going to have to keep an eye on her.

Steph was chatting to Paul about Hannah and the baby, and Will leaned in, using the opportunity to put his hand on my thigh.

'So, things seem to be moving forward with this interview.'

I looked over at Mat and was pleased to see he was pouring Claire some water, and I nodded slowly.

'What are you thinking?' he asked.

'Um… I'm thinking that if by doing it, and Mat is right, the press might give us some breathing space, and surely that's a positive thing?'

Will was biting his cheek, not clarifying what Mat had said.

'However, the thought of actually doing it is making me feel a bit sick.'

He smiled.

I put my elbow on the back of my chair, creating a wall from the rest of the dinner party. I wanted his input. I didn't want to decide alone.

'I know you want me to give you a solid response, but despite what Mat said, it's not guaranteed. Yes, it could mean they lay off us for a bit, but on the flip side, we might give them something innocuous, but they want the whole nine yards.'

I looked down at my lap, thinking.

'We might find that by doing this interview, the floodgates open, and everyone wants a piece of the pie,' he added.

I looked over my shoulder and down at the restaurant below. I spotted a couple of people looking up. Despite it being a *private* dining area, it was almost like we were on show, and it felt wrong that we were looking down on everyone else.

I was undecided and somehow more confused. Will put his arm across my shoulders, shielding us from the onlookers and put his lips to my ear.

'Sleep on it,' he whispered, 'after you've slept with me,' he said in a low, seductive voice which caused all the hairs on the back of my neck to stand to attention.

His hand moved further up my thigh as he kissed my neck just below my ear, and I closed my eyes for a second, before I realised we were suddenly surrounded by waiters. Damn it. I still hadn't had the chance to speak to him about Over the Wire.

Food began to appear on the table. It was so colourful and beautiful, with vibrant greens and bright reds, and vivid pink flowers mirrored the pink of the lampshades dotted around. Everyone started tucking in, apart from Claire, who had bypassed the eating stage, and I nudged Steph. She looked at me knowingly.

'We're gonna have to send her home before the club at this rate,' Steph predicted.

'If she goes home, someone will have to go with her,' I replied, thinking *someone* would need to be me.

Will leaned in again.

'Were you asking Mat earlier to get Claire drunk?' Will asked, obviously picking up on what we were talking about.

'No... and as you can see, she doesn't need Mat's input.'

'So, what was it then?' he pressed.

I looked over at Jake and Zara, they were chatting and laughing, and Jake had pretty much blocked Claire with his back. I looked at Will and then back at them. He watched them for a few moments and then turned to me.

'I hope she's not looking for a happy ever after,' Will warned.

'She's divorcing her happy ever after,' I replied, and Will gave me a half-smile.

'So, you instigated this?' Will asked.

'I may have asked Mat to send Jake in the girl's car,' I confirmed, and Will smiled, shaking his head.

There was a moment's pause while we ate. The Over the Wire contract was eating away at my subconscious, and I needed to get it off my chest.

'Can we talk about this modelling thing?' I ventured.

Will sighed as he took his time chewing before swallowing, and I bit my lip in anticipation, not knowing how this would go. Eventually, he turned to look me in the eye.

'I'm not happy about it, Lu.'

My shoulders dropped in disappointment. I really wanted to do it but not without Will's backing.

Will took my hand in his, drawing me in closer so I could hear him over the general hubbub of the restaurant.

'Look, I can see this is something you wanna do. So... sell it to me,' he said, quirking his lip and flicking his eyebrow up playfully.

'What?' I asked, smiling.

'Why is it important to you? I can guarantee that if you do this interview, you'll have a whole bunch of offers on the table to choose from, so why this?'

He kept the tone of his question light, but I knew I'd need to put forward a convincing proposal if he was going to consider it.

'Because... if I'm going to put myself out there, I want it to be worthwhile. I want to make a positive impact. I want women like me, who don't feel confident about their bodies because they've been comparing themselves to catwalk models all their lives, to overcome that and feel sexy and desirable.'

As I was talking, Will's mouth began to gape open, but I didn't let that deter me.

'I want women to see my stretch marks and wrinkles and the odd grey hair and realise that it's natural to look like that when you've had two kids and...'

He grabbed hold of my face and kissed me mid-sentence. I tried to pull away so that I could finish, but he wouldn't let go. Embarrassed, I began to feel my cheeks heat as I struggled to break free while he laughed against my lips.

Eventually, he released me, but before I could chastise him for interrupting me, he said, 'Okay, okay, you got me.'

My eyes lit up.

'But I'm coming to the shoot,' he added.

I grinned.

'Deal.'

As Mat had foreseen, the press was well established outside by the time we were due to leave. I looked over at Claire, trying to gauge how drunk she was and whether there needed to be a change of plan, but she seemed miraculously with it suddenly. Mat moved around the table and crouched down by Will.

'I'm gonna send Jake and Paul out with the girls first,' he said, and my breathing began to quicken. 'That leaves me and Fletch to be on hand for you guys.'

'Sounds good, what's the score out there?' Will asked.

'It's not just press... and being that Lucy is with us, I think we just get straight in the car,' Mat suggested.

'Definitely,' Will nodded.

Mat announced what the plan was to everyone else. Jake and Paul pretty much ignored him as this arrangement was clearly run-of-the-mill to them. Steph looked at me studiedly, and I shook my head. Claire, however, had other ideas.

'No! That's a rubbish idea. We want Lu with us,' she said as if she was in competition with Mat.

I looked at her, my mouth open, but before I could say anything, Steph just said, 'Claire,' in a warning tone.

'Don't *Claire* me, she's one of the girls,' she stated, and I looked at Will, utterly embarrassed by her behaviour.

'Claire, would you mind if Lu travelled with me? I haven't seen her all day,' Will asked, trying to smooth over the uncomfortable environment she had created.

She tutted and then said, 'Oh, you two, you're so fucking loved up.' With that, she picked up her bag and walked toward the exit.

She had no idea of the freedom she had by doing that.

'I'm sorry,' I said to Will as Steph squeezed my arm in a kind of good luck manner, and I smiled back at her before she caught up with Claire.

'Are you sure that's just alcohol?' Will asked, but it wasn't really a question, more of an observation.

We waited for the others to leave, and as the minutes ticked by, I became more nervous. It reminded me of the time at the London gig, which was bad enough.

'Okay, the cars in place,' Mat said, and I could see Fletch making his way back towards us.

The general atmosphere in the restaurant had changed. There was a strange hush as we headed down the stairs, and someone took a picture with their phone. It was as if that was the green light the diners had been waiting for, and literally everyone got their phones out.

As we approached the main entrance, I could see the crowd. There were so many people. Will pulled me in close, Mat positioned himself next to me, and Fletch stepped up beside Will.

The screams were ear-piercing, the flashes and the shouting constant. I could see the car, but then there was a big surge, and I lost my balance. Will held me up, but I let go of my clutch, and it fell to the floor. Mat saw it happen and dipped down to try to retrieve it, but someone grabbed my wrist and yanked my arm. Will shouted something, and Fletch jumped in to assist me, but then all these women were clawing at Will, grabbing his jacket, and pulling on his t-shirt.

I couldn't see Mat at all, the crowd cascaded around us, and I lost sight of the car. I wasn't sure which direction to turn. Someone grabbed my waist, but I didn't know if it was Will or not, so I resisted, but Mat reappeared behind me and pushed me forward, as Will took my hand and pulled me into the car forcefully.

'Fuck! Are you okay?' Will asked as he dragged me onto his lap, Mat following as Fletch jumped into the passenger seat.

He immediately turned to face us, 'Is everyone all right?'

I slowly lifted my wrist because it was stinging, my bracelet was broken, and I had a nasty gash on the inside of my arm.

'Shit, you're gonna need to get that seen to,' Mat said. 'Emergency Department,' he instructed the driver.

'Lu, say something,' Will said, brushing my hair out of my face, but all I could think about was my bag. It had my phone in it.

'You might want this,' Fletch said and handed my bag over the partition.

Mat took it on my behalf. I breathed a huge sigh of relief and wrapped my uninjured arm around Will, burying my face into his chest. Will kissed my hair and then put his head in his hand, sighing and shaking his head at the same time.

Mat had found a tissue for me to wrap around my wrist, but my skirt was already blood-stained. Will gently took my bracelet off and gave it to Mat to put in my bag. He turned my hand over to inspect the cut. It wasn't too bad. If I'd done it at home, I wouldn't have gone to casualty, but it did need dressing.

'I need to call Paul,' Will said.

'I'll call him,' Mat offered, grabbing his phone. 'Hey, yep, on our way to the ER, Lucy got cut.'

There was a pause, and I could hear loud music in the background.

'Hold on, I'll hand you over,' he handed the phone to Will.

'Hey,' Will said. 'They were fucking animals, Lucy got hurt... she's okay, just need to get it looked at.'

I could hear Paul saying something about Milly.

'Okay, man, we'll just have to see,' he handed the phone back to Mat.

I could hear my phone vibrating in my bag, and I remembered my promise to the boys.

'I need to contact the boys,' I said.

Mat passed me my bag, but my hands were shaking so much I couldn't even open it.

'I'll do it,' Will said, using his phone to ring Frankie.

They were none the wiser, as Will had to explain the whole thing, but as soon as I heard Frankie's voice, I began to well up.

'I think your mom might wanna say hi.'

Will held the phone to my ear.

'Hey Frankie, yeah, I'm okay. If I were at home, I'd just put a plaster on it.'

Playing the situation down in true parenting style. Will wiping my tears from my cheek and Mat turning to look out the window. Was he getting emotional too?

'I'll call you tomorrow, okay, have fun, love you, love to Pads.'

Will put the phone away, wrapping his arm back around me.

Mat coughed and said, 'We're here.'

A short while later, after being cleaned up, dressed and told I had a lucky escape as it was close to a main artery, we climbed back into the car.

'Home?' Will asked.

Having recovered from my adrenaline dump, I didn't feel like returning to Wills.

'No, I should at least go and see the girls. I feel like I've abandoned them,' I said.

'Lu, they'll understand if you wanna go home,' Will replied, surprised at my response.

'I don't want to go home. I want a drink and Mat? Can you tell Kieron we'll do that interview,' I said adamantly.

'Okay,' Mat said with uncertainty in his tone, looking at Will for confirmation. Will just held his hands up to indicate it was my decision.

I had to do something, it was getting out of hand, and if I didn't try, I might regret it. I sighed and looked out of the window, Will took my hand and squeezed it, and nothing more was said until we reached the venue.

It was much smaller than I'd expected. It was classified as a piano bar, and on the sign, it said, *Drinks, Dancing and Upscale Debauchery*. I could see by the clientele standing outside, either in the queue or smoking, that it attracted all walks of life, and I smiled. There was a pause before we got out, and I looked from Will to Mat.

'What are we waiting for? It can't get much worse.'

I had a sense of bravado about me, I was really done with it all, bloody skirt be damned. I just wanted to have a good time, but I sensed the guys were hesitant. I went to open the door myself, but Mat beat me to it.

'I'll do the doors,' Mat said as he hopped out and marched across the street to speak to the guy on the door.

Will got out, as did Fletch, and someone smoking, dressed in full drag wolf-whistled. I didn't know whether they identified as a man or woman, but they placed their hand on their hip while fluttering their eyelashes and said, 'Oh, look who we have here!'

Will turned back immediately, rolling his eyes and promptly picked me up and carried me into the bar. The bar stretched down the left-hand side, and there were tables and chairs to the right. At the very end of the room, there was a little snug, and that's where our group sat. It was so busy in the bar with people standing waiting for drinks and chatting that they barely noticed our arrival.

'Oh, thank God,' Steph said, standing as soon as she saw us. 'I tried to call. I've just been looking at the pictures. What the hell happened?'

Will put me down, and she gave me a huge hug.

'I'm fine, there was just a crowd surge, and it all got out of hand,' I said, and she looked at my dressing and then my skirt, her eyes widening.

'Sorry guys, I need Will and Lucy on that back wall,' Mat announced.

Paul kindly ushered everyone around so we could sit in relative safety. Claire was not happy about being moved and made it perfectly obvious by standing up and taking herself off to the toilets, huffing as she did so. I watched her walk across the bar, open-mouthed, as I slid in next to Paul. She had some nerve, that girl.

'Are you okay?' Paul asked, putting his arm around me.

'I'm fine, honestly. I think the hospital trip was slight overkill,' I said for all to hear.

I didn't want to keep going over it.

'The pictures look pretty horrific. Our fans are savage,' Paul said, looking at Will as they did a funny handshake. It was a thing between them.

'It's been a while since I've seen it that bad. It was Lu they grabbed first,' Will admitted.

'Shots?' Jake said as he arrived at the table with a tray and started handing them out. 'You get a runner,' he told me as he put two shot glasses in front of me.

I was so desperate to forget about the evening's ordeal and get on a level, that I picked up the first shot and downed it before he'd even finished handing them out. Everyone raised their glasses, clinking before we downed them in unison, just as Claire returned from the toilets.

'Oh, wait for me, why not?' she slurred, perching on the end of the booth bench and picking up her drink, spilling some of it on her dress as she did so. I ignored her, I needed to because she was pissing me off so much, I was going to say something I'd regret. She hadn't even asked if I was okay, mind you, neither had Zara.

Oh! I nudged Will's thigh and nodded to Jake & Zara. They weren't kissing, but their mouths were way closer than they needed to be while they were talking. He looked back at me and smiled.

'Do I need to start calling you Cupid?' he asked, and Paul twigged what we were talking about.

'Yeah, I was gonna ask you about that... so it's a thing?' Paul asked.

'I don't know, but it could be?' I replied.

Just then, Claire slid off the end of the bench, plonking onto the floor and smashing her glass in the process. I put my head in my hands as Steph and Mat got up to assist her.

'Come on, let's get you off to the ladies,' Steph said, shooting me a look.

I went to get up to help, but Will grabbed my hips and sat me back down.

'You need to stay here,' Will said sternly, and I looked at him, taken aback.

He wasn't in charge of me, and I was getting fed up with being told where to go and what to do.

'I'm sorry,' he said more softly, realising his instruction had vexed me. 'We can't make a scene.'

I looked along the length of the bar with my jaw set, trying to breathe steadily.

'Lucy, look at me.'

I closed my eyes, and Will gently put his hand on my cheek and turned my face to his, bringing his forehead to mine.

'Look at me,' he growled, and I opened my eyes.

His beautiful green eyes were staring straight back at me. My heart felt like it had skipped a beat.

'There she is,' and he kissed me.

I kissed him back and Will slid his tongue into my mouth. I melted into him, if we'd been anywhere else, I would have taken it further, but I was acutely aware that we were in public. Will drew back first.

'I'm gonna have to pull you onto my lap in a minute to avoid embarrassment,' he whispered.

'I wish we'd gone back to yours now,' I admitted, whispering back, and he smiled. 'I need restraining,' I added.

He pulled me onto his lap, and I giggled.

Steph and Claire arrived at the table. Steph sat her on a chair and went off to the bar to get some water. Claire was so wasted. I had no idea how she could still function.

'Well, Howdy, partners!!'

Someone shouted over the music, and we all turned to see Milly.

'Milly!' I said, hopping up, forgetting I was sitting on Will's lap for a reason, and he leant forward towards the table.

I flung my arms around her.

'How are you? Are you playing here tonight?'

'I am, but more to the point....' She lifted my arm. 'What happened to you?'

'Oh, it's nothing, really,' I said, waving it off as Steph arrived back.

'Milly, this is Steph.'

I allowed them to shake hands before I pointed towards Zara and then Claire, introducing them in turn.

'Here she is,' Claire piped up suddenly, 'with her *new* set of friends,' she slurred, and she gave me the bitchiest look.

I closed my eyes, humiliated that Milly had heard and apologised. She was making such a fool out of herself.

Claire cackled and added, 'You should be apologising to me, for bringing me to this shit-hole,' she said, gaining everyone's attention at the table.

My humiliation turned to anger.

'Claire, you're being rude,' Zara said, but it was as if she hadn't even heard.

'We should be at Avalon,' she added.

Milly nodded with her eyebrows high. I wasn't sure if she'd taken offence or not.

'Claire, will you stop being so ungrateful,' I said, putting my hands on my hips.

'It's not worth it, Lu,' Steph piped up.

'No, it's unacceptable. She doesn't deserve to be here,' I replied.

'Oh, would you listen to her? She's above us now, calling all the shots,' Claire said.

I had heard enough.

'I'm calling the shots because you're being a fucking, thankless bitch.'

'Ohhh, this is gettin' spicy,' Jake said with glee as Claire repeated the end of my sentence under her breath before using the table to hoist herself up.

She looked at me and then looked at my arm as if seeing it for the first time and frowned.

'You're the ungrateful one. You have it all,' she said, waving her hand around dramatically. 'Yet you are still undecided,' she added, pointing at me.

There was an unusual stillness that gripped the table. What the hell? What was she talking about? I looked at her, my jaw wide and shook my head.

'You don't know what you're talking about. I think you need to go,' I said, turning to Will, and he just looked down at the table.

Mat sighed audibly with frustration and stood up.

'I think we all need to go,' he said, getting his phone out.

I looked at Milly, unable to convey how gutted I was. It could have been such a fun evening, but it clearly wasn't meant to be.

'Don't worry, honestly. I think it will be a packed evening with or without you,' she said, nodding towards the queue.

I gave her another hug.

'Sorry about Claire. I wish you'd all met under happier circumstances.'

She pulled away and held my shoulders.

'It's fine. I'm sure I'll see them again at the gig,' she reminded me.

Bloody hell, everyone Will knew was going to this gig.

'Okay, guys, they're here,' Mat said. 'On me.'

I looked over at Will, but he didn't make eye contact. For fuck's sake, was he going to take Claire's drunken comment as gospel? Steph looked at me, reading the situation straight away.

'Do you wanna ride with us?' Steph asked.

I looked at Claire with disdain, but before I could answer, Mat put his hand on the small of my back to usher me out. I looked at Steph, imploring her to take the lead, but she didn't.

The ride home was awful. No one said anything, and the tension was almost palpable. Will was just looking out of the window, ignoring me. Paul and Mat were facing us but doing everything not to look. I felt like the guilty party for ending the night so abruptly. They could have all stayed out, and I could have taken Claire home and given her a well-deserved slap.

When we pulled up, Will got out of the car and slammed the door so hard that Fletch turned to look. I looked at Paul, who gave me a pained smile and then at Mat, who gave his shoulders the slightest shrug before opening the door to allow me to step out.

The girl's car pulled up, and Jake got out, offering his hand to Zara. Well, at least one thing had worked out this evening. Steph guided Claire towards the door, but she threw up in the flower bed before they made it. I shook my head and strode in.

Will was nowhere to be seen. Leaving everyone to sort themselves out, I went to the bedroom. Will was pacing. I walked over to the bedside table and put my purse down. Then, sitting on the bed, I started to take my shoes off.

'Do you want me to go and sleep in Steph's room?' I asked, mainly so we could start talking, more than anything else.

'I don't know. Do you want to go and sleep in Steph's room?' he bounced back at me in a sardonic way.

'Not really. I want you to stop being angry at me for no reason,' I said.

'I'm angry because your so-called friend seems to know more about how you are feeling than I do,' he said scathingly.

I stood back up and turned to face him.

'And you're....'

But he cut in before I could finish.

'Ever since we got here, I've been worried that you're gonna run, and you've reassured me time and time again, and now I discover that you're undecided? What the fuck, Lucy?'

His voice was getting louder, and I was sure everyone was listening to us from the kitchen.

'And now the whole fucking household knows, so at least there's no explaining to do,' he added.

'Can I speak now?' I asked, still cross that he'd cut in.

'The floor is yours,' he said, sweeping his arm out in front of him as if he was ushering me on stage and then placing them on his hips. 'I can't wait to hear what fucked up sham you're gonna make of this explanation.'

I shook my head, willing the words to come and feeling under immense pressure.

'So... you're gonna believe a pissed-up... woman?' I couldn't even refer to her as a friend at that moment. 'Who I haven't seen for weeks over the *private* conversations you and I have had?'

I purposefully emphasised the word private and spoke at a reduced level, hoping he would respond in kind.

'Well, it's surprising how the truth comes out when you're fucked up on coke.'

I looked at him. Did he know that for sure, or was he guessing?

'Well, there's no point in continuing this conversation if you're going to believe her over me.'

I went to walk into the bathroom to get ready for bed, but he grabbed my arm, forgetting that I'd hurt it.

'Ow!' I shouted and pulled my arm back, cradling it in the hope he hadn't reopened the cut.

It obviously shocked him, and he took a step back. I slowly looked back up at him, tears pricking my eyes.

'You know, if I were gonna run, today would have been the day, but instead, I agreed to an interview. Not for my gain. For ours.'

My voice cracked on the last word, and I couldn't hold on any longer. I quickly turned, heading into the bathroom and locking the door before the tears fell. I sat on the edge of the bath and grabbed a towel to sob into.

A few moments passed, and then he started banging on the door, making me jump.

'Lucy, let me in. I'm sorry, okay? Please, let me in.'

I just wanted to be on my own for a bit. I was so cross with Claire. She just didn't understand and had caused all of this. I wish she'd gone to Avalon alone and then gone home.

Just then, the sliding door that led out to the balcony opened, making me jump again, and Will stepped in. I looked up in shock and then looked back at the mascara-stained towel.

He exhaled loudly. 'I'm really sorry.'

He came and knelt at my feet, looking up at me.

'I jumped to conclusions,' he said, kneeling up. 'Is your arm okay?'

He slowly turned it over, but it was fine.

'I don't know how to put your mind at rest. I'm not going anywhere. I can't give you any more. You have all of me, and it doesn't seem to be enough,' I said, wiping my tears away. 'Yes, I'm missing the boys. Yes, I miss home, yes, I could really do with not being attacked by your deluded fans, but I'm still here, and I love you.'

I sniffed, and he moved the towel out of the way and hugged me.

'I'm sorry I doubted you,' he said, releasing me so he could see my face, and I sighed.

'We just seem to keep going around in circles,' I said, and he shook his head.

'We won't be once we've got this album down—it won't be long. We're nearly there. I think we'll have it done in time for the gig,' he said.

Wow, that was only a few days away.

'Really? That's amazing... a whole album?'

I was astonished.

'We've had everyone on it. The second we finish a track, we get the team working on it.' He looked up at me. 'I'm gonna get up now because my knees are killing me.'

I chuckled, and as he stood up, he pulled me up to stand.

'I'm sorry about Claire. I don't know what's gotten into her. I mean, she likes to have a good time, but I don't think I've ever seen her that drunk,' I said.

Will lifted his eyebrows. He thought that she was on something else. Where would she have even got it from? Now wasn't the time, I needed to go to bed, and she was probably passed out, anyway.

Chapter 23

I could hear a knocking, and it took me a second to register that the knocking was on the bedroom door. I pulled the sheets up around me.

'Hello?'

'It's me. Can I come in?'

It was Steph.

'Yeah, is everything okay?' I asked.

'Everything's fine. I just wanted to come and see you, check you're all right,' she said, walking towards the bed while I rubbed my eyes.

'I'm okay, we're okay, he just went off at the deep end,' I explained.

'Did he hurt you?' Steph asked suddenly.

'No, why? He wouldn't do that,' I said honestly.

'I just heard something and... was worried,' she admitted, and it was clear everyone had heard our disagreement.

'Has Claire appeared yet this morning?' I asked.

'Nope, and neither has Zara... I think she may have had a late night,' she said with a sparkle in her eye, and I smiled. 'Anyway, I think Mat needs to speak to you.'

'Okay, I'm just gonna jump in the shower.'

'THERE YOU ARE!' MAT said as I headed into the kitchen. 'They wanted to do this afternoon, but Kieron wants to prep you first, so I managed to put them off until early evening. I told them you were still recovering after yesterday.'

I looked at him, not quite believing this was actually happening, and I swallowed what little saliva I had left in my mouth.

'You haven't changed your mind, have you?'

I shook my head.

'Phew, I was worried for a sec. Anyway, you weren't up, so Will told me to arrange for it to take place here.'

'Here,' I said, nodding, my mind already splintered.

He put a coffee in front of me and then a hand on my shoulder.

'You okay after last night?' he asked, and I wasn't sure if he was referring to my arm or the argument. 'Paul said he can be... impulsive.'

Okay, so he meant the argument, and I wasn't sure how to respond. I mean, it was a bit weird that Mat was broaching the subject with me. Surely his allegiances lay with Will.

'I'm the TM, Lucy, my job will be to ensure everything runs smoothly, and you're a big part of that,' he said, guessing I was confused.

'I'm okay. He just needs a lot of assurance,' I said, and he smiled a knowing smile.

'Well, for the record, I think you're amazing. He's a lucky guy,' he said before dropping his hand and taking a call.

Was he being genuine or coming on to me? I shook my head, picked up my coffee, and headed out to the pool.

Early evening? My stomach flipped. It was nearly eleven already. What had I let myself in for? Niall O'Brien was coming here. Oh my God! I walked all the way to the end of the garden, trying to calm my nerves. Sitting down on the grass, I concentrated on my breathing. In through my nose, out through my mouth. Maybe lying down would be better. I looked up at the sky, there wasn't a cloud in sight. I could do with a long walk along the beach.

'Nervous?'

I sloshed my coffee all over my hand.

'Jesus, you startled me.'

It was Will.

'Sorry, I saw you from the window. What's up?' he asked as I wiped the coffee from my hand onto the grass.

'Nervous, yes,' I admitted, and he smiled and lay down beside me, holding my hand.

'Where do you feel most comfortable in the house?'

'In bed with you,' I said, and he laughed, rolling onto his side. 'To be honest, anywhere in the house as long as I'm with you.'

'Well, I'm here.' He put his arm across my waist. 'And remember, it's not live. If you fluff your answers, they can cut it out.'

'Don't you need to be strumming a guitar or singing or something?'

'What, while you get all nervous over Niall O'Brien? I don't think so,' he said, rolling on top of me. 'And besides, we're nearly done. I woke early and... strummed my guitar and sang something.'

I smiled, and he kissed me. I returned the kiss, and he tasted so good.

We hadn't had sex the night before, after everything that had happened, and I wanted him. We were kind of concealed but not enough, but we were interrupted before we could take it any further.

'Yo, Wilba, stop macking on your woman and get up here. We need you,' Jake hollered from the balcony outside the studio, and Will rolled his eyes.

'You're needed for strumming,' I said, and he grinned.

'I'll see you this afternoon. Kieron will be here at three.'

He kissed me and squeezed one of my boobs before jumping up. 'Later, Daniels.'

Steph was reading by the pool when I got back to the house. There was still no sign of the others, so after getting another coffee, I set up camp next to her, lying face down so I could play with the water like a toddler.

'Have you had some breakfast?' I asked.

'No, but I have eaten two biscotti, so I guess that could be classed as breakfast. You?'

'Me what?' I asked, distracted.

'Have you had some breakfast?'

'No, and now I'm too nervous to eat... it's happening, the interview.'

'Oh my God! Have you got to go to a film studio?'

'No, they're coming here.'

'Here? Are we gonna meet him too?' she asked, sitting up.

'I guess so,' I said, turning my head to see her face, and I laughed. She was excited.

'That's amazing. The kids are gonna be so jealous. I mean, they're jealous anyway, but this? Wow.'

'Yeah, you're right. The boys will be jealous, too,' I mused.

'Speaking of jealousy... do you think that's why Claire is acting the way she is?' Steph asked.

'How can she be jealous when Will has flown her out here, paid for a spa day and dinner so far, and put her up in his house? If she'd been left at home, I'd understand her feeling that way, but she wasn't, so she has no right.' I looked at Steph, and she looked out to the view. 'Do you think I'm being unreasonable? That argument Will and I had last night was mainly her fault.'

'Maybe there's something underlying, something we don't know about,' she said.

'Well, I hope it's not a coke addiction because that's what Will thinks.'

'Morning, Ladies,' Zara cooed as she walked out to the pool with a herbal tea.

'Zara. Good morning,' I said as she sat down. 'And how was last night for you?'

'Very good, thank you,' she said. I bit my lip. 'Oh, stop it.'

I laughed.

'I get the feeling one of the bedrooms was empty last night,' Steph said, and then to save her embarrassment, she continued. 'Zara, you will never guess who's coming here this afternoon.'

Steph explained, but the more they talked about it, the more nervous I became, so I slipped off to the bedroom to call the boys. It was good to speak to them. They were having such a fantastic time and had done so many activities. Mike must be shattered.

Sliding the balcony door open, I lay on the sun lounger to look at the view and try to clear my head. My arm was getting a bit itchy, and I was tempted to take the dressing off, but not before the interview. Thinking about what Steph had said, I wondered if Claire was okay, and I hoped she wasn't taking drugs.

At three o'clock, I was sitting with Kieron in the non-TV lounge.

'So, what I need from you is everything you *don't* want to talk about.'

'And what would you recommend I put on that list?' I asked. How was I supposed to know that? 'What does Will put on his list?'

'No questions about his family, Alysa... the baby,' he said tentatively, unsure whether he should have mentioned that.

'Okay, so those subjects....' And I stopped to think.

'Clever,' Kieron said under his breath, typing something on his laptop.

'As well as my ex and my boys... my clients?' I didn't know what else to suggest.

'Right, good, well, to give you an idea of what he will want to ask you, there's the girl next door aspect, but following last night's events, they'll no doubt wanna ask you about that,' he said, pointing at my arm. I looked at it again. It really was itchy. 'You can describe your feelings about the situation, but under no circumstances do you slate the fans.'

'Okay.'

I had been told.

'I know you're nervous, but they'll want to see relaxed Lucy Daniels, so just remember that it's not live, and we will be checking it before it goes out. The trick with interviews is to give the audience enough information to appease them, but not so much that you're left wide open,' he explained.

How was I to know how much information that was? Oh, God.

'I'm looking forward to this. It should be fun,' he said.

'I'm glad someone is,' I replied on a long exhale.

'Their main aim will be to make you comfortable. They want the best out of you. Don't stress,' he said, but rather than sounding reassuring, he just sounded a bit patronising.

An hour later, I was in our ensuite, I'd already been sick once, and I was splashing water on my face when Will came in.

'Hey, they're here,' he said, looking at my ashen face in the mirror as I patted it dry. 'They wanna do your make-up.'

I could see they'd already done his. His entire face looked matte.

'Well, that's good. Maybe they could make me look like I haven't just puked.'

He turned me around and kissed my forehead, which I was thankful for because I needed to brush my teeth. He got hold of my shoulders and put his forehead to mine.

'You'll be fine. I'll be right with you.'

'Is Steph melting in front of Niall O'Brien?' I asked.

'Oh, he's not here yet. It's just the production team.'

I had been sitting and having my make-up done for nearly an hour. I couldn't believe how much makeup they needed to apply a natural look. I'd had my hair done, and someone had just rolled in a rail of clothes.

'Can I not wear something of my own?' I asked.

'Honey, you can wear whatever you want, we just wanted to give you the option,' the lady said who'd arrived with the clothes rail. 'And it will be fun to try some clothes on, right?'

I could see right through her, there was a big fat no in that response, but she hid it well. I was just thinking of wearing some denim shorts and a tee, but I ended up in a sun dress that hit just above the knee with a halter-neck bikini underneath. They wanted holiday pool vibes.

'Niall is here,' someone announced, I hadn't seen before.

'Great,' the woman said, who appeared to be in charge. I thought her name was Bel. 'Are you happy to do the meet and greet here?'

'In the bedroom?' I asked questioningly.

'This bit isn't recorded, it's just where you guys get to know each other a bit off camera, and it'll be away from the rest of your house guests.'

'Okay,' I replied.

I guessed Will would be there too, so if he was happy with it, then I was. I could hear them coming down the hallway.

'This place is so cool. I've driven past it a few times and always wondered what it was like inside.'

I could hear Niall talking to Will. It was strange to hear a different British voice in the house and one that was utterly recognisable. The door opened as I stood up, and I held my breath.

'Here she is....' Niall said excitedly as he walked straight in with his arms outstretched to hug me. 'Can I hug her?... I'm hugging her.'

Everyone laughed, including me. He was a good hugger.

'Nice room,' he said, looking out to the view as Will put his arm around my waist. 'Shall we sit out on the balcony?'

Will gestured with his arm, confirming he was happy with that suggestion, and the three of us walked out. Bel slid the door back across to give us some privacy, Will and I sitting on the edge of one of the sun loungers and Niall on the other.

'They always get me to do this bit, to explain what's gonna happen, but if I'm honest, I don't know!' he laughed. 'We tend to wing it, try to make it look a bit more natural... natural as in, you'll open the door to me and pretend that you've invited me over... so natural that it's a complete farce.' We all laughed again. 'I understand you're pretty nervous?' he said, looking at me.

'Just a bit,' I said, swallowing.

'Let me run you through the vague plan. Bel thinks we should do your bit first,' he said to Will. 'She thought we could ask you a few questions about the up-and-coming album in the studio, possibly get some footage of the three of you jamming? Then, if it's okay with you, do a little tour of the house. The fans would love that.'

Will was nodding along as he made suggestions.

'And then,' he turned his attention to me. 'You and I can have a cup of tea, so cliché, but the viewers will love it, walk and talk through the gardens and then maybe have a game of pool... you've got a table, I understand?' He asked, directing his question at Will.

'We have,' he confirmed, slightly over pronouncing the 'we', and I closed my eyes.

There was the faintest of smiles on Niall' face, and it was evident that he was very perceptive.

AFTER THREE ATTEMPTS at the welcome, the fourth was apparently good. All Will had to do was open the door and say hi. Niall said exactly the same line every single time, and he made it sound so genuine that I was laughing after the third and fourth time.

The band headed to the studio with Niall while interviewing Will about the album. I watched on from behind set, my nerves causing me to run to the loo twice. Will was so relaxed, the lights and cameras not fazing him at all. They asked him questions about his preferred method of writing, his inspiration and the forthcoming tour.

Will then showed him around the house, but the focus was mainly on Niall and his reactions to what he saw. The artwork, the instruments, the awards, the view, the pool. It was very relaxed.

Everyone else was kind of being moved around the house to make sure they were out of the way for each scene. Jake and Paul had headed back into the studio to continue working, and I was worried that Will would be needed elsewhere.

Claire appeared wide-eyed, wondering what on earth was going on, and I could see Steph filling her in. I gave her a small smile. I knew we needed to talk, but now wasn't the time, but I didn't want her to feel awkward all evening.

We had a break while the camera crew set up in the garden, and we all gathered around the island in the kitchen for drinks and snacks.

'So, our bit is sort of done now. The focus will be more on you from now on,' Niall said, and I nodded, looking at the floor.

Will put his arm around my waist again. He was being so supportive.

'You'll be fine,' Will said.

'You will be,' Niall added. 'Get a drink down you. It might help calm the nerves.'

Will promptly passed me a glass of fizz, and I sipped, but I was also conscious that I hadn't eaten.

'Right, we're ready,' Bel said.

The make-up girl came and put yet more make-up on me while I took some calming breaths. The crew had set up a little area in the garden on a raised podium with two chairs and a table, the view in the background. We were to walk down through the garden while Niall asked me a couple of questions and then sat on the chairs to have some tea. The sun was just starting to go down, but it was warm.

'I might need a dip in your pool after this,' Niall said as he dabbed his brow with a handkerchief. 'Actually, that's not a bad idea… Bel, let's do a scene in the pool.'

I looked at him, my jaw open.

'Oh, come on, it'll be funny, we could sit in doughnuts… have you got any doughnuts?' he asked, turning to Will, who was already laughing at the prospect.

I just shook my head, I knew something like this would happen, and Niall squeezed me, he was really sweaty. We stood at the top of the garden, waiting for everyone to finish setting up. The clapper board went, and we began to descend slowly.

'So, what I really want to know, and I'm sure the viewers do too, is just how big Will Reynolds is?'

My jaw dropped again, and I immediately looked over at Will.

'That was a joke, that was a joke!' And we all started laughing. 'Just thought I'd break the ice…' he said to the camera. 'Because the glass of fizz we fed Lucy before this isn't working.'

He shook his head in an elaborate pained grimace, and I put my head in my hand, trying not to smile.

'Okay, okay…' he said, turning back to me. 'Seriously now… How did you not know who Will was? I mean, really?'

I laughed again.

'I just... don't look at that stuff. My son does all my techy things for me, and I don't buy magazines or use social media much,' I admitted. 'I knew the band because I'd heard them on the radio, but I guess it was a bit like when you see a picture of a DJ for the first time, and they look completely different to how you'd imagined... I just didn't recognise him.'

'But you know who I am?' he said.

'Well yeah, but only because you star in one of my favourite TV shows,' I said honestly.

'It's just astonishing. When did you find out, and how did you react?' he asked.

I thought back to our first date, which I didn't even realise was a date and began to smile.

'Ohh, there's a story here. Come on, Lucy, we all wanna know.'

'We were in a restaurant in my hometown....'

'Clevedon,' he confirmed. 'I've been there. Walked on the pier and everything.'

'No way.' And suddenly, it was as if we were just a couple of friends chatting, and the cameras weren't there. 'Anyway, a waitress asked for his autograph, which I thought was weird because he'd told me he was a writer and...'

'Woah, woah, wait!' he said, holding up his hands. 'He told you he was a writer!?' Niall asked and then rubbed his face in disbelief.

I smiled again and nodded, biting my lip.

'Will Reynolds, you little minx!'

The camera crew diverted their view towards him as he smiled and shook his head with embarrassment.

'Soo, that kind of let the cat out of the bag?' Niall continued.

'It did, but despite knowing the band, I didn't know *how* famous he or the band were. It wasn't until I got home after our first date that I actually looked him up.'

'Wow, and how did you feel?' he asked, and I had to take a moment because I wasn't ready for that question.

I went to say something but then stopped, and Niall was about to ask something else, but then I carried on. I looked Niall in the eye.

'I guess... it didn't matter... because I was already in love with him,' I saw Will smiling, and Niall lifted his eyebrows. Even the crew were a little taken aback.

'Woah,' Niall said, nodding. 'So, it was love at first sight?'

'Yeah,' I confirmed, a little shy to admit it.

'And cut!' someone said.

'Brilliant, that was great. Do you wanna make your way up onto the podium now,' said a guy standing to the side.

I breathed out, shaking my hands to release the tension and looking at the sky.

'You're doing just fine,' Niall said as we settled into the chairs, and once everyone was set, we started again.

'So, Lucy, I know you're nervous, and I thought, what could we do to make you feel comfortable?'

And he suddenly got back up and collected a tray which was already set with tea and biscuits and put it on the table between us.

'Look! Rich Tea and Nice biscuits.'

I laughed again as he poured the tea and handed me a mug.

'I love Nice biscuits!' I said.

'Me too, sadly, we couldn't get hold of any Hobnobs,' he said, sitting back down.

'Let's focus on you... what was your life like before you met Will?' he asked, dipping his biscuit in his tea.

'It was busy, like any mum, constantly working and when I wasn't working, doing family stuff or grocery shopping or walking my two dogs. Just a normal working mum.'

'And then Will just walked into your life?' he asked.

'Yeah... I wasn't even looking.' I took a sip of my tea. It was cold.

'And now?' he asked, and I knew what he was getting at. 'I mean, look at this place.'

I spotted another camera operator panning around to show the house.

'It was a shock. I didn't actually know about this place,' I admitted, and Niall threw his head back, laughing.

'Did it not come up when you searched online? Come on... you must have known.'

I shook my head.

'I don't look, I knew he had a place in Brooklyn, but I didn't know about this place until I got out here.'

'Wow! So, what, he wanted to surprise you?' Niall asked.

'I think he was trying to make it easier for me to accept.'

'Is that something you've found hard? Accepting?' And I had to think about how I would answer because I didn't want to appear ungrateful, but Niall added. 'I mean to suddenly have all of this put on your lap....'

'Yes. I didn't grow up with it or work for it. It was a bit like winning big at the casino or receiving a sudden windfall, I guess and... it didn't seem fair.'

'Fair?' Niall repeated.

'Yeah, not equal.'

'I'm desperate to ask Will how he thinks he handled this,' and I giggled.

The cameras panned around to him again.

'Badly,' he said, pushing his hand through his hair, causing the crew to laugh again.

'So, has that caused a bit of tension between you two?' he asked tentatively, and I knew he was asking me that because of my response to the 'we' comment earlier. I bit the inside of my cheek.

'On occasion,' I confirmed.

I didn't want to say anymore. What did he want? The details of our arguments?

'I bet,' he responded, lifting his eyebrows, alluding to the fact there had probably been some disagreements, and then he dabbed his brow again. 'Shall we take a dip in the pool?'

'If you want,' I said, smiling.

'And cut.'

I looked straight over at Will to check I hadn't said anything out of turn, and he walked over, putting his hand out to pull me up.

'Brilliant, guys, take a break. We're gonna set up by the pool. We'll be an hour or so,' the guy said.

Will kissed me and then took my hand.

'Can I offer you guys another drink?' he aimed the question at Niall.

'Anything's better than cold tea,' he said, and we headed back up to the house.

I looked at my watch. 'Maybe we should order some food in?' I suggested.

'Good idea.' Will smiled.

When we got back up to the house, Claire approached us immediately. 'I'm so sorry about last night. I am really grateful to be here. I've been feeling awful all day.'

'Apology accepted,' Will said straight away, and he left Claire and me to chat.

'Is everything okay? It's unlike you, and you were being really... unthoughtful,' I said for want of a better word that didn't involve bitch.

She started to well up.

'Okay, conversation for another time?' I said quickly, squeezing her shoulder, and she nodded, turning towards the bedrooms.

I glanced at Steph, and she gave me a half-smile before heading to the island to introduce herself to Niall.

I sidled up to Will and put my arm around him. I was really looking forward to spending some alone time with him. There was crew everywhere.

He turned to face me. 'I'm just gonna go and get the guys, you wanna come with me?' he asked, his eyes darkening as he said it.

'Sure,' and we left everyone to it, heading towards the studio.

'I just need to get something from our room,' Will said as we approached, and he pulled me in with him, pushing me straight up against the wall, kissing me fervently.

I breathed out, all of my tension leaving me and suddenly really needing him.

'Can I fuck you?' he asked without any preamble.

'Is that what you needed to get from our room?' I asked, laughing.

'Yeah... a fuck,' he said, looking straight at me with a wry smile appearing on the corner of his lips.

I looked at the door, and he immediately locked it.

'Turn around,' he said, and I did as I was told.

He pulled my bikini bottoms down but left them loose around my ankles.

'Bend over.'

Okay, this really *was* going to be a fuck. We were literally between the door and a chest of drawers.

'Hold on to the sideboard.'

I gulped as I did so, and he undid his fly. He nudged my legs apart with his foot and slid his fingers inside me. My breathing was already coming rapidly. He used the residue on his fingers to circle me, and my breath quickened before he thrust himself into me. An animalistic grunt emanated from deep within his chest.

'Shit, give me a second,' I panted, and he did, circling his fingers around me again.

'I'm gonna fuck you, Lucy,' he said as he patiently waited. 'Hard and fast, and I don't care if you come or not. I want to know that my cum is inside you while you're in that pool.'

Why was what he was saying turning me on so much? He was acting selfishly, but I didn't care. I wanted him inside me. I wanted him to fuck me. He started to move back and forth with gusto, and whether he wanted me to come or otherwise, I began to build straight away.

The ornaments and box of tissues on the sideboard were wobbling with every thrust. One of them toppled over, and I was concerned I wouldn't be able to hold on. I was so close, and his thrusts began to lose their rhythmic timing. My panting turned into tiny yelps as my climax began, and he covered my mouth with his hand to stop the noises from escaping. He silently pushed his release into me as I desperately tried to breathe through my nose.

When he was done, he leaned forward, grabbed a handful of tissues and pushed them between my legs as he pulled out. I stood there for a second in mild shock, still bent over and holding onto the sideboard while catching my breath. Will pulled my bikini bottoms back up after doing his fly and turned me to face him.

'You okay?'

'I think so,' I said, and he kissed me, pulling me into him. 'I'm glad I'm getting in the pool now.'

He laughed.

'That guy is crazy,' he said, while I sorted myself out.

I looked in the mirror quickly, pulling my dress back into place.

'I don't know what you were worried about, you're a natural,' he said, coming up behind me and kissing my neck. 'I love you.'

'I love you too,' and with that, he unlocked the door, and as we were about to step out, Jake, Paul and Mat were heading down the corridor.

They looked at us, and we looked at them, a little surprised. Jake looked toward the kitchen and then looked us up and down.

'For fuck's sake, you two,' he said, shaking his head, and they carried on their way, laughing as we fell into step behind them.

Will kissed my cheek, smiling as he did so.

'Oh, here they are,' Niall said. 'Pizzas have just arrived.'

Will let go of my hand, and Niall immediately put his arm across my shoulders.

'Bel's pleased with what we have so far, so it's time to have some fun.'

Chapter 24

Niall passed me a glass of champagne and picked one up of his own, letting go of me and clinking. It was so weird. I was in a room with Niall O'Brien, and it felt completely normal.

Suddenly all the lights came on, and it was almost like daylight out by the pool. Everyone squinted until their eyes adjusted.

'Five minutes,' someone called.

I managed to eat a piece of pizza and sip a little more fizz before they called us through. Despite being super bright, it was nice because everyone came and sat around the edge of the pool to watch. Someone had found two ridiculous doughnuts, one looked like it had hundreds and thousands on top, and the other had chocolate dripping down the sides.

A woman helped me onto the one with sprinkles.

'Rolling,' I heard someone call before the lady passed me my drink.

I spotted Niall at the other end of the pool handing his drink to someone before taking his robe off. He was wearing a pair of union jack Bermuda shorts, and suddenly he took a run and jump, holding onto his knees and dive-bombed into the pool, splashing me and everyone around, making us all shriek with laughter.

The lady was clinging onto my doughnut so that I didn't topple over, but Niall swam over to me and steadied himself on the other handle, making it jerk and causing me to shriek some more.

'Ahh, that's better,' he said before someone passed him the other doughnut. He made several false attempts at getting onto it, causing yet more laughter. But eventually, he managed to sort of jump, twist and land in one fluid movement.

Once everyone had calmed down, Niall and I sat there bobbing around. Someone tied ropes to each of the inflatables so that we didn't float too far away from each other.

'What better way to spend the day, in a rock star's swimming pool... under the sun,' he said, purposefully causing more laughter as the camera took a shot of the lighting against the night's sky.

'Anyway, Lucy, you said earlier that you had struggled to accept all of this,' he said, waving his arms around us. 'But what about the press, I think we can all agree, they've been hounding you a bit.'

I looked at my arm, which felt decidedly heavy, and then back at him. 'I wasn't expecting or prepared for it to be so invasive and frightening,' I admitted.

'I guess William here has practically grown up with it, whereas... pardon the pun, you have been thrown in at the deep end,' he said and then added. 'Oh, come on! That was funny,' he said, lifting his hands to get some response. There were a few sniggers, but the pressure was on for me to answer, and he shot the camera a pained expression.

'I haven't coped with it particularly well. There have been times when I thought we were alone and weren't.'

'Are you referring to the pictures taken at the apartment in Brooklyn... have you even seen those?' he asked suddenly, lightening the mood a touch, and I smiled.

'Yes, I was shown those. I tend to see the ones that might affect others in my private life... I'm not interested in the rest.'

There was a pause. He wanted more.

'Will tells me if I need to ring my children.'

There was another pause, and I felt under duress to say something more. I glanced at Will for a split second.

'My... mental health has been affected.' I breathed out audibly. I could see Will had sat up on his sun lounger, trying to gauge if I was happy with the questioning, and there was a look between Bel and Niall.

'You mention your children....' I had requested that we don't talk about my family, so I wondered where this question was going and was on high alert. 'Are you and Will thinking of starting a family?'

Will suddenly stood up.

'That's not permitted,' he said, putting his hands on his hips, and the tension around the pool was thick. Niall quickly lifted his hands, palms facing Will.

'Sorry, sorry, that wasn't on the list of subjects we couldn't discuss,' he said as he covered his eyes from the lights to see if he could see Bel. 'We can cut that out. We're cutting it out.'

I looked at Will, and he looked pensive. I spotted Bel walking over to reassure him, Kieron too, and Niall mouthed sorry to me. I lifted my hand to signify it was okay.

'Let's move on to a lighter subject.'

Will sat back down. Whatever Bel had said had done the trick.

'And what about the future? Where are you going to live?' he asked.

'Um, it's still early days, but I need to be in Clevedon for my boys, and... if we base ourselves there, I guess we'll visit here frequently to see Will's friends and family.'

This wasn't something Will and I had discussed, and I didn't want Will to think I was making assumptions.

'The sunshine hasn't lured you here as it did with me then?'

'The sunshine is amazing, but having a family is an unbridled commitment.'

'And you and Will?'

'Future-wise?'

'Yeah.'

I glanced at Will who was biting his lip and looking at me intently, and I couldn't help but wonder if he wanted to hear the answer to this question more than anyone else.

'Will and I are... committed to being together, so when he's not working, we'll be... with each other,' I said slowly and carefully.

'Well, Lucy, it's been an absolute pleasure to meet you and Will. Thank you for inviting us into your home.'

The camera took a shot of Will, lifting his hand with a single nod.

'Thank you, it's really lovely to meet you too,' I said honestly, smiling.

'Okay, cut, that's a wrap.'

As soon as Niall heard those words, he got off his doughnut and swam straight over to Will.

'I am so sorry. I wouldn't have asked that had I known it would cause upset.'

'It's fine, as long as it's cut,' Will said pointedly.

'We'll cut it after the previous question,' he confirmed.

Someone put a hand out to help me out of the pool, and somehow, I managed to get out without getting my arm wet. It was so itchy now I wanted to rip the dressing off, but Will was there before I'd even looked around, wrapping me up in his arms.

'You okay?' he asked, putting his forehead to mine. 'That got pretty intense, but you handled it really well.'

'I'm fine, glad it's over. Are you okay?'

'Yeah, that was my fault. I should have put that on the list.'

He kissed me, and we headed back up towards the kitchen. Paul and Jake were already getting drinks out for everyone, and I scarfed a cold pizza slice. I was so hungry suddenly. The crew were busy packing down but Will put some music on. He was obviously not heading back into the studio.

'I'm sorry that got a bit tense,' Niall apologised again. He genuinely felt terrible, and Will looked him straight in the eye.

'No, man, it was my fault. Please... stay. Invite your wife. Everyone is welcome to stay. It's time to relax.'

'Oh my God, really? Georgie will be stoked. She's a massive fan,' he said, pulling his phone out of his pocket, and I turned to Will.

'You're very relaxed,' I said, observing his body language and a slow smile spread across his face.

'We finished,' he replied.

'What? The album?' I asked, unable to hide my excitement.

'Yeah, recording anyway, there's still quite a bit to do, but we're ahead of schedule,' he clarified.

'That's amazing! Why didn't you say earlier? When you said you were nearly done, I didn't think you meant nearly, as in today, nearly,' I said, putting my arms around his neck.

'Because today was about you... but now, we celebrate.'

He kissed me on the forehead and then turned and got several bottles of fizz out of the fridge, taking one, and as if he was celebrating the end of a race, he shook it up and sprayed it everywhere, causing everyone to cheer and clap.

I didn't know whether it was the relief after doing the interview or the fact the band had finished recording, but everyone was in party mode. More and more people were turning up. I'm guessing the guys had sent out a few texts to gather the troops, and within an hour, there was little space to move. The kitchen, the dining area, the lounges, the games room, and the pool were all bustling with people. People I had never met.

I was just getting more fizz out of the fridge when the doorbell rang again. I looked at the security camera, it was Milly, and I flung the door open and wrapped her up in a big squeeze. She was obviously still in town following the gig. Behind her was a delivery guy, and he had several cases of champagne, wine and a box of vodka. Jesus Christ, who ordered them? This was going to be a very messy night. I signed for the delivery and ushered Milly and the delivery guy in.

'Awesome. Supplies!' Jake said as he gave Milly a squeeze.

The music was pumping, the alcohol flowing, and everyone seemed to be having the time of their lives. I sidled up to Steph and gave her bum cheek a squeeze. I had no idea where Will was. She responded in kind, and I looked at her, all doughy-eyed, because I was really feeling the effects of all the fizz.

'Come on, Daniels, we need to dance,' she said, and as if by magic, someone turned on a glitter ball in the games room, and we were drawn like moths to a light. Bonkers by Dizzee Rascal filled the room, and I grabbed one of the remotes sitting on the side. It was like finding gold as I cranked the music up, and a few people cheered and came to join us. Before we knew it, the whole room had filled with like-minded people spilling out to the poolside.

Zara and Claire appeared by our sides.

'If in doubt, look on the dance floor,' Zara shouted, and I laughed, realising they had been trying to find us.

I had the best time. My friends were all there, Will and I were good, and everyone was happy. 'Filthy/Gorgeous' by the Scissor Sisters came on the playlist, and while we were doing our usual silly dance-off, a pair of hands wrapped around my waist, and I assumed they were Will's. I pushed my hips back into his, but despite my state of mind, it didn't feel quite right and judging by the girls' faces, it was not Will.

'I am so glad you're wearing a dress this evening.'

'Stryker! What the fuck?' I said, spinning around. 'How did you get here so quickly?' But instead of answering, he kissed me square on the lips. I immediately pushed him back and gave him a hard stare.

He laughed.

'I'm staying with a friend nearby,' he explained.

The girls were all staring at me, wondering what the hell was going on.

'Stryker, these are my friends, Claire, Zara and Steph. Girls, this is Stryker. He sings for The Deck.'

He kissed each of their hands, and I watched each one of them melt as their eyes locked with his before he turned his attention back to me, wrapping his hands around my waist and pulling me in close.

'Dance with me,' he ordered rather than asking.

'Have you asked Will?' I checked, looking straight into his eyes.

'I don't need to get permission,' he assured me as Milly passed us by, catching my eye.

'Stryker,' she acknowledged him with a single nod as she walked by towards the kitchen.

Stryker pushed his leg between mine just as Make Me Feel by Janelle Monae dropped. He began to dance, and I couldn't be bothered to fight, so I went with it. Stryker gave me a wicked smile and then leaned in.

'I've been dreaming about this, Lucy. In fact, I've been dreaming about fucking you,' he said, his voice laced with seduction, but before I could reply, he lowered me over his thigh. It felt like all the booze I had consumed rushed towards my head, and my dress had ridden right up my thigh.

I had a moment to clock the girls' faces as they watched on, completely bemused, before he whipped me back up to face him.

'Just because you love someone doesn't mean you can't give them what they want.'

'What are you talking about?' I asked as he pulled my hips closer to his with one forceful hand, the fabric from my bikini bottoms rubbing against his tight jeans, and I gasped.

'Will loves an audience, always has, and I am more than happy to oblige,' he stated as if I should know this, but Will told me outright that he did not like an audience with his girlfriend. In fact, he chastised me once for being so brazen in public.

'I don't think that's the case anymore,' I replied, as self-assured as I could.

'Oh, come on, a leopard doesn't change its spots,' he said, taking the upper hand.

What the hell? Stryker had known Will for years, decades even, and I was beginning to lose confidence in my beliefs.

'He may not like it with a live audience but a hand-picked one... He's a fucking exhibitionist, Lucy.'

He pushed me away, leaving his words bouncing around in my head as he spun me around several times. My woozy state made me lose my balance. Pulling me back in with my back to him to steady me, he wrapped his arm around my waist and pulled my chin back with the other so that my ear was aligned with his mouth. I was feeling dizzy and more than confused.

'Let me watch you fuck Will.'

He let my chin go.

As I focused on the people on the dancefloor, Will was standing there, watching me. Milly stood by his side. She'd obviously gone off to find him. Will approached, and I was worried that he thought that I had instigated the dance, but when he reached us, he looked at me and then at Stryker.

'Can I have my girlfriend back now?' Will asked, staring at Stryker, there wasn't much malice in his voice, but it was definitely a warning.

I noticed Jake and Paul were on the periphery, and Stryker released me, holding his hands up like I was hot property, a smug grin and a glint in his eye, before he went off to get a drink. Jake shook his head as he passed them. The girls just stood there dumbfounded. Will pulled me into him, and I glanced at Milly. She winked. She had my back. I looked up at Will, my eyes wide, like I'd been caught doing something I shouldn't.

'He told me he didn't need your permission,' I said straight away.

'Did he now,' he said with a small smile on his face. 'What else did he say?'

I looked at the floor, I didn't know whether to tell him or not, but Will gently lifted my chin up to look into my eyes, waiting for my reply. I pushed up on my tiptoes so he could hear me.

'He said he had been dreaming about having sex with me, that he wanted to watch us having sex, that you like it, and a leopard doesn't change its spots,' I replied in a flurry, getting it all out there before lowering myself back down.

Will glanced over my shoulder, and I followed his gaze. Stryker was back, beer in hand, chatting to Paul, Jake and the girls, who were all swooning over him. Will slowly looked around the room at all the other people and suddenly took my hand, leading me out past the pool to the garden.

I wasn't sure if he was cross or whether he wanted to speak to me privately, but he was almost dragging me down the garden.

'I haven't got any shoes on,' I said as we descended, and Will scooped me up and carried me right to the bottom of the garden, the music getting quieter as we went and a ringing starting in my ears.

Pushing past some overgrown bushes, he set me down, and I realised I was standing on some decking. It took me a moment for my eyes to adjust to the darkness. We stood on a partially covered platform that jutted out, looking out across the beautiful view. All we could see now were a few lights in people's houses and above us, the night sky, twinkling away. Behind us was a cushioned swing seat.

'Why didn't you show me this before?'

This would be the perfect secluded spot for reading, a morning coffee or an evening glass of wine.

'I haven't been down here for ages. I kind of forgot it was here,' and he began to fiddle with the mechanism of the seat, locking it into place to stop it from swinging and then unfolding the cushions to create a bed.

'Lie down,' he commanded, and I did.

I watched as he took his jacket off and climbed up the bed, and I began to giggle.

'What's so funny, Daniels?' he asked, securing my arm above my head and looking into my eyes.

'Is this the rock stars equivalent of a quickie behind the bike sheds?' I asked.

Despite the darkness, I could see he was smiling.

'Maybe, but hopefully less quick. We did that earlier.'

He kissed me gently, but it steadily became heavier. I lay there, soaking up the moment, enjoying the feel of his lips on mine and feeling a little bit naughty that we'd sneaked off.

He hadn't responded to what I'd told him about Stryker, and my mind wandered. Did he enjoy people watching him having sex? Or was that something he used to enjoy? Surely anyone that played in a band was an exhibitionist in some way, but did that apply to their entire lives?

Will pulled away slightly, looking at me in the half-light.

'What are you thinking about?' he whispered.

'Just about what Stryker said.' I could see him smiling. 'Is it true?'

'Is what true?'

He was going to make me spell it out.

'That you like people watching you have sex? I'm confused because you told me otherwise at the festival.'

'I guess it depends on the circumstances,' he said as if that was an explanation.

'And what would those circumstances be?'

He laughed a little.

'You don't let up, do you?'

I didn't answer him. I was too tired for games.

'If it was someone I trusted. If it was private. If I was damn sure it wouldn't get leaked... yeah, I guess so.'

'So...' I took a moment to try to get my head around it. 'You would like to have sex with me in front of someone else? Exposing me to them?'

'Not if you weren't willing.' He sighed, and that sympathetic smile made its way back onto his face, which annoyed me. 'I don't wanna patronise you...'

'Well, you are, simply by looking at me like that,' I quickly interjected.

He grabbed my other arm, pinning both down to the mattress, narrowly avoiding my dressing, and shifted himself so he was fully on top of me.

'Lucy, I've told you before that I love our sex life, it's amazing, and we have a connection that no one can rival. I love that you're always willing to try new things. And I love providing the opportunity, but if you're not into it, it won't be enjoyable. For either of us.'

I gave him a hard stare. He hadn't actually answered my question.

He closed his eyes and let out a frustrated sigh.

'Yes, it turns me on. If someone is watching, it makes me feel superior somehow, that I am getting what that person watching wants. Having the opportunity to show you off like that, your beautiful body on display, knowing that they can't touch you, and I can.'

'So, it's a power thing?'

'I guess, partly, but it's mainly a trust thing. Trust between us and the people watching.'

'People?' I repeated, astonishment in my tone, and he laughed.

'People, person, whatever, it doesn't matter because there's a ton of other stuff we can explore if you're not into it.'

'What do they get out of it?' And I looked away when I realised it was essentially like experiencing live porn for the person watching. 'I meant, why would someone like Stryker want to watch when he could easily get a woman of his own?'

He smiled a devilish grin, and I realised at that moment that Stryker wanted *me*, and he couldn't have me.

A dormant lick of pleasure slowly swirled in my core at the dominance we had over him. With piqued curiosity, Will rolled his lips between his teeth and watched my eyes.

The feeling of pleasure merged quickly into confusion at why I would feel that way when Will had proved to me already that I liked to submit to him.

Will ran his thumb over my eyebrow, trying to decipher my thoughts.

'Don't label yourself, Lucy,' he reminded me. 'Be open. Trust me.'

'And what if I didn't want to explore anything else?' I tried to move my arms, but all I achieved was pushing my boobs up towards his face, and he looked down and smiled. 'What if you get bored?'

He pushed his pelvis into mine as if to prove a point. He was rock hard.

'That is never gonna happen. I will take your pussy in any way you're willing to give it to me.'

He kissed me deeply. Was he saying that because he wanted me to know that sex without all the other stuff was enough for him? Would I be comfortable with someone watching us? For goodness sake, I had only just become confident being naked around him. Will leant up on one elbow and undid his belt buckle, undoing his fly with one hand, not breaking the kiss.

I tried to move my hand down to touch him, but he tightened his grip. He slowly rubbed the end of his dick up and down the fabric of my bikini bottoms, teasing me, and then he gently undid the strings before lining himself up.

'I will never get bored with this, Lucy.'

He plunged himself into me, and I let out a scream. Holding himself there, kissing my neck and cleavage before pulling out again and sinking back down at a much more controlled speed. He set a slow, deep, rhythmic pace, and it felt divine. I wrapped my legs around him and could feel the breeze between our legs as I looked up at the stars.

He let go of my hands, and I immediately grabbed his arse, pulling him into me.

'You want it deeper, baby?'

'Yes,' I said, unable to avoid the neediness in my response.

He wriggled his jeans and pants down further and then knelt up, pulling my hips with him, my dress riding up as he did so.

'Ahh,' I breathed. It felt so good.

'And how would you feel now if someone was watching?'

'What?' I immediately pushed myself up onto my elbows, looking around.

'We're alone, Lucy, relax. I would never do that to you. I'm just putting it out there while you're in the moment.'

I lay back down and gulped. How *would* I feel?

'I could easily get Stryker down here. He's probably been looking for us, he knows damn well what we're doing, but he doesn't know this place exists.'

He took hold of my hips and pulled me in, deeper still, and then he took my hands, hoisting me up so I was straddling him, and he put his forehead to mine, my dress gently covering us.

'He wouldn't be able to see much,' I said, biting my lip.

'He would only see what we let him see.'

I took a deep breath in, unsure.

'We can send him back if you don't like it, he'll be fucking pissed, but I don't care,' he said, laughing a little at the thought.

'Okay.'

The confirmation was out before I'd allowed myself to overthink it too much. Christ, what was I doing? My fuzzy thoughts were all awash as Will lowered me back down to reach over to get his phone and pushed himself into me.

'Ahhh,' I breathed again.

'We're at the very bottom of the garden. You're only watching.'

He hung up and chucked his phone back down.

I was beginning to wonder if I'd made the right decision, my senses on high alert suddenly. Only watching? Was he hoping to share?

'Relax, Lucy, just concentrate on me... trust me.'

He set a steady pace again and knelt back up, pulling my hips toward him and making me moan.

'So, this is where you've been hiding out?' I heard Stryker say quietly, and I froze.

'Just sit over there and shut the fuck up,' Will said, waving across to the end of a stone wall.

I was rigid. It was as if we'd gone back in time to our first kiss. Will leaned over me again.

'Look at me,' he whispered. 'Keep watching.' His forehead was on mine, and he began to speed up a little. 'Concentrate on what you're feeling... the sensations... the breeze... the smell of the fresh night air.'

It was as if he was trying to make me go into a trance.

His fingers began to work their way down my neck, and his kisses followed. I looked up at the stars as he pulled the strap of my sundress down, and his fingers skated across the top of my bikini, squeezing my nipples through the fabric as they puckered up. I kept my gaze upwards, I did not want to look at Stryker, but I could hear him undoing his fly. Fuck, was he going to get himself off while he was watching? Will came back to my eye level, looking straight at me.

'Can I pull the cup of your bikini down?'

I took a sharp breath in, but Will didn't break our gaze. His eyes were hooded, he was enjoying this, and I wanted to please him.

'Okay,' I whispered, gulping.

Will slowly pulled it down, still gazing at me, immediately covering my exposed breast with his hand as his kisses descended once again. He devoured my nipple in his mouth, sucking and nipping it as he massaged it with his hand. He picked up his pace ever so slightly, and I reverted to looking at the stars.

I was starting to build, but I was trying to fight it for some reason. I didn't feel comfortable coming in front of Stryker, but I really wanted to give this to Will.

He slowly knelt back on his knees, sliding the other strap of my sundress down as he did so, and I felt exposed as he left my boob on display.

'Fuck.'

I heard Stryker say under his breath, and Will signalled with his middle and forefinger for me to keep looking into his eyes. He gently pulled the bikini top away, and Stryker sucked his breath in through his teeth. Will smiled. He was obviously enjoying the fact that Stryker was getting wound up.

He pulled my hips towards him, my boobs jiggling, and Will bit his lip. He did it over and over, amusement dancing in his eyes, and I was trying not to moan as he pushed himself in deeper, harder. Will put his thumb in his mouth and then began to circle me.

Jesus Christ, I bit my lip to stop any noises from escaping. I didn't want Stryker to hear me, but I was building for sure. I kept staring at Will, trying to push the thought of Stryker out of my mind. Will signalled for me to turn over. Would I feel more comfortable that way around? I guess it would mean Stryker couldn't see my tits jostling around.

Will leaned forward again, creating a barrier, and he slowly pulled out.

'Turn over, Lucy. I need you to come now,' he whispered.

Will stayed where he was as I wriggled over, and then he crawled a little closer to me. He lifted my knee up, out to the side and slid back in. I very much doubt Stryker could see anything apart from the sides of my boobs pressed into the cushions.

Will pushed his hand between my legs, collecting some of my arousal on his fingers and sliding them up to circle me once again. I was definitely climbing this time and fast, possibly because I knew Stryker couldn't see anything. He'd probably got bored and wandered off, and I was starting to relax.

I began to pant, and suddenly Will pulled my hips up and slammed into me. I screamed. I couldn't help it, and I couldn't work out if it was Stryker or Will that had said *yes* through gritted teeth. He pounded into me until I was right on the edge, and then he stopped. My orgasm teetered there, and Will held his dick just inside me as a small needy whimper left me.

I didn't know whether the wind blew the bottom of my dress up or Will lifted it, but I felt it gently land on my back and head, covering my upper body.

Will didn't move. He just waited.

'Come on, Lucy, give it to me,' he coaxed, knowing I was desperate for him.

I pushed my hips back and let go, Will stayed perfectly still, rock solid, so that I could move my hips in whatever direction I desired, he let me rinse my orgasm completely, and as I began to come down, he slammed into me again, coming pretty much straight away.

'Jesus... Fuck,' he said before pushing my hips down to the cushions with his own and covering my back with his chest.

His breathing was laboured, but as he caught his breath, he said, 'He's gone. Are you okay?'

Will slipped out of me and turned me onto my back, brushing my dress out of the way.

'Yes,' I said breathlessly. 'Was Stryker there the whole time?'

'He was... he came when you did,' he said, smirking.

'Oh my God, I can't believe I just did that,' I replied, covering my face with my hands. 'Niall O'Brien is up there,' I said in dismay.

'Lucy, you were fucking amazing. You milked my dick with that beautiful pussy of yours like a pro,' he said, smiling, pulling my hands back down. 'Stryker was in fucking awe.'

I closed my eyes, turning my head.

'Don't shy away from me, baby,' he said, gently moving my jaw, so that I was facing him. 'It was fucking hot.' He kissed me long and hard. 'I love you,' he said breathlessly between kisses, and I could feel him getting hard again. 'I wanna take you again.'

'COME ON, WE NEED TO get back up to the house. We've been down here for ages.'

Slowly unravelling ourselves from each other, I quickly put my bikini back on and readjusted my dress while Will sorted himself out. He lifted me up again to head up through the garden.

'What are you giggling about?'

'You're going to have to take me straight to the bathroom. Your load is literally pouring out of me,' I whispered, and he grinned.

Bypassing all the smokers, he lifted me into the air and deposited me onto the bedroom balcony, swiftly following by pushing himself up on the ledge and smoothly swinging his legs over the railings. He put his hand out for me, pulling me up to stand, and we slipped past the hot tub and into the bathroom, leaving the sound of wolf whistles and cheers behind us.

I quickly changed, and Will put on a fresh t-shirt. I was about to open the door when Will grabbed me, and I wrapped my arms around his neck.

'What?'

He kissed me with such force that I crashed back into the door.

'I fucking love you,' he said. 'I want you in my life forever.'

My heart skipped a beat, and I swallowed hard.

'Is it too early to say that?' he asked, and I looked him in the eye.

'No,' I said, tracing my fingers from his jaw, over his adam's apple and down to his heart. 'I feel the same.'

He looked down at my fingers and back up to my face, kissing me once more before opening the door and pulling me out into the corridor.

The party had moved on, and quite a lot of people had left. There were a lot of wasted people leaning over the breakfast bar or draped across sofas. A few people were still on the dancefloor, including Steph.

'You changed,' Zara stated as I was pouring myself a glass of water.

'I spilt my drink,' I said with a straight a face as possible.

Jake looked at Will.

'Yeah, right,' Jake said.

I flushed and quickly lifted my glass to my lips, turning to see they were holding hands and raised my eyebrows. Zara glared at me, so I averted my gaze and scanned the room. I was kind of looking for Stryker, but I couldn't see him. Maybe he'd gone home.

'Right guys, I'm heading off,' Stryker said from behind us, making me jump.

'Cool, cool,' Will said, shaking his hand. 'See you soon, man.'

He turned to me, and for a split second, I didn't know what to do. What was the etiquette for someone who had just watched you having sex? A handshake, a kiss? He pulled me in for a hug.

'Thanks for having me, Lucy,' he said for all to hear, making me squirm with the underlying reference, and then he whispered. 'Next time, I'm gonna kiss that British pussy of yours.'

I gasped, and he kissed my cheek. Stepping back and nodding, saluting the greater group before heading to the door.

Chapter 25

Oh, my head.

I lay in bed, looking out at the view, remembering the previous night's events trying not to move. Once Will and I had re-joined the party, there were drinking games, pool, and darts, one of the crew from The Night Show fell in the pool, and several others jumped in for a laugh, fully clothed.

Jake and Zara were openly kissing. So that was a thing.

Claire had gone to bed shortly after we had reappeared. We still hadn't had a chance to talk, but she had come to apologise again.

Paul got really drunk, and Will found him in the bathroom, passed out. He and Jake had to carry him to bed.

I met Niall's wife, she was lovely, but they left once things started to get really silly.

And there was more dancing, so much dancing, particularly Steph, Milly and me.

I gingerly sat up. I needed a wee, so I swung my legs out of bed and stood, only to sit straight back down again.

Woah! Major head rush.

I stood again and had to really concentrate on walking across the bedroom. I felt a bit weird, not just hungover, but I couldn't put my finger on it. Will was still asleep, snoring softly. I'd not heard him snore before. He was pretty drunk last night.

I headed out to the kitchen to get some water, and Miranda was already on the case with the clearing up. She'd employed the help of more cleaners as there seemed to be a team of them.

'Morning, Lucy,' she said brightly.

'Good morning, I'm so sorry about the mess,' I said, looking around at the state of the place.

'Don't apologise. It's my job. I've seen it in worse states,' she admitted, and I imagined she had.

A wave of nausea passed over me, and my palms felt clammy. I took a long, steadying breath and made my way to the cupboard to get a glass.

'Are you okay? You look ever so pale,' Miranda said.

I had another massive head rush as I turned towards the sink.

I could feel my legs going from beneath me and heard the glass smash as I collapsed on the floor. All I could see were what looked like black fish scales and then... nothing.

I LIFTED MY HAND TO my head, it felt sore, and my hand felt funny. There was something on it, and I opened my eyes. It was a cannula. What the hell? I tried to sit up.

'Lucy!' Will suddenly came into view. 'You're awake, thank God.'

He sounded concerned. I looked around, trying to piece everything together and failing. I was in a hospital room.

'You passed out, took a bang to the head. Your arm was infected, but they've put you on antibiotics.'

I looked down at my arm, which had a fresh dressing.

'Do you want some water?'

I nodded, and he brought a cup of water to my lips as a nurse walked in.

'Oh good, you're back with us. Lucy, my name is Brandy, and I'm your clinician. How are you feeling?' She asked assertively, checking my pulse as she did so.

'Um, my head hurts.'

'Okay, I'll get some pain relief arranged.' Brandy then turned to Will. 'Maybe Lucy would like a hot drink?'

She looked at him with her eyebrows raised expectantly. He looked back with a slight frown, seemingly realising he was being dismissed.

'Sure,' he said, looking at me quizzically before leaving the room.

The second he left, Brandy came to my side. I thought she was going to ask me if Will had hurt me.

'Lucy, are you aware that you were pregnant?'

I looked at her dumbstruck, mouth open and unable to breathe.

'I take it that's a no. You were about three or four weeks along, so it was early days, but sadly you have miscarried.'

Oh my God. How? I was on the pill and hadn't missed one because if I had, the days on the packet would be out of sync... but I had been sick. Several times, in fact. I hadn't even considered that. How irresponsible was I?

I couldn't tell Will about this. He would be so upset, especially after everything he said to me regarding the loss of his baby with Alysa.

Will returned to the room with two coffees.

'Well, everything's looking good. We should be able to discharge you later today,' Brandy smiled and squeezed my hand before leaving the room while Will put the coffees down.

'Everything okay?' he asked.

I just stared straight ahead. I couldn't look at him and lie, Will would see straight through me.

'Mmhmm,' I replied, and then I closed my eyes.

Was this why my emotions had been off the scale these last few weeks? I totally thought I was going insane at one point. The news was so fresh I needed a bit of time to get my head around it, so pretending I was tired was the only way. I led there. My thoughts shattered.

Jesus Christ.

I had Will's baby inside me... and now it was gone. An uncontrollable sob came out, and Will jumped up, sitting on the side of the bed and holding my hand.

'Lucy, talk to me. I'm worried about you,' he carefully ran his knuckles over my cheek.

'I just want to go home, please. Can you take me home?' I pleaded.

Will looked at me, he could tell something wasn't right, and I knew he was biting his tongue. He went out to find a nurse. I moved into the foetal position, and I could feel a big thick pad between my legs.

Once they had removed the cannula and the doctor had signed me out, Paul came to pick us up. The tension in the car was awful. I was on the verge of tears, and Will was pissed. He knew I was holding back on something.

The second we pulled up outside the house, I rushed in, not even stopping to speak to the girls. I got straight into bed, wrapping myself up tight in the sheets, sobbing before my head had even hit the pillow. Moments later, I felt the bed depress. Will was towering over me, and I just wanted to click my heals and be at home, my real home.

'Lucy, please don't shut me out.'

He sounded exhausted. Did I detect anger?

'What's wrong?' He tried to move my hand away from my face, but I resisted. 'For Christ's sake,' he said angrily, striding back across the bedroom, slamming the door. I closed my eyes and sunk further into the bed.

Sometime later, Steph came in with a tray of tea and biscuits.

'How are you feeling?'

'It's my head mainly. My arm is okay,' I said, void of emotion.

I think I was still in shock. I felt the back of my head again as I sat up, I'd bumped it when I'd passed out, and there was a big lump there.

'Do you want me to get you some more pain killers?' she asked, reaching across to get the paper bag that the hospital had sent my meds in. 'Will is really worried about you. He's gone out for a drive with Paul. He couldn't stand all the waiting around,' she admitted.

'I was pregnant,' I suddenly blurted out.

She sat down on the side of the bed.

'I didn't know, and now I've miscarried... and I can't tell Will. He's already been through enough, and what's the point, anyway?' I burst into tears again, and she wrapped me up in her arms as I sobbed on to her shoulder. 'This is all so fucked up.'

She let me cry until my heaving breaths began to subside.

'Okay, this is what we're going to do. When Will gets back, I'm going to suggest to the girls that we go out to give you and Will some space. Hopefully, Paul and Jake will get the hint, and then you'll tell him.'

I went to disagree, but she held up her hand.

'You can't keep something like this from him. It will kill you. It's really important that you tell him.'

I knew she was right, but the thought of it was breaking my heart.

'Drink the tea and take these.' She held up the pain killers. 'Eat the biscuits, have a shower, put a fresh one of these on,' she said, holding up a sanitary pad that the nurse had obviously put in the bag. 'And then you tell him, okay?'

'Okay.' I sniffed and then took a long, steadying breath.

I did as I was told, and when I walked back into the bedroom following my shower, Will was sat on the side of one of the loungers, and I stilled. The house was quiet, and he looked up at me. I took a staggered breath in and clutched my mouth with my hand.

He was in front of me in a flash, his hand gently resting on my waist and his other pushing my hair away from my face.

'Please talk to me. I've got the most awful thoughts going through my head.'

'Oh God, the last thing I want to do is worry you... upset you.'

Bloody hell, this was so difficult.

'Christ, Lucy, just fucking say it.'

'I've had a miscarriage. We've had a miscarriage,' I corrected. 'I didn't know. It was early days, apparently. I'm so sorry,' I said in a rush.

Maybe the quicker I said it, the less of a blow it would be. Will stood there, his mouth slackened. I could almost see him absorbing the information in slow motion in his eyes. He closed his eyes and then wrapped his arms around me so tight I couldn't breathe.

'Fuck, Lucy, I thought you were dying or something,' he admitted as the relief hit him.

I just stood there, feeling the warmth of him, the security he gave me, listening to his heartbeat, and I cried some more.

'Obviously, the miscarriage is... unbelievably sad. We would have made things work, but fucking hell, Lu, I thought they'd told you that you had terminal cancer. My world was literally falling apart.' He paused for a moment, trying to find the right words. 'I'm not gonna deny, a baby would have been... amazing, but it's you I want, Lucy. You are my world.'

I didn't say anything. I just stood there, letting him hold me. I hadn't realised what was going through his mind... and what he said about the baby. It made me wonder whether, deep down, he did actually want children, but now wasn't the time to address that.

'I'm sorry,' I said eventually. 'I guess it might go some way to explain why my hormones have been so fucked up recently,' I admitted, and he laughed a sigh.

'Can we lie down?' he asked. 'Maybe have a little nap. I am so fucking hung over.'

I pulled away slightly and looked up at him. He cupped my face, brushing the tears off my cheeks.

'Please don't shut me out like that again, I felt completely helpless, and my mind was on overdrive.'

'I'm sorry,' I said again.

He kissed me. It was so gentle, yet there was so much in that kiss, love and affection, and I kissed him back.

Eventually, he picked me up and carried me to the bed, spooning me, and after stroking my hair for a while, relaxing me and making me all sleepy, his hand travelled down my side and rested on my belly. I could feel the heat of his hand soothing me, and we silently lay there mourning something that never was before sleep took hold.

I woke to Will placing a tray beside the bed filled with fruit, biscuits, various drinks, and my meds.

'What's the time?' I asked, looking up at him.

'Just gone five. How are you feeling?' Will asked, and I sat up a bit.

'Okay... sore. Marble is not very forgiving.'

He sat down on the bed, and I continued.

'A bit bereft if I'm honest, it's weird, despite not knowing, I feel incredibly empty.'

He didn't reply, he just looked out at the view.

'Will?'

He turned and put his arm across me, propping himself up.

'How do you feel?' I asked.

He looked across at the tray as if contemplating his reply.

'Err...'

He was hesitating, and his voice wavered slightly. It was the first time I'd ever seen him falter over his words.

'Just say it, whatever it is,' I said, copying his advice to me when I'd struggled to find the words.

'I'm hesitating because I don't want to fuck things up between us but...' He paused and looked at me.

'You want to have kids,' I whispered, finishing the sentence off for him, and he closed his eyes.

'I honestly didn't think I did, but I think I've been suppressing my true feelings because of what happened in the past. And after today, if I'm being totally honest with myself, yeah. Yes, I think I do.'

He was searching my eyes, and I exhaled a breath I didn't know I was holding.

'What are you thinking?' he asked.

I was falling, tumbling back down this mountain I had been climbing. We had been climbing. He'd changed his mind? What the hell? He knew I had closed that window, and the thought of having a baby, the sleepless nights, the crying, the nappies, the exhaustion.

'Lucy?'

'I'm thinking... that we had the baby conversation weeks ago. That you said...' I couldn't quite remember what he'd said because my mind was reeling, but I vaguely remember there being a question hanging over the subject. 'I said that chapter in my life was over. This is a big change, Will... like a huge change of direction.'

I was really trying to stay calm, but I was getting a bit hot and bothered. Will was playing with the bottom of his lip, squeezing and pulling it like a child would do if they were being told off.

'Where do we even go from here?' I asked and went to get up, but he put his arm across me again. 'Fuck.'

'I'm sorry, it's just how I feel, and I want to be honest with you.'

'I need some space... some time to think.'

I pushed his arm away and went into the bathroom. Will didn't follow. He knew I needed to process what he'd said.

I went to the loo. My towel was saturated. Huge clots and so much blood. Christ. I looked up at the ceiling, and my eyes brimmed once again. Why was I feeling so emotional about this? Maybe it was just my hormones.

I stared at myself in the mirror. I looked awful, drained. A bandage around my head and a dressing on my arm. Not to mention the bombshell that Will had just dropped. I guess I was thankful that it came out now and not a couple of years down the line because we couldn't move on from there, could we?

We wanted different things.

'Jesus,' I blurted out thickly, catching it in my palm, and I sobbed, moving towards the shower and switching it on so I could disguise my crying, my grief, our loss....

When I realised I was on the floor, unaware of how much time had passed, I carefully took the bandage off and gently washed my hair in the sink. When I returned, Will wasn't in the bedroom, so I dressed quickly. Cautiously heading out into the kitchen, I was relieved to find it was empty. The girls were all sitting by the pool.

'Here she is,' Steph said, hopping up. 'How are you feeling?'

I had no idea if Will had told the others about the miscarriage, and Steph shook her head, signalling they didn't know.

'Yeah, okay,' I lied for their benefit.

'Come and sit by the pool,' Claire instructed. 'The boys have gone out.'

Out? What the fuck? I sat down carefully.

'Yeah, I can't believe the stamina of those guys. I'm done in after last night.'

'I'll make you some tea,' Zara said and hopped up.

'I'm just going to use the loo,' Steph announced, getting up, and there was a look between them all.

Something was up. I knew them too well.

'What's going on?' I asked Claire, and she filled her chest, sitting squarely to face me.

'I wanted to apologise again for my behaviour the other night.'

'You've already apologised, twice. It's fine, honestly.'

It was the last thing on my mind right now.

'I had a scan before we came out here.'

Wait. What? I looked up at her, but I didn't say anything.

'A mammogram and an aspiration. I know it doesn't excuse my behaviour, but I think I was drinking to forget,' she explained.

'So, they think you have breast cancer?' I asked, my eyes wide, moving over to her lounger.

'They don't know, but the signs are there. I don't get my results until we return to the UK.'

'And you've been harbouring all this since you got here?' I asked, dumbfounded.

'I didn't want to put a dampener on the holiday,' she admitted.

I wrapped my arms around her.

'Don't,' she said, pulling away, tears beckoning between us. 'There's no point until we know.'

'Okay. Fair enough.' I looked at her. 'And if you do...?'

'They set me a treatment plan, and we go from there. And if I don't, we party!' Claire said, and I laughed.

Steph and Zara headed back in.

'They know. I told them earlier,' Claire confirmed.

'Well, whatever the outcome, we'll all be here for you,' I said, and we had a little group hug. 'I don't know about you, but I need a drink.'

'Shouldn't you be taking it easy?' Steph eyed me suspiciously. 'What about the antibiotics?'

'I'll be fine,' I said, brushing it off.

I needed to do what Claire had done, drink to forget.

'Well, we may as well. It's our last night here,' Zara added.

She was right. What with everything going on, I'd forgotten that we were heading back to New York the next day.

A couple of hours later and we were all fairly tipsy. After topping everyone up, I flopped back down on the lounger, my head spinning a little, and I lazily looked over at Steph.

'Okay?' she mouthed, and I gave her a slow blink to confirm that I was.

Little did Steph know that Will had dropped a bomb on me before he left, and the more I thought about it, the angrier I became. Was it really the miscarriage that had made Will rethink his decision about kids? Or had he not been honest with me since the beginning? If I knew he wanted kids at the start, would I have ended it then? Would he have? Where did this leave us?

Suddenly the lads came bumbling back into the kitchen, Zara got up to greet them and offered them drinks, but I stayed put. Will looked over at me, his expression fixed, but I couldn't hold his eye and looked away.

Steph frowned at the exchange.

I couldn't handle the tension that had seeped in and gripped me, so I got up and wandered down the garden to escape it. I felt pretty woozy but reached the grass and sat down, looking at the night scene.

'Can we talk?' Will asked.

'I don't think that's a good idea right now,' I said carefully, trying not to slur.

It was likely I'd say something I'd regret, but he sat beside me all the same.

'What I said back there was stupid. It's you I want, Lucy. After you told me what happened, I allowed myself to think about the possibility of us having a baby, and I kinda liked the idea. I know that's not what you signed up for, and I get that, but it's not the be-all and end-all. You are my all, Lucy, my whole.'

'What you said was that you wanted to have kids. It's not stupid, Will. It's how you feel. It's inbuilt in us, and it's completely natural.' I stood up, wobbling a little as my head caught up with the movement. 'That's not going to change. You can't suppress feelings like that.'

Will stood up too, and went to put his arms around me, but I stepped back.

'It will come up time and time again,' I said.

I hadn't realised I'd raised my voice, and Will shot a glance back up to the house.

'Okay, maybe you're right. Let's talk about this tomorrow,' he suggested.

'Tomorrow, next week, next year... it will always be hanging over us.'

I was desperately trying to hold back on what I was about to say because it was breaking my heart, but my drunken ramblings had taken hold.

'I need to let you go.'

'Lucy, no!' he said, stepping forward into the gap I'd created between us, but he didn't touch me.

'Will, you need to find someone who will give you the family you yearn for,' I said as the sting of tears hit.

I couldn't quite believe the words coming out of my mouth, but I knew they were right.

'*You* are what I yearn for,' Will said thickly.

His words weighed heavily on my heart while I turned, crossing my arms and looking out at the view again, and it blurred as I sat back down. Why was he making this so much harder? Surely, he knew as well as I did that we couldn't carry on. We couldn't stay together. I didn't hear him go, but I felt it. I felt immediately hollow, and I keened into my lap.

Not much time passed before I sensed that someone was sitting next to me. It was Steph.

'You okay?'

I shook my head.

'What happened? Will looked really upset when he came back up to the house. The lads have all disappeared off into the studio.'

'I think we've split up,' I announced, another round of tears threatening as I heard my words.

'What? Over the miscarriage?' she sounded enraged.

'What miscarriage?' Claire asked as she and Zara joined us. I couldn't be bothered to explain. They'd have to catch up.

'No, over the fact that he's admitted he wants kids,' I said.

'Oh, fuck,' Steph said. 'Seriously?'

'Yeah, I think maybe he thought he could do without, but we all know it doesn't work like that,' I said, flopping back onto the grass. How on earth had I got there?

'So, you were going to have a baby, but you miscarried?' Zara asked, trying to piece it all together.

'I didn't know I was pregnant, and I miscarried, and now Will's told me he wants kids,' I explained.

'And you've split up over it?' Claire asked, shocked.

'I think so, we didn't actually say the words, but they were hanging there between us. He tried to assure me that it's me he wants, but this will just keep rearing its ugly head, won't it?'

I stated it rather than asking, trying to look up at the stars, but they looked more like white splodges that left trails if I moved my head too quickly.

'I'm not so sure it's the same for blokes,' Claire said.

'Yeah, they don't have that maternal clock like we do,' Zara added as if she was more qualified than me because she had five kids. Maybe she had a point.

'But he could have anyone, like, literally anyone. He could walk out of that door and girls would drop at his feet, openly offering to have his babies,' I said in my defence.

'Sounds to me like this is more of a crisis of confidence than anything else,' Steph said.

'Yeah, and he's already said that it's you he wants,' Zara added.

'Babe, I think you've jumped to conclusions. Go over and see him. Talk it out,' Claire suggested.

'And besides, would it really be that bad if you did have a kid with him? I don't mean now, but, in the future, like a couple of years down the line?' Zara asked.

I went to answer straight away with my automatic response, but I stopped and allowed myself to think for a second.

'If you had a baby with him... can you imagine, it would have the best of everything,' Claire said dreamily.

I was starting to get tired, and my body was not responding in the usual manner. I don't know whether it was the antibiotics, the booze or simply that I was exhausted.

'I need to go up there and go to bed. I am so drunk. We can talk in the morning.'

Chapter 26

When I woke, Will wasn't beside me, and a pang of disappointment struck me. Did he get up early, or had he not come to bed? We needed to talk. I jumped in the shower to freshen up and try to shake my hangover, I was way more wasted than normal last night, and I was kicking myself for saying what I'd said to Will.

As I stood there, letting the water sooth me, I thought about my conversation with the girls, instinctively placing a hand over my belly. Could I have a baby with him? He would make an amazing Dad. Thinking about it, the only thing holding me back was my age.

And maybe the fact that I had been striving for so long for a time when I could have some freedom and be in a position to be able to work a bit more to have some extra cash. The extra cash felt a bit like a moot point now.

I was suffering from this feeling of emptiness and loss, maybe because it was meant to be?

Once dressed, I headed out to the kitchen in search of Will. Jake was making a coffee, no sign of the girls.

'Hey, have you seen Will?' He looked up at me sorrowfully and nodded towards the garden.

Will was sat on the grass finishing up a call. 'Okay, that will have to do. Book it,' and he hung up.

'Hi,' I said hesitantly.

'Hi,' he replied monotone, but didn't look up. He just looked toward the view. 'I've booked you and the girls a flight, but the earliest first-class flight I can get for you isn't until the day after tomorrow from New York.'

What I should have asked was why he'd booked us a flight. Instead, I just said, 'We don't have to travel first class.'

He stood up and looked at me, and I was a bit taken aback. His eyes were red, and he looked exhausted. Had he even slept? He certainly looked like he'd been crying.

'The girls could travel commercial, but you can't. You'd get mobbed, and I don't want you travelling alone.'

'Right,' I whispered.

The realisation was that he'd decided that it was best we broke up. He was sending me home without him.

'You and the girls can use the apartment. I'll stay at Jakes,' he said matter-of-factly.

My mind was in free fall. I just stared at him blankly, unable to speak. He looked back and shook his head.

'You finally found the perfect excuse for an out.'

He strode back up to the house. What? This wasn't about me finding an out. This was about him changing his mind about wanting his own family. I was about to call him to tell him so, but then I heard an almighty crash. I ran back up to the house to see what had happened.

'Holy fuck, Will! Calm the fuck down,' Jake said as he grabbed him before smashing anything else.

The kitchen was covered in a sea of glass and bits of fruit, Will had obviously thrown the large glass fruit bowl on the floor. I looked across at him, my jaw open, and he looked back with fury. I wanted to run to him and tell him what I had been thinking in the shower this morning, but the glass obstacle course prevented me. Will went to take a step toward me, but Jake pulled him back, and there was a short tussle before Jake managed to guide him away toward the studio.

I fell to my knees and started to pick up all the larger pieces of glass, but the tears were falling, and because I couldn't see properly, I managed to cut myself within seconds.

'Lucy, I'll do that,' Jake said, coming back through. 'Oh shit, are you hurt?'

'It's just a...' but a sob replaced the rest of my sentence, and I began to shake.

Jake's hands appeared under my elbows as he helped to hoist me up to standing, moving me away from the glass and around the other side of the island where the sink was. He held my finger under some running water and then inspected it.

'I don't think you've got any glass in there, but you might wanna stick a Band-Aid on it,' he said, and I nodded through my tears. 'I don't know what's happening between you guys, but I'm sure you'll sort it out.'

I shook my head.

'I think it's too late,' I managed between my erratic breathing.

Jake didn't say anything more, he just found the sweep and started clearing up the mess, and I headed into the bedroom. I needed to pack. I silently and methodically packed my suitcase, trying to concentrate on the job rather than Will.

I did well until I picked up the bracelet Will had given me. The bracelet he'd purchased to apologise for our holiday becoming so stressful. The bracelet was the equivalent value of a deposit for a house in the UK. The bracelet that had dug into my arm when I was grabbed outside Tao, causing an infection.

I didn't want to keep it as a reminder of all those horrible memories. In fact, I didn't want any of it now. I dug the necklace and the earrings back out and left them all on the side.

Despite an overwhelming need to be at home in my sloppy joes with a cup of tea, I didn't want to leave there, it was so beautiful, and I certainly didn't want to go back to the apartment. The last time we'd been there was when we had fled for the villa. I didn't feel safe there, and Will wouldn't be with me this time. I guess I had the girls, and at least it would only be one night, I thought, trying to calm my nerves.

Just as I was zipping up my case, Will came bursting in, making me jump. I don't think he was expecting to see me, and he stilled, taking a breath in and holding it as he stared at me. I stared back, thunderstruck. This was my opportunity to talk to him. To tell him how I was feeling.

'Will, I...'

'I need to pack,' he announced, folding his arms, and I looked down at my case.

I lifted it off the bed and pulled the handle up. It was as if everything was happening in slow motion. As I approached Will, I put my hand out to touch his arm, and he recoiled, physically moving his whole body out of my reach as if I was about to burn him with a red-hot poker.

I gasped at his reaction.

He looked past me as if he couldn't bear the sight of me anymore, and I headed for the door. I was just about to pass through it when Will strode over to the bedside table.

'Are you not taking these?' he asked incredulously, pointing at the jewellery, and I looked down at the floor.

'I don't want the reminder,' I said quietly and Will put his hands on his hips.

'You don't want to be reminded of me?' He said, raising his voice a notch.

'It's not that...' I began, and he shook his head, staring at me with what, rage in his eyes?

'You don't want to be reminded...' he said, picking up the box that contained the necklace. 'Of when I asked you to be my girlfriend, and you accepted,' he said, nearly shouting.

He threw the box across the room, making me jump before picking up the next box.

I was aware that he'd caught the attention of whoever was in the kitchen because the babble of chatter had stopped.

'You don't want to be reminded of overcoming the struggle we went through when we first came out here?' he shouted, lobbing the next box across the room.

The bracelet fell out and clattered on the floor.

Paul and Mat had been walking along the corridor back from the studio and had both stopped about ten feet away, trying to make sense of the situation.

'It's not that...' I stammered, tears tracking down my face, trying to get a word in edgeways to explain why I was leaving them, but he was getting angrier by the second as he picked up the final box.

'You don't want to be reminded of the fact that I fucking love you, Lucy,' he yelled, throwing the box at me.

I had to lift my arms up to protect my face, but it landed at my feet.

Suddenly Steph was beside me, putting her arms around me protectively, as Paul barged past and grabbed Will's shoulders, but Will carried on. He was on a roll.

'That despite accepting me for who I am, despite me making plans for our future....'

Paul was physically holding him back, and Steph increased her protective hold around me.

'Despite me telling you my innermost feelings after losing the baby, you're prepared to just throw in the towel?'

I bit my lip, if the lads didn't know about the baby, they certainly did now, and I was getting cross, too, because he was broadcasting his feelings about our relationship across the entire group. I hated confrontation and being the centre of attention, but I couldn't just stand there and say nothing.

'I'm throwing in the towel because...'

I was just going to say that it was because he'd changed his mind about having a family of his own, but that sounded pretty lame compared to what he had just said.

He looked at me expectantly, along with everyone else, and I felt under pressure to put my side of the argument down. I tried to take a steadying breath, but the anger bloomed inside me.

'Because I've just done an interview to try to tame your savage fans, which was the most daunting thing I've ever done in my life, only to discover that I had lost our baby, due, may I add...' lifting my finger up as if to make what I was about to say more poignant, 'to one of your deluded fans.'

Will's jaw dropped and then he lifted his hands and placed them on the back of his head, anguish shot across his face, waiting to hear what else I had to say. I took a long-staggered breath, realising all eyes were on me, and I closed my own eyes to block them all out.

'I don't want the jewellery because that is what it symbolises for me. Loss.'

Will closed his eyes, and Mat was about to step in before either of us could expose ourselves to the group any further, but I held my hand up.

'And Will, despite all of that... I still love you,' I whispered because I could've heard a pin drop by that point.

Then I turned to Steph and sobbed.

'Okay, guys, let's take a break. The show's over,' Mat said, physically standing between Will and me while Steph guided me outside to the garden.

My legs buckled beneath me, but Steph managed to sit me on a lounger before I collapsed.

'Wow, that was quite a performance,' Steph said, crouching down to my level. 'Who knew you had it in you?' she said, trying to make light of the situation as Zara and Claire joined us.

'Now that is how to lay out an argument,' Claire said, and I looked up at her and then out to the view. She loved drama, that girl.

'I'm not proud,' I said, shaking my head sadly.

It wasn't as if I wanted everyone to hear what I was thinking and the ins and outs of why we were splitting up. I just wanted to explain to Will why I was leaving the jewellery.

'But you still love each other,' Zara proclaimed.

'It's not enough Zar, we've got twenty-four hours in New York, and then he's sending us back to the UK on a flight.'

'What, we're missing the gig?' Claire said in disbelief, and I nodded.

As if to signify the end of the trip, the doorbell went, and Mat opened the door to a driver, and the girls quickly scuttled off to finish packing. I looked at the view again, soaking it up one last time. Mat came out and hovered beside me.

'Will told me to let you know that you and the girls will be travelling together to the plane.'

A short sharp breath expelled through my nose, and I closed my eyes.

'What are you, like the messenger now?' But as soon as I'd said it, I felt guilty. 'I'm sorry,' I said earnestly.

'It's okay. We all know the immense pressure you've been under,' he said, putting a hand on my shoulder. 'I'm sorry about the baby.'

I hated the fact that everyone knew exactly what was going on between us, and I was angry with myself for getting so wound up.

'I'm gonna go and wait in the car,' I said.

My case wasn't there, so I figured the driver already had it.

He was waiting outside by the car and nodded to me as I stepped in. The girls eventually joined me, and we set off. I just looked out of the window, allowing my tears to silently fall. Once we arrived at the airfield, I quickly got out and headed to the plane. I just wanted to get this over and done with.

The six-hour flight felt like an eternity. The girls and I were down at one end of the plane and the boys at the other. The atmosphere was dreadful. Nobody said anything for at least the first hour or so, and then Mat broke the silence and got everyone a drink. I noticed Will opted for cola while everyone else had alcoholic drinks. I ordered a double vodka, and Will looked over at me.

I tried calming my nerves about returning to the apartment, but they were blooming inside me. I felt sick, fidgeting, tapping my foot, biting my lip, and doing anything to keep myself in the moment.

'Are you all right?' Steph asked, holding onto my hand.

I glanced over at Will, and he was still watching me as I tried to keep my breathing under control. I closed my eyes, and all I could see was the view from Will's breakfast bar in the apartment. Looking out to the balcony and across to the New York skyline. My anxiety was beginning to take hold.

I began to do the breathing exercises Roxy had taught me. And I thought about home. The view from my kitchen into our garden. The boys, their beautiful faces and even the thought of their bickering brought me comfort. And Luna and Grayson, how I longed to sit on the sofa between their warm furry bodies.

My breathing began to calm, and I forced my body to relax. Sleep. I just needed to sleep. In forty-eight hours, I would be in my happy place, and until then, I would dream about it.

The next thing I knew, the captain was announcing our descent, and I woke with a start. My eyes immediately found Will's. He was staring straight back. Had he been watching me the whole time? I tried to hold his gaze, but it was too painful, and I looked down to find the seatbelt to clip myself in.

The moment we landed, Will got up and stood by the door, waiting for the stewardess to open it. He glanced at me while she went through the unlocking procedure, holding my gaze for a moment. There was so much in that look, so many unspoken words, so many emotions.

He took a breath in, and for a moment, I thought he was going to say something, but just then, the door opened, the light flooding in, accentuating his jawline and the bottle green of his eyes. He swallowed, tearing his gaze away and stepped out.

I slumped back in my chair, his departure lacerating my heart like a stab wound. I was completely hollow. The following few hours seemed to happen around me. Like I was on autopilot.

I numbly hugged Jake, Paul and Mat. Saying a final farewell before Steph guided me toward the waiting car. I vaguely recalled seeing Terry standing by the other car, but I didn't have it in me to smile.

We eventually arrived in the apartment, and after showing the girls where everything was, I took myself off to bed. I wanted to be alone to grieve not only for the baby but also for our relationship. I kind of knew deep down that it would never last. Will had just done a bloody good job of making me think it could work.

I don't know how long I'd been asleep, but I woke suddenly when Steph sat on the edge of the bed.

'Hey, sorry to wake you. I just didn't want you to wake up and wonder where we were.'

I shivered, and she pulled the covers over my shoulder like a mother would for her daughter.

'We're gonna head out. I'm not even going to attempt to talk you into it, but Jake called Zara, and he's gonna meet us in town and be our guide for the evening.'

'Okay, sure, do whatever you want,' I croaked. 'Just don't waste your money and go up the Empire State because if I'm honest, the view from here is better.'

'Good to know,' she said, giving me a weak smile. 'There's some left-over pizza on the island if you're hungry.'

I shook my head and closed my eyes again. A silent sign to leave me alone, and she took the hint.

After tossing and turning, I eventually managed to get back to sleep, and when I woke a few hours later, it was dark, and the apartment was empty. My tummy groaned, and I realised I hadn't eaten anything all day, and then I remembered the pizza.

I got up, realising I was only wearing a camisole and some briefs, so I wrapped one of the blankets around me to keep off the evening chill and ventured into the kitchen.

I was just about to bite into a slice of pizza when suddenly, a deafening alarm started going off. A red light above the elevator began flashing, and then an automated announcement came over the tannoy system.

Stay calm.

Please make your way to your place of shelter.

Do not panic.

This is a non-combustible building.

And then the alarm kicked back in.

What the hell?

Where is the place of shelter?

Was there a fire somewhere?

The announcement sounded again, and despite its efforts, I was starting to panic. Will and I hadn't gone through fire regulations when we were there last. I mean, who the fuck goes through fire regs when you stay at their place?

The alarm sounded again.

Should I go out onto the balcony? My stomach tightened at the thought. I was sensible enough to know I shouldn't go in the lift. Was there a secret staircase? I was almost positive there wasn't one from the apartment. Maybe it was outside. But that would mean I'd have to go out onto the balcony.

Oh God.

The alarm was so loud it was making it almost impossible to think.

I started pulling drawers open in the kitchen. Maybe there was a document somewhere showing where the place of shelter was. Or how to get out if the fire spread. In my panic, I was literally pulling the contents of the drawers out, not caring that it was landing on the floor.

Once I'd emptied them, I spun around, searching for other possible places. The cabinets by the TV were next.

Stay calm.

Please make your way to your place of shelter.

Do not panic.

This is a non-combustible building.

'Shut up!' I shouted at the automated message. It was making it even more difficult to concentrate.

Once I'd exhausted all the places I thought sensible to keep fire reg documents, I spun around and stared at the balcony. My nemesis. My breathing was laboured. I was still clutching onto the blanket that was now half wrapped around me and shaking.

I took a big breath in.

'You can do this, Lucy,' I whispered to myself.

Despite the mayhem around me, I slowly began to walk towards the windows. Desperately trying to keep my senses together. I reached the door, and just as I was about to pull on the handle, there was an odd bleep, and the alarm stopped.

I stilled, frozen with my hand still clutching the handle.

Thank you for your cooperation.

Normal activities can resume.

As the breath I had been holding left my body, I turned my back to the door and slid down it to the floor. Collapsing in a heap at the relief that the emergency was over. My hearing was muffled after the loud alarm.

I must have only been there for a few moments when I thought I heard the lift ping.

'Lucy?' Will called, his voice laced with concern.

Before I'd replied, he came striding into the kitchen, and he saw me in a crumpled heap by the window.

'Lucy, baby,' he said, immediately scooping me up and nuzzling into my neck.

He was out of breath, and I could feel his heart hammering against my torso. I wrapped my arms around his neck and held on tightly as he walked us over to the sofa, sitting down without letting go. I should have asked why he was there, but I figured he'd probably been alerted about the emergency on his phone.

'Why are you out of breath?' I asked.

'Because I ran here from Jakes,' he replied between breaths. 'You know, you could have just called. You didn't need to set the fire alarm off.'

A small laugh bubbled up and escaped me, and as if seeing the apartment for the first time, Will began to look around.

'What the fuck happened in here?'

'The announcing person kept telling me to go to the place of shelter, and I didn't know where that was, so I was frantically searching for the fire drill documents.'

He began to chuckle, and as if he had been hit with a mild case of hysteria, the chuckle turned into a laugh until he was bellowing uncontrollably. I began to laugh too. It was contagious. And before I knew it, we were clutching our bellies when it became painful. As our laughing subsided, Will looked at me, biting his lower lip.

'So, for future reference, this,' he said, gesturing his hand around the apartment, '*is* the place of shelter.'

'Oh,' I said.

But the mere mention of the word *future* caused the elephant in the room to expand and suffocate the lightheartedness of the moment.

There was an awkward period of silence as we both gathered our thoughts, and then I looked up, about to speak just as Will did the same, and we both laughed again.

'You go,' Will said, ever the gentleman.

My mouth went dry. The tension consuming. What I said next would determine our future. I took a short breath in several times, readying myself to speak, but the words wouldn't come.

Will smiled genuinely, knowing I was struggling and silently willing me to just say it. I shuffled around to straddle him, getting caught up in the blanket as I did, but I wanted to look him straight in the eye.

'I love you,' I said simply.

There was a pause, and Will bit his lip as if he was physically stopping himself from interrupting.

'I want to be with you,' I continued. 'Forever,' I clarified. 'I want you to be in my view wherever I look.'

He closed his eyes as if what I had just said was cleansing his soul, but when he opened them again, they were glassy.

'Even though you lost the baby because of me?' he said, a single tear dropping onto the blanket between us.

I shook my head, 'No.'

'Yes, Lucy. The fans, the assault, the infection.' He sniffed and released a shaky breath.

I scooped his face up in my hands.

'You can't blame yourself for that. That was out of your control. I know it was one of your fans, but you can't take responsibility for what they do and say. I don't hold you personally responsible for that,' I said, smoothing my hands over his face.

He looked at me with big eyes. We were both avoiding the issue that had set this clusterfuck of events in motion. Will rubbed his hands up and down my thighs a couple of times, searching for the right words, and then he closed his eyes and took a deep breath.

'I do want a kid with you, but if it means I can't have you, I'm willing to forgo that because I love you and want *you* above anything else.'

Tears were pooling in my eyes at the enormity of what he was saying.

'Will... I had a serious think about the baby thing. I do not deny that I'm concerned about my age and its health implications, but maybe, later down the line... if it felt right, we could try for a baby.'

Will laughed through a sob and drew his eyebrows together.

'You'd be willing to have another baby? For me?'

'For us. Yes,' I said confidently. 'Although that has some bearing on the future plans you have for us.' I said, drawing upon the point he'd raised in our argument, and I frowned with a smile, trying to lighten the seriousness of our conversation.

'Well, for now, you're just gonna have to trust me on that one,' he said, not willing to confirm anything.

'So... we're gonna make a proper go of this, with the view of having a family in the future?' I asked to clarify.

'With the view of adding to our family in the future,' he said.

I smiled. I went to kiss him, it felt so natural, but then I stalled, hesitating about taking the lead.

'Kiss me,' Will instructed.

I did, with force, and I heard a small moan as his hands slowly snaked around me, drawing me in close.

Our kissing became heavy, our tongues exploring each other's mouths as if we hadn't kissed in weeks. His hands smoothed over my camisole before pulling it off so that he could pepper kisses below my collarbone.

His touch was becoming dominant and rough, and I could feel him rock hard beneath me.

'Will,' I whimpered. I was still feeling delicate after everything that had happened, and he immediately eased his grip, sliding his hands under my thighs before scooping me up and carrying me into the bedroom. He gently lay me down and lay by my side, leaning over me.

'Are you okay after earlier? I thought you were gonna have another anxiety attack.'

'I'm fine. I just felt like the closer we got to New York, the closer the walls were caving in on me.'

'You want me to contact Roxy again to see if she can help?'

I nodded.

I guess it wouldn't hurt, and being that I'd now done the interview, maybe she could help me with some more coping strategies.

'What's happening with the interview, by the way?' I asked.

'I dunno, they're probably editing it. Kieron'll let us know so we can sign off the final cut before it goes out.' He kissed me chastely and then added. 'I really appreciate you doing that, it was really brave of you, and I know that it put you completely out of your comfort zone.'

I put my finger against his lips to stop him from talking. I knew he was only saying all of that because of our argument, but he took my hand and placed it on the bed.

'And how are you feeling about the miscarriage?'

I took a breath in at the mention of the word.

'Sad... it's always sad, right?'

He nodded.

'I guess if I'd known, it would have been a lot harder. Grieving for something that I didn't know was there feels strange, but then I guess my body knew it was there all along.'

Will was just looking into my eyes sorrowfully.

'My boobs are really sore,' I added, and he glanced down at them and then back to me, a small smile appearing on his face.

'What?'

'If it's possible, they're bigger,' he said, his eyes dancing over them again.

'Will!' I said, attempting to swipe him with my free hand but as usual, he caught it and pinned that one to the bed too. 'I'm also wearing the most unladylike pad you have ever seen.'

'Noted,' Will said as his hungry eyes returned to my boobs, and then he kissed me. He kissed me like it was the first time we had ever kissed, exploring my mouth and devouring it before moving down to my swollen boobs.

Chapter 27

I leapt out of my skin as the bedroom door burst open. Steph, Claire, Zara, and Jake came tumbling in.

'Lucy! We've been burgled!' Steph hissed in a drunken slur.

'What?' I said, sitting up, the movement causing Will to stir.

Our limbs were all tangled up together with the sheets.

'There's paperwork everywhere,' Jake added before flicking the light on.

I squinted and watched all their faces morph from anguish to shock to embarrassment. I looked down to discover that Will's behind was on full display.

'We haven't been burgled,' Will mumbled into the pillow. 'Lucy just decided to empty all the drawers.'

Claire snorted through her nose.

'Yeah, we can see that,' she said as everyone started giggling, me included.

Will lifted his head and realised what we were all laughing about before face-planting the pillow again, completely disregarding his appearance.

'Come on girls, it's time for bed,' Jake said. 'Glad to see you two have made up,' he added, giving me a rueful smile.

I WOKE NATURALLY THE following morning. Will was fast asleep. He must have been exhausted because he'd barely moved since we were woken unexpectedly. He looked gorgeous lying there, his hair all mussed up, his eyelashes fanning his cheeks, and I slowly disappeared under the covers, taking full advantage of his morning glory.

I wrapped my fingers around him, gently pulling down so not to startle him, and I could feel him hardening under my grip. Sleepily he moved onto his back.

Perfect.

I wriggled further down. Licking and kissing the end of his dick, I could sense him stirring, so I took him in my mouth.

I felt the covers being lifted, and I looked up as he peeked under, eyes shining, and I took him deep into my mouth.

'Fuck,' he said, raising his hips towards me, and I slowly came back up, grazing my teeth along his shaft before taking him in again. Will exhaled. I moved my fingers down to his balls, his skin puckering under my touch, and then I grabbed them, making him jump. I looked up again, and he was watching me, smiling and shaking his head.

I increased my pace, working the top with the flat of my tongue every now and again. Will put his fingers through my hair, cupping the nape of my neck, encouraging me to take him deeper. I didn't disappoint.

'Christ, Lucy, I'm gonna come in a minute.'

I just looked at him again with more determination as his hips took over. His thrusts became more erratic as he used his hands to keep my head in position, and then I felt the warm salty spray on the back of my throat as I drank him in, revelling in his pulses.

I climbed back up, hovering over him and smiled.

'That was one mighty fine way to wake up,' he said, and I laughed at his mock Texan accent. 'I love watching you with your lips around me.'

'Do you indeed. Good morning, Will.'

He grinned.

'Good morning, Beautiful.'

I lay beside him, resting my head on his chest as he pulled me in close, and I sighed happily. This is what I lived for, moments like this, of pure contentment and happiness.

'What are you thinking about?'

'How content I am right now, at this moment,' I sighed, and he smiled.

'Yeah, it's pretty damn cool.'

There was a knock at the door. I closed my eyes and shook my head in disbelief, and Will laughed, pulling the covers up and over me.

'Yep, come in.'

'Sorry, I hope I didn't wake you,' Zara said.

'Not at all. Everything okay?' Will asked.

'Yes, perfect, thank you, I just wanted to let you know that we are heading into the city. Steph said you probably didn't wanna come, so we thought we'd hit the shops before it got too hot.'

'Sure,' I replied. 'I'm happy chilling.'

'Okay, well, we'll see you when we get back.'

'Zara?' Will asked. 'Can I ask you a favour?'

'Of course, anything.'

'Give me a sec,' he said, climbing out of bed, and Zara quickly shut the door, realising he was naked.

'What are you up to?' I asked as he dragged some boxer shorts and jeans on.

'Never you mind,' he replied before slipping out of the bedroom.

He was up to something, but I left him to it and headed into the bathroom. I was pleased to see that the bleeding had abated. I could do without the constant reminder that I'd had a miscarriage every time I went to the loo.

Will came back in while I was showering and watched me while he brushed his teeth. I purposefully lathered up, washing my body slowly. Smoothing my hands over my breasts and between my legs, lingering there for a while, and occasionally catching his gaze before turning to rinse. As I reached for the shampoo, I felt him behind me.

'That was quite the show, Daniels,' he said, and I smiled as he fed his arms around me.

'Glad you enjoyed it,' I replied seductively, and I began washing my hair.

'You know, you would never have done that when I met you,' he observed, and I stilled. Was it too much? 'I love it. I like that you feel confident around me. It shows you trust me.'

He turned me, lifting his hands up to rinse the suds off my hair.

'Your body is beautiful. I am one lucky man.'

He lifted my chin and kissed me. I responded eagerly. I wanted him.

'Come on, your time's up. I need to shower.' And he physically moved me out of the flow and stepped under.

Damn him.

'I'm gonna cancel your flight home. I'm guessing the girls will want me to cancel their flights too.'

'I'd imagine so. The girls were pretty disappointed when they thought they would miss the gig.'

He nodded, and I left him to it.

Coffee. That's what I needed. I quickly put my underwear on and grabbed a cardi to stave off the morning chill. Someone had picked all the stuff up from the floor and put it in a huge pile on the breakfast bar.

I set about making the coffee, switching the sound system on and playing a bit of Bill Withers while I figured out how to use the enormous machine. As I was scrolling through all the options on the screen, I sensed Will had come into the room.

'What would you like?'

'Anything, if you're gonna serve it to me like that.'

I leapt out of my skin, turned, and quickly covered myself up. It was Jake. He sat down on one of the stools on the other side of the breakfast bar, laughing.

'Shit, I didn't realise you were here,' I said.

'Obviously,' he chuckled, smiling as Will came through.

He nodded to Jake and then smiled at me with amusement as he took in my attire. I stood there for a moment, unsure of what to do, Will clearly didn't care that I was half-dressed in front of his friend, but I felt awkward.

I decided it was best to get dressed, so I went to head back to the bedroom, but Will grabbed me and sat me on the island. I yelped as the cold marble made my skin prickle.

'Where are you going?' Will asked, but rather than waiting for me to answer, he kissed me, pushing himself between my legs.

'Bye, Jake,' he said, pushing my cardigan off my shoulder. I watched as Jake picked up his keys and wallet, shaking his head while Will kissed my neck.

'Bye, guys. See you later.'

Jake pressed the lift button, but before he'd had the chance to get in, Will pulled the cup of my bra down and licked my nipple.

'Will,' I scolded, and he smiled as Jake disappeared from view.

'What?' he asked, smiling with amusement. 'That'll make his walk home difficult.'

I giggled, and Will picked me up and took me back into the bedroom, setting me down on the floor at the foot of the bed. He pushed my cardigan off my shoulders as he sat down on the end of the bed in front of me and trailed kisses along the waistline of my knickers as I combed my fingers through his hair.

'I'm assuming your little performance earlier, and the lack of padding means you're okay with this?'

'Yes,' I said breathlessly.

He lifted one of my legs, placed my foot beside him, and looked up at me as he pulled my knickers to one side. I could feel the air cooling my wet centre and licked my lips in anticipation. He smiled up at me before running his index finger through my opening and then popping it in his mouth to clean it off.

'So. Fucking. Sweet,' he said before leaning forward.

Will's tongue followed the same path as his thumb had, and I moaned. Using his tongue to alternate between licking and sucking me, it didn't take long before I was panting, and my fingers were fisted in his hair.

'Rock that beautiful cunt on my face, baby.'

His words were so crass but so fucking hot, and he started fucking me with his tongue, wedging his nose onto my clit. I moaned again as he guided my hips back and forth, encouraging me to rock over him.

'Oh, fuck,' I murmured as I felt myself building and took over the rocking motion myself. He hummed with satisfaction, and then using his thumb to slide through my opening, covering it in my arousal, he pushed it into my butt, and I stopped moving at the sudden intrusion.

'Don't fucking stop. I wanna feel you shudder all over my tongue.'

He grabbed my hip, forcing me to rock again, pushing my knee out to the side to open me up further and fucked me with his tongue again. With each rock, his thumb moved in deeper, and he was swirling his nose around my clit.

'Oh God, oh God, I'm coming,' I said and grabbed the back of his head, holding him just where I needed him to be while I rubbed myself against him until my pulsing clit was sated.

I looked down at Will, and he was sporting the biggest, salacious grin one could wish for, and I immediately coloured up.

'Don't you dare be embarrassed about that,' he said, gently pushing me back slightly so he could stand. 'I nearly came in my fucking briefs.'

I laughed, and he kissed me, but I pushed him away. 'You are covered in me,' I said, turning towards the ensuite.

'Aha, just the way I like it,' he replied, wiping his face with his fingers and licking them as he followed me.

I HAD UPGRADED MY CARDIGAN to a dressing gown and sat at the island with a coffee, scrolling through some pictures the boys had sent me from their holiday. I looked up at Will.

'Are you nervous?' I asked, and he stopped pacing and texting, which he had been doing for the last ten minutes and stared at me.

'Yeah, I guess so,' he said, breathing out, and I frowned.

'That's unlike you for a local show. It's just friends, isn't it?'

'Yeah, it's probably because we're showcasing the new stuff,' he replied, brushing it off and then changing the subject. 'Are there any specific drinks you want on the rider tonight?'

'No, I don't think so.' I replied.

'Okay, I'm gonna have to leave around six, but Terry will be here to collect you and the girls at eight. There's likely to be press, but it'll be managed, and Terry will take you in. Will you be cool?'

'What about fans?' I asked purposefully, not confirming that I would be okay because I was immediately shitting myself.

'You know what? I'm gonna get Terry to organise some backup.'

Then he wandered off with his phone again.

The girls arrived back, all chattering at once. There had clearly been cocktails involved during their shopping trip. They had so many bags.

'Are you gonna fit all of that in your suitcases?' I asked.

'Lu! It's not all for us, we bought you an outfit, and we all think, well, hope you'll love it,' Zara said.

'Yeah, we figured since you couldn't go shopping, we'd bring the shopping to you!' Steph added.

'We can always take it back if it's not right,' Claire said.

'Aww, thanks, girls, that's really thoughtful,' I said as Zara was fishing around in one of the bags to do the big reveal.

She pulled out what initially looked like a slinky sequin scarf and held it up. It was a dress. A very short dress, covered from top to bottom in dark marine blue sequins. I took it from her, holding it up.

'It's beautiful... I mean, does it come with a bottom section?'

They all laughed.

'I told you she'd think it was too short,' Steph said.

'You will look stunning in it, and you can pair it with your ankle biker boots,' Claire said.

I looked at it again and sighed.

'Thanks, guys.' As I was turning it to see the back, I spotted the price tag. 'What the... this is nearly two thousand dollars,' I said, my mouth popping open.

'I paid for it,' Will announced as he joined us.

'Will!' I said in dismay.

'What?' he said, shrugging, feeding his arm around my waist. 'I wanted to treat you.'

He kissed me on my temple.

'Thanks, ladies.'

This had clearly been planned, and then he leaned in.

'I've gotta go. I'll see you in a couple of hours.'

I looked at him, breathing in and held my breath.

'You'll be fine, I promise.'

And with that, he left. Suddenly I felt sick. I quickly passed the dress to Steph and hot-footed it into the bathroom. A few moments later, Steph opened the door as I perched against the vanity unit and rested the back of my head on the mirror.

'You okay?' she asked.

'Oh babe, I'm just really nervous. There's going to be press and fans there, and after the last ordeal... I'm just not looking forward to it,' I admitted, and Steph quietly tutted.

'Gosh, do you remember when we went to the gig in Bristol? You were so excited and in awe of him, and now you're throwing up for fear of getting papped,' she mused.

'I know, it was so much easier then,' I said.

'Go and put that sparkly dress on and some makeup to cover up your post-puke hue, and let's have a good night.

I'm ready and poised to punch anyone's lights out who even attempts to touch you,' she declared, and I laughed.

'Thanks, babe.'

When I got into the bedroom, I lay the dress over the stool by the dressing table and spotted my broken bracelet, only it wasn't broken anymore. Will had obviously got it fixed. I looked around for a note and saw a bottle of fizz in an ice bucket on the bedside table. I walked over, and there was a card.

I can't wait to see you in that dress tonight… I can't wait to see you out of it too. X

I smiled.

PS Please wear the bracelet.

I poured myself a glass and got myself undressed.

Joining the girls an hour later in the kitchen with a topped-up glass, Claire wolf-whistled when I walked in. I flushed, smiling shyly. The dress was way shorter than I would have ever chosen for myself, but I did feel good in it.

'You look amazing,' Steph said.

'As do you lot. Look at you all.'

Everyone had made a real effort, and it felt like we were the Sex & The City girls for a split second.

I smiled, and Steph lifted her glass. 'Here's to an awesome night.'

'To awesome nights,' we all chimed, and they told me about all the shops and bars they'd visited.

It sounded amazing, but it wasn't long before I saw the lift light come on, and Terry appeared. He immediately ushered me to one side to brief me on the plan, but I knew the drill. The girls would get out first, two security guards were meeting us there, and they would be on either side of me, with Terry behind. It sounded so over the top for a five-metre walk across the street, but also reassuring.

Chapter 28

The girls were visibly fizzing by the time we arrived at the venue.

Terry turned and said, 'Okay, ladies, if you could walk straight into the building and then wait just inside while I get Lucy in.'

Claire lifted her hand in a salute while the others giggled.

'We'll see you in there,' Steph said with a wink.

Zara looked me in the eye and squeezed my arm. 'Be careful,' she said.

They stepped out, and I could see the flashes and hear the shouting before I'd even moved towards the door. Terry ducked his head in and put his hand out for me. I took it, holding my breath, and as planned, two security guards flanked my left and right, and Terry put his hand on the lower part of my back as he guided me forwards.

Upon realising it was me, the flashing went wild, and I could hear people calling my name, but no one approached. I was hoping my dress hadn't ridden up. They all stayed behind the barriers, and despite feeling a little dizzy, we were through the doors and in the foyer in seconds.

'Okay, ladies, you're free to go in,' Terry said, nodding at me with a small smile.

Without further ado, Claire opened the double doors to the main auditorium, and we all walked in. I spotted

Will straight away. He was chatting to someone, but I couldn't see who it was. He looked up as we entered, and his face lit up into a huge grin, and my heart skipped a beat.

He beckoned me over, and as I walked, I could see the bar on the right, running down the entire length of the room. It was stainless steel with stools running all the way along, and it reminded me of a massive version of Will's kitchen island in LA.

Behind Will was the stage. I was expecting it to be relatively low key, like the one they played on for the acoustic gig when we first met. This was a proper stage. The auditorium floor was flag stoned, and there was barely any seating. In fact, the venue was much bigger than I had thought it was going to be. I thought it was just meant to be family and friends.

'Lucy,' Will said, placing his arm around my waist and whispering in my ear. 'You look fucking hot.'

And then he looked back at the man he was talking to.

'Ian, this is Lucy, Lucy, Ian.'

I put my hand out to shake his.

'Ian plays in the same band as Stryker.'

'Oh yes, The Deck, it's great to meet you,' I said, smiling warmly.

'You too. I've heard a lot about you.'

I blushed, wondering just how much he had heard. Stryker appeared at my side. He looked at me, jaw lax and took my hand, pulling me away from Will and making me twirl as if I were one of those tiny ballerinas that hid in all the cool girl jewellery boxes when I was little. He kissed me on the cheek.

'That is an incredible dress,' he said, staring straight at the top of my thighs.

My cheeks heated immediately, and Will laughed before pulling me back in.

'I'm not sure it's strictly classified as a dress,' I said, pulling it down. 'I have a feeling they ran out of fabric.'

They all laughed.

'Well, I think you look amazing in it,' Will said, kissing my neck as another man approached. 'Quinn! Good to see you, man. Quinn, this is Lucy, Lucy, this is my manager.'

'Oh, hi, great to meet you.'

'You too, Lucy,' he said, shaking my hand firmly. 'Lovely to finally meet the woman who has this one wrapped.' He nodded towards Will and gave me a warm smile which I returned. 'How are things going with Mat?' He asked Will.

'Really good, he's a nice guy, and we're looking forward to working with him.'

'Good, well, I won't keep you. I'm looking forward to hearing the new tunes.' He shook Will's hand before disappearing into the crowd.

The girls joined us, Claire handing me a glass of champagne, and there were more introductions. The room was filling up, and Will smiled and nodded to people as they came in. I could tell he was getting itchy feet, and I thought he would excuse himself, but instead, he said, 'We've just got to go and say hi to a few people, excuse us, and he took my hand.'

Half an hour later, I had been introduced to so many people, and it felt weird that they all knew who I was.

There was no way I'd remember any of their names. There were friends from school, people he'd toured with, friends in the industry, and even cousins I didn't know existed.

Then I spotted someone familiar. It was Cara. I'd completely forgotten she was coming, and Thomas had joined her.

'Cara!' I gave her a big squeeze and then kissed Thomas on the cheek. 'It's so lovely to see you again. I'm so glad you made it.'

'She's the only reporter allowed in this evening,' Will said with a warm smile, and I could see Cara's beaming smile.

This would be huge for her and her writing profession, and Thomas looked at her with pride. I glanced at Will and smiled. He knew the impact this would have on her career.

After having a catch-up with Cara, I finally made my way back to the girls just as Jake joined us with a large tray of shots. My God, I was already feeling the effects of the champagne and was about to refuse, but Jake handed me one.

'Glad to see you're fully dressed now, although...' he glanced down at my legs before he moved on to the next group, giving me a wink.

I shook my head and knocked the shot back. I would have to get used to people looking at me with hardly any clothes on. Could I really do the modelling thing? Will returned, holding another glass of fizz for me.

'I'm gonna be wasted if you carry on feeding me these,' I said, and he smiled.

'We're gonna go on shortly, so we're just gonna head out back for a minute. We'll play about five tunes and then have a break before going back on later. You gonna stay with the girls?'

He glanced over my shoulder as I nodded, and I followed his gaze. Terry was standing in the wings.

'I thought you knew all these people?' Wondering why Terry would need to be there.

'I do. I wanted Terry here,' he smiled and kissed me briefly.

Oh, now he was treating him like a friend rather than an employee, I couldn't keep up, and he headed towards a door to the right of the stage, Jake and Paul following suit.

'Hello, you!'

That was a voice I recognised. I turned to see it was Milly with Leo, Hannah, Mat and a girl I didn't recognise joining us too. Mat introduced me to his girlfriend, Emily, and I introduced Hannah to the girls, and Steph shot me a glance the second she started firing questions at her. It was so predictable, and I couldn't help but chuckle. They would never be friends.

The lights dimmed, signalling the imminent arrival of the band, and everyone turned. The stage lights came up, and they all headed onto the stage to raucous cheers, clapping and whistling. Will approached the mic.

'Hey, hey, just wanted to say thanks for coming out tonight and to Al for allowing us to use The Pound again. We love it here.' He strummed his guitar several times to check the tuning and then added. 'I hope you like the new stuff.'

He stepped away from the mic. Jake counted them in with his sticks, and they launched into the first track. It was fast, it was heavy, and it had a booming beat. I hadn't seen them play in a while, and I'd forgotten how energetic Will was on stage. He just loved it, and his enthusiasm transferred to the audience.

I thought the new tunes were brilliant, and despite them being heavy, the choruses were melodic and catchy. There wasn't the usual draw from the crowd to be at the front of the stage because the venue wasn't packed, and it was nice to have a bit of space to appreciate the music and tap my feet.

After a few songs, I was feeling the effects of the alcohol, but I was determined not to get too drunk, so I snuck off and went to the bar to get some water. The bar was dead, so I got served straight away.

As I waited, I looked down the length of the bar and spotted Stryker and Milly. I was about to walk over to say hi, but something stopped me. Their body language looked odd. Milly had her arms crossed protectively with her back to the bar, and Stryker somehow seemed closer than he should be, looking down at her with his hand on the bar.

The bar attendant put my glass of water in front of me just as one of the songs came to an end, and in that short moment, before the next song began, I caught a snippet of their conversation.

'If you possessed an ounce of consideration, you'd be aware that she would have been eighteen last month,' Milly exclaimed.

'And why do you *still* think I give a fuck?' Stryker seethed.

I glanced over at them just as I heard Milly yelp, and her head jerked to one side. Stryker was pulling his hand out of Milly's hair and it looked as though he was readying himself to slap her.

What the fuck?

I strode over to them at speed.

'Hi guys,' I said brightly. 'You not watching the show?'

Stryker immediately stepped back.

'Lucy,' he said with a false grin. 'We were just having a little catch-up.'

I looked at Milly, her sleek bob all askew and tears swimming in her eyes. I needed to think of something quick.

'Oh, I'm sorry to interrupt. I just wondered if I could borrow Milly, I've got a favour to ask.'

'Sure, I'll catch you later, Milly. Lucy,' he said to bid his farewell, nodding as he left us to it.

Milly slumped the second he was out of sight.

'Are you okay?' I asked.

'Yes, absolutely fine,' she said, sniffing and trying to swipe the unshed tears away undetected. 'How can I help?'

She obviously didn't want to talk about it, and I didn't want to make her feel awkward by admitting I'd overheard. But my suspicions about Stryker being the one that fled before her abortion had been confirmed.

'Oh... um... I just... I wondered if you could give me some advice about... piano lessons. Paddy is thinking of taking it up.'

As we weaved back into the crowd, she suggested some online courses Paddy could do that would mean he could learn at his own pace, but my mind was elsewhere.

Stryker was threatening Milly, but why? And why hadn't Milly ever divulged who the father was? Maybe he had some hold over her, or she simply didn't want people to know.

Either way, I'd seen a different side to Stryker and didn't like it.

The band finished another banging tune, and then Will approached the mic again.

'This next song...' he said breathlessly and took a second to compose himself. 'Is one I wrote for my girl.'

He shielded his eyes from the stage lights to see if he could see me just as we reached the girls, and the lights came up a bit on the audience. Everyone started to turn, and Claire grabbed my arm while my cheeks burned, and Will locked eyes with mine. He laughed, he could see I was feeling wholly self-conscious, and he added.

'You are my inspiration, Lucy... it's called, *My View*.'

The song was about other people's perceptions of me, and each verse highlighted a different group, the press, the fans, and our friends, but the chorus was his view of me. I was fighting back the tears as it was, and as the band entered into a more choppier section of the song, Will was singing about my courage and loyalty, my acceptance of him, and it was too much, and the tears began to fall.

The song came to an end, and I had my head in my hands from embarrassment and trying to hide my tears.

Claire put her arm around me as Will said, 'I knew she'd cry, we're gonna take a break.'

As I wiped the tears from my face, Will hopped over the monitors, jumped off the stage into the audience, and came running over. Claire released me as he approached and he wrapped his arms around me, shielding me from everyone's stares. He gave me a moment and then pulled back, wiping a few remaining tears away from my cheeks with his thumbs.

Then, cupping my face with his hands, he said, 'I'm afraid your embarrassment doesn't end here.'

'What?' I asked.

I didn't know what he meant, and then he dropped down onto one knee and took a box out of his pocket.

Oh.

My.

God.

My hands went straight back up to my face to cover my gaping jaw. Several people gasped around us, and a wave of hush slowly fell upon the crowd.

He looked up at me, 'Lucy Daniels...' He paused to clear his throat. 'Will you marry me?'

My cheeks were so hot, and I was rooted to the spot, utterly lost for words.

Will smiled and said, 'I mean, I know you struggle to find the right....'

'Yes! Yes, of course I'll marry you,' I replied, remembering myself, and Will closed his eyes as everyone in the venue erupted.

Getting the ring out of its box, he slid it onto my finger, and I didn't even look, I was still staring at him, astonished. He jumped back up to kiss me, and everyone cheered. He pulled away, placing our foreheads together again and smiled at me.

'I totally wasn't expecting you to do that,' I said, shaking, and the tears returned, but they were happy tears. 'I love you.'

'I love you too,' and he took half a step back, and did a funny theatrical bow to everyone as another round of applause rippled through the audience.

Steph grabbed my shoulders and screamed in my face as she wrapped me up in a huge hug, batting Will away in the process, and a few people laughed. Paul and Jake were shaking Will's hand as Steph lifted my hand to inspect the ring, and the girls huddled around. It was the first time I'd had a chance to look at it myself. I knew straight away who it was by. I could tell by the craftsmanship.

It was really unusual, there were actually two rings. A diamond-encrusted band that came to a point at the top where a huge pear-cut diamond nestled. The other was a band that mirrored the line of the first and had two wings that didn't quite meet in the middle. Together they created the shape of a butterfly or moth.

The girls were oohing and ahhing, and when I took a closer look, I noticed that the wings were tiny replicas of the angel wing shells we had found on the beach, and I looked up at Will. He was staring straight back, waiting for the penny to drop and my mouth popped open. Then, he took my hand, gently pulling me towards him.

'Sorry girls, I'm just gonna take this one out back for a sec.'

He pulled me through the crowd to the door at the side of the stage.

Once we got into the dressing room, he exhaled, and it was evident he'd been quite nervous.

'When you didn't respond, I totally thought you were gonna say no!' he said, trying to push his fingers through his matted, damp hair.

'I was just so shocked, I couldn't speak,' I said, still reeling.

'Do you like it? The ring?' he asked.

'Will, I love it, it means so much... so personal. Did you have it made?' I asked, and he smiled.

'I did. Stephen Webster himself helped with the design, in fact he's here tonight.'

'Oh my God, really?'

'Yeah, I'll introduce you to him later,' Will took my hands, interlacing our fingers.

'Lucy...' he said, waiting for my gaze to lift from my rings to his face. 'I know the last few days have been tough, but I want you to know that it's you I want.'

I looked at him carefully. Did he ask me to marry him because of the baby and the argument that ensued?

'Will, this isn't because of the mis...'

'No!' He looked at the floor, a little coy. 'I knew I wanted to marry you after the festival.'

I pursed my lips to stop myself from smiling, and he looked back up.

'I asked the boys before we came out here,' he admitted. 'They told me I had to ask your Dad.'

My jaw dropped open again.

'I want to spend the rest of my life with you, Lucy, with Frankie and Paddy. You've all made me feel so welcome, made me a part of your family... our family, and the fact that you're willing to maybe add to that in the future is... dope,' he said, nodding with a smile, and I laughed.

He looked like he was high on something.

'I love my song,' I said, putting my hands around his neck.

'To be honest, most of the album is about you, and we wouldn't be here performing it if it wasn't for you.'

His arms entangled themselves around me, and he kissed me. I could feel his heartbeat thumping against mine as his hand travelled down over my arse. He didn't have to travel much further to reach my skin, and he took full advantage, taking my arse cheek in his hand and deepening the kiss.

'This really is an incredible dress, I could literally turn you around and fuck you right now,' he breathed, but just then, there was a knock at the door.

Jake walked in with his hand over his eyes.

'Are you decent?'

We both started laughing.

'Guys, congratulations, but there is a whole room full of people out there wanting to congratulate you as well.'

'Gotcha,' Will said, taking my hand and leading me back out of the room, while Jake held the door open for us and winked.

I THOUGHT WE HAD SPOKEN to everyone, having the same conversation over and over. Will was so good at saying the same thing and making it sound so authentic each time. I let him lead, showed my ring at the appropriate moment, and smiled a lot. We eventually made it back to the girls. Paul, Hannah, Jake, Milly, Leo, Mat, Emily, Cara and Thomas had all gravitated towards them.

'We really should get back up there,' Paul said.

'I know, you're right,' Will agreed. 'I'm just going to kiss my fiancée.'

And he did as they all did a collective ahhhh.

While they played, yet more people came to congratulate me and I chatted some more to Cara. Rolling Stone had been stoked that she'd landed such an exclusive interview and gig review and had already begun negotiations regarding a more regular feature.

The final song ended abruptly, and everyone cheered and clapped. Will grabbed the mic.

'Thank you to every single one of you here tonight, you've all played a part in our lives, and we're so grateful for your continued friendship and support. Good night!'

The band high-fived as another round of applause ripped through the crowd and then left the stage, and everyone began to chat amongst themselves excitedly.

I turned to speak to the girls, nearly bumping into someone, and was about to apologise when I realised it was none other, than Alysa. What the hell was she doing there? Surely Will hadn't invited her.

'Oh, look, it's the girl next door,' she said to no one, other than herself.

She looked a little worse for wear, her hair wasn't as perfect as usual, and she'd done a rubbish job with her bat wings, they were kind of wonky around her eyes.

'Why are you here?' I asked her outright, and she snickered.

'I work for Rolling Stone now, I'm reviewing the show,' she said in a rehearsed manner.

'Well, that's a lie because I know for a fact that the only reporter allowed in tonight is a friend of mine.'

Not wanting to point Cara out but knowing she was right behind me. Steph appeared at my side. She didn't say anything but showed her support.

'Oh, I see, so you're calling the shots now,' she said, her voice rising slightly and attracting the attention of a few nearby people.

'I think you need to leave,' I suggested.

She was clearly not in a good place mentally.

'I think that's an excellent idea, Alysa,' Mat said, suddenly appearing on my other side.

She laughed, a bit like a witch, and it struck me how much she looked like one.

'Would you look at that? It's my replacements,' she said, pointing from me to Mat. 'First the girlfriend, then the job.'

Terry quietly came up behind her but didn't make himself known. She looked at me with such hatred and then whispered.

'He'd even tried to replace the baby.'

My face fell. How did she know? Had Will told her? Everyone immediately around us had fallen silent, and I was vaguely aware that Will, Paul and Jake were making their way back through the crowd. Of all the people to let the cat out of the bag, my scalp prickled, fury didn't even cut it.

'You are so bitter,' I said with venom, shaking my head. 'You need to go because I never want to see your face again,' I added, and she sneered.

'I'm not bitter. I'm grateful for getting my life back.' She leaned in, lowering her voice. 'Do you know what? After delivering that baby, I told them to burn it.'

I saw Will moving quickly towards us out of the corner of my eye, but he was too late. I pulled back and thumped her right in the face, splitting her lip. Terry caught her as she toppled backwards while I looked at my hand because it felt like it was going to fall off. Terry dragged her away as she spat a gob full of blood out of her mouth.

I looked back up to see everyone looking at me aghast, Will mainly, but his shocked face turned into a massive grin, and he began to slowly clap, everyone following suit until it turned into applause. I immediately went red, Will grabbed me, pulled me in for a hug and announced, 'I fucking love this girl.'

'I'll get some ice,' Mat said and headed to the bar as Will lifted my hand to inspect it, I was beginning to shake following the adrenalin rush.

'How did she know?' I asked him.

'Know what, about the gig?' He obviously hadn't heard the entire conversation.

'About the miscarriage,' I whispered.

'She knew?' he said, frowning at me. 'Did she say something?'

'Yes, and I don't know how many people heard,' I said, looking around, starting to panic that it would be leaked.

Jake approached.

'Make sure you remind me not to cross your path,' he said with a wolfish grin, and I laughed nervously. 'I thought I saw that bitch backstage earlier, but then I thought I'd had one too many shots.'

I looked at Will, and he frowned.

'Paul asked how you were feeling after the miscarriage when we were backstage,' Will recalled and we both realised she must have overheard their conversation.

Mat returned with some ice in a towel and wrapped it around my hand. Steph joined us too.

'Does everyone know about the baby now?' I asked her.

'No, I don't think so, they're all talking about the wallop you gave her!'

Thank God.

'Is your hand okay?' she asked, and I lifted the ice off. It looked a bit swollen. 'Bet you're glad you're not left-handed, otherwise, she'd have an impression of that ring on her face.'

I laughed. That would have been quite fitting.

The band went off to do the rounds with Mat and Will's manager, Quinn, the general buzz about the place regarding the album was fantastic. A few people I'd met earlier came over to congratulate me, and I hoped I'd remembered all the names correctly.

Eventually, Will made it back, looked at me, and leaned in. 'Okay, I'm all yours, what do you wanna do?' I looked at him seductively but then Mat stood up on an old beer crate.

'Okay listen up, after party slash engagement celebration is at Kayto's, everyone's welcome.'

A resounding babble of excitement filtered through the crowd. Will looked back at me and bit his lip.

'I guess we kind of need to be at our own engagement celebration,' I said, a little disappointed that I didn't quite have him to myself yet.

'I'll make it worth your while, and besides, we've got Paris yet,' he said with a wink.

'What? Paris!' I asked, stunned, and he grinned.

'Call it a post engagement gift. We can fuck as many times as you want, and no one will disturb us.'

I quickly looked around to check no one had heard and Will chuckled.

'Come on, Terry will take us. Oh, and take your rings off. I don't want the press to know because I've asked Cara to officially announce it in her article.'

Chapter 29

Kayto's was so cool, it was a roof top venue with a pool, there were padded neon cubes which could be used to sit on individually or pushed together to make a long bench. And the pool had beds, actual floating double beds.

The bar itself was inside, outlined with neon lighting and the entire ceiling was covered in disco balls. It had a really sexy, hipster kind of vibe about the place, and the DJ booth was nestled between the indoor and outside areas. We had the entire club to ourselves. We stopped by a pillar in the bar area while everyone filed in, and the sound of their chatter slowly filled the space.

'What can I get my fiancée to drink?' Will asked with a twinkle in his eye, and I laughed.

'Um, anything other than champagne, I'm feeling a bit giddy,' I replied, and he headed straight over to the bar.

'I haven't had the chance to check out the ring yet,' Milly said, as she arrived at my side. 'Let's have a look.'

'Oh, Will has the ring, he didn't want the press to see,' I explained, and she rolled her eyes, making me smile.

'You looked utterly shocked,' she admitted.

'I was, I am. I really wasn't expecting him to ask. We hadn't discussed it. It was a complete surprise,' I replied honestly.

'Well, it's obvious that he's completely smitten, I've never seen him like this before, and the way he looks at you...' she trailed off and I looked up at her. 'If he could have love hearts for pupils.'

We laughed and Will returned with our drinks.

'Hey, Milly, did you enjoy the show?' he asked, kissing her briefly on the cheek.

'It was brilliant, I enjoyed the proposal more though. Very romantic, Reynolds,' she said, shoving him. 'But where's the ring?'

'Oh yeah,' he dipped his hand into his pocket and pulled them out, pushing the rings back on my finger, kissing my hand and wrapping his arm around my waist as Milly clutched my hand to look.

Someone I couldn't remember the name of took Will's attention for a moment and I quickly asked Milly if she was okay after earlier.

'I'm good, honestly,' she said forcing a smile.

I rubbed her arm affectionately trying to convey I understood.

'How's your other hand?' Will asked, pulling my focus back to him and I lifted it, it was a bit swollen, but I waggled my fingers around to prove it was okay. 'I can't believe you hit her!'

'She fucking deserved it, I've always detested that woman,' Milly revealed.

'She had it coming. What she did...' I trailed off, knowing my words would catch in my throat if I continued.

I didn't know how much Milly knew, I figured quite a bit, but I didn't want to say it, so I just shook my head. Will smiled but I could still see the sadness in his eyes, and I had to cough away the restriction in my throat, taking a sip of my drink to disguise my sudden emotion. Milly smiled sympathetically and excused herself.

'Hey, don't let her get to you,' Will said, bringing his forehead to mine and smoothing his thumb along my collar bone.

Music suddenly filled the room, Hey Ya! By Outcast, so I leaned in.

'I'm not, I won't,' I promised, taking a quick breath in as the back of his hand brushed past my nipple. I put my free hand around his neck and kissed him.

'I really want you,' I breathed, and he smiled knowingly.

'We can't leave yet, plus I definitely want to discretely touch you up on one of those floating beds,' he divulged, and I laughed. 'Come on.'

'Fine,' I said, and he pulled me onto the dancefloor where a few people had already started to gather. We danced, but we were constantly being interrupted by well-wishers. Steph and Claire arrived on the dancefloor, and they sauntered over.

'May we take this dance?' Steph asked Will, and I smiled as he lifted his hands up, stepping away.

He took my glass out of my hand and headed off, leaving us girls to it, as Jungle Boogie by Kool & The Gang began.

'I'm sorry if this trip hasn't been quite the holiday you were expecting,' I said for them both to hear.

Claire shook her head as if to implore me not to apologise and Steph leaned in.

'Babe, we've had the best time, do not apologise. And besides, apart from shopping, we haven't spent a penny!' She winked at me and then her eyes widened as an arm wrapped around me.

'Dance with me,' Stryker whispered in my ear seductively.

I instinctively glanced around the room for Will. Our eyes locked, and he tilted his head as I tried to convey my uneasiness. I closed my eyes for a second. He'd watched as Will had thrust himself into me... he'd watched me come.

I grimaced.

'Don't have a crisis of conscience on me, Lucy,' Stryker murmured in my ear. 'I've seen your pretty pink pussy, and I want to make it all wet and ready for me.'

He spun me around to face him and smiled, while I gaped at him, his eyes boring into me with intent.

And then I thought about Milly.

This was not happening.

'Do you know what Stryker? I've been wondering how you can reach your fifties and be so carefree.' I didn't actually know how old he was, probably early forties so I hoped that stung. 'And I've just figured it out. It's because you're a selfish arsehole, and only ever think about yourself.'

His mouth opened as he let out a short laugh.

'What's going on?' Will asked, appearing at my side.

Stryker's serious gaze boring into me, waiting to see what I was going to say.

'Nothing. I just don't want to dance with Stryker.'

Will frowned, looking from me to Stryker, obviously confused at my sudden change in demeanour around him, and probably knowing that I was holding back on something.

'Okay, your heard her, Stryker,' Will said, looking at him with his eyebrows raised.

'Fine,' he said and sauntered off to the bar.

Will turned me to face him.

'What am I missing?' he asked.

'I'll tell you another time.'

He drew back slightly to look into my eyes, willing me to tell him.

I sighed at his persistence and leaned in.

'He was the reason Milly went home.'

'Milly's gone?'

'No, I mean back in the day. She didn't leave because she couldn't handle the knock backs. She left because Stryker did a runner.'

'That doesn't make sense, Lu. Milly wouldn't have left unless...'

He trailed off, piecing everything together, obviously recalling the events that happened all those years ago. He pulled back to look at me again. His face was serious and his eyes, his eyes looked almost black.

'That fucking cunt,' he said slowly and clearly.

I was surprised at how angry he was, but then I guessed he was thinking about all the times Milly had supported him during his loss and how she'd never mentioned it.

'Will, now's not the time to make a scene.'

I wrapped my arms around his neck, drawing him into me, partly to stop him flying off the handle.

'It's not your fight,' I added.

'You're right, but I *will* deal with this.'

Before he could expand, we were interrupted yet again with more well-wishers. I excused myself to nip to the loo, and when I returned Will was chatting Jake.

'Your wish is my command,' Jake said to Will, winking at me.

'Come to bed with me,' Will said, smiling from ear to ear.

I laughed. I knew exactly what he meant.

'These are so cool. I might get one for the pool in LA,' Will mused as we bobbed around on the bed, watching all the guests chatting at the bar and dancing as Will lay on his back with me beside him.

'Do you think we've been here long enough to sneak off unnoticed?' I asked.

'Why, you need something?' Will asked, purposefully winding me up.

'I need my fiancé.'

Just then, there was a commotion on the dancefloor, and I propped myself up onto my elbows to see what was happening. As the crowd moved out of the way I could see Stryker had been restrained by a security guard, Leo was standing in front of him but before I could see what happened next, the bed rocked, and Will rolled on top of me.

My arms collapsed, and the bed bobbed ferociously as Will pressed his lips against mine. I wriggled to break free and see what was happening because people were beginning to scream and shout, but Will pressed his whole body against mine effectively stopping me from witnessing anything.

HE KISSED ME, HIS HANDS gliding down my dress, past the hem and down my leg, before he changed direction and came back up between my thighs. I closed my eyes. I had been thinking about this moment all night. I wanted him, and I pushed my hands up into his hair and kissed him fervently, and he hummed with satisfaction.

The low ebb and flow of some sensual music that Will had put on when we arrived home, filled the space of the open-plan kitchen, diner and lounge.

I moaned as his finger slipped inside me again and my body kind of slackened, immediately surrendering to his touch. His arms increased their grip in response, supporting me.

'I have wanted you all night,' I admitted breathlessly between kisses, and then cringed as I heard the words escaping me. I would never have said things like that before, internally maybe but never out loud, but Will encouraged me.

'And what exactly do you want?' he asked while he pushed the shoestring strap off one of my shoulders.

'I want you,' I repeated, and he smiled.

I knew this wasn't the answer he was looking for but what was I supposed to say? Everything I thought about saying sounded so stupid, needy or slutty and it was best I kept them to myself. The only time I ever let things slip was when Will literally had me at the point of orgasm, when I would do or say anything for him to continue.

Suddenly Will pushed me back onto the sofa and bent down to unzip my biker boots, letting them clatter to the floor and then he lowered the lights even further so that my eyes had to readjust. He slowly climbed up, hovering over me, not touching me and I wondered why he was hesitating. I grabbed a hold of his t-shirt and pulled him towards me, but he resisted.

'Tell me what you want me to do.'

Shit, I thought I'd got away with it.

'Kiss me,' I said.

Even that sounded foolish, but he kissed me before I had time to overthink it. It was just a regular kiss, nothing more, nothing less, and despite my efforts to deepen the kiss physically, he did not respond. He was going to make me ask, but I felt so awkward, I broke away.

'Will,' I pleaded.

'Tell me,' he demanded.

'I want you to kiss me... harder.'

Oh God, that was... but his lips pushed into mine and with such force it made me moan. His tongue, his lips pressing against mine, just how I liked it, but the rest of his body was still hovering, and I became desperate for his touch. I couldn't stand it anymore.

'Touch me,' I managed between kisses.

'Where?' Will asked, and I sighed with frustration. 'Come on Lucy, you can do this.'

'Caress me,' I said.

'Where,' he growled.

'My neck... my tits...'

Christ, that sounded slutty, but his hand was already travelling down my body.

'My hips, my thighs.'

He did exactly as I asked, kissing me too, and then repeated the very same thing on the other side. I wanted him to linger on my boobs, and play with my nipples like he always did, but he didn't. Instead, my body responded, arching my back and pressing my boobs up to him but getting no relief as he stoically hovered there. He continued to kiss me.

'I want you to press your body against mine,' I said out loud, surprising myself as he pushed his whole body into me, and I could feel him hard against my pelvis.

I wanted him inside me but not yet.

'Touch my tits,' I asked, and he pushed his palm against one, kneading gently.

'Fuck,' I whispered, looking up at the arm of the sofa with frustration. 'Not through the fabric,' I specified, and he smiled, pulling my dress down along with the cup of my strapless bra and the feel of his warm hand on my skin sent a bolt of energy right through me.

It wasn't long before the frustration returned. He wasn't doing anything with my nipples just stroking and massaging and I wanted to speed things up.

'Take off your clothes,' I suddenly blurted out.

'All of them?' he checked.

'Yes,' I hissed, 'and hurry up.'

I could see him smiling, doing his very best not to laugh, and I shook my head. Once he'd stripped, he climbed back on top of me.

'Where were we?' he said to himself, as he mechanically placed his hand back on my boob and went to kiss me again. My breathing was rapid with annoyance.

'Pinch them,' I said quickly.

'Pinch what?' he asked, feigning ignorance.

'Aaahh, my nipples, Will! Fuck!' and I suddenly sat up, pushing Will away with the palm of my hand on his chest.

'I can't do this, Will, whatever it is you're trying to get me to do, it doesn't come naturally to me, I feel awkward, and it's just making me really angry.'

Frustrated tears pricked my eyes.

'Shit,' Will closed the gap between us immediately, cupping my face. 'I'm sorry, I just wanted you to explore your innermost thoughts. I want to give you what you want.'

'You do, you always do,' I sighed, I was tired, it had been a long night. 'I just want to make love to you. I don't want mind games. I just want you.'

He nodded and then I felt bad, I knew he didn't mean to make me cross, he was just playing, and I needed to say something to rescue the night.

'I like it when you tell me what to do,' I said shyly.

He looked up into my eyes.

'I like it when you're... rough with me,' I whispered, and he smiled. I took a breath in to say something else and then bottled it. He stood and then scooped me up, heading towards the bedroom.

'Do you like it when I fuck you hard?' he asked.

'Yes,' I replied honestly.

'Do you like it when I bring you to the brink, and then bite down on your nipple so hard that you buck your hips, offering me your pussy?'

'Yes,' I said, my voice wavering, my insides clenching.

'Do you like it when I fuck your ass and make you come by stimulating your clit with my fingers?'

'Yes,' I whispered as he lay me on the bed.

'Do you like it...'

He began as he suddenly yanked my legs down, causing my dress to ruck up.

'When I flip you over...'

He carried out that very action, tugging my knickers down.

'Pull your hips back...'

Which he did with such force that I yelped.

'And slam into you before you're ready?'

'Ahhhh, yes,' I screamed as he did just that.

'Good, because I am going to do all the above right now... and I want to hear your release, Lucy, we have the apartment to ourselves for at least a couple of hours.'

Chapter 30

'Are you not going to pick up?' I asked when I saw Stryker's name on Will's phone.

'I'm not ready to speak to him,' Will replied, sitting on the stool next to mine at the breakfast bar.

The girls had gone out to do some sight-seeing and after a lie in Will and I were waiting for a delivery of pastries.

'Did you tell Leo?'

'Yes,' he said simply, owning his decision by staring at me as he sipped his coffee.

I chewed the side of my cheek, unsure how I felt. It wasn't really any of our business and if I'd known Will was going to tell Leo I probably would have kept it to myself. Milly had obviously kept that secret for years. It was private, and I felt guilty.

'Don't feel responsible. There's more to this story than you know.'

'Oh,' I said frowning.

'Leo has asked Milly for her hand in marriage on more than one occasion and she has always declined. He knew that something had happened in her past that she couldn't move on from and it was killing him. There are only so many knock-backs a man can take, and he admitted to me when we were at Paul and Hannah's that he was considering ending it.'

My jaw dropped.

'I know Milly loves Leo, and I wasn't prepared to watch two of my best friends end their relationship because of what Stryker did.'

I didn't say anything, it wasn't my place to pass judgement. Will had known them for years, so I had to trust him that he knew best.

'Imagine if the tables were turned, I'd be pissed if Leo knew something and held it back from me.'

He had a point.

Will gave me a half smile, knowing he'd won me round, and I rolled my eyes.

'So, you're just going to ignore Stryker?'

'I'll speak to him, eventually. I wanna speak to Milly first, there's gotta be a reason why she never told anyone.'

I lifted my coffee cup, and the sunlight caught my ring. I wasn't used to seeing a ring on that finger. Will spotted me looking.

'Speaking of phone calls, I'd imagine there are two young men waiting to hear from you.'

Frankie picked up after one ring.

'Well?'

'I said yes!'

'Yay,' I heard them say together, and I think I heard them high-five.

Paddy was very excited that *Will Reynolds* would be his stepfather. I left them to tell Mike, which was probably a cop-out, but what the hell, what could he say? I later received a text from him.

WTF, Lucy! Errr, congratulations? I hope you know what you're doing.

And that right there was proof of why I didn't tell him myself.

I also contacted my Mum and Dad who were delighted for us. And last but not least, Paige to let her know I wanted to accept. She was over the moon. She would send the contract over and get Nikki from Over the Wire to email me with all the details. I was excited about the prospect. This could be the beginning of something big.

It was time to say goodbye to the girls. Will and I would be travelling back in a couple of days, stopping over in Paris on the way. It seemed excessive that the pilot would basically have to turn around and collect us separately, but the girls needed to go back to work and their families, and Will had some work to do before we left. So, Terry collected them from the apartment, and we planned to have a full debrief of the trip a couple of days after we returned.

The apartment felt so empty after they'd gone, and I felt a bit low. Will had a hard job cheering me up, and it didn't help that he would be busy with work for the next few days. I was clearly moping around too much because he came back through to the kitchen on his phone.

'So, can you make sure that everyone is aware that Lucy will be joining me and make the necessary arrangements? Thanks.'

'Who was that?' I asked.

'Mat,' he replied.

'And what am I joining you for?'

'Well, anything that I can't do here. The interviews and the photoshoot... I don't want you hanging out here, feeling like you're a prisoner in your own home.'

I was about to say it wasn't my home, and Will lifted his hand before I could speak.

'And before you say it, you agreed to marry me, so sup it up.'

My mouth popped open in mock horror as he leaned across the breakfast bar.

'You're gonna have to get used to it now,' he grinned cheekily.

The lift light came on.

'And you're gonna have to get used to telling me when you've invited people over.'

'Touché,' he said as he kissed me on the forehead. 'It's Kieron. He's come to show us The Night Show footage before the final edit.'

I did not enjoy looking at myself on the TV, but I couldn't believe how seamless it all was, knowing what had happened between each cut, and it only lasted about fifteen minutes. All that for fifteen minutes of television.

'You realise this will have to air before announcing your engagement. Otherwise, they'll be pissed,' Kieron said.

Christ, even our engagement had to be scheduled.

'So don't go wearing that in public,' he said, pointing at my rings.

He had such a way about him. He reminded me of a school teacher.

'Cara will be announcing it in her review of the gig, so it's probably best to liaise with Rolling Stone,' Will said.

'Oh, I'm not sure that's a good idea. A review and an engagement? It might overshadow the album launch, and where has this *Cara* sprung from anyway?' Kieron asked.

'Well, it's not just a review. I've done an interview for her too, so it's more of a feature,' Will confirmed.

'An interview?' Kieron spat.

The conversation started to become heated, and I slid off my stool, but Will caught my hand, pulling me into his side as if we were a united front.

'You've never done an interview for Rolling Stone. You've always made it clear that it's *no comment*, all the way.'

'Well, it turns out a leopard *can* change its spots, and besides, Cara is a friend,' Will said, smirking at me, his comment making me think back to Stryker's appraisal of Will.

'You could have let me know,' Kieron huffed.

'I just did. I think we're done here....' Will announced.

Bloody hell, this was awkward. Kieron looked at me and then back at Will.

'We'll see you tomorrow,' Will said, dismissing him.

'We?' Kieron asked.

'Yes, Lucy will be joining us.'

Will looked at him with a hard stare as I looked at the breakfast bar, and Kieron went to say something but then thought better of it.

'I'll see you both tomorrow then,' Kieron said eventually and began to gather his things.

He and Will had a short conversation about what to say to The Night Show team while I cleared the coffee cups away, and he left.

'Will, that was really awkward, and he's going to resent me now,' I said with my hands on my hips.

'Sorry, the guy needed putting back in his box,' he replied, feeding his arms through the loops I'd made with mine.

'He's just trying to do his job,' I said, and Will kissed me on the forehead.

'Come on, I told Mom we'd take her some lunch... and don't take those rings off. If we get snapped, it will only be rumours until we announce it officially.'

I guess all the key people would know once we'd seen his mum.

We had to get up super early the following day and be at one of the New York rock radio stations by six. The traffic was so busy already, I wondered whether it would have been quicker for us to walk.

We met Paul, Jake, Mat and Kieron there. Jake looked worse for wear, and I wondered if he was missing Zara. Mat handed out passes, and we were ushered through a network of corridors before arriving outside one of the studios.

When it was time to go in, there weren't enough seats for all of us, but Will insisted that I go in with them and sit on his lap.

'I'm quite happy waiting out here.'

Jake pulled me in, putting his arm around me, and said, 'Whatcha gonna do, sit out there with Cranky Kieron? You're one of the family now.'

I closed my eyes, wondering what Kieron's face looked like.

The interview was fun, they played a couple of the tunes from the new album, and the DJ asked the band questions about the songs. It was all very light-hearted, and then he directed the questioning at Will.

'Now the next tune, My View, is a little... softer, I'm reluctant to say ballad....' Will laughed, 'because it's not, but it's not as heavy as the others. If I'm not mistaken, having listened to the lyrics, it could be classified as a love song. Is that what it is?'

I wasn't sure whether Will expected the questioning to become so personal, but it didn't seem to faze him.

'I guess so, but it's also a song of struggle,' Will explained. 'The media have utterly harassed us since we arrived here, it's a disgrace, and I cannot wait to get back to the UK.'

There was a moment of silence as Will's reply was absorbed. A bold statement on a US radio station.

'So, will the UK become your permanent residence?' The DJ asked, and I could see Kieron on the other side of the window, almost jumping up and down to get Will's attention. He was not happy with his answers.

'My girlfriend lives in the UK, and I wanna be with her,' Will replied, not entirely answering his question. I realised at that moment that we hadn't actually discussed our living arrangements.

Kieron suddenly slumped, and I realised he was getting concerned that Will would mention the engagement.

The DJ went on to ask Paul how he felt it would affect the band. Paul brushed it off, explaining that the world of technology nowadays meant they could live anywhere in the world and still write music together. The fact that Will had been living in LA for the last couple of years had little impact on their creative output.

The rest of the day followed a similar pattern during other interviews. The band answered personal questions so vaguely that no one would know any more about their private lives than someone who had just met them. And Kieron panicked every time our relationship was discussed.

We all ended up at Will's apartment... our apartment and the lads had a few beers to wind down. Paul headed off after the first beer to get back to Hannah, and Kieron used the opportunity to make his excuses. Mat expelled a massive sigh of relief when he went.

'Did you say something to Kieron? He's been spitting feathers all fucking day,' he asked Will.

'He's a dick, and if he doesn't sort his shit out, I'm gonna ask Daisy to find someone else,' Will said. 'He's just worried about the press getting hold of our engagement announcement before The Night Show airs.'

I looked at Jake. He was sitting on a stool, turning his bottle around on the breakfast bar. Moving away from Will and Mat's conversation, I sidled up beside him.

'Missing a certain someone?' I asked in a hushed voice, and he looked at me, pushing his breath out of his nose and shaking his head slowly.

'I dunno, Lu, her situation sounds complicated,' he admitted.

'Five kids and a shitty divorce is pretty complicated,' I agreed. 'But if you like her....' He released his breath as if he'd been holding it in for too long. 'I guess it depends on whether you want five kids and an angry ex-husband in your life.'

I wasn't trying to put him off. I just didn't want Zara to get hurt. She'd been through enough.

'Five kids,' he repeated. 'The ex I can deal with. I've dealt with enough, but *five* kids?'

I smiled sympathetically. He had some serious thinking to do.

The following day was the photo shoot for the album cover, the team were great fun, and it was such a laugh. Everyone was mucking about, and it was so nice not to have Kieron breathing down our necks with his negativity. I hoped my photoshoot would be just as relaxed.

Then, everyone decided to go out for dinner, I was hesitant, and Will took me to one side.

'Lu, we need to live, we can't stay cooped up in the apartment, and Terry will be on-hand.'

Paul suddenly appeared at our sides.

'I'm gonna get Hannah to come and meet us. Please come. It will probably be our last opportunity before you go home,' he said.

He was right, and I wanted to see Hannah before we left. It ended up being a lovely evening. Jake had recommended a small establishment, he knew the owner, and the other patrons either didn't know the band or didn't care. It was the first time I'd felt comfortable being out in public in a while.

At the end of the night, I found it hard to say goodbye to everyone. This is what our life would be like, saying our goodbyes to people all the time.

'The thing to do when you have to say goodbye to people is organising when you're gonna come back,' Will said when we got home. It reminded me of what he'd said about our relationship once. 'You know, we could come back out for the holidays? It's a pretty different vibe in the snow,' he said, putting his hands on my hips.

'By holidays, do you mean Christmas?' I asked.

'The very same, we could bring the boys out... I mean, if that fits with Mike?'

'Well, he has just had them for four weeks, so maybe...' I brushed his fringe out of his face. 'Um... we haven't actually talked about you moving in,' I ventured, and Will bit the inside of his cheek. 'I mean, I'd like you to... if you want to?' I said quickly, and he sort of frowned and smiled, a look I couldn't quite decipher.

'Okay... cool,' he said.

'Cool?' I asked, and it was my turn to frown.

'Mmm hmm,' he added before kissing me, and I got the distinct impression he was hiding something.

Chapter 31

I was surprised to see their offices were in a shared building. Rolling Stone was iconic, but I guess magazines were becoming a thing of the past, and despite them having a website, etcetera, you didn't need office space to write an online article.

There was a frisson of excitement as Will entered, but Cara was there to meet us, and she showed us through to a room where two executives were waiting. Will shook their hands, and I managed to refrain from giving Cara a massive hug and kept it professional.

'We are honoured to be printing this for you.'

One of them said while the other pulled up the proofs on a huge screen that appeared crisper than the view from Will's bedroom window in LA.

'I hope I've balanced the article well. The engagement is huge, and I know we're extremely privileged to have this exclusive, but it is primarily the interview and album review,' Cara said.

'Cara, don't sweat. It's all good,' Will assured her. 'The gossip sites will be all over it once this has gone to press.'

There were three pages, a picture of the album cover with the review straddling the first and second, and little snippets of lyrics were written in bold. I was surprised at how quickly the images from the shoot had been finalised, but I guess they were on a tight schedule. There was another picture of the band and then a blank space which I assumed would be for an advert. The last page had a smaller picture of Will on his own, followed by the interview. At the very end, she had written.

Here at Rolling Stone, we are very excited and thoroughly ecstatic to announce that Will proposed to his girlfriend, Lucy Daniels, at the launch show, and she said yes! Congratulations, Will and Lucy!

There was a small picture of the two of us, it was a candid shot that had been taken at the photo shoot of us looking at each other, and they'd somehow managed to capture Will's adoring eyes while I smiled. It was a flattering picture for once.

'Happy?' Will asked me.

'Um, sure… if you are?' I said, not quite knowing why he was checking.

'Well, there's gonna be seven hundred-thousand people looking at that picture of us,' he said, and one of the men coughed a tiny cough.

'Actually, we're predicting a million this month.'

He swiped the screen, and the front cover came up. There was a portrait of Will with Rolling Stone written just above his forehead, he looked hot, and I took a breath in and held it. He had his leather jacket on but no t-shirt, so you could see a bit of his pecs. The look they'd caught in his eyes was striking yet loving, and it was a look I'd seen so many times.

Exclusive *The 'king Band's New Album and Will Reynolds on Music, Life and Love.*

'What do you think?' one of the execs asked.

'I think I need a copy of that picture,' I said and then realised the question had been aimed at Will, and they all laughed while I went bright red. Will pulled me in to help hide my embarrassment, but I was mortified.

'I think we're good,' Will said with a chuckle. 'Send the final version over to Kieron.'

'Great, well, it's been a pleasure,' one of the execs said.

We all shook hands again, and Cara showed us back out. She came outside with us and then gave me a huge hug.

'Thank you so much,' she said. 'Safe journey home.'

'Will you stop thanking me? This is all your own hard work. You and Thomas must come over to the UK, stay with us,' I said.

'We'd love to,' she replied before shaking Will's hand, and he pulled her in and kissed her on the cheek. It was her turn to be embarrassed, and she scuttled off back inside.

'Paris?' Will asked, smiling, and I beamed back before he kissed me.

'Will Reynolds?' someone said, and Will opened the car door to let me in.

'Sorry dude, plane to catch,' and he hopped in too.

Will had a message from Kieron just before we boarded to say that The Night Show was going to air the following day. I was a bit gutted because I had thought it would have been nice to watch it with the girls and make a night of it, but instead, we were going to Paris. Okay, maybe I wasn't gutted.

A few hours later and I was nodding off. The seats Will and I had could be folded flat into a double bed, and we lay on our sides, Will spooning me.

'Don't go to sleep,' Will whispered in my ear, and he pressed himself against me.

'Will, I'm not having sex with you here,' I said as his hand slid under the waistband of my pyjama bottoms, over my hip and between my legs.

'I've put the do not disturb sign on,' Will said.

'Oh great, so now they think we're fucking even though we're not,' I replied as he slid his fingers inside me.

'Well, if they think we're fucking, we may as well,' he said, tickling my ear with his lips.

'What if there's an emergency?' I asked as he began to circle me.

'We'll die fucking... so rock and roll.' He pushed himself up against me before swiftly lowering his sweatpants and lining himself up. 'Okay?' he said, asking permission.

'I can't believe I'm doing this,' I murmured, and he slid inside me, taking that as confirmation.

'Just imagine if all our adoring fans knew....' he whispered while holding my hip in place and thrusting himself hard inside me, causing me to gasp. 'That the girl next door was fucking her fiancé above their heads,' he said before doing it again.

I yelped, and he pulled my pyjama bottoms down past my knee and then lifted my knee while pushing me half onto my front. He had way better access and rammed himself into me again, it was deep, and I screamed.

'Lucy...' he chastised me. 'The steward will hear us.' But I could hear the smile in his voice before he did it again. It was as if he wanted them to hear me, and I tried hard not to make any sound but failed.

He lifted my knee further and thrust himself in deeper. I mewled loudly. I couldn't help it. Will grabbed the blanket, gathered it up into his fist, and shoved it in my mouth. I couldn't believe he'd done that, but it kind of felt sexy, wrong but sexy. He picked up his pace and pushed one of his knees between mine, giving him some leverage and pumping his hips.

'Touch yourself, Lucy. I want you to make yourself come while I fuck you.'

He grabbed my hand, put my fingers in his mouth, and then shoved them between my legs.

'Circle yourself,' he demanded.

I was surprised at how wet I was. It was as if he'd poured lube on me. I moved my fingers around him, and he suppressed a groan, so I did it again, but he grabbed my hand back and held it against the mattress. All the while fucking me with such force that my head was hitting the armrest.

It struck me that he was lost in the moment, not caring for my well-being, chasing his high, and I smiled to myself. I made him feel that way. My yelps were being masked by the blanket. His thrusts lost their consistency, and then picking my hand up again, he pushed it back between my legs, but this time he kept his hand there and guided my fingers around me, not trusting me to do it myself without touching him.

Once our climaxes were imminent, he finally let go of my hand and grabbed onto the armrest to pull himself in deeper. The veins in his arm were bulging with the force of his grip. I used my fingers to rinse every last ounce out of my orgasm while Will forced his release into me, grunting as he did so.

There was a moment of stillness, and as if Will suddenly checked back into reality, he pulled out and flipped me over. Concern on his face as he yanked the blanket out of my mouth.

'Holy fuck, Lucy...' he said, shaking his head in disbelief. 'Are you okay?'

'Um... my mouth is a bit dry,' I said, trying to lick my lips.

'Jesus Christ....' He leaned down and gently kissed me. 'They said it would be intense, but I fully fucking checked out.'

'Well, if I knew who *they* were, I'd be inclined to agree,' I said, frowning. Who the hell was he talking about? He brought his gaze back in line with mine.

'They... like, no one... just a conversation from years back when I was touring. These guys were boasting about how amazing it was, having sex in the air,' he clarified.

'And you've never done it before?' I asked, struggling to believe him.

'Never... never had the opportunity. You say that like I'm some crazed, male nymphomaniac.'

I lifted my eyebrows as if to confirm that's exactly what I thought of him, and he laughed. He kissed me lovingly, and I kissed him back with passion.

'You never cease to amaze me,' and then he added, 'I wonder how many people we've flown over while we've been fucking?'

I laughed.

When we landed, Will led me to the exit with his hands over my eyes, the steward opened the door, and a rush of oppressive heat hit me as Will removed his hands. On the runway, there was a red open-top tour bus like the ones you see packed with tourists, but this one was empty. I turned to Will frowning, and he had a great big grin spread across his face.

'I felt guilty about you missing out on the New York touristy stuff, so I thought we could do some sightseeing around Paris.'

'Will! This is amazing,' I said, laughing as our luggage was piled into a car to be taken to wherever we were staying.

We boarded the bus, and I ran straight upstairs to sit right at the front of the top deck, like an excited teenager on their first bus trip without their parents. Will was chuckling to himself as he sat beside me.

We spent the next couple of hours chugging around Paris, sharing a pair of those crappy earbuds to listen to the tour guide. Will told me some stories about the band touring around Paris in the early days. I told Will about my only trip to Paris, a school history trip. The teachers had told me and my boyfriend at the time off because we had tried to get into each other's dorms.

'How old were you at the time?' he asked.

'I suppose I was fifteen, maybe?'

'Lucy Daniels!' Will said like a teacher. 'And I had you down as a good girl when you were at school. What would you have done had you made it without the teachers knowing?'

'I don't know, probably just felt each other up or something.'

'What would you have liked to have done?' he asked in that low, seductive voice, but I was literally saved by the bell as the bus stopped and the engine was switched off.

'Shit, we're here,' Will said.

'Where?'

Will took my hand and led me back downstairs, thanking the driver and wishing him a good night before stepping off.

'I'm taking you to one of my favourite places in Paris. It's a bistro and a good friend of mine runs it.'

'Will, I'm not dressed to go out to dinner.'

My mascara had probably worn off in the heat, and my sundress that I'd slipped on before we landed was all crumpled from the bus. Will looked me up and down.

'Baby, you look beautiful, and besides, it's not a fancy place. It's chill.'

I didn't have time to argue because we had arrived, and Will was pulling me into the bustling bistro. He was right. It was understated, a little run down if anything, and was situated on the corner of a street that had a mix of little cafés, bars and restaurants.

'Will!' a man called.

I turned to see a guy around the same age as us, drying his hands on an apron before putting his hand out to shake Will's and draw him in for a hug. He was tall, with a blond top-knot and fuzzy stubble around his pointed jaw.

'Fabien, my man,' Will said as he embraced him. 'This is Lucy, ma magnifique fille,' Will added, pulling away and gesturing to me.

'Oui, mon Chérie,' Fabien said as he took hold of my shoulders to look at me and then kissed me on each cheek, saying, tres bien, to Will over my shoulder.

My cheeks flushed as he drew attention to us before ushering us along to a table for two, chattering away in French to Will, and to my surprise, Will was responding with ease. Suddenly Fabien grabbed my hand and lifted it up.

'Qu'est-ce que c'est?'

I looked at Will, a little shocked, but Will was chuckling.

'Fabien, Lucy is my fiancé. I asked her to marry me just before we left the US.'

'You are kidding me,' he said, reverting back to English and looking from Will to me and back again. 'Remi,' he called, and a waiter came striding over, speaking to him in French again and then continuing in French as he spoke to Will at speed. Will was laughing and held his hands up, gesturing to me.

'Pardon, pardon, Lucy, we celebrate, oui?'

Remi arrived back with a bottle of Laurent Perrier, and Fabien took it from him, reaching behind the bar for three champagne flutes and pouring us each a glass.

For a moment, I thought Fabien was going to join us for the evening. Still, once he'd downed half a glass of champagne, he left us to tend to the rest of the patrons. As we sat soaking up the Parisian culture, I marvelled at how quickly Fabien moved around the place. Despite not being able to understand him, I could tell he was genuine, and liked by both the customers and staff. He had a broad smile and a sense of ease in everything he said and did.

Will had met him at a venue in Paris they'd played at years ago. As he was finishing up his shift, he was working the bar there and offered to show them around to some of the lesser-known local bars to keep them out of the limelight. It sounded as though they'd had a very good night.

The food was superb. I had the tuna served with an Asian-style sauce and, of course, frites. Will went for pizza. I mocked him for coming all this way and having pizza, but then I guess my choice hadn't exactly been traditional. I noticed Will wasn't drinking, and to be honest, I hadn't drunk much either, opting for water due to the humidity. All we'd had was the glass of champagne, and neither of us had finished it all.

When we said our goodbyes to Fabien and thanked him for a wonderful evening, it was dark out, and I was pleased to discover we could walk to where we were staying.

We walked away from the high street, turning into a quieter road, and we ambled along hand in hand, content in our own thoughts, taking in the tall buildings and the cobbled streets. Turning again, Will led me down another road, narrower and deserted.

I was unsure whether the street was used by cars or if it had been pedestrianised, but suddenly Will had me pinned up against a wall. Kissing me hard as if he'd been waiting to do it for weeks. It was wet and fervent, our salty sweat and saliva mixing as we chaotically took what we wanted from each other.

I lapped him up eagerly, exploring his mouth with my tongue as he pushed himself into me, trying to gain some relief from his steel-like erection. He was clawing at my chest, squeezing my nipples through the fabric and grazing his teeth down my neck when we heard voices nearing. He quickly grabbed a key from his back pocket and unlocked the door we were standing by.

I looked up in awe as the huge, heavy wooden doors swung open into a beautiful internal flagstone courtyard. Large green pot plants and a small wrought-iron table and chairs illuminated by the moonlight decorated the space. Will hastily pulled me along to the other side of the courtyard through another door draped with billowy curtains.

He shoved me back up against a wall just inside and began to empty his pockets onto a sideboard, kissing me all the while. Snatching my purse from me, dropping it on top of everything else, and quickly getting to work on the buttons of my dress. I couldn't really see the apartment as the only light was the moonlight, but that didn't deter us. We knew where each other was, and that was all that mattered.

As my dress fell to the floor, he wrapped his large warm hands around my neck and waist, hoisting me up as I curled my legs around him. He sunk his teeth into my neck just above my collarbone, and I cried out. He growled as he ground his hips against me and then suddenly released me.

'Get on your knees,' he gritted out.

'What?' I was totally taken aback by his tone.

'Lucy,' he said with a sardonic laugh. 'Do as you're told.' He began to undo his fly. 'We've been surrounded by people for weeks, and I've finally got you on your own, with no chance of interruption. Now get on your goddamn knees.'

He capped off his demands with the sweetest of kisses to soften the blow, and then whilst he expertly whipped his dick out with one hand, he pushed my shoulder down, forcing me to my knees with the other.

I knelt there, stunned for a moment as he gently took my jaw in his hand and looked down at me, a strange mix of dark desire and delight flashing in his eyes as he licked his lips, looking at mine, willing me to do the same. My tongue slowly traced my lips on autopilot as if they were under his spell, and then he languidly ran the tip of his cock over my lips with his pre-cum as if it was some sort of lip gloss.

He smiled down at me wickedly and, staring straight into my eyes, he held the base of his cock and slid his other hand around the back of my head, angling me just so before slowly, smoothly feeding his dick into my mouth. Further and further, he went until I could feel him at the back of my throat. I was desperately trying not to gag. I instinctively tried to move my head back, only to discover that my head was butted up against the wall. I looked up at Will, imploring him with my eyes to move back as they filled with tears, and then I gagged.

'Oh, baby, don't gag. You'll make me come,' he said, his eyes closed briefly with pure pleasure written on his face. My breathing was coming quickly through my nose as I panicked, thinking he'd completely lost it. I gagged again and could taste his saltiness as my tears rolled down my face.

I was about to push him away when he finally let go of his dick and pressed his hand against the wall, drawing himself back out slowly, like it was the last thing he wanted to do. Using the wall to help steady himself physically while he used his other hand to delicately trace the lines of my tears with his index finger. A confusing mix of dominance and tenderness. He stepped back a fraction, popping free and giving me a moment to catch my breath.

'So, fucking good, baby, you take me so well,' he said silkily. I looked up at him, not quite knowing whether to be cross with him for purposefully making me gag, or be delighted with his praise. Still, the look he gave me of raw lust made my anger dissipate immediately.

'Now, are you going to suck me, Lucy, or do I need to fuck your mouth?'

My lips were around him, and I was sucking hard before he'd even had a chance to consider option two. I was too wary of his mood to take the risk, and he smiled down at me knowingly. This fucking guy and his sexual alter ego. I took him in deep and sucked, dragging my teeth back up his shaft in an attempt to show him that two can play at his game.

He thumped the wall with the side of his fist.

'Yes, Lucy. Again!' he demanded, and he thrust himself into me, taking back control.

I clenched my teeth around his base as he drew back out and growled. Christ, the man was an animal. 'Suck,' he practically shouted, anger lacing the word, and I did as I was told while he fucked my mouth.

The wet sounds filled the room as he pounded into me, missing the target several times as he lost control, popping out and slopping saliva and pre-come over my chin and cheeks.

'Fuck,' he growled out, suddenly grabbing me by the throat and dragging me up to standing. He spun us around and started marching across the room, forcing me backwards and causing me to stumble. He still had me by the throat, and I was scrabbling to stay upright. If he wasn't staring into my eyes with pure wonderment, I'd be fearful of him, but this uninhibited, unrestrained side of him was making me feel so incredibly desired. I loved the fact that he wanted me so much. He was losing his mind.

The backs of my legs hit something soft, and I fell backwards. Will shucked his jacket off and then disappeared into what I could only assume was the bathroom. The light cast a shard of bright yellow into the room, and I realised I was on the bed. He returned with two bathrobe sashes.

'Take your panties off.'

I decided now wasn't the time to pick him up on his terminology and shakily took them off, slipping my sandals off too. He came to stand in front of me at the end of the bed.

'Move back and spread your legs.'

I followed his order. He began to loop one end of the sash around my leg, just at the top of my calf and repeated the same on the opposite side with the other sash. My breaths were coming in short rasps as I realised his plan.

Slowly passing the loose ends of the silky sash through his fingers, he then wrapped it once around the corresponding foot post, repeating the process on the other side. He carefully pulled until my legs were spread as wide as they could go, the fabric sliding around the posts like a pulley system.

He grabbed hold of his t-shirt at the scruff of his neck and dragged it over his head in one fluid movement before climbing on top of me. He looked deep into my eyes. I couldn't help but glance down, his jeans and boxers still around his thighs, framing his perfect dick. When I looked back up, he was smirking at me.

'Not yet, Lucy.'

He kissed me chastely before moving back down, nipping as he went. Feeding both of his hands under my hips, he yanked my torso down, slackening the sashes, the relief in my hip joints causing a surge of warmth to my groin. But the moment I felt the relief, Will pulled the ends of the two sashes towards him again, the fabric gliding around the foot posts, pulling my knees out to the side. I gasped at the sudden exposure. The air cooled my arousal.

'Jesus, baby, you like me being rough with you, huh?'

I didn't respond. Even if I tried, my breathing probably wouldn't allow for a cohesive sentence. I could feel my arousal slowly pouring out as Will watched in amazement, stroking himself. He pushed himself off the bed, turned and nudged the bathroom door open, allowing more light to flood in, essentially putting a spotlight between my thighs.

As if he couldn't make me any more uncomfortable, he returned, and while tugging himself off, he swiped his middle finger through my arousal, coating it and then slid it straight into my butt hole. I gasped again and bucked against the intrusion, the sashes whipping back around the foot posts with the movement.

'Keep still,' he commanded and tenderly pulled on the sashes again.

He then pushed his thumb from the same hand into me and pinched the two together.

'Ahhh,' I cried out, more with the frustration of not being able to move my hips than anything else, and I grabbed his wrist with my hand.

'Don't you dare fucking come. You are not fucking coming until I'm pumping my grain into you.'

'Well, you'd better put your dick inside me because....'

Whop!

I lay there for a split second in shock, wondering what the hell had just happened, and then the sting of heat erupted on the side of my breast.

'Ahhh,' I cried again, my hands immediately covering it. Out of the corner of my eye, I saw the leather tongue of a riding crop before Will removed his finger and thumb and crawled back over me.

'Don't. Fucking. Come.'

He pronounced each word in a gruff voice, lifting my hands away and shoving them above my head.

'Move them, and I won't let you come at all.'

I had well and truly been stunned into silence. Had he lost it? He just fucking struck me with a riding crop. He'd smacked me before, using a spatula once in the kitchen, but a crop?

Will carefully lowered the cup of my bra, delicately licking the heated flesh and gently blowing on it, helping it to cool. He then pulled the other cup down, taking my nipple in his mouth and sucking hard. The pain of the sucking steered my concentration away from the heat. The heat now shifting from pain to pleasure. The two feelings were unifying.

Moving back down, he removed the rest of his clothes and returned his attentiveness to my pussy which he could probably see was quivering in anticipation.

'Holy fuck, why have I been holding out on you? You fucking love this.'

The wet patch forming under my arse was making the sheets cold. He suddenly lapped me from one end of my opening to the other, in one long wide, measured lick, causing me to suck in air through my teeth.

'My God, you taste so good,' he murmured as if he'd licked an ice cream for the first time.

He used his fingers to wipe the remaining residue from his chin and lips and licked them clean. I was so busy watching him lick his fingers I hadn't realised he'd lined himself up.

Once his fingers were clean, he carefully and precisely placed his hand around my neck, his thumb pressing uncomfortably into the v between my collarbone and his fingers taking purchase at the back above my shoulder blade. My breath was coming quickly again, wondering how many more breaths I would be able to take before the pressure became too much.

I was looking into his eyes, he into mine, me checking he hadn't lost it completely, and Will watching with a level of intense scrutiny. Just as I thought I couldn't take it, Will rammed himself into me so hard. He eased the pressure on my neck and fucked me.

I'd never felt him so hard, so big, and he did not let up. Each time he withdrew, I could feel the ridge on the bell of his cock rub against my pubic bone adding a sensation that was causing my clit to quiver before he slammed back in again. I was climbing fast.

'Don't fucking come yet,' he hissed, but I couldn't help it. My body had taken over.

Placing one of his knees on the end of the bed to give him more purchase, he fucked me deeper still. Suddenly his hand was right up under my jaw, pressing firmly against the arteries below my ears, and he pumped me harder, using his knee and my jaw as leverage to fuck his cock deep into my core.

'Come for me now, baby,' Will commanded.

Several things happened at once, Will removed his hand, and my upper body was tossed around like a ragdoll with every thrust.

'Let me feel you.'

My lower body anchored in place, unable to gain any purchase other than my pussy on his cock. A monumental wave of euphoria surged through me as my insides clutched around his shaft like a vice. My orgasm going into hiatus.

A ringing in my ears.

A feeling so intense it gripped me.

'Yes, fuck! Holy fucking Christ.'

I looked at Will, wondering what the fuck was happening as I felt his cock convulsing inside me. Staring back at me with astonishment and fascination, I fell off the proverbial edge. I knew my body was thrashing around, and I had no control over it.

At some point, Will must have released my knees because I was grinding my release against him with everything I had. My entire body was like a live wire, absorbing every touch and magnifying it.

'Lucy, baby... I'm gonna... fuck.'

The wash of ecstasy that consumed me was the last thing I remembered.

I WAS NAKED, WILL'S arms and legs were wrapped around me, and it was still dark. I lifted my hand to my neck, and with the movement, Will stirred.

'Hey, beautiful, are you awake?'

'Aha,' I rasped, and I shivered.

Will pulled me in close, wrapping the blankets around me tightly, but the shivers turned into trembles, and my entire body began to shake. What was wrong with me?

'Will?' I whispered with concern.

'It's okay, baby, you're doing fine. It's just your body readjusting.'

He held me tighter still, absorbing the judders with his own body.

'Try to relax. Think about your breathing. Have you ever done box breathing before?'

'A couple of times.'

'Okay, let's keep it simple. I'll count for you.'

He began to count, and although my breathing was staggered, to begin with, it soon dissipated along with the trembling. As my body started to relax, I pressed my ear up against Will's chest and listened to the rhythmic beat of his heart.

Chapter 32

My first thought was, why does my boob feel sore? Will has behind me, spooning me, one of his legs between mine and his arm draped over my hips. I needed to pee. I carefully lifted Will's arm, only for him to pull me in tighter, and as the blanket brushed against my nipple, I winced.

'Will, I need the loo.'

He mumbled incoherently but released me, and I gingerly padded to the ensuite. It was spacious, with a chequered tiled floor and a marble suite with traditional brass taps and accessories.

As I sat there, my mind wandered to the previous night's events. I smiled as I thought about us kissing outside on the street and then pursed my lips when I remembered how commanding he'd been. I suddenly recalled the crop as I pulled the chain for the loo.

I bolted over to the guilt-framed mirror and looked at myself.

'What... the... William Reynolds!!' I shouted.

'Shit,' I heard him say before hearing the distinctive sound of his palms brushing against his nine o'clock shadow while his footsteps got closer.

I was still gawping at myself in the mirror when Will entered. I had faint bruising at the top of my sternum where his thumb had been pressing. The outer side of my right boob looked like someone had slapped me with a pallet knife. I had a love bite by my left collarbone. Not to mention the fingertip pressure marks and smaller bite marks where he had nipped my breasts and inner thighs.

I was panting, and not in a good way. As my gaze rose back up my body, my anger rose with it, and then our eyes locked in the mirror. He was biting his lip, looking at me intently, and that was when I lost my shit.

'What the fuck have you done to me? Are you seeing me right now?' I shouted, turning to him and gesturing my hand up and down my body frantically. 'I look like I've been assaulted.'

Even in my anger, I realised that now was not the time to compare these bruises to the one his brother had left me a couple of months ago.

'I don't know if you've noticed, but it's fucking hot out there, and I'm gonna have to wear a boiler suit if I want to leave this place any time soon.'

I looked down at myself again, cupping my boob to take a closer look at the red mark the crop had left.

'You used a *crop* on me, Will, a fucking riding crop!'

Will just stood there, completely naked, his arms crossed and one hand holding his chin. And then I looked down. The fucking arsehole was hard. My jaw dropped again as I shook my head, giving him a look of disgust, and he dropped his hands and brought them up as if he was going to hug me.

'Ahh,' I screamed in his face and shoved him out of my way as I barged past him, stomping back into the bedroom, muttering to myself about finding the crop.

'Lucy,' Will warned as he hot-footed after me, but he was too late.

I located the crop just beside the bed. I rushed over to pick it up, Will in close pursuit, and as I turned to wield the weapon, the sound of the crop sliced through the air, Will tried to catch it, and in doing so, the end of the crop slapped his palm hard.

'Ahh,' he bit out against the sting and stood still for a moment. He looked at me with fire in his eyes, and I looked back at him with satisfaction in mine, still holding onto the handle.

He yanked on the crop, jolting me toward him, wrapping his free arm around me, and crashing his lips against mine. I struggled, trying to break free, but in doing so, I lost grip of the handle, and it fell to the floor between us as Will wrapped his other arm around me.

I struggled some more as he walked me backwards towards the bed and had me pressed against it within seconds, kissing me hard. I bit down on his lip in frustration, knowing my efforts were futile, and he dragged his mouth from mine.

'You wanna hurt me, baby? Well, come on, I'm all yours. Give me your best shot.'

He released me, hovering over me and waiting for me to slap him or punch him. I stared at him, trying to catch my breath, but I couldn't do it. It wasn't in my nature to lash out. Instead, I did what any other respectful woman would have done in my situation.

'I hate you!' I screamed in his face, and he laughed at me, crashing his lips back into mine.

I wriggled and kicked my legs as hard as I could while he tried to restrain me. Eventually, he grabbed hold of my hands, holding them against the bed. With one quick thrust of his hips, he was inside me, and we both stopped, our chests heaving, staring at each other.

Our breathing slowed, and Will gently brushed the hair out of my face. He kissed me. It was tender, and loving, and sensual. I closed my eyes, and he slowly, carefully made love to me. Caressing every bruise, kissing every mark, and murmuring lyrics to me as he professed his love until the rage I felt had completely evaporated.

THAT AFTERNOON, AFTER finding some floaty cotton trousers and a wraparound halter-neck top that covered most of the blemishes, I allowed Will to take me out.

We walked around a beautiful park called Parc Monceau, watched the little kids on the merry-go-round, marvelled at the pretty bee garden, and sat on the grass under a tree with ice cream. My sunhat, his aviators and baseball cap and his knowledge of the lesser-known areas of Paris working to keep us out of the limelight.

He also took me to a bakery called Aux Merveilleux and bought me what I can only describe as a gooey marshmallow cake. It was melt-in-the-mouth delicious.

When dusk fell, we went to a bar that yet another friend of his owned. It was below street level, intimate with dark furnishings and low lighting. We sat in the back corner opposite each other on a small table for two, a bottle of wine and a candle between us.

'So, have I managed to show you a good time in Paris?' Will asked.

'If by good time you mean the mouth sex I had at the bakery earlier, then yes.'

'Mouth sex?'

'Aha,' I said, grinning.

'That's the overriding memory you have of our time here?' he asked, and I could tell he was trying to ascertain what my thoughts were over the previous night's activities.

I leaned in.

'Well, I don't need memories for the other stuff. I have bruises instead.'

Will had the decency to look down, but his bright green eyes were defiant when he looked up.

'I'm not gonna apologise for that,' he said, interlacing the fingers from his right hand with my left.

'I didn't ask you to,' I said in a hushed whisper.

The corner of his lip lifted into a smile, and he leaned in closer still, searching my eyes and lifting our interlaced hands to his mouth.

'I want to do those things to you again,' he whispered.

I laughed nervously and swallowed while he brushed my knuckles over his lips.

'I honestly don't know what to say to that,' I admitted.

'Say yes,' he said without hesitation, not once breaking eye contact. 'Trust me,' he implored as he kissed the inside of my wrist.

I was stalling.

'How can I trust you not to lose it?'

'I won't,' he declared with a devilish grin.

He dropped his gaze to our hands and began to kiss the tips of each of my fingers.

'No alcohol,' I stated suddenly, deciding there and then that should be a rule.

He stilled and looked back up.

'Is that your only stipulation, Lucy Daniels,' he asked disbelievingly.

'I don't know what other stipulations I should have, William Reynolds.'

My words becoming wispier by the second.

He laughed.

'Okay, so we make the rules as we go.' He kissed me on the lips. 'I'd happily knock alcohol on the head completely if it meant coming twice again.'

'What?'

He gave me a wicked grin.

'Your orgasm last night, you came, and then I came... and then you... you suspended it somehow.'

He looked down at the table, frowning for a second, trying to work out how to explain it.

'You were free, liberated, in sub-space... and fuck.' He shifted in his seat, clearly being turned on at the thought of it. 'It was fucking hot... and I came again... and you...' he took a breath. 'You were so fucking beautiful.'

The last word caught in his mouth, and he coughed.

'Will,' I whispered with concern, trying not to draw attention to us.

He fed his fingers into the hair at the nape of my neck and pressed his forehead to mine.

'To witness that... knowing that I got you there... it was an honour, and I really fucking love you, Lucy Daniels. You're my everything. My view.'

Tears were pooling in my eyes, hearing the compassion in his words, and I cupped his face and kissed him.

'We need to go now before I make a fucking scene,' he said swiftly, knocking a tear off his cheek.

I giggled as Will left a wad of euros on the table, and we went in haste.

WILL WAS IN THE BATHROOM when his phone buzzed on the bedside table. I glanced over at it. It was Paul. I was going to pick it up but thought better of it. Then my phone started ringing, and I rooted around in my bag until I found it. It was Paul again.

'Hello?'

'Lucy, is Will with you?'

'Yeah, he's in the bathroom. Do you want me to get him?'

'It's Iris.'

The colour drained from my face as Will came out of the ensuite.

'Hold on.' I held the phone out for Will. He looked at me, frowning when he saw Paul's name on my phone.

'Paul?'

Will slowly sat down and closed his eyes.

Will's Mum had a heart attack, she was stable and had been given blood thinners, but they were keeping her in for observation.

'You should see her,' I said, sitting beside him and touching his thigh.

'You'll come with me, right?'

I bit the inside of my cheek and gently rested the palm of my hand on his jaw. 'Will, I can't. I have work. The boys are due back, I'm sorry.'

Will scrunched his eyes up, knowing there was no way around it.

'Go and look after your Mum.' I kissed his lips delicately. 'I'll be waiting.'

He pulled my forehead to his, his glassy eyes looking into mine. 'This wasn't the plan,' he said before kissing me, pressing his lips firmly against mine.

After Will had made a ton of phone calls, it was decided that I would take the plane home that we had been planning to take together, and he booked a seat on the next available first-class flight back to JFK.

We were waiting in the pretty courtyard for our cars to arrive. My flight was leaving from Paris and Will's from Charles de Gaulle. Will had his arms around my waist, mine around his neck.

'A guy called Nick is going to meet you at Bristol airport,' Will said.

'Nick?'

'He's *the help* in the UK, and I want you to promise you'll use him whenever you need to.'

'Okay,' I agreed. 'I really hope your Mum's okay. Send her my love.'

Will's face contorted before shaking it away. I could see he was deeply worried about her, and I really didn't want him worrying about me.

'She'll be okay... I'll be okay... Okay?'

He laughed and then kissed me just as we both jumped at the sound of a horn on the other side of the door.

'I love you, my girl next door.'

The driver beeped again. The Parisian drivers had no patience. They were worse than New York.

'I love you too.'

He kissed me one last time, and just like that, our perfect bubble popped, and we went our separate ways.

Nick was a nice chap. He had a military background. He'd served in the Foreign Legion for five years before working in the Metropolitan Police. He'd retired early after injuring his shoulder a few years ago and had been offering private security ever since.

Will had obviously given him the passcode for the house because he didn't need to ask what the number was when he pulled up outside the new security gates. There was a smattering of press outside, Will had warned me this would likely be the case as The Night Show had aired. He collected my luggage while I opened the front door and popped it just inside before giving me his card.

'Call me if there's anything you need, anything at all.'

'Thanks, Nick. Enjoy the rest of your day.'

The dogs were going crazy having heard my voice, and the house sitter came to greet me. We had a quick handover before she left, and then I went to fuss the dogs. They were so pleased to see me, licking my face and running circles around me.

There was a huge pile of post on the kitchen worktop, and I turned the coffee machine on as I opened all the letters that didn't look like junk, and I stilled. There in my hand was a letter from my solicitor confirming that the divorce had been settled. I took a breath in and held it. I couldn't quite believe it. I thought about the end of one era and the beginning of another as I glanced at my engagement ring.

'Mum?'

I looked up suddenly. The boys were back. Frankie and Paddy came piling in, followed by Mike. I flung my arms around the boys, tears springing to my eyes. It was so good to see them.

'Where's Will?' Paddy asked.

'He had to fly back home. His mum had a heart attack. She's okay, but he wanted to be with her.'

'Oh,' Paddy said, brushing the subject away easily, clearly not understanding the enormity of the situation, before firing questions at me about The Night Show they'd watched just before they flew home. All the while, Mike leaned up against the fridge freezer with his hands in his pockets, looking decidedly awkward. And then Frankie lifted my hand to look at the ring.

'Wow! How much did that cost?' Paddy asked.

'Um... I don't know,' I said honestly.

'You're not supposed to ask that, you div,' Frankie said, giving Paddy a playful shove.

'How about you take your cases upstairs and unpack, I'll make us some lemon slushies, and then you can tell me all about your holiday?'

'All of our clothes need washing, so we may as well leave them down here,' Frankie said, and I rolled my eyes. 'I'm dying for the loo, though,' he added, turning on his heel.

'I need it first. I'm desperate,' Paddy whined, racing after him.

A few moments after they'd left, Mike pushed himself away from the fridge freezer and nodded at my hand. I thought he was gesturing toward the ring, and I was waiting for a snidey comment.

'You got the letter then?'

Oh. I was still holding it.

'Er, yeah.'

'Just in the nick of time,' he said with a hint of sarcasm.

I smiled, but it didn't reach my eyes. I wasn't sure what he wanted me to say to that. Or do. I put the letter down.

'You could have run it by me.'

'Sorry?'

'The engagement. You could have given me a heads up.'

'Mike, I didn't know he was going to propose. It was a surprise.'

'What? And you just said yes?'

I breathed out a short, frustrated sigh and looked away from him. What was he expecting me to do? Call him and check if he was on board with the idea?

'Yes, I said yes. I love him.'

He laughed mockingly, and I gave him a hard stare.

'You've only known him a few months, and I suppose you're going to tell me it's got nothing to do with that fat rock on your finger and his net worth.'

I shook my head in disbelief.

'Because that's what everyone thinks,' he continued.

I couldn't believe what I was hearing. I was too tired and weary from travelling to hold my anger in.

'I don't care what everyone thinks. I don't care what you think. You need to leave and, in future, just leave the boys at the door.'

With that, I headed out of the kitchen, collected my case and began to drag it up the stairs, but Mike followed me and stood at the bottom.

'You know, you should really get the low down on Will Reynolds before you sign a marriage certificate,' he said, looking up at me with a smug expression.

'What are you talking about?'

'Maybe you should ask the man himself? Or better still, his brother Ben. Will's got an injunction against him.'

'An injunction? An injunction for what?'

'I'm not at liberty to say, but it brings into question why Will is famous and his brother is a nobody.'

There was a pause while he let that sink in.

'You really think you can trust someone, *marry* someone, after three months of knowing them? You're more naïve than I thought.'

With that, he laughed at me as if I was some sort of stupid bimbo who had been taken for a ride and leisurely sauntered out of the house.

God, he was such a jerk.

I stomped up the remaining staircase, letting the bottom of my suitcase thud against each stair and then threw it on my bed. I flopped down next to it.

Mike's words were rolling around in my head. Was he alluding to the fact that Will was famous because of his brother in some way? And Will had an injunction against him to stop the truth from coming out?

If it was anyone else making those allegations, I'd brush it off, assuming it was jealousy, but Mike had ways and means of finding this information out. His mother was a KC, for goodness sake.

And the fact that Will had looked after his brother for all these years kind of made sense if that was the case. Was Will paying for his brother's silence?

Maybe Mike had a point. Three months wasn't any time at all. How could you know someone, like *really* know them, in that amount of time?

The last few weeks had been like a whirlwind. Paul and Hannah's wedding. Discovering Will was so much more well off than I had realised. The press. The time we spent at the beautiful villa. I saw a shrink, for goodness sake. Paul and Hannah's baby. Los Angeles. The album. The girls coming over. The interview and then the miscarriage. The gig, the engagement and the modelling contract.

Paris.

It was as if Will and I had raced through all the things a normal couple would have to deal with in a lifetime in just under a month. Like our relationship had been on fast-forward, and all of a sudden, someone had pressed stop, and the room had fallen silent.

I looked down at my ring. It was so beautiful. And a lot of thought had gone into the design. But had I been swept along with all the glitz and glamour? The excitement of being with a rockstar. The stunning properties. The lavish gifts. The opportunities. The romantic proposal.

Being back home made it all feel like a fairy tale.

There was a weird feeling in the pit of my stomach, as if Mike's allegations had physically made their way into my belly and were swimming around. I couldn't help it. Doubt was beginning to seep in, and it wasn't a nice feeling. When everything had come to the surface about Alysa and the baby, I'd asked Will if there was anything else, and he'd assured me I knew everything.

So, why wouldn't he tell me about an injunction? What was he hiding? And if he was hiding that, what else could there be?

THE END... FOR NOW

Please take a moment to leave a review, as an independent author it would mean the world to me.
To find out what happens next in Lucy & Will's story sign up to my mailing list for updates and be notified of launch dates, free bonus scenes and new titles:
www.rblackwrites.com[1]
Follow Rebecca Black on social media:
https://www.facebook.com/profile.php?id=100082847830078
Instagram:

RBLACKWRITES22

It's Yesterday's News is the last book in The Hearsay Series which will be available in October 2023

1. http://www.rblackwrites.com

Acknowledgments

Once again, I must give a big shout out to my husband who has not only helped me by reading and giving me feedback on the original manuscript but has also been on hand when I've done trade fairs and has constantly been my sounding board when I've needed to run through scenes and discuss plot ideas.

Victoria Straw, you are so much more than my editor, more of a mentor and always available to answer my novice-like questions. I love that you picture yourself sat with Lucy and her friends with a glass of wine. And I love your frank and honest feedback, particularly your attention to detail when it comes to the raunchy scenes.

Olivia Handley, thank you for doing the final proofread on this one, in-between a ton of other commitments. If you want something done, ask a busy person! I don't know how you manage it.

Ashley Santoro, the cover designer, I promise the next one won't be such a strict deadline.

And last but not least, my readers, I wouldn't have gone on to publish My Girl Next Door had it not been for your encouragement and enthusiasm. My ARC team especially, thank you for all your feedback and reviews.

About the Author

Rebecca Black was born in Croydon, London in 1978, moved and has lived in the west country since 1987.

She left school without passing English at GCSE level and worked in the hospitality industry until she had a family.

In May of 2020 she was diagnosed with breast cancer, had a lumpectomy and went through chemotherapy and radiotherapy. It was during her recovery that she discovered a love for romance novels – the smuttier the better!

For Christmas 2021 she received a keyboard iPad cover and decided to write a couple of letters of thanks to try the keyboard out. Once complete she went on to write a romance story of her own.

She didn't intend to write a book but thirty thousand words in she decided she'd check how many words the average book had. Two weeks later she had the first draft of her first book written!

Printed in Great Britain
by Amazon

25644131R00283